BY DEEPA ANAPPARA

The Last of Earth
Djinn Patrol on the Purple Line

CO-EDITED BY DEEPA ANAPPARA

Letters to a Writer of Color

THE LAST OF EARTH

THE
LAST OF EARTH

A NOVEL

DEEPA
ANAPPARA

RANDOM HOUSE
NEW YORK

Random House
An imprint and division of Penguin Random House LLC
1745 Broadway, New York, NY 10019
randomhousebooks.com
penguinrandomhouse.com

Grateful acknowledgment is made to HarperCollins Publishers and Faber and Faber Limited
for permission to reprint an excerpt from "Little Gidding" from *Four Quartets* by T. S. Eliot,
copyright © 1936 by Houghton Mifflin Harcourt Publishing Company, renewed 1964
by T. S. Eliot; copyright © 1940, 1941, 1942 by T. S. Eliot and copyright renewed 1968,
1969, 1970 by Esme Valerie Eliot. Rights outside of the United States are controlled
by Faber and Faber Limited. Reprinted by permission of HarperCollins Publishers and
Faber and Faber Limited.

Names: Anappara, Deepa author
Title: The last of Earth : a novel / Deepa Anappara.
Description: First edition. | New York, NY : Random House, 2026.
Identifiers: LCCN 2025031606 (print) | LCCN 2025031607 (ebook) |
ISBN 9780593731352 hardcover acid-free paper | ISBN 9780593731376 ebook
Subjects: LCGFT: Historical fiction | Novels | Fiction
Classification: LCC PR6101.N325 L37 2025 (print) | LCC PR6101.N325 (ebook)
LC record available at https://lccn.loc.gov/2025031606
LC ebook record available at https://lccn.loc.gov/2025031607

Printed in the United States of America

1st Printing

FIRST EDITION

BOOK TEAM: PRODUCTION EDITOR: *Cassie Gitkin* • MANAGING EDITOR: *Rebecca Berlant* •
PRODUCTION MANAGER: *Samuel Wetzler* • PROOFREADERS: *Julie Ehlers, Anya Getschel,
Katie Powers, Russell Powers*

Book design by Barbara M. Bachman

Interior map by Helen Cann

*Title page images from Adobe Stock. Left to right: Buddhist mural: Elena Ray, Landscape:
rcausino, Snow leopard: white_whale.*

The authorized representative in the EU for product safety and compliance
is Penguin Random House Ireland, Morrison Chambers, 32 Nassau Street,
Dublin D02 YH68, Ireland. https://eu-contact.penguin.ie.

This book is dedicated to:

My father TK Prabhakaran,
my mother Yesoda Anappara,
my nephew Param

and

my sister Divya Anappara
(in memory)

I am bound by the illusion of Time and Space.

—RUDYARD KIPLING, *Kim*

And still deeper the meaning of that story of Narcissus, who because he could not grasp the tormenting, mild image he saw in the fountain, plunged into it and was drowned. But that same image, we ourselves see in all rivers and oceans. It is the image of the ungraspable phantom of life; and this is the key to it all.

—HERMAN MELVILLE,
Moby Dick; or, The Whale

We shall not cease from exploration
And the end of our exploring
Will be to arrive where we started
And know the place for the first time.
Through the unknown, unremembered gate
When the last of earth left to discover
Is that which was the beginning . . .

—T. S. ELIOT,
"Little Gidding"

THE LAST OF EARTH

REPORT OF A ROUTE-SURVEY MADE BY PUNDIT *—, FROM NEPAL TO LHASA, AND THENCE THROUGH THE UPPER VALLEY OF THE BRAHMAPUTRA TO ITS SOURCE. BY CAPTAIN T. G. MONTGOMERIE, R.E., OF THE GREAT TRIGONOMETRICAL SURVEY, IN CHARGE OF THE TRANS-HIMALAYAN SURVEY PARTIES.

———

Read, 23 March 1868.

EXPLORATION beyond the frontiers of British India has, for many years, made but little comparative progress, and (as far as Europeans have been concerned) has been confined to points not many marches beyond the border.

A European, even if disguised, attracts attention when traveling among Asiatics, and his presence, if detected, is now-a-days often apt to lead to outrage. The difficulty of redressing such outrages, and various other causes, has, for the present, all but put a stop to exploration by Europeans. On the other hand, Asiatics, the subjects of the British Government, are known to travel freely without molestation in countries far beyond the British frontier; they constantly pass to and fro between India and Central Asia, and also between India and Tibet, for trading and other purposes, without exciting any suspicion.

In 1861 it was consequently proposed to take advantage of this facility possessed by Asiatics, and to employ them on explorations beyond the frontier.

---

* The two pundits still being employed on explorations, their names are, for obvious reasons, omitted.

1.

MISFORTUNE ON THE MOUNTAIN PASS—
UNEXPECTED VISITORS—THE CAPTAIN'S AMBITIONS—
LAST NIGHT AT THE BORDER

———

THEY WERE ONLY AT THE BEGINNING OF THEIR EXPEDITION, AND already they were three men and twice as many sheep short. The captain said the men who deserted the camp, like most natives, lacked nerve. About the sheep no one was certain, but high up on the mountain pass snow leopards were known to sneak into wind-rocked pens at night and vanish with their prey silenced between their teeth. The bearers were spooked because when the white mist lifted at dawn, they saw neither animal tracks nor blood and, behind the boulders, they found no bones or carcasses.

Balram watched them scuttle away from the camp, their sullen faces reddened by lashings of wind. They mumbled about the smell of the netherworld in the air, creatures that were half-animal and half-human whose knotted fur carried the mustiness of long-buried wants.

It fell on Balram, as the captain's right-hand man, to dispel their fears. He supposed he could confess to feeling light-headed himself, a fate inescapable at this height. He could remind them of his previous travels, when he had encountered specters rising out of the mist only to realize such visions were the work of exhaustion and insufficient air in his lungs.

All these words he ought to say.

He didn't feel particularly inclined to say them.

A clank caused Balram to turn around. Pawan was packing his knives and ladles, muttering curses to himself. Face as smooth and shiny as a baby's, though the mouth on that boy could put a drunk to shame. Balram snapped his fingers and gestured that he should hurry. Pawan scowled but hoisted his sacks over his shoulders and walked away in a clatter of pots and pans, a squabble an indulgence neither of them could afford when their breathing was so ragged.

They were now midway through the Mana Pass, a gap in the Himalayas that was nearly as formidable as the snow-cloaked mountains it cut through to form a passage to Tibet. At eighteen thousand feet above the level of the sea, here they were closer to gods than mortals, but this proximity to the divine had brought them no blessings, only burdens.

Balram kicked dust over the remains of the previous night's fire. The light was full of shadows, the sky heavy as a bog. There were no fetters on his ankles. Then why did it feel as if he had been tied down to the coarse logs of his own funeral pyre?

The captain bellowed at the men to gather around him, his shouts necessitated not as much by anger as the unruliness of the wind. The nine bearers left in their group, and the two shepherds, flocked together, sacks and trunks at their feet.

"If you return home without a formal letter of discharge from me, carrying my signature, you'll be punished severely," the captain warned them now. Plumes of white breath laced his words. "You'll be sent to prison—as your friends who have deserted us will find out soon."

Despite his fluency in the language, the manuals he read on masculine and feminine nouns, and the companionship of native women whom white men called "sleeping dictionaries" owing to the twofold nature of their responsibilities, the captain's Hindustani had a strange inflection to it, the whiff of vast oceans no one could cross without losing caste. His threats sounded comical because of his manner of speaking, but the bearers kept their eyes downcast. They knew the native's role well; they had played it all their lives. Jumped out of the path into a ditch when a white man's carriage spat a cloud of dust in the distance. Readily arched their backs when condemned to flogging for improperly greeting an officer. Polished the boots flung at their faces for nodding off after midnight while fanning their English masters.

"If you imagine you can escape detection, say by traveling to Calcutta and finding employment on the docks, let me remind you, the Survey has detailed records of your families," the captain said. "They will experience the full force of the British government's fury."

Balram examined the ground again. He saw footprints but no animal tracks. The three missing bearers had most likely stolen the sheep and retraced their steps, having decided the expedition was too perilous for them to undertake. Balram ought to have sensed their disquiet. Gyan would have. Gyan used to say that Balram had spent so much time with white men, he had imbibed their manners and vocabulary, and his thoughts were no longer his own but of a race that would never see him as an equal. The memory of it tensed the muscles in Balram's back. He wished he could give Gyan a clout on the head and clasp him to his chest.

He bent down to wipe the ash off his boots. His belongings, tied up in a bundle on his back and fastened across his chest, swayed to the side. The heat of a sharp gaze scalded his face. He looked up, chest thumping, expecting to lock eyes with a snow leopard, its thick tail assuming the curve of a sickle, wool snared between its bloodstained fangs. But behind the creaking rocks, all was still.

AFTERWARD THE CAPTAIN TOOK Balram aside and said, "The men were idle for too long. Their heads have filled with clay."

"We're making good time," Balram said, an itch beginning in his throat that felt like ants scurrying up to his mouth. "Took me the same number of hours to cross the pass last time."

"How can you speak of hours when we were detained at Mana for weeks?" the captain asked, his saffron robe flapping in the wind. "All that time we squandered, waiting for the Tibetans to decide if India is a fit country to have relations with, you have forgotten it already?"

"The pass was closed on account of snow, sir. The Tibetans couldn't help it. Besides, they worry we will bring smallpox with us, or war. They want to first ascertain nothing has gone wrong on our side of the border."

"You don't have to repeat every lie the Tibetans tell," the captain said.

Balram kicked a pebble into a tributary of the Alaknanda that curved below their path. For much of their journey through the pass, they had followed the river, whose waters swelled the Ganga farther down south; but here it was slight, no more than a sea-green vein that appeared to be hewn into rocks. At first its banks had been carpeted with scarlet and yellow wildflowers, but now the earth was bald, and as dreary as the sky.

"When I was a small child, I knew summer was beginning not from the skies but from the sound of sheep bells ringing," Balram said. "It was the sound of traders guiding their animals to the pass. I used to dread it because it meant my father would leave for Tibet." As soon as he said these words, he wished he hadn't. "Our traders sell grains and dried fruit and tobacco. After a long winter, Tibetans wait for their arrival."

"Not with bated breath," the captain said.

"They do take their time once the snow melts," Balram tried to explain to the captain again. "But they're merely being cautious."

The wind hissed in Balram's ears, but he heard Durga's voice, pointing to the lack in his head that kept him from speaking when he should, and garrulous on those occasions when tact demanded silence. He smelled the sesame oil she dabbed on her cheeks each night and wondered if her arms were aching now from hours of thrashing clothes against the rocks by the river.

Always he carried her reproaches with him as he walked. At first he had believed it to be a certain sign of madness in him. But then, one evening, trading stories with Gyan about Tibet, his friend had put him at ease with a confession: he too heard the voices of those he had left behind. On occasion their laughter and screams goaded him, burning his ears as if gods were shoveling hot embers into them. He said such sounds could tempt you to leap into a crevasse if you didn't watch out. Just as sailors across the high seas were enticed by sirens, those scaling the Roof of the World were tempted by the call of the abyss.

Now his friend too was only a voice inside Balram's head.

But not for long, Gyan whispered in a rusty tone, and Balram felt Gyan's ghost thumb draw a damp line across his cheek.

THE CAPTAIN HAD SPENT many years surveying the Karakoram mountains, and so the high altitude and the capricious weather on the Mana Pass didn't bother him. But in the disguise of a Hindu priest, his gait was clumsy. The unfamiliar folds of his robe taunted him and caused him to nearly lose his footing. Seeing him struggle, the bearers discreetly turned their heads. Bands of snow, uneven like ribs that had snapped and healed crooked, coated the steep ridges flanking the river.

"I wonder where they have reached," Balram said. "The three boys who ran away before dawn."

"Cowards," the captain said, waving the notebook in which he sketched their route. "Don't speak of them again. But our provisions, the sheep we lost, we will be all right without them?"

"There will be plenty of butter tea and tsampa once we cross the border."

"Yes, of course. We will be fine," the captain said, as if it was Balram who needed the reassurance.

Out of the corner of his eye, Balram saw the captain pick at a stain on his robe. Then he licked his fingers and dabbed at it with something like fury. When fretful, the captain took to polishing his own person as if he were a silver goblet, a gesture ill-suited to the disguise he sported to escape detection by Tibetans. Balram couldn't ask the captain to stop. Or could he? The farther they were from Hindustan, the murkier the rules that separated men from their lieges. Balram had never been on a surveying mission to Tibet with a white man.

It was silent for a moment, then the wind uttered its incantations again, loud enough to raise the dead.

ALL DAY BALRAM WAITED for the captain's recriminations, but they never came. White mist rolled down the mountains and pressed its icy fingers against his throat. Had he better prepared the men for their passage to Tibet, perhaps their expedition wouldn't have gone so awry at such an early stage.

In the weeks they had spent in the village of Mana, snow falling over the mountains with the steadiness of a heartbeat and every stream turning blue, he had conveyed to the men the broad strokes of the captain's ambitions but hidden the Englishman's true mission, and his own too. He told them the sole objective of their journey was to map the course of the river that began as the Tachok Tsangpo, the Horse River, near Mansarovar and meandered through southern Tibet and eventually transformed or didn't transform—this was the question they were deputed to settle—into the Brahmaputra in Hindustan. The entirety of their journey would pass in the proximity of rivers: here the Alaknanda; beyond the Tibetan border the Sutlej; then the subject of their expedition, a river so great Tibetans simply referred to it as the Tsangpo, the River. As the captain was the deputy superintendent of the Great Trigonometrical Survey, and oversaw all Trans-Himalayan survey parties, he was naturally at their camp to direct their arrangements.

When the captain dyed his hair black with Chinese ink—perhaps the same indelible ink that officials in China used to brand the faces of criminals—and stained his skin brown with iodine and the juice of black walnuts, Balram said white men did this everywhere, in America they painted their faces black and sang onstage, and people paid money to watch them, and he couldn't explain such madness—could they? The bearers took him at his word. Away from the captain in their tent at night they laughed about the captain's costume when they thought Balram was asleep, but one night he said, "Should I tell

him about the giant bald spot on the top of his scalp? That he ought
to paint it black too?" He was mocking the captain for the first time,
a thrill coating his tongue thick and sweet like jaggery, but his tone
must have been severe, because the bearers were quiet.

Only on the morning of their journey, in the death-blue darkness
before dawn, had Balram revealed to the men that the captain too
would be accompanying them to the land that expressly forbid those
of his race. The bearers objected. Hadn't a lama from Shigatse been
sewn into a sack and flung into the Tsangpo, the very river they
would follow, for helping a Christian missionary? Hadn't bandits
shot an English explorer in the head in the Changtang grasslands and
attacked his servants? Balram said Tibetans themselves spread such
tales to keep white people away. They didn't want the British or Russians preaching Christianity, or annexing their country and calling it
a colony. He said Tibetans wished to remain free, and the men agreed
that was a good thing. He said the terrain of Tibet—the unbridled
currents of the Tsangpo, the winding gorges and steep glaciers in its
path—was harsher than its residents, and the men grew anxious. He
said he knew the land well. If only the men who fled that morning
had believed him.

Now Balram observed the bearers, but none behaved suspiciously.
They walked in single file on the narrow path that appeared to hover
above the Alaknanda, their eyes fixed on the ground until the trundle
of a stone, the sputter of the wind, or the crackle of the mountains
caused them to look around as if a beast stalked them. He had condemned these men to their possible deaths—and for what? So an Englishman could map the path of a river. So he could find his friend
who had traveled to Tibet three years ago on a surveying mission and
never returned home.

Anyone who went that long without sending word was most likely
dead. But one morning Gyan's parents had interrupted Balram's lesson at school to tell him a trader had sent word that their son was a
lama's slave in Shigatse. Not long afterward, other traders had come
home with similar stories: Gyan was being held in a monastery in

Shigatse, on the path of the Tsangpo; Tibetans had caught him spying for the English. Balram had to find out if it was true. How could he not? Between them was a bond men and gods couldn't name.

They had grown up in the same village and trained as surveyors together. When they were children, Gyan's mother had glistened rotis with butter for Balram, said, *poor boy, how you must miss your parents, you have been tested by the gods so early in life,* and tilted his chin to the sky with a thumb as coarse as a woollen blanket. She parted for a few moments the heaviness that curtained his eyes even at noon, hushed some kind of want that otherwise rumbled inside him. Gyan, fretful when his mother's attention wavered from him, once upturned a pot of milk and, as his mother and sisters mopped the floor on their blistered hands and rasping knees, smiled wickedly at Balram, brought his toes to his mouth, and licked the white drops spattered on his feet. Envy went both ways. At their school below a banyan tree, Gyan was always the first to solve sums, and each time the teacher praised him, Balram nudged him in the ribs as if to cheer him but with such vigor Gyan's wiry frame collapsed.

Balram wasn't one for wistful reminiscences. But if not for him, Gyan wouldn't have disappeared.

The captain had intended for Balram to follow the Tsangpo three years ago, but when Balram's son's illness worsened on the eve of his journey, Gyan had volunteered to go in his stead. Some might call it the will of the gods. Some might call Balram fortunate, but when had fortune favored him?

Be quiet, Durga whispered, her breath warm in his ear.

A fine story, but it's not the whole truth, is it, Gyan said.

Balram spat out the dust the wind propelled into his mouth. In one of those slow-turning hours at the village of Mana, when the sun's appearance had lent a golden glow to the slate roofs of houses, and butterflies whorled above scarlet rhododendron flowers so rich with honey it slickened the petals, he had dared to hope for an unremarkable journey through Tibet. It wasn't in his nature to hope and, now that his miscalculations were laid bare, with the ease of a bird

returning to its nest at twilight, dread folded its wings and slipped
right back into the groove it had carved in his mind a long time ago.

THE CAPTAIN HALTED THEIR march as the hours advanced toward
dusk. He ordered the bearers to camp for the night, rested his back
against a boulder, and asked Pawan for tea. To keep the captain occupied, Balram told Ujjal to fetch the captain's drawing materials,
hidden in the false compartment of a trunk. But Ujjal dawdled.

Conversation had been scant from the time they entered the Mana
Pass two days ago, the air being treacherous and the paths overlaid
with patinas of ice and frost. But now Ujjal stood with the other bearers, talking freely of the men who had vanished that morning—into
the mouths of monsters perhaps. The mist curled thick around them,
its whiteness turning them into black silhouettes.

"Ujjal, the captain is waiting," Balram snapped.

The young man crossed his hands over his chest and, half-
squatting, pulled his own ears like a child atoning for stealing butter
from his mother's kitchen. Though he was short and as thin as a reed,
Ujjal's hands could wring rainwater out of stone, and his exertions
made him look ridiculous.

"Stop that nonsense," Balram said, and Ujjal stood still, his carriage so upright he could have passed for a sepoy. "Go and open the
trunk."

The others looked amused by Ujjal's antics; smiles plucked at the
edges of their blood-spotted, wind-scoured lips.

"The tents and sheep pens"—Balram's gaze shifted from one
flustered face to another—"do you expect them to go up by themselves? Who's going to collect dung for the fire?"

The bearers dispersed. Balram followed Ujjal to the spot where
sacks and trunks had been heaped together in a slovenly manner. The
captain would be angry if he saw that the men had ignored his instructions to pursue order at all times. Ujjal rescued the captain's
trunk from the tottering jumble and set about opening it.

By the slender loop of the Alaknanda, the lone pony in their group kicked a bearer and made to jump across the river. The shepherds, running after the animal, clacked their tongues and cursed. In the uproar, almost all of them missed the two strangers walking toward them with nervous smiles. With the tip of his boot, Balram nudged the open trunk shut. Its lid nearly slammed against Ujjal's wrist.

"Should have acted quicker," Balram said. That was the teacher in him speaking, unable to let a moment vanish without retrieving a moral or a precise lesson from the faint scuff of time.

"Compass-wallah, you heard what everyone thinks about the captain's disguise," Ujjal said. "He'll be found out."

Balram glanced at the strangers, bowls tucked beneath their sheepskin coats, above their cummerbunds. Must be in need of milk or flour. They were already speaking to the bearers beating down tent pegs into the rocky ground.

"Isn't the wind dreadful?" the older of the two men said as Balram approached him. His accent was that of a man from the hills, and he seemed to have noticed that the bearers deferred to Balram. Gray gathered in his hair, above his temples; his teeth, when not black, were tainted yellow.

"Are you from Badrinath?" Balram asked.

"Joshimath. A day's walk from Badrinath as the crow flies. How did you know? Are you from there too? I don't remember seeing you before."

The man's questions needed no answers. He seemed nervous, and eager to fill silences. Sure enough, deterred not at all by Balram's uninterest, he said, "The old woman we're serving, she's from Punjab. She's traveling to Mansarovar to go around the holy lake."

"Mount Kailas too," the younger of the two said.

"And you have run out of milk already?" Balram asked.

The older man smiled but looked mortified. The younger man held Balram's gaze and said, "We can see you have many sheep. Can't you spare any milk?"

"We have fewer sheep today than we had yesterday," Ujjal said unnecessarily. "Snow leopards maybe. Demons maybe."

In front of them the shepherds caught up with the skittish pony and threw themselves against its saddle.

"Ujjal," Balram said, "get them some milk, will you?"

The men brought their wooden bowls out of their coats. Ujjal pointed them in Pawan's direction. Pawan turned a jug upside down and shook it vigorously to make a point of its emptiness. "These animals don't make enough milk for us to share," he said.

But the sheep were strong and hardy. They had grazed on the rich grass of Mana and gathered together now to form a circle of bleating, dirt-caked fleece, the worsted packs they carried still slung across their backs. The process of tying the bags was time-consuming, so the bearers chose not to relieve the animals of their burden each night. If the sheep minded, they gave no indication. The ewes that stretched on pebbles had the manner of memsahibs lolling in their parlors.

"See what you can do," Balram told Pawan.

"What's the reason for your journey to Tibet?" the old man asked.

"Don't be fooled by their size," Ujjal said, pointing at the sheep. "They're carrying weighty loads of wheat and rice, which we will trade for borax and wool."

"You're traders then?" the younger man asked, his eyes considering their well-worn clothes.

"Traders, yes, but pilgrims at heart," Ujjal said, looking at Balram for affirmation, or praise. Their secret hadn't been revealed.

"If you're headed toward Mansarovar," the older man said, "we can make our way together. Our numbers will stop bandits from attacking us."

"We have to stop frequently," Ujjal said, repeating the words Balram had taught the men so that their group could avoid scrutiny, and company. "You'll tire of our traders' ways, and your old woman won't be pleased if she has to wait with us for weeks."

Balram felt the hair on the nape of his neck prickling, and he prodded at it with his fingers. No one was watching him. The burning in his gullet must spring from his fears—not of wild animals and bandits, but those he couldn't bring himself to express.

Don't be afraid, I'm not dead yet, Gyan said.

But I could be, Gyan said.

Balram saw the captain bearing down upon them, the scowl imprinted on his face so vicious it cut deep furrows between his eyebrows. Here was a man unaccustomed to waiting, whose every other utterance was an order of some sort, who even in his sage's costume couldn't hide the superiority he had gained solely by the circumstances of his birth.

The bearers bowed, involuntarily perhaps. Balram excused himself and hurried to the captain's side. He stood in front of the captain to block him from everyone's view, and drew himself to his full height, though it still left him a foot shorter than the captain.

"Sir," Balram said in a whisper, "Pawan couldn't bring your tea because we have visitors. They may gather from your Hindustani, or the color of your skin, that you're not who you claim to be."

The captain bristled, as if it was unfair of Balram to have such a poor opinion about his disguise. With his notebook he pointed to his voluminous robe, his skin stained brown if only in jagged patches by iodine and walnut juice and the sun, and the wire-gauze spectacles that hid the green of his eyes. "I look like you," he said, stepping forward and nearly tripping over a rock.

"Please, sir, do oblige this humble servant's request," Balram said. Durga would have told him it was the right thing to say. The captain's forehead smoothed.

Balram ushered the captain toward the bearers closest to them and placed him in their midst. They stood a few feet apart from the captain, fearful. The captain leaned away from them, nostrils quivering as if they stank of rot. It occurred to Balram that his mission was foolhardy. He didn't know how he was going to rescue Gyan. He had thought that once he found his friend in Shigatse he would convince the captain to part with his gold coins and pay for Gyan's freedom. But what was a native's life worth to an Englishman? A single cowrie shell, an anna, a gold coin, or nothing?

The visitors were preparing to leave, the younger man holding a bowl between his hands with such care he could have been carrying a diamond-encrusted crown. Balram dashed back to their side to bid them farewell.

"It appears the snow leopard, or the demon, took your best sheep," the younger man said. The volume of milk in his bowl was modest. "For your sake, I hope it doesn't return."

BALRAM WISHED FOR SILENCE that night. Each hour of the day had been tallied, as if life was an extended entry in an accountant's ledger, measured in paces taken, distances bridged. Now to sleep. But how could it come? The blanketed bodies of the men lay side by side, another ear no more than a whisper away. Their numbers had reduced by three, but the tent didn't feel any roomier. Gusts of wind sent shivers up spines that throbbed from carrying sacks and trunks. Balram had unwrapped the puttee around his legs in the evening to check for signs of frostbite. He wished he had thought to enfold his feet in cloth again before lying down.

The air smelled foul, all reeking mouths and armpits. The shepherds were outside, sitting by a fire whose flames cast shadows that skimmed the tent's fabric like stones on water. The bearers chattered, unable to sleep, the panic of that morning clinging to them still.

Not for the first time, Balram wondered if it had been an error on his part to hire men of the same caste who spoke the same dialect and worshipped the same gods. By tradition smelters of iron and copper, they had observed the ruinous conditions of their fathers' lungs and purses and decided to forego the vocations fate had imprinted onto the lines on their palms. Recasting themselves as porters and coolies, they ferried pilgrims from plains to temples on the summits of mountains. They were inured to the altitude and bitter cold, and willing to brave landslips and snowstorms, but apparently not what they considered to be interventions from another world. None of them had been to Tibet before, but when Balram sent out a call for bearers in Dehra and Mussoorie, promising high fees half of which would be paid in advance, he hadn't insisted on men with knowledge of that land; he had in fact considered their lack of experience an advantage.

They had no friends in Tibet with whom they would be tempted to share the captain's secret, thereby guaranteeing, in as far as such things could be guaranteed, their silence.

Englishmen picked men whose castes forbade them from consorting with each other, thus eliminating the likelihood that the bearers would join hands and conspire against their masters, but Balram had pursued the opposite course of action. He had persuaded himself that the bearers would get along if they could eat and drink from the same bowl, and sleep under the same canopy. The journey was arduous and long—three months to Shigatse, where he might find Gyan, a year or two if they were forced to carry out the captain's plan and follow the Tsangpo into the gorge. Either way Balram had deemed it unlikely they would last even a week without fellowship and good humor. But his plans had come to nothing. Three men had already broken rank. A revolt was brewing. He could hear it now in the voices rising around him.

They were right to leave.

You wish you had joined them?

You might as well wish to spend the rest of your life being chased by the police.

It's not like them to leave in secret.

Perhaps their brains were addled by the heights.

They have climbed mountains before, as have we.

They have been killed.

All three, by one leopard?

They ran away, is all.

Not without telling me.

We were friends.

I know his parents well.

I knew *his wife.*

A spell of nervous laughter followed the last claim, but it stilled quickly. Ujjal usually sang or hummed at this hour, until his voice faltered or his tunes were smothered by snores. But there were no songs in the tent tonight. Only waves of fear, rising, ebbing, rising again. They were like soldiers on the night before a battle: alert, fearful, seeing everything, seeing nothing, mere flesh to be cut down by swords.

"Will we suffer Gyan's fate?" Ujjal asked. Balram recognized his voice in the dark and guessed the question was addressed to him. The men had heard about Gyan at the Survey. It was Balram's job to reassure them, but he didn't know what saying Gyan's name might do to him—cut his tongue in half, burn his eyes, paste a smile on his lips, stick in his throat like a horse in a crocodile's jaw.

"That bastard is dead," Pawan said.

How dare he, Gyan hissed in Balram's ear.

"He's too strong to die," Yogi said.

"How can you be certain?" someone else asked.

"The captain said Gyan fought a snow leopard with his bare hands," Yogi said. "The captain tells me things."

"Everyone knows you're a liar, Yogi."

"I bet Gyan chanced upon a gold mine in Tibet and decided to stay."

"Maybe he has a dozen wives there."

"I have one wife, and she drives me mad."

"He's dead. Dead," Pawan pronounced at the top of his voice.

"I heard he's a prisoner," Jagan said.

"Better to be dead than to be locked up in a Tibetan prison, isn't that right, Compass-wallah?" Ujjal said.

"How many times must I tell you not to call me that," Balram said, sitting up to scratch his chest, his parched skin crumbling to powder like a dead moth's wings. Gyan had been the first to call him Compass-wallah, a title reserved for English surveyors, but now even the captain and the bearers had picked it up. "If the Tibetans find out the true nature of our—"

"We know," Ujjal said.

The wind rustled the tent again. Balram grasped the edges of his blanket. The sensation was of being in a goatskin raft spun around by vicious currents. He remembered the Tibetan myth that all of earth was once submerged under the sea, a story that must have begun when nomads found marine fossils on mountain peaks. The nomads believed Tibet had surfaced when the sea waters retreated. It seemed to Balram that the sea was returning now to claim what once belonged to it. All the journeys he and Gyan had undertaken to chart rivers and mountains so that the captain could fill the blank space that was Tibet on his map—what purpose had they served? Certain claims, imperious ones, had been made, about defending the British Empire from Russians who would annex Tibet to conquer Hindustan. But the lines the captain drew on paper appeared to Balram to be no more than a child's scribbles on mud. If the earth shrugged, mountains would cleave, rivers would surge, seas would swallow cities and fields alike, and every map would be rendered incoherent.

Balram gathered his blanket around his shoulders, stood up, and stepped over the men and sometimes on them, eliciting curses and screams. He was glad to part the tent's folds. The animals were quiet in their knee-high enclosure hurriedly built with stones and rocks. The shepherds now turned to face him, their hands raised to the fire for warmth. He looked over to where the captain sat by another fire that blazed orange. He didn't have to share his tent with nine men like Balram did, but sleep was eluding him too for whatever reason.

The captain wasn't the first white man to attempt to enter the Forbidden Kingdom. Missionaries and explorers had slipped into Tibet before him. Those who survived had written accounts of their faith or daring. If Tibet opened its borders to foreigners, Balram suspected these explorers would lose their interest in the country; its appeal lay not only in its isolation and altitude but also in this prohibition.

"It's in the nature of white men to believe they own the world, that no door should be shut to them," his father had said when Balram was a little boy. His father had been a trader who called no man his master. But as a teacher at the Government Vernacular School for Boys, Balram drew his salary from the British government. For eight years, he had absented himself from the school every so often to conduct secret route surveys across Tibet for the captain, and now the captain wanted to see Tibet with his own eyes.

"Sir," Balram said. "Can I get you something?"

The captain gestured at Balram to sit.

A metal contraption glinted in the captain's hands. His compass. He liked to say that it had been in his pocket when he sailed from England at the age of twenty-one to join the Bengal Sappers and Miners, from where he was assigned to the Survey. The captain looked his age now, perhaps the same age as Balram, three or four years shy of forty. But the compass shone as if it had been purchased yesterday, the glass unmarked and wiped clean of grime and smudges. The captain slipped on its brass lid and placed it on a leather-bound book.

Something screeched in the darkness, startling them. But the sheep were quiet. The harsh noise stopped.

The captain tapped the book with his knuckles. "Herodotus claimed that he wrote *The Histories*"—the captain cleared his throat— "*in order that the actions of men may not be effaced by time.*"

Balram said nothing. In his papers about the Tibetan explorations that the captain submitted to the Royal Geographical Society in London, which he had read out to Balram, he had described Balram as a "pundit," a title inspired by his other life as a teacher; an "intelligent Asiatic," a creature apparently so unusual as to be considered with the same curiosity as a talking monkey; and "a promising recruit" who nevertheless remained nameless, though the captain insisted this was only so Balram's safety wouldn't be compromised in Tibet.

"If Gyan's mission hadn't taken such an unfortunate turn," the captain said, "he would have charted the course of the Tsangpo— from the gorges of Tibet to the northeastern frontier, if that is indeed how the river flows."

One of the shepherds, the youngest of their group, a boy still, sang in a low voice as he raked the fire. The older shepherd pissed into the rocks, an unending stream. Balram raised a brow.

"Is it Gyan who has you in such a bad temper?" the captain asked in a genial tone. "You're grieving his absence still, as you would, I suppose." His beard girded his cheeks and concealed his neck, but his ears were long and protruded outward unflatteringly, giving the impression that he was listening avidly even while sleeping. When he moved his face into the darkness, these peculiar features merged with the shadows. The fire revealed only patches of his hands.

"I always imagine the worst at the beginning of an expedition like this. But the more I walk, the less I fear the outcome," Balram said.

"I thought by now you would have changed your mind about me being part of this expedition," the captain said.

"It's dangerous, sir," Balram said. Durga would have told him to keep his mouth shut, so he added, "If you'll pardon me for saying so."

"Yet here we are," the captain said, pocketing his compass. Then, tapping *The Histories* again, he continued: "You think me arrogant for wanting my name in a book like this. For wanting to be the first man to chart the route of the Tsangpo and discover where it meets the sea. The first to answer one of the most perplexing questions of our times: is the Tsangpo in Tibet the same as the Brahmaputra in India?" He rolled the words in his mouth before he uttered them, as if judging their taste and finding them flavorsome on the whole. "But why have you left your home?"

"Why, sir?"

"Don't play the fool, Compass-wallah. It doesn't suit you. You could have refused when I asked you to travel to Tibet the first time. How long ago was it now?"

"I don't remember, sir."

"But plenty of years to change your mind, wouldn't you agree?"

"Yes, sir."

"I didn't summon you with a blade at your neck, did I? You agreed of your own accord. It's in your bones, you see, as it's in mine, this restlessness that torments us so. Why else would you choose to be here when you could sleep in your own bed, be dry when it rains, warm when it snows? Your teacher's salary is meager, I know, but it's more than adequate to fill your stomach with wine and meat, or whatever it is that you like to drink and eat."

"Yes, sir."

"And yet: you spend a month in comfort, and you find the world has become dull. You can't rinse the chalk off your hair, the ink from your fingers. Your students are too loud, your children too." Balram glanced at the shepherds, who seemed to be listening intently, but he could be wrong. They were dark forms behind the sputtering flames into which they threw the occasional twig. And was that a head peeking out of his tent, or was he imagining that too? "You're fond of your wife, but even she——"

"Sir, you speak the truth, sir."

"Some men are happiest when they don't have to move an inch from their hearths. But for some of us, to sit still is to feel the weight of six feet of earth on our chests."

"Yes, sir."

"I didn't leave England because I was an undesirable in my own country."

"Yes, sir."

"This charade of yours may trick your wife, Balram, but it has no place here."

"Yes, sir."

"Listen, I don't claim to be without vanity. If a hundred years hence, say history remembers my contribution, say the Tsangpo were to be named after me—not that I seek such an honor, bear in mind—but say it were to happen, I imagine my spirit will be pleased. But my ambitions alone, they're not worth much. The reason we risk our lives, it's for——"

"Queen and country, sir."

"Yes, think of how it will extend our trade. And the Russians who advance closer to Tibet every day, snatching any khanate they can? Our maps will help repel them. But first and foremost, we're here as men of science. Across the world, as we speak, explorers are commanding boats through pewter waters to discover the mouths and sources of the Nile and the Niger, the Zambezi and the Mekong, all of us merely following in the footsteps of the ancient Persian king Darius. According to Herodotus, Darius the Great sent an expedition along the Indus River to find where it joined the Indian Ocean. He understood that the routes of rivers are significant—they change how we ferry goods and people, what crops we cultivate, and what we eat. Our little drawings will one day reshape the world."

Flames twisted in the captain's eyes, set too close to each other, sunken and intense like a fanatic's. Balram was glad the captain couldn't see his expression in the darkness.

"The routes you and Gyan mapped for us, the descriptions you brought back from your previous journeys to Tibet, they're easily the best we have. Father Desideri toured these parts in 1715, but there's little in his account about Tibet that's of interest to the geographer, and a great deal instead about how he crossed rivers by holding on to a cow's tail. Indeed, you'll find that the most useful piece of advice in his recollections is that cows help travelers ford rivers."

Balram smiled, but he stopped the smile from brightening his voice. "We don't have cows, sir."

"And we will know soon enough how we fare."

2.

I HAVE MARKED THE date of this entry with great confidence, but I must ~~confess the secret to you, Ethel~~ admit that M— and I can no longer be certain if it is a Monday or a Friday. We are fortunately much more competent at telling the time by the sun and shadows, though I suppose even a child could perform this task with sufficient instruction.

I could not write last night owing to a storm. All of yesterday we marched on the Nirpani, or Waterless, path, which has gained a reputation for being treacherous. For long sections, it is less than half a foot in width. A stumble and we would have fallen down a thousand feet or more. I did not find the track particularly difficult.

We came across a waterfall, whose presence on the "Waterless" path M— could not explain. He has walked this route many times before, as a bearer and guide for pilgrims and traders, but does not think to warn me of what lies in wait.

Saw no animals except goats. No birds. Spectacular views. Mountains brightened by filaments of cirrus clouds in unexpected colors: salmon, violet, crimson, gold. We encamped by the Kali River at sunset. The dreadful storm arrived soon after. I had to hold on to the posts of my tent to keep it from collapsing.

We will reach Garbyang tomorrow. Then: Tibet.

~~M— is certain I will escape detection because I look like a native. He speaks as if this is a compliment. Ethel, do you remember how often Mother called me Mongrel? Once or twice~~

~~you protested when she cast a slur upon my appearance~~
~~within your earshot. You claimed a kinship with me that I did~~
~~not deserve or earn, I who did not even see you die. Your~~
~~husband told me that toward the end of your life, you were in~~
~~such pain that your lips curled into a permanent frown, but he~~
~~also said no weakness emerged in your character. In the face~~
~~of the hardships you endured, my own challenges with the~~
~~weather and wilderness appear unworthy of setting down on~~
~~paper.~~

A MONTH AFTER HER fiftieth birthday, Katherine Westcott walked
on a mountain track that was as narrow as the snake king coiled
around Lord Shiva's blue-tinted throat. She was dressed in an ankle-
length Tibetan robe inconvenient for the demands of her day but
preferable to the corsets and petticoats she had to wear in London or
Darjeeling. Over her long gray hair she had tied a bonnet picked up
from the ground on a previous journey through Tibet. It was a
ghastly thing, the bonnet, lined with fur that must have been white
when it was sewn and was now brown and fell out in tufts that remained threaded in her hair like wilted jasmine. But she was willing
to wager it had talismanic powers after a ruffian servant had failed to
harm her within a week of it coming into her possession. The bonnet
lent her appearance an air of frail bones and unseeing eyes, but she
could still match the pace of the young man who accompanied her.

The path was tedious. They had to climb up stairs carved out of
rock, numbering in the hundreds, only to descend twenty steps or
more, then undertake yet another ascent. The folks who lived near
these parts called the track Nirpani, or Waterless, on account of the
lack of springs for the traveler, though below them coursed the Kali,
the roar of its swift waters a taunt to the thirsty. If one peered over
the cliff, the river would appear as molten silver, but neither Katherine nor her companion were keen to risk a fall.

"Careful," Mani said, turning to watch her ascend the steps.

"I don't need *you* to tell me that," Katherine said, waving him forward. She spoke sharply, discerning in his tone his fear that her feet, flecked with purple veins where the blood ran cold, wouldn't carry her much farther.

Mani smiled as if he approved of her mild rebuke, and ran his hands over his scalp, shaved before they started their march three weeks ago and already covered with an outcrop of short, bristly hair. His skin stretched taut over his frame, emphasizing, on his face, the hollowness of his cheeks, but in sharp contrast, the muscles on his arms were thick and firm owing to the nature of his employment. He claimed to be eighteen, looked younger, acted as if he was much older, and received Katherine's inquiries about his home or family in silence, only stating that he intended to renounce the world soon and become a monk. She suspected he had agreed to accompany her (*a woman!*) because she had spent a year at a monastery in Kalimpong studying Buddhist scriptures.

"It's going to rain, mother," he said now, gesturing at the opaque, gray clouds rising above distant peaks like a groundswell of the ocean.

"This is why we have a tent," Katherine said with more conviction than she felt.

It had fallen on Mani to carry the tent, though she expected him to sleep outside come rain or snow. If Mani thought this arrangement unjust, he had not said so. In keeping with their disguise of mother and son, he addressed her as *mother* with the reverence of a devotee paying obeisance to his favorite goddess—perhaps a hint of mockery smudged his courteousness, but she who was no one's mother didn't care to dwell on it.

The two of them were at the very edge of the maps men had made. Lines that traced villages, towns, mountains, and rivers, ended here, and Tibet, a space that appeared as smooth and white as a pearl, began. The river that corkscrewed below them split the land into Kumaon and Nepal. On the Kumaon side, where they now marched, the rugged mountain slope was gray-hued and barren, excepting the occasional green bursts of shrubs, dewdrops on their bare branches crystallized into startling ice flowers in the shade of overhanging rocks. Across the river in Nepal, trees sheathed in creepers directed their branches toward the water. Wild goats balanced precariously on rocks to feast on the shrubs growing out of every cranny.

Katherine paused to catch her breath, and Mani stopped too, sticking his little finger in his ear to scratch some itch he couldn't seem to reach. Then he patted a boulder. "Come, sit," he told her. "Get some rest." He wiped his fingers against his coat and, from his sack, brought out a long strip of dried meat, tore it in two, and offered her the bigger portion. Such a gesture would be unimaginable in an expedition group where servants had their own food and utensils and rules of caste and class and religion; they wouldn't dare sit next to their English masters, or speak to them, as Mani did. "Take it, mother. You need the strength," he said, and she accepted without looking at him. "Why did the monks in Kalimpong agree to teach you?" he asked, having determined perhaps that he knew her well enough now to inquire about private matters. "Usually they don't even speak to women."

"You'll have to ask them."

"They must have given you a reason."

"Maybe they taught me because they're kind. Learned. Devoted to prayer." Katherine chewed the meat, which was salty and tough. "Witty too."

Dark clouds loomed over them like demons threatening to possess their souls. Mani's manner reminded her of the way natives inquired into each other's affairs without shame or embarrassment. Accompanying her ayah as a child, Katherine had heard about the pustules on a teacher's scrotum, and a maid who had children with three different neighbors, her husband surprised none looked like him but never suspecting his wife of infidelity. The native's curiosity, and appetite for gossip, were galling, but perhaps without malice.

"The monks knew I wanted to visit Lhasa," Katherine said now, "but that I didn't even make it to the Tibetan border because a British officer refused to let me pass. They must have felt sorry for me. I imagine they were also impressed that a foreigner, even if only a woman, knew about Buddhism and wanted to learn more."

"But what's the reason for your interest in our books when you have the Bible?"

Katherine clicked her tongue in annoyance; really the boy ought to know his place. "Why do you want to be a monk?" she asked.

"It's a kind of freedom," Mani said as thunder rumbled in the distance. "To belong to the whole world and not just a village. To pray for everyone on earth instead of just me, or my family."

His freedom sounded like servitude to her. At the Kalimpong monastery, she had hoped for deliverance—but for herself. She had imagined that being around monks who forsook every desire known to man would calm her restive mind, but that hadn't come to pass.

The first raindrop brought Mani to his feet. Katherine returned her half-eaten ribbon of meat to him and he folded the whole of it into his mouth. Then he helped her hoist her sack, and she said, "The young monks in Kalimpong were not at all like how I imagined monks to be. They made each other laugh, even during the debates about Buddhism they held every afternoon in the courtyard. Or as they polished stone floors—you must have seen how difficult that task is. They have to drag a large rock, wrapped in sheepskin, from one end of the room to another. They would be bathed in sweat from the effort. Still, they were always cracking jokes." Mani, his cheeks swollen with meat, couldn't speak, but pointed his thumb at his own chest as if to say he could be witty too.

They walked in silence, the clouds sprinkling raindrops, a choppy wind hissing in their ears, Katherine remembering her time in Kalimpong. Her sister had been alive then, even if bedridden in Edinburgh.

Katherine had written to Ethel about the Buddha's gospel, and the monks at the monastery who were sometimes only six or seven and already learning to be indifferent to life and death but not gossip, asking her if it was true that she was going to marry a Bhutanese prince visiting Kalimpong and wasn't he much younger than her? Ethel found these letters so delightful she convinced her husband to share them with one of his friends who ran a small publishing house in

London. To everyone's surprise, including Katherine's, *Letters from the Foothills of the Indian Alps* had done well, bringing her a hint of fame, and suspicion too—how could a woman travel alone without a husband, or chaperones?

Her mother had asked Katherine this question when she first sailed to the East at the age of nineteen, utilizing a small portion of the inheritance Father had left her. Ethel had said Katherine could look for a husband in India, but it was curiosity alone that prompted Katherine's return to the country of her birth, which she remembered only in jagged fragments. On that journey, she discovered that the traveler's life, without responsibility or attachment, suited her. Watching the gray ocean from a ship rocked by furious waves, or the emerald of paddy fields as her shoes sank into mud, she felt anchored to the universe by some vital force she couldn't describe. Since then she had explored the Orient at every opportunity and, in all those years, she hadn't troubled herself with the task of letter-writing. Weeks passed before she even remembered she had a sister. But fate, that impertinent burglar, had connived to repair their frayed bond with Ethel's illness.

Katherine had written to Ethel during her second attempt to reach Lhasa too. This time her journey had begun on the banks of the Mekong in Burma and concluded in a town in eastern Tibet from where she could glimpse the sacred peak of Khawa Karpo. Her good fortune ran out there after her thieving servant revealed her identity to soldiers, who escorted her back to the border. They could have hurt her or killed her. Instead they were polite. The bonnet she had picked up from the dust during that expedition must have acted as a charm and saved her.

On her return to London, Katherine published the letters written during her expedition, and miraculously this compilation too did well, despite Katherine confessing in the preface that the letters had been delivered to Ethel by her own hand, there being no post fit for purpose in Tibet. The second book firmed her reputation of being a female explorer, as exotic and dangerous as a Bengali tiger or an African elephant. Katherine welcomed such acclaim as a woman explorer could be expected to receive—never on a par with men. But in her letters she portrayed herself as modest and religious and insisted that even on a mountain she dressed like a lady.

Then Ethel died.

Katherine had been in Calcutta at the time, planning a third tour to Tibet. In the bright heat of grief that scalded her flesh, she thought she would never write again. She didn't want to enter into a correspondence with Frederick about her travels, though she wasn't averse to sending her husband notes requesting money or expressing gratitude for supporting her financially. Frederick brooked no ill will against her for her absences, or her indifference to household matters. Some said he encouraged her to travel so that he could entertain a certain fine-looking cousin in her absence, but that didn't strike Katherine as a great calamity. She had married him at the late age of thirty-five, when her inheritance was dwindling.

She missed Ethel's funeral, but guilt made her return to London. She set about making her home with Frederick, as if God would forgive her once she had remade herself into a good wife. She visited Ethel's husband and her nieces often, and they responded politely but not with warmth. She longed for Tibet, but didn't admit it. Instead she sought the thrill of entering a new world by writing fiction for the first time.

Her novel, only loosely inspired by Walter Scott's *Waverley,* told the story of a misguided English boy in India who befriends a prince and has to choose between his friendship and country when the prince rebels against the East India Company. It was published quickly and enthusiastically, but received with disdain. *An unsuccessful addition to the world of fiction,* wrote a reviewer, and Katherine, her face flushing with indignation now as these red-stained words drifted toward her like feathers torn from a bird's wing, wondered if her keenness to become the first Western woman to reach Lhasa was spurred by pride and notions of revenge, or by her desperation to be far from a world that she cared for but little. In London she was forced to acknowledge the lack in her life, the absences that furnished her dreams with the shape of the sister she had lost, the mother who had never known how to love her, and her own failure to be a *successful addition* to society. But—and here she breathed deeply and exhaled as if to recover full command of her nerve—she had never yearned for what others wanted, not the comforts of children and marriage or cashmere and diamonds. Her place was here, in movement, in desolation. (And if the publication of her letters had given her a taste for fame, a possibility that her name might remain on earth after her last breath, was that so wrong?)

Mani was watching her again, with concern. She reverted her gaze to the path that slanted down toward the river. One step in the wrong direction and her foot would find no purchase. Her heart fluttered, but she charged ahead.

An hour, or two, passed. Darkness seemed to descend along with them. Raindrops pattered down, confining her vision to no farther than a few feet. Thunder rattled the mountains and shook a few boulders loose, rendering their passage even more unsafe. Her bonnet channeled the rainwater into two rivulets that ran down her cheeks.

"Mother, why don't you take my hand?" Mani asked.

Katherine shook her head, though the slope was far more precipitous than she had imagined. She wondered if her ambition would be her downfall, as some in London had prophesied. *What was she thinking? A woman in the winter of her life scaling the steps of the Potala Palace?*

The rain quelled the sound of their footsteps. It seemed to Katherine that the earth was moving, sliding under her feet like a reptile. The river sounded closer. But it was a thousand feet below, or had they already descended that far down the mountain? The path seemed to have evened out.

"See the gorge?" Mani shouted to make himself heard over the rain. "Once we pass through it, there will be an incline where we can camp."

The rain lashed down on her with such force she felt she was drowning.

"Waterfall," Mani said. "Here the track goes under a waterfall."

"I thought this was meant to be a waterless path," Katherine said after they had arrived on the other side, unable to convey the full extent of her irritation on account of her chattering teeth.

"Only when the weather is dry," Mani said. "In the rain, waterfalls are common—I warned you about this several times, mother."

Katherine reminded herself that she ought to trust him. Mani had walked on this path before and crossed the Lipulekh Pass to reach Mansarovar and Lhasa. Besides, she had hired him on the recommendation of the deputy collector of Almora, whom Mani had accompanied to the Tibetan frontier the previous year. She had been unlucky with servants in the past, but thus far the deputy collector appeared to be correct in his appraisal of Mani as an honest attendant.

A perfect gentleman, the deputy collector. Handsome too. No doubt the last Englishman she would see for months. She had neglected to tell him her journey would take her to Lhasa, and instead given him cause to believe she would be conducting an ethnographic investigation of tribal settlements by the border. If made aware of her plans, the British government would have claimed that a diplomatic problem would likely arise from her presence in Tibet and refused yet again to grant her permission to explore the country. For the same reason, she hadn't informed the Royal Geographical Society about her tour. The men in the Society didn't admit women as fellows, and believed the female of the species was too incompetent to contribute geographical knowledge. She couldn't plead with these risible men for permission or support. Fortunately, for money she once had her inheritance, and now she had Frederick, and he didn't require an accounting of expenses to open his wallet.

Katherine walked past the gorge to the slight rise where Mani set about pitching her tent. Holding a sack over her head as if it was a parasol, she gave him instructions that he dutifully obeyed. Perhaps he preferred not to argue with her, as lone servants were liable to do on such journeys, because his heart was set on monkhood. Perhaps it was because of the substantial fee she had promised to pay him on their return to Almora, a quarter of which he had already collected as advance. In any event, he hadn't protested when she told him of the true nature of her journey.

Now he finished setting up the tent and blinked the rain out of his eyes. She waved him off. Inside the tent, she wrapped herself in her camel-hair blanket, the only item of bedding in her sack that wasn't soaked, and sat down on the damp ground. Ingeniously sewn inside the blanket were watertight pockets in which she carried money, and small notebooks and pencils sheathed in oilskin. Hunger strung up her innards in tight knots, but in this rain flint and steel wouldn't yield sparks however forceful the strike.

The emptiness in her stomach was a mild inconvenience compared to the fullness of her bladder. She couldn't wait for the downpour to stop. She shrugged the blanket off her shoulders and prepared to be drenched again.

KATHERINE FELL ASLEEP SITTING upright, her damp hair spread over her shoulders, her exhaustion so great the discomfort of her position ceased to matter. A storm was raging outside, but the wind and thunder sounded dull. A few moments or hours later, she woke up with a start, her breath locked in her lungs, the lid of a coffin above her eyes. *Oh, death has come for me,* she thought, *too soon yet also too late.* She saw Ethel, and called out to her. Then it occurred to her that the storm had caused her tent to collapse, and its canvas was bearing down on her face, smothering her. A temporary impediment that could be easily resolved—unlike death. Still, these days, on too many mornings, she opened her eyes uncertain if she occupied the world of the living or the dead; only a thin curtain appeared to separate the two, and it was as if she drifted between these realms in her sleep.

She crawled out, the canvas heaving, something snapping, ice sticks jabbing her in the eye; but from where? She would have a word with Mani today. Such poor workmanship was unacceptable.

Once outside she dusted her knees and elbows. The wind had cleared the clouds in the sky. Rich shades of crimson tipped the edges of the horizon. Almost dawn, but she could have done with a few more hours of sleep. Her head ached as if nails were being hammered into her skull. She touched her scalp and realized the rainwater she hadn't wrung out of her hair the previous night had deviously turned to ice. Strands of her hair must be standing out like icicles.

"Mani," she called out. The wind muffled her voice. Beneath the collapsed tent were her prized possessions, her sack and her blanket, without which she now shivered. At the beginning of their trip, she had instructed Mani to stay within shouting distance, should she require his assistance in the dark, but perhaps last night, because of the storm, he had been forced to wander farther to find a cave for sheltering. For the briefest of moments, shame, or something like it, chafed against her heart. Should she have asked him to stay in the tent? But a woman couldn't be expected to share a cramped space with a man-servant, that too an Oriental.

Katherine wandered down the gorge, shouting his name. Rocks hurled her words back to her. Here, underneath peaks that didn't bend even for the sky, she began to feel as small and insignificant as a pebble. Was this where her adventure would end? Was this all she would ever be, mere bones to be discovered by a pilgrim in a year or two? These fears whipped warm blood into her ears, but she couldn't allow herself to be frail of spirit.

You don't need Mani, she told herself. *You can travel to Tibet alone.*

But she couldn't even cook. When Katherine first came to England as a child, her mother had told her the mistress of the house ought to set a suitable example for domestics to follow. Even then Katherine's character had a rebellious taint to it, and she had refused to accompany her mother as she did her morning rounds of the kitchen and other rooms to see all was in order. Afterward at home and during her travels, there had been housekeepers, maids, and bearers to look after such trivial matters, which scarcely required her supervision.

Ahead of her was the waterfall they had passed at night, white as milk. She saw now that the force with which it had fallen on her and Mani had been blunted by an overhang that directed the water away from the path and into the river. She couldn't determine the height of the cascade because a thin haze rose from the flanks of the mountains, covering the peaks.

By the waterfall, a man washed his dark-brown hands in the silver-white waters of the Kali. His hair was tied at the top of his head, and his beard was lustrous and black. He must be one of those mystics who sequestered themselves in a Himalayan cave to find enlightenment, stepping out only to conduct their ablutions. But he dispelled her impression by swearing at the river in Hindustani. "Do you have to be this cold?" he asked the currents, as if they could answer.

Katherine glanced up at the slopes for Mani. The morning light was soft, with a penitent, bluish edge to it.

"Fine morning," the man said. "May the sun keep us warm today."

Katherine hesitated, wondering if she should greet him or not. The wind cast the waterfall's spray across her eyes in the guise of a million tiny stars, and their frostiness on her skin felt like sparks.

"Are you lost, ma-ji?" the man asked, smiling roguishly at her as he flicked the water off his hands before wiping them dry against his clothes.

This wasn't the time to be dismayed by such trifles, but to tell the truth, the man, though younger than Katherine, wasn't so young that he ought to address her as mother. She stared at him frankly and saw the strands of white in his beard and hair, which she had missed from a distance. Then, remembering the state of her own hair, she let her hands hover above the ice sculptures on her head, and found herself laughing at the ridiculousness of it all.

The man took a step back. He raised his hands as if to show he intended no harm, the smile still parting his lips. Katherine decided that his nose was too long and his inscrutable eyes a strange color that was neither green nor gray, and his lips too thick despite being half-hidden by his mustache and beard. But surprisingly, these unappealing parts when put together made for a handsome face.

"Your hair," the man said, furrowing his brows.

Katherine looked around frantically for Mani. In these mountains, as in cities around the world, a husbandless, sonless woman was treated without a touch of solicitude. Mani's presence alone would have deterred this man from speaking to her.

"On your head," the man repeated, "grow trees of ice." He gestured with his hands that she should follow him. "Come with me, ma-ji," he said, and Katherine winced. "My camp is behind that hill. You need to dry yourself by a fire. Otherwise you'll catch pneumonia." His voice, though low, had a commanding tone that puzzled her.

If the attention of men had been disagreeable to her during her early travels and as much an obstacle to her ambitions as the monthly curse, she had no reason to be fearful now. The curse hadn't visited her for a while, and neither had the chills and feverish heats and wakeful nights that had followed its departure. Thorny hair sprouted on her chin, which had once been smooth. Men, even those older than her, *particularly if they were older than her,* were indifferent to her. They were unlikely to violate her person, though she still had to watch out for the thieves among them. Her present circumstances, however, were beggarly. Free of possessions, she was like Diogenes the cynic, falling asleep where she could, eating what she could. Even if the stranger hoped to steal, what could he take from her, she who had no beauty, youth, or money?

Still, it was unsafe.

She ought not to follow him.

She followed him.

Over his plain, straw-colored shirt, he wore a nomad's red-and-white shawl pulled together at the waist by a girdle, from which hung a knife sheathed in leather, and a few charms. It wasn't unusual for nomads from Sikkim to be armed with knives, but Katherine could tell from his features that he wasn't born in the mountains.

They arrived at his camp, marked only by a waterproof sheet, a dismantled tent, and a fire that was about to die but which he now revived with lichen and twigs. Then he stood away from her. By some process she couldn't explain, he seemed able to conceal himself in plain sight. It brought to her mind an insect that had startled her near Almora. On her leaning against the trunk of a tree, the insect, as long as her palm and with its shell the same color as the tree's peat-colored bark, had scrambled up, thereby disclosing its presence.

Katherine sat down by the fire. Who was this man, she wondered, a trader or a pilgrim, a bandit or a spy, the only ones who walked on this path over the Himalayas to Tibet? He had no caravan, no sheep, no goods to trade; no prayer beads moved between his fingers, no prayers misted his lips. The ice in her hair thawed and water trickled down her face.

"Not so close, mother," the man said. "Your hair will catch fire."

"How old do you think I am?" she snapped at him, wiping her face against the sleeves of her robe, not attempting to hide her temper or her accent and regretting it all at once. Buddhist monks, and even Mani, would have been dismayed by her vanity, her failure to leash her anger, but she couldn't overlook the unsuitable honorific that seemed to slip so easily from this man's tongue.

"What are you doing here?" he asked—gently, she noticed, as if to calm a snarling animal. "Alone in these mountains?"

"We're pilgrims. My son is with me. I was looking for him when I saw you." She spoke slowly, worried that the gender of verbs didn't match the nouns. Her ayah had taught her Hindustani when she was small, on summer afternoons when the house was quiet, and it was odd how swiftly those lessons came back to her along with memories of green parakeets and golden marigolds and the fiery vermilion on a deity's forehead, these colors so intense in her mind's eye it seemed to her that she always lived in two places at once, and two different people lived beneath her skin.

"You're a pilgrim?" the man asked.

Katherine heard the disbelief in his voice. *What are you, where are you from, who are you:* her appearance had always prompted these questions unless she was in the presence of a personage who could dispel the other's confusion. In England, she had been white at her father's side, her complexion an anomaly that could be overlooked against the cut of their fine clothes and the delicate whiteness of his skin. In Hindustan, when as a child she had followed her ayah around the garden, a newly hired gardener had taken her to be the ayah's daughter, and told the ayah she was lucky to have a generous mem-sahib who gifted her daughter good-as-new English dresses.

"Did you travel here from Dehra or Calcutta?" the man asked now.

"What about you?" Katherine said, something telling her he wouldn't give her an answer, and he shifted his weight from one foot to another, and the flicker of his body in her watery vision told her she was right.

"Terrible place, this," he said. "If you slip and fall, there's no one to rescue you."

"In that case you must take special care," she said. "My son will be here soon. He has gone to fetch firewood."

Her head was beginning to feel lighter, but her robe was simultaneously growing heavy with the meltwater from the ice in her hair. Then she heard Mani's voice. She stood up quickly and waved her hands though she couldn't see him. "I'm here," she shouted. Her voice was too feeble to carry over a distance. "That's him," she told the man. "My son."

"I don't see him," he said. He brought a threadbare but clean shirt out of a bundle and offered it to her. "Dry your hair." He pressed the shirt into her hands, his long fingers brushing against her skin, his expression innocent though his eyes sparkled with what could have been mischief. She couldn't tell if his overfamiliarity with her was deliberate or unintended. Social conventions in London didn't restrict those in the mountains. Here the people were wild but simpleminded, and men and women mingled much more freely than in other parts of the world.

Her hands moved the man's shirt over her hair. There was the animal scent of him in the fabric, which wasn't as clean as she had thought. It roused in her a longing that ought to surface only rarely in women her age. But Ethel's death had unhinged her. With nothing to tether her mind to the world, it flitted between fear and anger and desire, like a ghost that could pass through stones.

"Shall I?" the man asked, pointing at the shirt in her hands. "Let me help you."

She flung the shirt at his face and he caught it deftly, laughing as if he sensed her anger was merely an act. Something drew her to him as the ocean was pulled toward the moon, but she ignored the degrading impulse and walked in the direction from which she had heard Mani's voice.

"Wherever did you go?" she said when she spotted Mani standing a few feet from the waterfall, his hands rubbing his prickly scalp as if to coax a wish-granting genie to emerge from his skull.

"Mother, I thought the storm had taken you," he said.

He looked so relieved to see her that Katherine forgot the sharp words with which she had resolved to admonish him. The last person who cared if she was alive or dead had been Ethel.

"What is this, on your head?" Mani asked. "Did you sleep out in the rain because the tent collapsed? You must have called for me. I'm sorry I didn't hear you."

"Don't do it again," she said, lifting the ends of her hair where shards of ice still clung to the strands.

At the camp, Mani folded her blanket and tent and managed to gather dry moss in sufficient quantity to build a fire. On the mountaintops the sun's rays were amber-colored and languid. But around her brooding shadows still stole the shapes of rocks.

While Mani boiled water in the one pot he carried, Katherine found a natural privy enclosed by rocks to piss and shit. Then she returned to the river to wash herself as best as she could, simultaneously anticipating and dreading a second meeting with the stranger. But he wasn't there. The river had blotted out his footprints. In spite of herself, she felt disappointed. Perhaps he had only been an apparition concocted by her febrile mind.

Back at the camp, Mani had prepared a breakfast of tea thickened with roasted barley. Called suttoo or tsampa, the barley was a staple among travelers, its advantage being that it was already partially cooked and therefore saved one both time and fuel; in Tibet twigs were scarce, and food took twice as long to prepare on account of the altitude. A mouthful of the tsampa, from the wooden bowl that served as her cup, saucer, and plate, steadied her limbs.

"I saw a man," she told Mani, "not far from here."

"I saw him too."

"You did? I wasn't—"

"We must keep our distance from strangers, mother. Unscrupulous people on this route steal from traders and pilgrims."

"Where are these traders and pilgrims?"

"There will be many now that the weather has improved. And we don't want anyone to find out you're really from London."

For a few pressing moments, his words caused doubts to assail her mind again. Lhasa seemed too far; only a couple of Englishmen and male European missionaries had reached the holy city since the beginning of time, and she wondered if those of her sex were indeed too frail for such an arduous undertaking. Perhaps the altitude or the cold would kill her. Vultures would feast on her corpse in a ravine or on a hilltop. Then, the tsampa warmed her throat, and the vines of dread binding her chest slackened. She reminded herself that in her travels, as in her writing, it had served her well to look no further than the next hundred steps, the next hundred words. And for shame, how could she even consider what would happen to her corpse? The philosophers she admired had been scornful of ceremony. Diogenes had asked for his body to be thrown out of the city walls and fed to dogs.

Was her life in London better than this? In Frederick's house the same questions were put to her at the same hour every day: what she desired to eat, which dress she wanted to wear, how thick visiting cards ought to be. Others enjoyed the monotony, or delighted in buying new gowns and lace-bordered handkerchiefs every other day, but to her it was a trial. The surprises she encountered in her journeys might be irksome (she thought of the stranger) or pleasant (she thought of the stranger), but only at the edge of the precipice could one appreciate the true value of life. Or did she believe so because of a flaw in her character, a deficiency she ought to remedy?

"We mustn't linger," Mani said. "The route will grow steeper before it levels. At Garbyang, we'll find provisions, but the place is overrun with Tibetans at this time of the year, and their yaks and sheep. The Taklakot jongpen's men will likely be in disguise among them, to find out if there are any sahibs about, trying to sneak into their country. Of course, it's unlikely they'll notice you, but we must be cautious." As he spoke, Mani worked away to push her tent into his sack. She understood he was voicing his thoughts so as to plan his actions. He wasn't applying to her for advice; he didn't seem keen to receive it.

The sun rose higher in the sky, at last offering warmth. The rocks, varnished by the rain, shimmered. Though still far from a soothing melody, the river no longer sounded as if it was raging.

"What is sunshine but a divine coat for those too poor to afford sheepskin?" Mani said, chortling to himself.

Katherine scraped her bowl clean with her fingers. She could eat with her hands like a native, her mother had always said, mouth twisted by scorn. Dead now for over a decade, and still whispering truths in her ear.

Mani heaped their vessels in a rag and said he would rinse them at the river. Katherine warmed her hands over the fire. Her hair was still damp, but her headache had dulled.

After Mani returned, he secured her bundle to her back with a rope, fashioning straps that he looped around her shoulders. The weight of the sack cut into her skin. Shading her eyes, Katherine squinted into the distance. Her vision was not what it used to be. The mountains loomed ahead, conspiratorial in their silence.

3.

———

NO WALL OR FENCE MARKED THE END OF THE MANA PASS.
They stepped from one country to another and the land was as forlorn, and the wind as harsh, as it had been a moment ago.

Balram shaded his eyes. Seven, maybe six, years ago, he had stood on this very spot with Gyan, nothing around them except for a flighty herd of antelopes in the distance, the sun scalding their eyes. Gyan had pulled Balram toward his chest and clutched his hair with a viciousness that Balram thought petulant, and then they had gone in opposite directions, each of their footsteps claiming different regions of a country that wasn't theirs for a white man. Now, some part of Balram ached with want, for the burning in his scalp as Gyan departed with a strand or two of his hair like a talisman to tie around his wrist.

"Is this it?" the captain asked, a brightness in his eyes that one could mistake for madness. "We're on the Roof of the World?" His robe was in tatters where it had snagged on rocks, and he looked even more beggarly than before. He had exchanged his notebook for the accoutrements of a pilgrim: a japa mala that he called the rosary and a Tibetan prayer wheel that he spun in the same direction as the hands of a clock.

"The jongpen of Tsaparang must have set up an inspection camp farther ahead," Balram said, as if apologizing for the lack of pageantry at the border.

The wind howled, scattering his words. The landscape was magnificent in its desolation. It mocked them with its sudden dips and rises, and by altering its hues as a chameleon would so that no sooner had the eye settled on red than it appeared to be gray or purple. Balram gazed up at the white clouds drifting across the blue sky and wished they would carry a message to Durga or Gyan. But while a cloud would oblige the exiled spirit in Kalidasa's *Meghdoot*, yearning for his beloved, mere mortals like Balram couldn't hope to bend its ear.

"Do you think the jongpen himself will make a personal appearance?" the captain asked now. "Must have no time left, that man, after entertaining Russian spies. Tibetans are fools if they think they can form an alliance with the Russians against the British Empire."

"I doubt any Russian has made it beyond the Pamirs, sir."

"Can't put anything past them," the captain said, sacrilegiously attempting to remove the dirt under a fingernail with the bud-like tip of his prayer wheel. "Tashkent and Samarkand are now with the Tsar."

"Sir," Balram said gently, and indicated with a turn of the wrist that the captain should refrain from employing the prayer wheel as a tool for personal grooming.

"Right," the captain said, his tone as prickly as a wounded cat, and wiped the wheel's tip against his robe. "Seeing as the bearers are catching their breath, we have sufficient time to measure the latitude here. Balram, the sextant?"

"Tibetan soldiers may arrive here at any moment, sir. We don't want to make them suspicious. Once we're in an isolated area, perhaps then?"

"I suppose that's the more prudent course," the captain said, as if he was the one doing Balram a favor.

Balram missed the luxury of traveling alone, when he was accountable for no one but himself. On his own, without sheep and bearers to worry him, he was quicker too. Having Gyan with him hadn't altered his pace either; their steps had matched, and so had their thoughts. When they trained together, Gyan would offer

Balram water the exact moment he realized he was thirsty but before he had reached for a goatskin bag. About to slip on a tricky slope, he would find Gyan's hands arresting his fall. A cut in Gyan's hand would result in a dull ache pulsing beneath Balram's skin. In the village some cackled they were like a married couple, and it didn't matter to Gyan, him never having married, but Balram could tell Durga didn't like hearing it much.

His mind was now darting around like a dragonfly and he wanted to pin it down. How long would it take him to find Gyan? Shigatse, where Gyan was said to be locked up in a monastery by the Tsangpo, was at least a three-month walk from here for their group. On his own Balram could have scrambled across passes and peaks in less than a month, but the animals needed half a day for grazing on the occasional clusters of grass they came across, and there was no avoiding that.

The captain asked Balram to fetch him water from a goatskin bag tied to the spirited pony, but before Balram could oblige him, Yogi hefted the bag and produced a bowl so the captain could drink from it decorously. Then Yogi hovered around the captain, bashful black eyes glittering and hands running nervously over his hair as if he was serving a princess. Balram had seen his kind before, men who believed in the superiority of white skin, men inclined to make themselves appear slight so that their stooped backs would let the white man feel twice as tall.

"You look frightful," the captain told Balram once he had slaked his thirst. "But so must I."

He licked the blood crusted on his lips, recovered the stump of a pencil and a creased scrap of paper from the folds of his robe, and scribbled on the fragment. Then he deposited it inside the prayer wheel, altered for this purpose at the Survey headquarters. In appearance it resembled the pilgrim's prayer wheel whose golden cylinder, carved with elaborate flowers and sacred words, was affixed to a weighted chain and rotated on a wooden rod. But the captain's prayer wheel contained, in the place of mantras, his notes. Balram had carried a similar one on his previous journeys. Each evening he would

reorder the fragments inside the cylinder, poring over them as a
scholar would. Occasionally a dreadful fear would take hold in his
mind that his measurements were erroneous, but if it had kept him
awake at night in his first year of surveying, time and practice had
made him more certain of his skills and instincts.

"My distances for this region adhere closely with your calculations," the captain said, "if I'm remembering them correctly, of
course."

These words sounded to Balram like the rasps of a knife against
whetstone. "You taught me to walk," he said rather gruffly, but the
captain didn't seem to hear the belligerence in his tone.

"A slight exaggeration, your mother would note."

"Died when I was born, sir."

"Is that so? But didn't you say . . . Never mind. I must have been
mistaken."

The rosary, wound around the captain's left wrist and hand,
moved awkwardly between his fingers. Survey-issued like the prayer
wheel, it looked ordinary and was scratched as if the captain had been
praying with it since his childhood. But its beads numbered one hundred instead of the conventional hundred and eight in the japa malas
favored by Buddhists. To track distances, the surveyor slipped a bead
every hundred paces. The tenth bead was a size bigger than the other
nine, making it easier for the fingers and the mind to keep count.

Before their first Tibetan tours, the captain had instructed Balram
and Gyan not only on the correct way to employ these devices, but
also to walk such that they covered almost a mile in two thousand
paces, each pace being thirty-one-and-a-half inches. They had practiced this walk for months, a rope tied around their ankles, its tensity
against their skin telling them if the foot had been placed forward at
the right distance.

"Is this why you wanted me to join the Survey?" Gyan had said
one morning as they sweltered in a wintry breeze after marching up
and down the same path a hundred times, and Balram thought Gyan
meant the way in which their bodies were entangled, thought he had

sensed the pleasure Balram found in it. "So I can suffer like you," Gyan continued, and Balram felt something like relief that also tasted muddy like disappointment.

It was true that he had convinced Gyan to work for the captain. Gyan was smarter than most white men, but what did that get you in a land that was no longer yours? The title of a clerk, a junior position in the army, a dresser in a hospital, and these jobs that didn't tax his intellect Gyan simply wouldn't do. Instead he had taken to wandering the streets, spending far too much time with itinerant boys who taught bears to dance, or the falconer's son who was known to be a wastrel, and on many evenings the two had been seen entering the woods together, to trap birds, they said, even if they always returned with their hands empty. Gyan's mother begged Balram to help her son. When Balram suggested the Survey, Gyan agreed, perhaps because Balram had spoken of the long hours he would have to spend alone, walking under the sun and the stars, in snowstorms and hailstorms, counting the steps in his head like a secretive, shameful prayer darting from his mouth to the ears of gods.

The captain had believed Balram when he said Gyan would make for a good surveyor, and that a Swedish explorer would enlist him otherwise. Before the captain recruited him, Balram had collected rudimentary details about Tibet's topography for the Swede who had wandered into his school, looking to hire a native who could endure Tibet's altitude and had a sound grasp of geometry and algebra. In his own mind the captain competed with the Swede for both mastery of the region and the men who could map it, and so Gyan—whom the Swede had never heard of—had found himself with a job at the Survey.

Balram's bond with Gyan changed in the years they worked together. He couldn't tell how, the changes being near imperceptible. Together they encountered wilderness and strangeness, and saw aspects in each other's character that only proximity to death could reveal. Sometimes they felt as if they were the only two people in the world. Everything else vanishing. Balram concealed his wants, something he had learned to do as a child. Still, a new intimacy had emerged between the two of them, shimmering dangerously; to Balram it had felt like the edge of a knife pressed against his throat.

"I must have a word with the bearers," Balram said to the captain now. "Remind them not to speak out of turn and unwittingly give us up at the inspection camp. That goes for you too, Yogi."

"I would never," Yogi said.

"Why would they speak against us?" the captain said. "No man who worked for me has ever turned against me—if we disregard the events of yesterday. Which we must, because they were cowards. Even during the height of the Sepoy Mutiny, my native surveyors chose to remain with me, and our map-making in Kashmir progressed well."

Balram, watching the captain twirl the prayer wheel, had to admit he wasn't cut from the same cloth as other masters. The Englishman who started the Great Trigonometrical Survey across Hindustan was known to have flogged his bearers, being of the view that corporal punishment was *odious* but necessary. The captain admired that man, and his assistant after whom the Royal Geographical Society had renamed the highest peak in the world four years ago, but he loathed their methods for instilling discipline.

Much more likely to wield a book than a whip, the captain looked happiest when describing how one could calculate altitude from the boiling point of water, or measure latitude with a sextant. He was fastidious about records, scrupulous in the care of surveying instruments and, in direct contrast, surprisingly lackadaisical about the affairs of his heart, there being some truth to the rumor that in Calcutta, Simla, and every other village in Kashmir was a woman and a half-caste child who could lay claim to his name. But Balram couldn't see how the captain's flaws or merits could endear him to these bearers whose livelihoods remained precarious whether the earth was deemed flat or round. The span of the Indian Ocean, belted by land in Ptolemy's map of the world or allowed to greet the Pacific in the maps of Islamic geographers, had no bearing on their lives. What had Gyan said once? *A map may anoint a man Tibetan or Kumaoni, but it can no more alter his soul than the wind can scatter the constellation of stars in the sky.*

Balram walked toward the bearers squatting on the ground. They warned each other of his approach with nudges. He gestured they needn't stand, as they felt compelled to do when the captain addressed them, and they looked at him as if the thought hadn't crossed their minds.

"Are the goatskins full?" Balram asked Naga, the quiet, emaciated-looking bearer from whose hollow eye sockets Yama, the God of Death himself, seemed to peer out. Balram had put Naga in charge of water collection despite his feeble protest. He wasn't a bhisti, Naga had said; he wasn't even a Musalman. It was the most Balram had ever heard him speak.

"Naga, why pretend you can't hear the Compass-wallah?" Ujjal asked. "Your job is to ensure we won't die of thirst. That doesn't make you a bhisti. The colonel is the bhisti."

"Colonel?" Balram asked.

"On account of the pony's airs, we have anointed him Colonel," Ujjal said, laughing at his own little joke. "He's the highest-ranking officer in our party."

"The bags are full," Naga said hoarsely, flinching as if the sound of his own voice was disagreeable to him. Balram wondered if he ate little so as to disappear. His pockets were swollen with nuts and dried fruits, an endless supply of food that he shared with others and never partook of himself.

"I was telling them a story I heard in Mana," Jagan said.

Balram pressed a finger on the two half-inch creases that Durga said had deepened like scars between his eyebrows. He was wary of Jagan; the young man had an excessive reverence for nature that hinted more at madness than mysticism. He even had the appearance of a tree, with his timber-colored skin, canopy of curly hair that couldn't be tamed with oil, thick limbs that stretched like branches, and a beard that advanced across his cheeks with the ponderous hesitancy of moss growing over bole.

"Jagan wants us to avoid Toling," Ujjal said.

"No doubt he will tell me why," Balram said.

Jagan looked like he had changed his mind, but then said, "A trader I met at Mana saw a bearlike beast in Toling, carrying a boulder the size of a hill on its shoulder. Its footprints were four times wider and longer than ours." The sun lit his voluminous hair from behind, turning patches of it copper and gold, seemingly conferring upon him the blessings of gods.

"What is it that you want?" Balram said, fixing the men with a stare that they returned without wincing. "It's not as if I hired the lot of you through lies and deceit." He paused, aware this was exactly what he had done.

"We agreed to enter Tibet," Pawan said, "but not with a white man. The Tibetans will take one look at the captain and know the truth. What if they throw us into the Tsangpo for helping a foreigner?"

"I don't remember you complaining when you collected your advance," Balram said. "Your wages are high because it's a dangerous mission."

"But you can choose a less dangerous route," Jagan said, kneading his left elbow. "We don't have to pass Toling to reach the Tsangpo."

"It's safer than wandering through tracks I haven't walked on before," Balram said. The men muttered under their breaths. "I don't disagree that caution is vital in a journey such as ours," Balram continued. "Fear is good. Fear keeps us safe. But I'm old enough to know that if you keep worrying about a shadow darkening the horizon, you're bound to miss the crocodile at your feet though it be ever so plain."

Why do you sound like an Englishman? Gyan asked.

Balram felt a sense of exhaustion constrict his chest. They had crossed a border they couldn't see but whose presence they couldn't dispute. One could argue then that belief alone could similarly render an invisible beast corporeal. Besides, not everything could be sundered into triangles and arcs with theodolites and sextants. The universe had many dark recesses, and a man's life was too short to illumine each one of them.

"The captain is a smart man," Balram said, because it simply wouldn't do to confess his ignorance. "His views are not shaped by superstition but by modern science. He believes no more in monsters than I do in miracles." *And if that doesn't stop me from wishing for a miracle*—an image of Inder, his son, his third and last child, distant, implacable, tugging at Durga's silken hair with such vehemence tears dampened her cheeks, arrived like a lightning flash, and vanished just as quickly—*at least I needn't admit it to others.*

The sun burned his face, and Balram wished he could divest himself of his coat, but the wind was sharp against his neck. He took out the felt cap he had bunched into one of his coat pockets, and pulled it down his forehead. It offered scant protection. *Gods forgive me,* he thought. *Don't let me be the reason wives become widows.*

"Will you force us to march to Toling?" Jagan asked.

"Really, Jagan, a wily merchant made up a story about a monster to scare you away. That's all. No need to make a fuss about it," Ujjal said. "If fewer traders visit Gartok, that man will secure a good bargain. You must have told him you were a trader yourself, and he decided to frighten you. He clearly succeeded without exerting himself too much."

Jagan smacked Ujjal on the head. Ujjal curled his fists, and Balram bent down to restrain him as the other bearers sucked their teeth. Out of the corner of his eye, Balram saw the captain watching the squabble, Yogi whispering in his ear.

"Stop this at once," Balram said, smiling as if the men were merely teasing each other, but the strain of it hurt his lips, brittle as dried leaves. "We mustn't argue. This is how expeditions fail. This is how good people end up in Tibetan prisons. Jagan, whether there are beasts or not, fear won't stop the trader who spoke to you from going to Tibet and bartering his wares—why should it stop us?"

"I didn't say a word until now. I didn't want to cause panic in our party. If three of our men hadn't disappeared on the pass, I would have never brought it up," Jagan said.

"I appreciate your tact," Balram said, drawing up a hasty plan in his mind. "Look, we can't avoid Toling altogether, but we won't stop there for the night." It seemed to be an acceptable compromise. Balram placed his hand on Jagan's shoulder and said, "I'm glad you reminded us to treat this land with respect."

"I feel it here," Jagan said, tapping his left elbow with a knuckle. "A pain I have learned not to ignore. It comes with the greatest regularity before misfortune strikes, just as clouds foretell rain. A frightful calamity awaits us."

"A gray sky doesn't always result in a torrent," Balram said.

THEY SAW NEITHER PEOPLE nor animals on their first march beyond the border. The bearers bore the strain the altitude placed on them without complaint, but Colonel, the pony, was nothing but trouble, kicking off dust in its attempt to return the way they had come. If its racing prowess had gone unnoticed before, now it was undeniable as the shepherds chased after the animal, stumbling over boulders, the rattle of their lungs as loud as their breathless shouts. By the time they caught up with the pony and persuaded it to return, half its load had scattered on the ground. Balram helped the shepherds gather what they could, and told them not to worry about the water that had spilled from the goatskin bags; they would soon come across patches of snow the sun hadn't yet melted.

"We'll face many problems big and small every step of our journey," Balram told Samarth, one of the two shepherds, who was thirteen or fourteen, certainly no older than fifteen. His head only reached Balram's chest, and all his bones were so loose and pliable his limbs appeared to be held together by fine threads. Balram wouldn't have brought along someone so young on such a perilous trip, but when he recruited the older shepherd, Rudra, he had claimed the boy was a distant relative who would starve to death if left to fend for himself. "I don't care if he dies," Rudra had said heartlessly, "but it would be a pity, don't you think?" So Balram had relented, because he saw something of himself in the orphan, or maybe he saw Inder, or the boy Inder could have been. The bearers weren't as patient with

Samarth, who tended to run around the camp, legs and hands knocking into trunks and pots.

By the path they walked, the skull of a yak, stripped of flesh and fur, gleamed bald and white above a pile of mani stones. These reminders of death, of impermanence, were everywhere in Tibet, but the prayer *Om Mani Padme Hum* scrawled in Tibetan between the horns invested the skull with sacredness too.

"If it had been higher, the stone heap would have made for a capital object to take a compass bearing," the captain said.

Always he seemed to think about surveying, the position of stars, the distance between two landmarks and the heights of mountains, his mind never meandering like the rivers he followed, the world perhaps appearing to him to be intersected by the curved bars of latitude and longitude. Gyan must have worked for the captain as long as he had because he admired the captain's rigor. But that couldn't have been the only reason.

I stayed at the Survey for you. Is that what you want me to say? Gyan taunted him.

Gyan hadn't been one for small talk or long discussions, unless he had a gallon of drink in him, but now it seemed he couldn't stop. Of the seven trips they had made to Tibet for the captain, they had traveled together on only two occasions. On other surveys they had parted at the border, or at the Survey office, to enter Tibet from different regions, Gyan from Nepal and Balram from Leh, the captain's reasoning being that if one was detained, at least the other could continue surveying the country.

Once, after bidding farewell to Gyan, Balram had walked up the path, thinking he wouldn't see his friend for another six months or a year; they never knew how long their expeditions would last, or if they would return alive, being at the mercy of the weather and their bodies. At a bend he turned around on an impulse and there was Gyan, standing and watching him, a severe expression on his face. Balram had waved in an indifferent fashion and walked ahead. Later, slipping his hand into his pocket, he had found two jalebis that Gyan had wrapped in a leaf and left for him, their stickiness already seeping into the fabric of his coat. He couldn't imagine how or where Gyan had managed to purchase these. Balram had made each piece last as long as it could, its sweetness on his tongue dazzling like lightning.

The captain stopped walking, his thumb and index finger paused on a bead of the rosary. Perhaps he was too awestruck by yet another change in the character of the country to count his paces.

"Never seen anything like this before," the captain said, pointing at the ravines and mountain ridges that resembled the spines of primordial animals cloaked in dust. Where the sun fell squarely on the slopes, these appeared to have been cast in sand, likely to crumble if a hawk as much as rested its talons on a jutting shoulder. Elsewhere, the ridges glittered as if a thousand gold coins had been concealed in their furrows. Behind these were mountains the color of coal, their peaks cased in smooth, satin sheets of snow.

The wind tugged at Balram's coat, whispering, it seemed to him, the Tibetan chant he had glimpsed on the yak skull.

"Only a few months ago I visited Calcutta," the captain said. "I walked around its parks. I attended banquets and drank wine that was ridiculously dear and beer that was almost boiling. I slept in a delightful bedroom at the Bengal Club and took baths in a tub. Baths, remember those? How indulgent." Then, as if reminded he was speaking to someone who had only ever known the still waters of a pond or the currents of a river, he shook his head. "The life we had before, how easily it can blur as we wander. Calcutta seems like a lie. This"—he pointed at the cliffs the wind had wrought into fantastical shapes—"is all that is true." He stepped forward and the rosary click-clicked. "You see, Balram, this is why I'm glad we're surveyors, not writers. Our numbers will never lie. Our numbers are eloquent. Our numbers will impress others with their fidelity to nature."

"How so, sir?"

"I told you once that I found a certain missionary's account of his time in Tibet lacking, because bad health and adverse weather caused him to judge this country harshly. Our prejudices, our yearning for home or comfort, may thus taint our words, but they can't alter our surveys. You can't rebut routes and maps with arguments."

"Is that true?" Balram asked.

"Why wouldn't it be?"

"Of course," Balram said.

Good, hold your peace, Durga said.

But Gyan had shown him that no matter how scientific their dispositions, ultimately their eyes sketched the maps, not their surveying instruments. Didn't al-Idrisi's world map place Mecca at the center of the world? Didn't Mercator's projection of the globe distort the size of countries so that the ones white men called home appeared bigger than those in Africa? For years Balram had accepted the map of the world as true until Gyan pointed out that the same map would be accurate if Hindustan were to be at its very top, and England below, the earth being a sphere after all. But how could Gyan, or Balram, place all the blame on white men when they themselves weren't above reproach? Many of the captain's existing maps of Tibet had been knitted together by tracing the movements of their feet on this sacred ground, their bodies merely instruments to undertake measurements, engineer's chains forged from pliant bones and sinews and clothed in skin and flesh.

Balram had been proud he could conduct a survey with none of the modern instruments that English officers had, but he had also known that to map the country without their permission was a betrayal of Tibetans, more his kin than the English. So surveying to him had always been a source of pride and shame.

The captain's thick, dyed brows were knitted as he watched Samarth retrace his steps toward them with all the elegance of a heron stuck in mud. Balram wondered if the boy had counted the sheep and realized that one, or more, were missing. A bearer named Mor cautioned Samarth to be careful. "We're meant to walk quietly so as not to draw attention to ourselves, but even a deaf lion could hear your racket," he said.

Samarth stopped in front of the captain and wheezed out a series of words, his mouth half-full with a roti he must have saved from that afternoon's meal. A Tibetan inspection camp was less than a mile ahead, he said. "Should we turn back?" he asked.

"What for?" Balram said. Then, indicating the crumbs of food stuck to the edges of the boy's mouth, he said, "Clean it up." The boy used his thumb to deftly channel the food back into his mouth.

"We weren't planning to sneak in, Sam," the captain said. "Remember? We're going to let them examine us and our possessions."

Balram was surprised by the kindness with which the captain spoke to Samarth, but kept his face impassive.

"Go back to the front," Balram told the boy. "I'll be there in a minute."

The captain ruffled Samarth's hair and, with a pat on his shoulder, sent him stumbling back to his sheep.

"I heard the men are whispering about my disguise," the captain said. "They're worried I'll be caught."

"Sir," Balram said. "You shouldn't believe everything Yogi tells you. He works hard, but he thinks he's better than everyone else."

"Doesn't matter what he thinks," the captain said, testily, smoothing down his robe with his knuckles. "I'll be fine, of that I am certain." In his eyes flickered the full range of human emotion: pride, fear, excitement, apprehension.

4.

I HAVE BEEN IN Garbyang for two nights. M— and
I were compelled to halt and seek shelter after two days of
heavy rain made me quite ill. Our hosts, whom M— knows
from his previous journeys to Tibet, have fed us such enormous quantities of meat that I now feel restored in body and
soul. Fortunately, they are not suspicious of my presence
and believe I'm a pilgrim eager to see Mansarovar and
Mount Kailas.

This afternoon I sought the curative properties of open air
and managed to take a walk around the village. I was struck
by the number of women smoking tobacco outside their
houses. If a passing young man caught their fancy, they did
not hesitate to hoist their skirts above their ankles and kick a
stone in his direction. They see themselves as equal to men, a
sentiment I wish I saw more among the ladies of England.

I believe this laxity in moral code is a result of Tibetan in-
fluence. Trade between the two regions being frequent, the
people of Garbyang still pay taxes to Tibetan officials and are
more susceptible to immoral Tibetan codes than the civilized
practices promoted by the British government.

There was much excitement in the village about a dance
that serves as an opportunity for men and women to find suitable partners. The "ballroom" where the dance is usually
held looked like a hovel with not much by way of creature
comforts. The liaisons formed at this disreputable place are
responsible for the illegitimate toddlers seen stumbling on the

grass without the hands of an elder to steady them. Naturally
I decided not to attend the dance, despite the opportunity it
afforded me to observe native ceremonies.

FOR MOST OF THE day the weather was foul. Without the sun, there
was no telling the time; hours blurred into each other as did the views.
Katherine could have passed the Garden of Eden and not known it.
She was damp and shivering and half-stupefied. Around her neck she
felt an iron chain whose clasp her fingers worked furiously to undo.
When Mani said she was delirious, she recited lines from *King John:*

> *I will instruct my sorrows to be proud.*
> *For grief is proud, and makes his owner stoop.*

Dusk arrived without warning. The clouds that had concealed the
sun gave way to swirls of thick, white fog. Mani wanted to inquire at
the village about an English doctor. "We're more likely to encounter
a Christian missionary," Katherine said, and Mani didn't disagree. A
sturdy constitution allowed visitors to scale the Himalaya, but only
travelers who served God were compelled to make a home in these
inhospitable heights. Katherine wondered what the missionaries,
bartering away a life of comfort, received in return. A square foot of
heaven for every heathen saved?

Blasphemous, these thoughts. When she had published her first
book with letters about the monks in Kalimpong, some had accused
her of abandoning Christianity and endorsing paganism. Katherine
couldn't explain that if one traveled the world as she did, it became
clear that each person's god served them. Such a provocative statement would have offended her readership and so, when she went to
church every Sunday with Frederick, she insisted she had chronicled
the monks' rituals only as a form of ethnography. Even if she wished
to be honest, she couldn't have described what drew her to Buddhist

texts or why she found the notion of impermanence, central to Buddhism, appealing. Was it because she had no sense of self?

Oh, she was delirious.

Her eyes refused to stay open as she stumbled forward, grasping at ghosts. Gunshots echoed across the sky. Below, the river's squall was equally threatening and loud. Her foot struck a rock, and a pain almost sweet and piquant floated up her veins. The air smelled not of rain but of smoke. Something was burning, her flesh maybe, but already it smelled like rot too. Through half-open eyes she saw the fog rippling down the slopes, hushing the gasps of trees. She sank under the heaviness of her sack and found herself being propelled forward by the slipperiness of the earth, which having yielded to the rain was more clay than stone. She flailed her hands about but couldn't find a boulder to arrest her fall. She was slipping into the netherworld. Soon she would be under the earth, where her flesh would become bones. The roots of cedar trees would weave a scarf over her clavicles, and worms would emerge from the sockets of her eyes.

Then she felt Mani's hands hooking underneath and around her shoulders and lifting her up. He grunted from the effort, but managed to hoist her to her feet. Her robe was askew and her boots loose and she felt the drunkenness of the fever thrumming in her veins. Never before had she fallen ill on her travels. In London, she had been known to prescribe over dinner a journey to the East as a cure for any decline in one's faculties and limbs. But perhaps now she was too old, too frail, to endure weather so inclement and circumstances so adverse. Lhasa would remain an unfulfilled dream, and the twinge in her chest made her think how strange it was that a mere dream could have the substance of a person whom one longed to see but couldn't, the shape of its loss palpable, as if one had wandered into the room of a dead sister and discovered in her journal a note that she had left for herself and to which she would now never return.

IN THE EARLY MORNING the clanking of pails shook Katherine awake. A crevice in the window shutters admitted a lone sunbeam into the room. She listened for the ticking of the clock before consciousness returned to alert her that she was no longer in London. But where was she? She pushed away the blanket—her own, she noted, without relief. Her nose twitched as it took in the sour and sharp smells of dung, smoke, and incense. She had become habituated to the fragrance of cedars and the fresh scent of dew and earth swollen with rain. From the floor below came the thuds of hooves, and the grunts and bellows of cows or yaks. Of the previous night she had no recollection beyond nearly falling off a mountain, and the fever, now thankfully broken, that had befuddled her.

The light was faint, but sufficient for her to grasp that the room was heaped with blankets and bundles of clothes and blocks of dried meat. A woollen rug on the floor had served as her mattress. Next to it was a deerskin trunk on which a cotton quilt lay neatly folded, for her to use should her blanket prove inadequate against the cold. Its presence suggested kindness. Perhaps this was the dwelling of someone Mani knew.

Katherine's legs buckled from the exhaustion of the journey and the fever. Her feet were bare. Crusted over her blisters and sores was a green paste that smelled medicinal. She wondered if Mani had applied it and felt a fondness for the boy that she recognized as naive. He *had to* take care of her; his wages depended on her good health. How deranged her mind must be on this journey, her first tour after Ethel's death, for her to imagine that insignificant gestures from strangers—the offer of medicine from a servant or a cloth from a passerby to dry herself—appeared as markers of affection.

Past a low doorway, she climbed down a ladder that shook with each one of her wary steps. At the foot of the ladder were cows, yaks, and dzos, a cross-breed of the yak and the cow, watching her curiously as they chewed their cud. Flies buzzed above the piles of dung on the ground that she stepped around, nostrils pinched. After all these years of traveling around the Orient, the native's deficiency in cleanliness still appalled her.

Outside the stable, a woman carried a pail of water into a hovel. The smoke that coiled out of its door suggested it served as the kitchen. The woman's turquoise and coral necklaces clattered as she walked, and if she noticed Katherine she gave no indication. Katherine had no intention of following her into the kitchen, where the native woman might expect her to fetch water or slice vegetables or pluck feathers from the carcass of a hen.

Two men sat away from the stable door on a rug spread on the ground. A little boy with ruddy cheeks climbed over them as if they were boulders and grew disappointed when they didn't sit still. The men looked similar enough to be father and son.

Mani emerged from the kitchen, a steaming bowl in his hands. The child stopped troubling the men to watch him. "Do you remember what happened last night?" he asked Katherine as he handed her the bowl, tea filled to its brim. "It started raining again—a torrent."

Katherine took a sip of the tea, rich with yak milk and sugar and as restorative as any bottle of medicinal syrup could claim to be.

"This kind gentleman here offered us a bed," Mani said, bowing in the direction of the older man, whose face had been marked vigorously by the pox. "He always opens his house to pilgrims—for a small fee."

Katherine gazed up at the house that had sheltered her without her knowing, and the mountains that soared into the sky behind it. The house was no palace but grand for these parts, a two-story affair with stone walls and a slate roof, doors and windows arranged in such perfect symmetry that it was pleasing to the eye as a painting might be, though admittedly she was no connoisseur of fine art. From nowhere a sense of vertigo seized her and she swayed. The ground beneath her feet wasn't as firm as she would have liked it to be.

Mani helped her sit on the uneven stone steps that led down from the front door.

"Am I right in thinking that, while almost unconscious, I climbed a flimsy ladder to the room in which I woke up?" she asked Mani.

"Not exactly," he said.

The native men were speaking to each other about tilling their fields or trading with Tibetans; Katherine couldn't follow their dialect. She imagined them, and the woman who was now in the kitchen, carrying her up the ladder, with Mani's help. How embarrassing. The tea in her bowl was swiftly losing its warmth.

"You should rest here for a couple of days," Mani said. "They won't mind."

"What if they discover I'm English? Even the government doesn't know I'm planning to travel to Tibet."

Mani gently flicked away an insect that had climbed up the sleeve of his robe. "The path over the mountains from Garbyang to Tibet is short but difficult," he said. "It will be snowing, and it is so high up there you'll feel exhausted after five steps." His eyes observed her hands, trembling in the morning wind. "Remember we have to walk all the way to"—he lowered his voice—"Lhasa. At your age, you have to be cautious. Regain your strength first. These are comfortable quarters you have here."

"I appreciate your candor," Katherine said. "But I don't need a lecture on the infirmities of old age, and certainly not from you."

"Say you reach halfway up the Lipulekh Pass and find that you can't take another step. What then? Do you expect me to carry you over the mountain?"

"Why not? God knows I'm paying you enough," she said.

"You're every bit as stubborn as my sisters, and my mother," he said, and it surprised her, the revelation that this monk-to-be had a family, and that he spoke as if she too was a part of it.

The fever must have weakened her mind because she heard herself say, "I'll stay another night, but then we're leaving."

KATHERINE WASN'T PARTICULAR ABOUT what she was offered to eat, having decided early on in her life that she would express no sentiment apart from gratitude to those who spared her a task as loathsome as cooking. But, if not beset with European prejudices, even the most fastidious of gourmands would have struggled to find fault with the lunch their hosts served: vegetable dumplings so airy and light one could eat ten in the blink of an eye, millet bread glistening with ghee, tender slices of lamb roasted with dried berries from

China that stung the lips and numbed the tongue, and rice beer that was sweet and bitter and tasted not all that different from ale. With great restraint Katherine didn't address the feast like a savage, though she wasn't coy about accepting second helpings either.

After the meal, Katherine found herself alone, the others having repaired to various corners of the house. Mani had issued strict instructions to her to rest, but sleep had deserted her, and feeling stronger on account of the enormous portions of meat consumed, she set out for a walk.

The fever's malevolence remained in her blood and slowed her steps. For a brief moment she imagined the vertiginous climb over the Lipulekh Pass that awaited her and saw herself stuck at a midway point, as Mani had predicted. Always this fear burbling in her like a brook. *Worry about it tomorrow*, she told herself.

Garbyang was small despite being a prominent trading post. The path on which she walked tapered toward the edge of a plateau whose steep slope raced to meet the Kali a few hundred feet below. Flat-roofed houses faced the direction of the river. The rain had perfumed the air and brightened the colors of nature so that leaves were no longer plain green but emerald green, and flowers weren't merely red but swayed in the breeze with the fieriness of rubies.

In her place, a male explorer would have noted down the temperature, the altitude, the direction of the wind, and the habits of natives, to be collated and later presented and debated in London societies. But Katherine remained indifferent to record-keeping of that nature. Now, hobbling down a stone path, she wondered if she should reconsider her methods. With Ethel gone, her travels couldn't be conveyed to the reader in the epistolary form. A rigorous accounting of all that she saw might earn her the respect of her male counterparts; a scientific outlook in her jottings might encourage the Royal Geographical Society to dispense with its rule barring women from being fellows.

But—

Katherine wasn't keen on description that relied on numbers instead of words. What authority would the boiling point of water confer upon her writing that her impressions themselves couldn't? She had to trust that her readers would find her plain observations to their taste.

At the entrance of the village stood a trading house of sorts. Mani had told her that Tibetan traders preferred not to travel beyond Garbyang, their yaks being unable to survive for too long in altitudes below ten thousand feet. This middling village had thus become the site for all barters between Tibetans and Indians. It seemed a Tibetan delegation had already arrived at the trading house, which Katherine took to be a good sign. The snow on the mountains had melted sufficiently to render the path between the two countries passable.

No one paid her much attention, other than to greet her with a hand raised up to the chest as the Tibetans did, a gesture that looked as if they were asking for alms but which was the equivalent of inquiring if one was well. Women returning from fields with bundles of grass or twigs on their heads smiled at her, taking her to be an elderly pilgrim perhaps. Their faces weren't hidden behind veils, and their expressions weren't bashful. Katherine had heard that these free-spirited women, and their intermingling with men, caused a great deal of offense to English officers in the plains. They had taken to describing Garbyang, the last outpost of the British Empire, as a place of disrepute. *If that's true, I belong here,* she thought.

On the outskirts of the village, she found an isolated spot where bees and butterflies shared the honey of wildflowers that carpeted the slopes in shades of white, yellow, and violet. The sun was warm but mellow, the breeze pleasant, and the sky blue. She sat down on the grass. Some distance below her were the ruins of an abandoned settlement. Creepers twisted around the walls of broken houses. Shrubs raised their inquisitive heads through cracks in the roof.

Katherine listened to the bells of the goats cropping the grass and the soft thuds of pine cones falling from trees, rhythms as soothing as birdsong at dawn. Already she felt her strength returning to her. What good fortune to be able to witness such beauty, to be alive and well. In her mind's eye she saw Ethel, and guilt blazed through her veins like a comet.

"You again? It's almost as if you're following me around," a voice said.

Katherine looked up and saw the smiling face of the stranger by the waterfall. His skin seemed to have become even more sunburnt in the hours since she saw him last. It was now a rich, luscious brown that caused his teeth to appear startlingly white. His shiny hair floated over his shoulders, down to his chest. He bowed theatrically and, without seeking her permission, sat down next to her as if they were old friends. His clothes seemed to be the same as those she had seen him wear before, but his knife was absent.

She wondered if she smelled of dung, and was mortified at the prospect. Mani would have told her to worry instead that the man would see through her pretense, on account of either her accent or her features.

The stranger's gaze had an intensity that made her feel as if every flaw in her appearance was being held up to the light: her nose was too flat; her left shoulder was higher than the right; and the curve of her stomach was too pronounced even if she inhaled and held her breath. This was new. In all her years of traveling, she had never worried about how she appeared to native men, having learned in her youth to keep them at a distance so they wouldn't take her to be one of their kind. Her brief indiscretions had been with Europeans who said they found her looks *unusual but striking,* and her spirit *wild but charming.* These traits some of them would have despised in their own wives, but on their travels they allowed themselves an expansion of their minds, certain that such a sentiment, like the dalliance itself, would be fleeting.

"Well then," the stranger said as if picking up the threads of a conversation they had left unfinished. His fingers twisted around the yellow-tipped grass, and Katherine noted that he had a rich man's hands; no dirt under his nails, which glistened as if varnished. "Are you headed to Mansarovar?" he asked and, when she didn't answer, he said, "Of course, where else will you be going if you're taking this route?"

"Is that where you're going?" she asked.

"I imagine so."

"You're not certain?"

He squinted at her, the gesture bringing out the crow's feet around his eyes. She ought to dislike him. He was arrogant, too certain of his position in the world, a trait common in an Englishman but unexpected and loathsome in a native. Already she knew she would portray him as drab and slow-witted in her journal (if she chose to write about him at all).

The ruins creaked. Fragments of slate tiles fell from the roof, raising columns of dust. Sunbirds rose shrieking from a tree whose trunk nudged a palsied stone wall. A shrub spewed out a boy and girl, clothes tangled, hair disheveled. They laughed, plucked at the grass in each other's hair and, eventually noting the presence of Katherine and her companion, looked at them curiously, all the while maintaining an air of self-possession. They appeared not at all ashamed of the scent of intimacy that clung to them like musk. The boy even put his arm around the girl's waist as if it was the most natural thing in the world. A distressing warmth spread across Katherine's chest.

"You must realize it's unusual for a woman to travel alone," the man said to Katherine as the couple receded from their view. "But admirable. Most women"—he stopped to correct himself—"why, even men, find these heights difficult to climb on their own and hire bearers."

"I didn't see any bearers in your camp," Katherine said. "And I told you I'm not traveling alone. My son is with me."

"Of course."

The man must think her a liar, the son a cautious invention to protect herself from men like him. Her fingers cast about her forehead for her bonnet, to pull it down and conceal her nervousness, but she had left it behind. Her hair felt coarse, like the husk of a coconut. She wished she had smoothed it with oil or dyed it black. How drab she must seem to him now, a splodge of gray in this landscape of a hundred vivid colors.

"You must bring him to the dance tonight," the man said. "Your son."

"What dance?"

He raked his fingers through his hair, thick as treacle, and tied it up in a topknot. His tunic strained around the muscles of his chest. Katherine stood up abruptly, wishing she could hold on to something, even if only her bonnet. But what was solid or certain in her itinerant's life? No person, no object, could tether her to this world that she inhabited only in name. She passed through cities and villages and homes leaving nothing of herself behind; even in the London house there was no sign of her except for her clothes in the wardrobe.

"There will be dancing and singing tonight, at a hall near the trading house. And excellent chhang to drink."

"Sounds like an unsuitable place for a woman."

"Every woman in this village will be there. And you don't have to stay for long."

"I'm tired," she said. "I'll be asleep by sunset."

THE LAST RAYS OF the sun gilded the peaks of mountains as Katherine reached the hall. She didn't need an address; songs, shouts, and drumbeats told her where the dance would be held. Regretting accepting the invitation of a stranger (whose name she hadn't sought, and which he hadn't offered), she entered a spacious but unfurnished room. A fire burned in a pit in the middle, and around it the youth of Garbyang sat decked in what appeared to be their best clothes and jewelry. Some of the young men and women were drinking and smoking, and already the liquor was encouraging them to become less decorous. Their voices rose with sparks; skirts fluttered well above ankles.

An elderly woman with wrinkled skin crisped almost black by the sun, her neck bent under the weight of the turquoise and coral chains she wore, pressed a bowl of chhang into Katherine's hands and asked if she was from the Punjab or the Deccan.

"Calcutta," Katherine said, and the woman seemed delighted.

"Welcome, welcome," she said. "I hope you won't find our evening dull—we can't match the excitement of Calcutta, of course not." She reached forward and pressed a finger against Katherine's upper arm as if to judge the ripeness of a peach.

"What are you——" Katherine started to say, but the woman said approvingly, "A man's strength, but the posture of a queen."

Katherine gulped the liquor quickly, catching sight of the stranger by the entrance, surrounded by a bevy of women of all ages who commanded his full attention. He was holding the hand of a fair, bright-eyed girl who looked no older than seventeen, and drawing what appeared to be lines on her palm. Listening closely, Katherine realized he was listing the things she needed to fetch from the storeroom—chhang, wine extracted from various fruits and flowers, dumplings or perhaps bread—and the name of each object he inscribed in invisible ink on her palm. The girl's cheeks reddened and her eyelashes fluttered hastily, but she didn't push him away and, when he finished his impossible demands, he twirled her around to the beat of a song someone was singing and the women, even those who must be Katherine's age, laughed. In London or Calcutta he would have earned a slap for such behavior, but here the natives were so simple-minded they weren't offended by his impropriety. He caught Katherine's eye and winked. In the light of the leaping flames, the stick figures painted on the walls appeared to be dancing, though this could have been the effect of the chhang she had imbibed too quickly.

She thought with regret that she should have listened to Mani; he had advised her against participating in the evening's festivities. This was an immodest place, replete with temptation, hardly suitable for a lady, and certainly unsuitable for him, almost a monk. Yet he had offered to accompany her, and she had refused, because she didn't want him to see her with the stranger. If, at the end of their journey, Mani told the Almora deputy collector about her and the native man, no doubt it would reach London with the next steamer.

"She's going to do the parikrama around Mount Kailas," the stranger told the women, pointing to Katherine, referring to the circumambulation of the sacred mountain undertaken by pilgrims that she had no intention of doing. "Her son is resting after a long march in the rain."

"She's from Calcutta," the elderly woman who had given her chhang said, and the others exclaimed with wonder. "She's related to the Rajputs."

"I'm afraid you're wrong," Katherine said.

"The Dogras then," the elderly woman insisted to the others. "You can see from her bearing and the way she speaks that she belongs to a royal family."

"Is your husband with you?" one of the women asked.

"Only my son," Katherine said.

"You should have brought him along," someone said.

"They're going to the home of Lord Shiva. She wants her son to think only of God, not girls," the elderly woman said, her chains clattering.

"He's eighteen," Katherine said. "You know what boys are like at that age." From the corner of her eye she saw the stranger turn his head ever so slightly, but his attention remained on the beautiful girl by his side.

"We're here to stop these young people from misbehaving," a woman said. "Join us, why don't you. Just stare at the boys if they get drunk, cuff them on the ear if they leer wickedly at girls."

Evidently the woman took her to be one of them, but it only made Katherine feel that she was an alien; she had no tribe to call her own, here or in any corner of the world.

Around the fire the boys and girls were merry, singing and dancing, feet stamping on the floor and hands swaying in the air. Every once in a while a matronly woman separated a couple she deemed was up to no good.

The stranger continued to flirt with women far younger than her, no self-consciousness or shame in him. Disappointment edged the flash of anger that moved through Katherine's chest like a blade. Why had she not been sensible enough to see him for what he was? How had she allowed herself to forget that he was only a native, unworthy of spending even a moment with her? The singing inside the hall grew plaintive, despite the joy on the faces of the women. Katherine pushed past others to make her escape from the smoke-filled room.

In the plains the monsoon had greened fields and swollen rivers, but up here seasons followed a different calendar, and it was still summer, if only in name. She trembled in the wind that swept down the Himalayas and carried the scent of snow-coated peaks. The light of a full moon, hanging so low that Katherine could see the birthmarks across its silver face, dimly outlined the village.

It occurred to her that she had reverted to an old habit without realizing it, as if she were merely slipping her arms into the sleeves of a much-loved jacket. After she had received a letter in Calcutta saying Ethel was dead, Katherine had searched the faces of the men around her for one who would serve as a distraction. What followed was an attempt at an affair with a gentle, elderly Englishman who had been an accountant with the East India Company, and it had ended in humiliation for the two of them, owing to his age, and hers too perhaps. Still, her undignified behavior then could have been attributed to poor judgment in the face of anguish. She had no such acceptable excuse now.

These short and false pleasures deceive us, Seneca had said, *and, like drunkenness, revenge the jolly madness of one hour with the nauseous and sad repentance of many.*

But what was life without these *short and false pleasures?* And would Katherine be here, in these mountains, if not for deception?

"Did you find the singing to be too loud?" she heard the stranger ask.

"I thought it was beautiful."

He laughed. "You didn't understand?" he asked.

"Understand what?"

He removed the thin blanket he wore over his tunic and Katherine thought he would offer it to her out of gallantry, which only seemed right as she was shivering. But he wrapped it around his neck as if it was a scarf.

"One might say their songs are unfit for the ears of a lady. They're full of obscenities," he said.

"That can't be true."

"I agree there's some merit to the argument that it isn't obscene to describe the exact way in which a woman can bring a man pleasure."

Katherine felt heat rise in her cheeks. "I could have gone without knowing that," she said, her voice as steady as it could be.

"The dialect in these hills is hard to follow, for a reason perhaps." He laughed again, then said, "Let us take a short walk, yes? It's a clear night, and some fresh air will do us good."

He strolled forward on a path that seemed to have known only the hooves of goats. How presumptuous of him to assume she would follow him, but he was right, of course. A faint scent of earth and chhang clung to his skin. His hair fell down in elaborate ringlets that would have been the envy of any woman in London. It was silkier and softer than her own hair, which was more like a bird's nest. He moved silently, bringing to her mind the image of a lion weaving through grass as it stalked its prey. In contrast she was ungraceful and loud, no lightness in her tread and her breathing so clamorous as to be heard a mile distant.

Behind them the houses slipped into darkness, except for the glow of a lantern raised near a window to guide someone home. On occasion a whistle echoed in the air. The stranger said it was an invitation to those in nearby villages to join the dance. A cloud caught on the moon, and its color shifted from white to gray.

They reached the summit of an acclivity and, looking down, Katherine saw the gleaming silver scales of a river. On the spine of the mountain that loomed in front of them, separated by the breadth of the river, a light waxed and waned, then danced all the way up to the peak. When it reached the crest of the mountain it disappeared, its wick pinched by invisible fingers. Her skin tingled, touched by a ghost.

"All of us are haunted by what we have lost," the stranger said, as if he had seen right into her heart. "Not just the loss of our loved ones, but our homes, our fields, our freedoms."

His voice sounded different, a grittiness to it that was almost frightening. The cold drummed against her bones, and she shuddered. Who was he, and what did he know about her? She could hear the snarls of a wolf or a jackal, birds fluttering their wings, and monkeys chattering sleepily on branches. Where terraced fields had been cut into the spurs of mountains, stalks of millet that had grown to a man's height swayed in the breeze, the earth's sighs released as their rustles.

"Legend has it that not too long ago an English officer stayed here for a few days to hunt deer," the stranger said. "He saw a beautiful village girl and tried to claim her. She told him her heart was with another. One night the officer had his way with her, up there in those mountains. In the morning he found she had turned to stone. Frightened, he ran away. For many weeks afterward the boy she loved searched for her, even at night, until he fell over a cliff and died. He wanders these hills as a ghost, looking for his love. It's the light of his lantern that we see up there on that mountain."

"Why would a ghost need a lantern?" Katherine said in her firmest voice even though her legs trembled. Sweat prickled her palms. "I must get back," she said. She felt certain the stranger had seen through her skin into her veins, where her blood pulsed thick and impure. If only she could cleanse herself of all sin—but the sin was not hers alone, but her father was a good man who had done right by her, but he was nothing like the Englishman in the stranger's story, but he could be, but he couldn't be. The circumstances of her birth were a mystery she didn't want to solve.

The stranger led her back to the village in silence, walking two steps in front of her, seemingly lost in thought. When he told her the story of the ghost he had looked at her not with sadness but as if he was commiserating with her for some harm done to her that she didn't deserve. But she was fifty and she had had a reasonable life and there was no reason good or bad to be ashamed of who she was or even to think of how she had been brought into the world.

They descended a steep path, and he extended his hand toward her, but she refused his help with a shake of the head. The air was cold and crackling. He kept turning back to keep an eye on her, maybe because he thought she was old and prone to slipping, and then idiotically she did stumble, no doubt distracted by his concern, and in a moment he was by her side, holding her above her elbows, steadying her as her head tilted toward his chest and his warm breath rippled over her face. His grip was strong but he held her softly. She looked up at him and saw the surprise in his eyes, as if he sensed—only now—her want.

Behind him she saw a house floating in the sky, and pointed at it in astonishment. He too turned to look and, as soon as he did so, the moon came out of the clouds and she saw the faint outline of a mountain slope on which the house had been built. Then the wind disarranged his hair and clouds enclosed the moon again. The mountain was once more cloaked in darkness, but the house itself, brightened by lanterns or candles, appeared to be suspended in the sky, a preternatural celestial object. Katherine felt as if she too was floating, yet another ghost.

Outside the dance hall, the revelry appeared to have become even more jolly. The man offered to accompany her to the place where she was staying, but she refused, and he didn't persist. Already his eyes were on a tall, slender woman whose cheeks glowed with youth and sweat.

"What's your name?" she asked him. She would likely never see him again, and yet she was anxious to grasp a part of him to herself, like a visitor purchasing a keepsake to commit to memory a holiday before the journey home.

"You can call me Chetak," he said, but only after a pause so lengthy it made her think he was lying.

5.

———

PAST CARAVANS OF SHEEP, YAKS, AND PONIES, BALRAM MADE his way toward the Tibetan officials presiding over the inspection of bags, animals, and people. They were ensconced inside a white tent of the kind favored by rich merchants from Lhasa. Here the air was laced with the scent of tobacco that traders shared with the officials. In Balram's pockets were stone toys shaped like ducks that he would supply as gifts for the officials' children, and fistfuls of coral beads for their wives.

At this hour the sun was white and scorching, but the Tibetan guards were hardened men, swashing about with their swords and matchlocks, eyes unblinking. The camp heaved with the pesky bleats of goats and sheep, the grunts of yaks, the neighs of ponies, and the chatter of men.

Balram strained to hear what the traders were saying. Gyan had told him one could identify credible information from gossip. But now Balram overheard nothing of note, only the dispute over a calf's parentage that had an entire town taking sides, and elderly pilgrims appealing to passersby for tea. A group of boisterous porters placed bets on whether a woman, the beauty of their village, would leave her husband and children for her brother-in-law in Lhasa. Traders quibbled about the length of time it took Tibetans to scrutinize a caravan's worth of goods. Someone said the officials were conducting exacting checks, resulting in long delays, because they had been warned a foreign spy would attempt to enter their country. These words took the air out of Balram's lungs, and he would have collapsed but for a man who helped him onto a blanket folded to form a cushioned seat on the ground. "I must get going," Balram said, though his legs were liquid. The man, whom Balram surmised was a Kashmiri trader on account of his fair complexion and fur hat, held a parasol over him and warned him about sunstroke.

"We have to suffer because they're looking for a white man," the trader said.

"Is it a Russian?" Balram asked.

The trader directed the question to others and it transpired that the white man the Tibetans were looking for—with such qualities as villagers might ascribe to a sly fox or a crocodile—was in fact the Swedish explorer whom Balram had once worked for, and whom the captain considered his rival. Years ago the Swede had claimed he would be the first man to track the great rivers of Hindustan whose sources were thought to be in Tibet, not just the Brahmaputra but also the Indus and the Sutlej, as if the task was no more demanding than following a puppeteer's strings. It seemed the foreigner hadn't yet given up on his dream. In rivers the white man saw not water not silt not rocks but commerce or an image of themselves so striking they couldn't look away.

When blood returned to his limbs, Balram thanked the trader. "May your silks fetch you an excellent price," he said.

The captain was standing near the bearers, a saffron cloth wrapped around his mouth and nose. Balram had made him exchange his more expensive wire-gauze glasses for yak-hair spectacles, their gauze netting so coarsely plaited that it likely pricked the eyes. It hadn't improved the captain's disguise. "They're expecting a white man, but it's not you, sir," he said.

"Impossible," the captain said, voice muffled by his veil. "The viceroy's office would have informed me if another British subject was planning an expedition to Tibet. I would have been notified by the Royal Geographical Society."

"It's the Swede, sir. The one who first employed me."

"He's here?" The captain squared his shoulders. "Did you tell him about my plans? Or did you speak freely of our mission when you searched for bearers in Dehra?"

"I haven't seen him in years," Balram said. "But you must turn back now, with the men, rather than risk capture. I can map the river myself."

"I won't be turning back, Balram," the captain said. "God will protect me."

The camp appeared so vast that the herd of sheep huddled at the other end seemed to be no wider than Balram's thumb. Admirably the bearers didn't stare at the two of them, and instead diverted the attention of strangers who wandered over to their group by sharing snuffboxes and asking questions about the conditions on the mountain passes the visitors had scaled to reach this camp in Tsaparang from Leh or Kashmir or Simla. They exchanged remedies for blisters: linseed oil, kept in a dark container and never exposed to sunlight, or a thick paste of flour and water or, if neither could be found, a touch of yak dung. When passersby outstayed their welcome, a bearer named Chand, thin as a stalk but with the appetite of an elephant, removed his boots and socks and showed them the dreadful state of three of his toes—so benumbed and stiff from frostbite that he claimed others could hammer a nail into them without as much as a whimper passing through his lips. He invited visitors to try, but thankfully no one took up his offer. Out of pity, some offered him fried bread or raisins that he devoured in one swift gulp before other bearers could lay claim to them.

"Sir, the Tibetans will be on their guard, not just here but everywhere," Balram said.

"I'll remind you to adhere to our plan," the captain said. "It will be a great disappointment to our colleagues at the Survey if the Swede achieves *our* goal." He then walked toward Yogi, thumbing his rosary far too quickly for it to seem saintly.

This was the way the world worked. The white man had a want, and to sate it brown men gave up their lives. How many native men had died triangulating Hindustan for the Great Trigonometrical

Survey? Balram didn't know because no book, no map, recorded their names or numbers. No peaks were named after them. Their bodies rotted at the bottom of swamps, in the bellies of the crocodiles and tigers that roamed the forests they had hacked through, their movements slowed by the theodolites, engineers' chains, leveling staves, and flagpoles they carried. Balram once heard the Survey superintendent describe the deaths as "a consequence of the country being unhealthy," as if the men couldn't outrun tigers because they had been too plump or too thin. Was this what the captain would say of the bearers in this foolhardy expedition? Was that how he thought of Gyan? Or would he remind Balram that English officers too had died of cholera and dysentery and malaria?

The bright blue sky darkened, mirroring his mood. Balram looked up, but there were no clouds. Toward the horizon, whorls of dust rose like waves from the ground.

THEIRS WAS ONE OF the last groups to be taxed. As he rounded up the bearers who smelled of sweat and snuff, Balram tried to reassure each one of them by repeating the same words: *nothing to worry; we'll be out of here soon; we'll be safe because our gods are with us.*

He didn't tell them that the last time he had prayed to gods was soon after his son was born. "A boy after two girls," he had told Gyan then, "a boy to continue my name." In the months that followed, when it became apparent that the child was not of this world, he accompanied Durga to temples and watched holy men smear ash on Inder's forehead. They looked into his blank eyes, insisted they had evicted the spirit that possessed his soul. Even as Balram dispensed coins into their cupped palms, he knew this to be untrue. Durga continued to bargain with bloodthirsty goddesses, sacrificing goats at temple altars. No remedy remained untried even if it tumbled from the mouth of a quack, her trials acquiring a feverish urgency when neighbors began to bar their children from going near their house. Village elders warned others a glimpse of Inder would bring passersby years of misfortune. Parents worried it wasn't safe to send their children to a school where the father of a demonic child was a teacher. Gyan took to calling the villagers names. He made his parents and relatives visit Balram often, so that others could see no curse befell them later, a gamble if ever there was one. His parents must have expected to catch the pox and, when they didn't, word got around the village quickly that the boy was harmless, just that the gods had been distracted when they made him and so a piece of him was missing, a limb turned the wrong way, clay in his bones, a hole in his skull that caused all his words to leak out of him before his tongue could catch hold of them.

Gyan was never timid or faltering around Inder, not the way Balram was. Gyan could talk to the boy, tell him stories or sit next to him as Inder played in the mud or watched clouds drift in the sky, drool spilling from the corners of his mouth that Gyan mopped up with the sleeve of his shirt. Gyan encouraged Durga to speak of Inder, and didn't mind the hope curling and uncurling in her sentences, none of which ended with the caveat Musalman employed: *God willing.* One day Inder will speak. One day Inder will walk without limping. One day Inder will smile. *God willing. God willing. God willing.* Balram silently mouthed an approximation of the Musalman expression each time Durga voiced an impossible dream, until one day he realized no God planned to intercede on his son's behalf. Then without telling anyone—even Gyan—he chose a peripatetic life for himself because he couldn't bear to be around the hope Durga carried in her fist like an amulet. To Balram, hope had all the comfort of a dagger stuck between his ribs.

"Trust the gods," he said to the bearers now. "And let me do all the talking."

His arms itched and he scratched his skin with vigor. He wanted to locate the exact point from where he could lift it up from his flesh in its entirety; once he sloughed it off, he would make himself anew.

"Stop that," the captain said, his grip piercing like a hook on Balram's shoulder. Balram reluctantly rolled down his sleeves to hide the fresh dots of red on his wrists.

The captain sauntered alongside the porters with his rosary and prayer wheel as if to walk into the house of the enemy was no different from a leisurely stroll around a rose garden in Kashmir. But the bearers were nervous. Ujjal whispered to Balram that the captain's legs, visible through the folds of his robe that swayed with each of his steps, looked too white. Balram asked the captain to wear a Tibetan chuba, which they had procured for him at Mana and whose hem came down well below his knees. Its thick fabric forced the robe to stay in place.

"Keep an eye on the captain," Balram told Ujjal, and the boy nodded quickly, his expression grave, the joker in him having vanished.

They were all watching the white man as if he was a baby about to be snatched up by a hawk, while somewhere beyond this camp Gyan was alone, no one to whisper kind words to soothe him in his prison.

The dust storm was racing toward them, already stinging their eyes. Balram looked at the horizon through a glaze of tears and couldn't tell where the sky ended and the earth began, the air the color of a tamarind pod.

They stopped outside the Tibetan officials' white tent, where alongside tobacco Balram now smelled shit and piss and vomit. The long wait must have disrupted the visitors' bodily functions. Around them the sheep cried and the pony sneezed.

The Tibetan officials asked Balram where his group was coming from, at which market they intended to sell their wares, and how many men were in their party. Balram spoke quickly: *coming from Badrinath through Mana, heading to the Gyanema market to sell grains and woollens, we have nine, no, ten bearers, two shepherds, one pony, beware of that rascal, don't go too close to him or he'll kick, the sheep number sixty-two, no, fifty-six. Six died on the pass. It was very cold.* He gifted the officials the toys and the coral beads in his pockets that they readily accepted, asked after their children, complimented the cut of their chubas and the make of their boots. Or did he praise the make of their chubas and the cut of their boots? In previous journeys he had hardly ever had any trouble, his Tibetan being fluent, but now words lay knotted in his throat and his left eye twitched, a dark warning no different from the ache in Jagan's bones.

Balram directed the bearers to open the trunks and spread out the contents for inspection. The captain, full of bluster, allowed himself to be seen by the Tibetans. "You," a Tibetan soldier said to the captain, drawing his sword out of his sheath. Balram panicked and said, "He's our bearer even if he's dressed like a priest. A devotee of Lord Shiva." Ujjal ran to the soldier, touched the tip of his sword, drew blood, and cried out, the lacerating dust allowing tears to easily flow from his eyes. The soldier watched him in disgust, sour hisses between his lips. Jagan and Yogi and the other bearers rearranged themselves so that the captain vanished from the soldier's sight.

Two groups of traders from Leh rushed toward the officials' tent, papers in hand, pleading to be let through before dusk. The Tibetans asked the traders to camp nearby for the night and return for inspection in the morning, and the traders protested, and the Tibetans said they would be barred forever, and the traders apologized. Balram was grateful for the distraction.

The Tibetans prodded their trunks, but didn't perceive the secret compartments that hid the captain's surveying instruments, his gold coins, pistol and rifle, cartridges, Herodotus, and notebooks. One of the officials asked Balram to buy pashmina wool worth a hundred rupees from him. Balram did so promptly, fearful any hesitation would cause the official to look at their party more closely. He settled the taxes they were meant to pay. A soldier asked for yet another count of the animals, a task made near impossible by the dust. Still, the Tibetans persisted. While they waited for the numbers, Balram told the officials about his father, who had made as many as five journeys back and forth each summer when the pass was open, trading grains and sugar for wool and salt. "If the pass wasn't closed in November, off he would go again, even if the snow came up to his knees," he said. An official asked, "Did you accompany your father?" A reckless smile spread across Balram's lips even though his heart ached. "I was too young," he said. "He died when I was seven." The officials looked at each other, their expressions inscrutable. "I

traveled with my uncles to Gyanema as soon as I was old enough,"
Balram said. "I have been here at least thirty times. I can find the path
to Lhasa in the dark."

It sounded like a boast, but it was only a fact. Mountains and hills
and lakes were like signposts to him, the shape of a ridge or the mouth
of a cave telling him where to turn left or right. The Tibetans knew
what he meant; like his father and uncle and his ancestors before
them, they too traveled without maps.

Balram inquired after the jongpen. The officials said the jongpen
had visited in the morning but left quickly on account of his ailing
wife. Balram said he would pray for her good health. He asked if
coral would likely fetch a higher price this year. They grunted in the
affirmative. He said he hoped to watch the annual horse race at Gartok, and did they know the names of the horses most likely to suc-
ceed? The officials said Balram and his party were free to enter their
country, wearying of his questions perhaps.

If the bearers were pleased, they gave no sign. They repacked the
trunks quietly. Another band of dust moved through them, the rust-
colored motes like embers in Balram's eyes.

THEY STUMBLED FORWARD FOR an hour, blinded by the dust storm,
their desire to be far from Tibetan guards outweighing the wish for
shelter. The road was deserted; others must have wisely made camp
to escape the inclement weather. Ujjal sang through the dust, a chaste
song about a man pining for his lover. Balram wished he could talk to
Gyan about these men, and this journey. Gyan had always understood him as no one else could. Walking home one evening after a
long, stiflingly hot day at the Survey office where he had heard English officers disparage natives for ruining the instruments they carried, Balram had stopped at the market to pick up fruit for the night's
meal. Durga and their children were away at her parents', and he was
alone at home. At the bazaar an insolent English officer berated a
butcher for having sold his servant a cut of lamb for its real price,
without a discount. The butcher fell at his feet to apologize. The

officer kicked him as if he was a stone lying in his path. Balram's stomach turned and he left without the fruit, most of it having blistered or rotted in the heat anyway. When he reached home with an ache in his temples ticking against his skin, he found Gyan waiting for him with a gift: a jar of ice he had made himself with saltpeter purchased from a merchant who cured meat for the English. Balram remembered the coolness of the jar as Gyan held it to the back of his neck, the heaviness in his head dissipating like clouds in the wind. Afterward they had drunk water cooled with the ice and, sitting on the charpai outside, watched the night suspend bright stars in the sky.

Through veils of dust Balram now saw stabs of green pierce the brown landscape—the poplars that grew by the Sutlej River and whose wood roofed Tsaparang's houses.

The captain nudged Balram's elbow with his prayer wheel.

"The wheel is sacred, sir," Balram said.

"Might it be possible to send a letter?"

"To whom?"

"The Swede. One of the bearers can take my message to his camp."

"Saying?"

"I'll ask him to leave."

"It's only a rumor. The Swede may be oceans away right now."

"We can find out."

"Our men aren't spies. Tibetans may chance upon the letter, then you'll be caught."

The dust storm halted without warning, carrying Balram's voice to the men, who turned to look at him. He mustn't disagree with the captain in their presence. Without leadership each man would do as he pleased, and the results would be disastrous. He bowed his head and, linking his hands below his chest in a gesture of atonement, said, "Our bearers don't speak Tibetan. They'll only invite suspicion if they inquire about a white man. Let it not go to waste, all the good work you have done. You are in Tibet at last. Isn't it astounding?"

The light turned orange, the dust that lingered in the air muting the brightness of the sun. They walked in silence until they reached a narrow channel of the river. Balram had suggested to the captain that they follow the Sutlej's path upstream to the holy Mansarovar, from where the Tsangpo was none too distant. He had an inkling Gyan would have followed the same path, which they had taken on a previous journey.

"I mustn't wash myself," the captain said, his eyes traveling along the winding river. "Serves my purpose to appear as sooty as a chimney sweep. Who knew I would miss a warm bath more than the touch of a woman."

The captain sat down in the shade of poplars, brought out a scrap of paper from inside the prayer wheel, and scribbled on it—paces covered or notes on the weather and the landscape. He ordered Pawan to boil water so that he could calculate the altitude, and had the bearers bring out his thermometer for measuring the boiling point. Would Balram ever know such single-mindedness, such devotion to a cause, such ambition? The captain often studied his sketches and notes even as he ate, as if food alone couldn't sufficiently nourish him. Perhaps a man could be so passionate about maps or words or music only if he wasn't encumbered with worries about money, a lost friend, a mute son.

Samarth pranced in the river, splashing water on the bearers who in turn cursed him. The shepherd Rudra threw a cube of sugar—reserved for the pony perhaps—toward him, as if training a pet monkey or a bear, and the boy expertly caught it in his mouth. Balram felt an unjustified twinge in his chest. Inder, almost Samarth's age, still couldn't eat with his own hands and, if Durga didn't feed him, would starve to death.

Laughter rose from the bank, the men expressing their relief at having crossed the first Tibetan outpost. Chand massaged his toes with cold water to increase circulation, hoping perhaps that feeling would return. Balram didn't think the poor bastard had a chance. Gyan had lost a toe to frostbite. Had it been it in Thok Jalung or Gyanema? He couldn't remember. Harish, one of the bearers, a fair-complexioned man who claimed his ancestors were royals—the Guptas one day, the Rajputs another day, even the Lodis and the

Mughals when it took his fancy—pulled out a knife from his coat pocket and began to trim his nails. Rana, a stout but muscular fellow who could always be found next to Harish, took a pinch of snuff from a box and drew it into his nostrils.

"A filthy habit," Harish told him. "It will kill you at this height."

"Not if the height kills me first," Rana said, "which, you'll agree, is more likely."

Naga, quiet as ever, filled pots with water, spilling not a drop, casting barely a ripple in the river. Ujjal professed his love to the pony through a song: "Without you, Colonel, I'm a tree cut in half, a bird without wings, a sky without stars."

"A true poet," Jagan taunted him. "Bound to become more famous than Rumi or Ghalib."

Holding his thermometer, the captain got up to hover around the bubbling pot of water. The steam made his dye run. He stepped back and issued instructions from a safe distance, frowning at the numbers Pawan relayed to him.

Balram felt at a remove from all of them, as if he was observing the world through a glass case. Did he alone notice how the land crackled like parchment? Now that the dust was beginning to settle, he couldn't rid himself of the sense that he was being watched. Always in Tsaparang an unsettling feeling came over him of being surrounded by hundreds of termite nests; every mound resembled an anthill, its slopes pocked with black caverns. What creatures lived inside them? Snow leopards, snow lions, beasts man hadn't yet named.

The captain summoned Balram with a hooked finger, a piece of paper fluttering in his left hand.

"We can't, sir," Balram said, meaning to thwart the conversation before it started. "A letter will be intercepted, and you will be imprisoned or killed."

"You're right," the captain said.

Though surprised by the captain's change of heart, Balram checked the impulse to ask why.

"What we can't afford to do now, however, is dawdle," the

captain said. "The Swede can't be allowed to win this race. We must proceed quickly. The shepherds must come up with a better plan to feed the sheep. We can't give up precious hours to graze the animals."

"The sheep will escape from their pens at night looking for grass if we don't feed them."

"I'm not suggesting we starve the animals, or the men. But I must insist that we spend our hours much more judiciously. Ask the bearers to prepare for our next march."

"We'll start early tomorrow. I'll make sure of it."

"We must leave now."

"If we leave now, we'll reach Toling at midnight. Maybe even later. The men fear strange nocturnal creatures have made Toling their home. They'll run off, sir."

"The men will do what I ask of them."

"We can visit Tsaparang's Summer Palace before dark. You'll see the most beautiful Buddhist paintings on earth, and the palace itself—"

"Have you mistaken our expedition for a holiday?"

"I thought you might want to sketch the palace, sir. Note down its characteristics for the Royal Geographical Society."

The captain, eyes gleaming with malignance, returned his paper to the pockets of his robe. He clapped his hands to release a sprinkling of dust. "You're a competent surveyor of land, but"—he advanced closer to Balram and jabbed his finger into his ribs—"you have no measure of men. The bearers supply you with idiotic tales about monsters and, as a bee might set upon a flower, you drink it up. You don't know how to earn their trust or respect. For a man who has lived in this world for as long as you have, you display an arrogant disregard for how it turns."

Balram noted with dismay that the bearers were listening intently.

"You'll tell the men to pack up, and you'll do it now," the captain continued, and set out in the wrong direction as if prepared to make his way to Toling, maybe even the Tsangpo, all by himself.

In Dehra the captain had been quiet and introspective, more likely to cajole the surveyors he trained than threaten them, but it seemed to Balram that since they had entered the Mana Pass, two men had taken up residence within the captain: one a kind and rational person, and the other a tyrant, the two battling each other as demons fought against gods.

Balram removed his cap and ran his hand over his hair, cut close to the scalp for ease of upkeep, though Durga disliked it being so short. He had sworn to her that he would grow it long after the expedition, which would be his last: that too a promise he had made, which Durga had received in silence, disbelief flaring in her eyes. He didn't blame her. Their time together was passing without him bearing witness. He was always at his school or at the Survey or in Tibet. When he was with Gyan, he didn't yearn for Durga; but when he was with acquaintances as he was now, he missed her—her touch, her hopefulness, even her faith—though no more than he missed Gyan. Was it a fault in him that he couldn't think of Durga without also thinking of Gyan, or was it that the want in him was like a white man's want and could never be hushed?

A steady hand squeezed his shoulder. Ujjal smiled at him warmly. "If we hurry, we'll pass Toling before evening," he said.

"Even a flying chariot wouldn't make it to Toling in that time," Balram said.

Ujjal whistled. "A chariot? I would be happy if I could ride a donkey."

"Yogi, bring the captain back, will you?" Balram said. "We're meant to go east, not west."

"Look at him," Ujjal said, shading his eyes to watch Yogi. "You'd think he was running after a beautiful girl. What would his wife make of it if she were to see him like this? I heard she's already quite unhappy with him."

"Why?" Balram said, startled, but he didn't want to know. His conversations with the bearers were only about the tasks he had assigned them. Just as the captain saw him as a surveying instrument, he identified bearers by their functions.

Look at you, Gyan said, *emulating the master.*

"Yogi has a great affection for whores," Ujjal said.

"Never mind," Balram said quickly.

Other bearers gathered around him, but they didn't complain about the impending march. They understood the white man's orders had to be followed. Only Jagan said, "A great tragedy awaits."

"The tragedy is that you can't shut up about it," Ujjal said.

"Let's see what you have to say when a monster breaks your legs."

"By any luck I'll be too dead to hear what *you* have to say about the matter."

"If we stick together, we'll be safe," Balram said. "Remember the captain has modern guns—a pistol, and a Snider-Enfield rifle, the same rifle English troops use. He's not a trader whose fingers are only good for counting coins. He's a skilled marksman, even at long range."

"If he spoke to me the way he spoke to you, I wouldn't be singing his praises," Ujjal said.

"That mouth on you—it will get your head on a spike one day," Jagan told Ujjal.

The sheep bleated, ears flicking back and forth, alert. The pony was behaving well for a change, as if intimidated by the sand-colored ravines around them. They were a ragged lot in this fantastical landscape. For a moment it felt to Balram that he had, by mistake, stepped into someone else's dream.

6.

~~OUR WALK TOWARD THE~~ Lipulekh Pass ~~took us past Gunji,~~
~~one of the last settlements on the Indian side. Here we met~~
~~enthusiastic dancers and drummers. M—— said the natives~~
~~were celebrating the vanquishing of a man-eating tiger. The~~
~~account of the hunt that the villagers narrated to him was~~
~~ghastly, but I wish I had witnessed it myself to enliven the~~
~~pages of this journal.~~

A few miles south of Gunji, one of the last settlements on
the Indian side, we came across a group of men wielding
stones and axes as if embarking on a medieval ritual. On inquiring we were told they were hunting a man-eating tiger
that had so far killed a dozen villagers, including children and
women.

Many moons ago, I had accompanied a wealthy Englishman on a judiciously arranged hunt in Bengal. His reti-
nue included elephants, guards, maids, cooks, washermen,
tailors, and two dozen bearers who carried beds, tables, and
provisions for the kitchen. A few of these servants had their
own servants.

It can be easily imagined that the hunt in the Himalayan
hamlet bore no resemblance to the only other tiger hunt I had
ever witnessed. Unlike Englishmen, the natives were dreadfully frightened.

After an hour's march we perceived the tiger sleeping in
the shade of a gigantic boulder. We stood a fair distance from
the animal, but four villagers rather foolishly, if boldly,

skirted around the boulder and scaled it. From their vantage point they dropped axes and stones onto the animal's head. I will not go into much detail about its death except to say that a great deal of pain must have preceded it. Even with its skull and limbs broken, and blood gushing out of its wounds to redden the earth, the animal roared so loudly that I thought I would go deaf. It managed to injure two villagers before it died.

The tiger was then laid out on the ground, and villagers struck victorious poses around it, prompted more by relief than excitement. It measured nine feet from its head to tail. In its youth it must have been a magnificent beast.

THEY STARTED THEIR JOURNEY across the Lipulekh Pass early in the morning, before the sun's rays could melt the frost and slicken the track as if with oil. A strong wind blew across the mountains and flung a coat of snow onto the ground. To Katherine the chilly welcome was familiar and exhilarating. Once again Tibet had cast itself in the role of an inattentive host, planting an icy kiss on the cheek before leaving guests to their own devices.

The slopes around her were bare. At nearly seventeen thousand feet above sea level, trees couldn't be expected to survive. In India her ears had become accustomed to the chittering of crickets and the howls of jackals, but here only the loudness of her breath, and the wind, broke the stillness of the land.

Mani chanted prayers that escaped his lips in white coils, and stooped down often to place prayer stones atop existing heaps. These cairns, which defied gravity all along the edges of the track, had been left behind by pilgrims and traders for good fortune and to mark the sacred aspect of the land they were about to enter. For Hindus and Buddhists and Jains and those who practiced the Bon religion, Tibet was as holy as Jerusalem; on the peaks of Tibetan mountains resided gods, and in the waters of its lakes and rivers, absolution could be found. This sacredness felt palpable to her in the angular mountains that hurt the lungs to climb, in the passes where prayer flags fluttered as loud as pounding hearts, and in the monasteries where the many faces of the Buddha soothed distressed minds. One might be tempted to mock the practitioners of Hindu and Bon religions who believed Tibet was the meeting point between the earth and the heavens, but standing on the pass right now, Katherine felt as if she had wandered into that very space suspended between the earth and the sky.

She stepped into Mani's footprints, conceding to herself that he knew where the ground was most firm. Her eyes watered from the cold, and the wind pushed her around. She slipped often. When she looked back, her set of footprints appeared ghostly, as if a spectral form floating behind Mani had on occasion decided to perch on the ground. When she looked ahead, the edge of his reddish-brown robe was disappearing around a bend. The boy seemed impatient or bored by her slow pace. She tried to walk faster, but couldn't. Her lungs refused to fill with air and her heart leaped against her ribs. She stood on the empty path, attempting to catch her breath that evaded her like a sneaky fruit fly in summer. Sunlight brightened the peaks of mountains but brought no warmth to the wind. From a distance came the sound of fireworks. What festival was being celebrated now? Looking around she saw ice loosen from a white peak and sled downhill with a loud crackle. The arrival of summer, merriment in the mountains, and here she was, feeling as if she was about to die. Thirst parched her throat, but she couldn't drink water. She would retch if anything passed her lips.

Mani retraced his steps with a swiftness that she envied. "I thought you were right behind me," he said, scooping raisins out of his pocket. "Food will give you strength."

Just as she had expected, the sweetness of the raisins made her even more nauseous. Shadows moved in the periphery of her vision. Nowhere else were hallucinations so assured as in Tibet. In her previous journey, before her servant revealed her identity, she had been surprised to come across cottages surrounded by ornate gardens. Robins flew into shrubs pruned in the shapes of elephants and came out holding berries in their beaks, spilling juice as red as fresh blood. But when she looked around after resting, of course there had been nothing.

Now Katherine saw a man with two heads walking toward them. She touched her talisman, the bonnet over her head. Tibetans believed divine beings sent bad weather and phantasms to discourage sinners from visiting their holy land. And here were the gods, reminding her that she was unequal to the task.

"Pilgrims," Mani said.

The two-headed figure in front of her separated into a man carrying over his shoulders another man with a gaunt face. When they came closer she saw that the man being ferried was blind. His wasted limbs, no wider than tendrils, were curled around the bearer's torso.

Mani spoke to them in their dialect. More ice thawed in distant peaks and crashed to the ground, but the boy didn't even turn his head. His manner calmed her too; he knew these mountains better than she did—she had to believe that.

After the pilgrims left, she asked Mani, "Surely these bearers don't carry men all the way to Kailas, and around the mountain too?"

"We're used to it," Mani said. "Last year I carried an old man to Kailas and we did the parikrama—Tibetans call it the kora—three times in a row. Mind you, he was a lot less heavy than some of the trunks I've hauled around for English officers."

Where is your nerve, Katherine asked herself. If natives could climb these mountains, the equivalent of their own weight on their shoulders, couldn't she scale the pass just once? In Tibet there would be no cabs for hire, no trains that would obligingly cover several miles in an hour.

"Much more comfortable to sit by a fire in Simla, isn't it?" Mani said. "Safe too. I can't imagine another woman in your position undertaking such a dangerous journey. You're doing well."

Katherine pulled down the long sleeves of her robe. The cold had numbed her fingers. Her faculties too, because she didn't dispute his patronizing comment. They walked slowly, Mani happily chatting away, perhaps to keep her from dwelling on whether her body could keep pace with her ambition.

Her head ached from the altitude. By foregoing the warmth of a fire, the comfort of a hill station where other Englishwomen spent their summers, what was she hoping to achieve? Even now with her lungs hollowed by the heights, she wanted to reach the Potala. In her mind's eye the palace appeared luminous, capable of revealing truths she couldn't otherwise grasp. In Lhasa, the Place of Gods, all the disparate parts of her would come together without shame or anger and she would be made whole (she hoped).

Your faults will follow you whithersoever you travel, Seneca had written in one of his letters to Lucilius. *You flee along with yourself.* So perhaps that was all she was doing, and there would be no respite for her even in Lhasa.

They met a group of traders returning from Tibet with their purchases of salt and borax. Mani managed to cajole from them, for the cutthroat price of a fistful of his precious raisins, a walking stick for her. It was taller than her, and coarse where it fit into her palm. But the snow had begun to turn into muck in the sunshine and the stick steadied her footsteps.

Being absorbed in the act of putting one foot in front of the other, Katherine didn't lift her eyes from the ground for a while. When she did so, she gasped. Without her noticing it, the sky had become cloudless, and below her, Tibet's extraordinary landscape gleamed in the sun. Others wouldn't believe such beauty possible in a land so severe, so bereft of trees and flowers and all things fecund. But this was a country that refused to be defined by its lack and, notwithstanding its desolation, served as a feast for the senses. Every shade of the rainbow, be it violet, red, yellow, or green, could be matched to an incline. Just as the colors in the sky changed with the sun, so too did the hues on this parcel of earth that was Tibet.

Mani pointed to a path. A mile or so ahead of them a row of men made their way downhill toward Tibet. "Shall we?" he asked and, without waiting for her reply, began the descent.

Clutching her walking stick, Katherine joined him. She wondered if it was the brilliance of the sun, capable of penetrating into the deepest recesses of one's soul, that made pilgrims believe Tibet was the land of absolution. Such clarity in the light left no nook for sin to hide itself, and threw into sharp relief one's foibles. If the time after Ethel's death had felt to her as akin to being held in a purgatory, would she, Katherine, find redemption here? Would she be reborn once she had immersed herself in the waters of Mansarovar? The wind hurled grit into her eyes and brought her mind back to the more mundane matters at hand.

AFTER WALKING A DISTANCE of no more than six miles that occupied eight of their hours, Mani pointed out to Katherine a Tibetan outpost: a cluster of black yak-hair tents encrusted with dirt and steadied with numerous poles and ropes. Katherine wondered if they should skirt the outpost, but the only way to avoid detection was to climb up a towering ridge and then down, and she was so exhausted she didn't think she could manage it. Mani said they should speak to the Tibetan officials and ask to shelter nearby instead of attempting another climb in the near-dark. Katherine recognized this choice to be strange and perilous, but she also knew any journey was made up of hundreds of such unlikely decisions.

"I doubt they will suspect you," Mani said. "It's not as if you dipped your face in brown dye—I heard a white man did that to enter Tibet, and he was still caught."

"A ridiculous story," Katherine said, "and no doubt untrue. You shouldn't repeat lies if you plan on becoming a monk."

"You're scolding me," Mani said, looking delighted. "You must be feeling better."

It exasperated her that he behaved as if he was older than her. But now that they had climbed down a few thousand feet, it was true that her headache was mild, almost gone.

Guards sat playing cards at the outpost, matchlocks by their side. They waved Mani in the direction of a tent, and he told her to wait.

With his shoulders drooping and head bowed so that he would appear suitably obsequious, he walked into the officials' tent. The wind, loud against its black canvas, strained the knots on the ropes.

Katherine sat on a boulder, clutching her stick as if it was a rifle. Though the guards didn't even look at her, an irrational (or entirely rational) fear struck her that she would be exposed momentarily. The prospect of discovery didn't terrify her; instead it soured her mood. At this very moment when her journey could end, the desire to see Lhasa surged in her. Who was she if not an explorer? What purpose did her life hold if it was confined to London? She patted the pocket formed by the folds of her robe, as if hoping to chance upon a flask of brandy a self she couldn't remember had secreted for a moment such as this when she needed to shore up her courage, and detected instead the shape of her notebook.

Before she started writing to Ethel, Katherine had recorded her travels in her journals, but discovered quickly that her words, while seemingly profound in the moment of writing, in truth veered between too insipid and too frank. Over the years, her notes, stained a pale yellow by the heat and a moldy green by the monsoon, never transformed into an engrossing account of a lady's travels in the Orient as she had hoped.

It was only by writing to Ethel, in the early days of her sister's illness, that Katherine had alighted on the appropriate tone. When they were still children, she had on occasion tried to shield Ethel from their mother's tempestuousness. Though older than Katherine by two years, Ethel was a sensitive soul, easily affected by sharp words and raised voices. Katherine wasn't above ridiculing Ethel's anxious manner, but she took pity on her sister too. Her practice of diminishing the turbulence of their parents' marriage in front of her sister had given Katherine a flair for altering the truth that stood her in good stead while she wrote the letters. She knew what to redact so as not to cause Ethel grief or offense, and what she should embellish to elicit a smile. If the world Katherine saw was unruly, her words smoothed and contained it for Ethel's eyes.

Now, without her sister, did Katherine even know how or what to write? Hadn't her novel been a stupendous failure because, without her intended reader in her mind's eye, her sentences were as discordant as a tune concocted by children beating on drums? She felt the impossibility of writing for men and women with whom she had nothing in common. What she knew: how to steer a pony across a brown river, how to sleep on grass sparkling with frost, and how to survive for days on tsampa alone. Stories about these travails were unlikely to appeal to those who would much rather read about snakes and snake charmers, tigers and tiger hunts, and the art of disciplining native servants.

"Mother," said Mani. "They have asked to speak to you. Just nod, and leave the talking to me."

Inside the tent the air was sticky with the smells of yak butter tea and sweat. A group of Indian traders waiting for the Tibetans to complete certain formalities greeted her with folded hands but talked to Mani alone. She was too nervous to listen to them, but she saw them punctuate their sentences with forceful gestures and expressions.

With her walking stick and silver hair (and the uncertain color of her skin), the Tibetans didn't perceive her as a threat. When a guard eventually inspected her sack, he didn't rummage through her garments to see what she might have hidden beneath them.

Mani said his farewells and took her elbow to guide her forward. She resisted the urge to push him away. The first obstacle had been surmounted, with barely any ceremony.

Outside, Mani pointed at a hill and said its incline would protect them from the wind. The blisters on her feet itched and hurt. The hill was too far. One forgot exhaustion as fear pulsed up one's veins, but always in the aftermath came a great crashing, blood draining from the limbs as if the body was no more than a carcass strung up at the slaughterhouse. She let Mani march ahead to pitch her tent, and hobbled behind, dragging her walking stick.

At the campsite, Katherine removed her boots so the air would cool the fire blazing up her feet. Moonlight flooded the lees and knolls, softening the sharp edges of hills. She ate the tsampa Mani had made, by the fire Mani had kindled. He bandaged her feet after applying a medicinal oil to her wounds. She told him he was nothing like her last servant. He didn't seem pleased; it was almost as if he didn't want to be reminded of his lowly position and this charade of being mother and son suited him. But she had said it more for herself so that she wouldn't grow attached to the boy.

The wind's swiftness was only marginally impeded by the hill. Mani brought out her camel-hair blanket and wrapped it around her shoulders. He sat by her side, chanting Tibetan prayers, and her eyelids grew heavy with sleep.

FOR THE SECOND DAY in a row, they set out before dawn, huddled under blankets. An early departure was essential. After a good night's sleep, Tibetan guards might consider their faces anew, and the sun might cause cracks to appear in their friendly veneer.

By the time darkness lifted, they were nearly two miles from the outpost. The sky's indigo shell had turned a soft blue tinged with rose and yellow, and the light revealed green swaths of land. Pigeons with white bars painted across their tails, red-billed choughs, and ravens and skylarks flitted through fields in search of food.

"Barley crops," Mani said, dutifully playing the role of her guide. He pointed out the irrigation channels that brought the waters of the Karnali River to the fields.

Mani's feet were quiet on the shingle strewn across their path, and he moved as silently as an ant—just like the man who had told her his name was Chetak. She supposed she wouldn't see him again. It was a relief. Her mind should only be on Lhasa.

Weather-beaten chortens lined the track. Mani stopped occasionally to circle one in a clockwise direction to pay his respects. Katherine wondered what prayers or relics each chorten held, or if some were tombs of high lamas, but she didn't ask Mani, not wanting to hear lengthy explanations when she was still half asleep.

At one end of the barley fields, in the foothills of mountains, flat-roofed houses huddled together. Bouquets of prayer flags tied to branches were planted in each of the four corners of the roof for luck, and firewood for the winter stacked in pleasing diagonal patterns all around it. From these homes came the sounds of ordinary life, the crying of babies and the placatory voices of mothers and the barking of dogs and the clanks of cowbells. Mani dawdled, speaking to every farmer on his way to the fields. They were preparing for the harvest festival, he explained to her afterward, pointing to horses decorated with tassels that would take part in races.

A little boy with a snotty nose began to howl on seeing them. His mother, walking behind him with a basket over her head, snapped at him to be quiet. Mani spoke to the woman gently, making her smile, and charmed the sniveling child with a magic trick that involved prying a coin out of his ear. Katherine quickened her pace, nudging stones away from her feet with her walking stick. Let Mani catch up with her once he had conversed with strangers to his heart's content.

The path descended toward a stream that Mani had indicated earlier they should ford. White clouds decorated the blue sky like flounces of tulle on a satin dress. The land rose and fell, all jagged teeth and crooked elbows. Beyond the barley fields the earth favored russet and ashy tones.

Katherine took off her boots and wool socks before stepping into the stream where it appeared shallow and suitable for crossing. The water was piercing cold. The hem of her robe grew damp and heavy; she was unable to lift it up, her hands encumbered by the stick and her boots. As she lurched forward, a black smudge grew in the corner of her eye. Turning to the left, she saw a yak charging toward her. Katherine splashed along the water, flailing her stick, heart about to separate itself from the cavity in her chest. Was her fate to be gored to death by a yak in the borderlands of Tibet?

She panted across the stream, climbed a steep slope, and stopped only after reaching the highest point. On the other side of the hill was the Karnali River, its currents so rapid that merely looking at the water caused her head to spin. She closed her eyes and heard the soft clumps of mud falling on Ethel's coffin, only this time she too was lodged inside the wooden box, parts of her twisted and fitted into the space as one might roll up a shirt before squashing it into a trunk. She was pressed up against something cold and icy, and realized belatedly it was Ethel's pale, blue-veined arm.

Katherine felt her breath steadying. Who knew the proximity of death could be comforting too? She looked around. The yak had halted below, distracted by a tuft of grass. The stream she had dashed across joined the Karnali ahead of her. Past steep ravines and cliffs specked with caves was the Taklakot fort, soaring toward the sky. Where was Mani? And how would he get past this wretched yak?

She pulled on her socks and boots, beat the dirt out of her robe, and wrung the water out of its hem. A movement in the shoulder of the ridge caught her eye. Only a few feet away from her, a man dressed in a filthy robe was scrambling up the slope on all fours like an animal. Lifting himself to his full height, he arched his back and stretched his hands. Noticing her, he bowed. Katherine bowed too. Then he lifted his robe to reveal his manhood, a puny little thing almost disappearing into a dark clump of hair.

The man took a step forward, his robe still lifted up to his chest, a leering grin on his face. Katherine heard the river below her feet. Behind her the yak and in front of her this man, both dispatched by some higher power to test her mettle. She gripped the walking stick firmly, its splinters sticking into her skin, and swung it at the man, missing him by a mere inch. He jumped back with a squeal, and let his robe fall to his ankles.

"An implement that small is an embarrassment you should hide even from your wife. It should never see the sun, or the moon," she told him in Hindustani, a language he might not know.

The man grinned at her, then scurried down to the river, cackling, as if there was no greater joke than the debasement of the self.

"Who was that?" asked Mani.

"This walking stick isn't fit for purpose," Katherine said. "I have to pull splinters out of my hands every hour."

Behind Mani the yak glared at her, the interloper. It had let Mani pass unmolested.

SINCE GARBYANG, MANI HAD developed the annoying habit of conversing with passersby for unreasonable lengths of time. Something in his manner or words made Tibetans mistake him for a wise monk, and Tibetans were always respectful of monks, even if they were no older than six or seven years of age. Katherine had heard that the Great Lama, whom the Tibetans called the Dalai Lama, was only thirteen.

When Mani spoke to the Tibetans, they shared their troubles with him, and in turn he reassured them that their fields would yield gold, or that a sickness in their grandmother's bones would pass with the weather.

Now, only a mile from Taklakot, they were stopped by a man whose horse had disappeared three days prior. Mani told him the animal was still alive. "But remember, its survival depends on how swiftly you proceed," he said.

By adding such caveats to his predictions, he ensured he would never be wrong; if the horse was dead, it was because the poor owner had been lackadaisical in his search. Katherine considered it a fact of life that one could undertake a chore wholeheartedly and still be found wanting.

"Must you talk so much?" she asked Mani afterward.

"You mustn't go off by yourself just because I stopped to speak to a villager," he said. "You should have never attempted to cross a stream by yourself. What if the currents had been strong?"

A servant would never question the master's actions, and yet here they were, bickering like mother and son. "It appears you've forgotten that you have been entrusted with my care, not that of every Tibetan you meet," Katherine said.

"I'll do better, mother," Mani said at once, his voice contrite yet firm. "But so must you."

Katherine scoffed at his words. Must be something in the Tibetan air that caused servants to hold such exaggerated ideas above their station. In no other corner of the world would a foreigner be so beholden to a native; the servant, observing this unnatural reversal of fortune, felt compelled to assert himself as he wouldn't dare in a parlor in Calcutta. But she also had to admit that Mani wasn't like the bearers who had accompanied her before; those men had no interest in scriptures or even the landscape, while Mani seemed at one with the mountains and the plains and the rivers, finding them as sacred as Tibetans did. To Mani every hill had a heartbeat that he could hear.

The Taklakot fort grew in size as they approached the town, its walls seemingly fusing with the ridge on which it stood. Katherine wondered how water was carried from the river that snaked hundreds of feet below the fort to its ramparts above: through a hidden rope-and-pulley system perhaps. Then she heard women singing, their voices if not exactly melodic then quite pleasing in rhythm and vigor. On walking farther, Katherine saw that these women had been tasked with supplying water to the fort. They filled pots at the river, balanced these on their heads above strips of cloth coiled so tightly as to resemble ropes, and began an onerous journey up the ridge. The women were graceful, and not a drop spilled from their pots, which remained affixed to their heads as if secured with nails. Their feet must know each pebble on their path, as they climbed without looking down or stumbling. Katherine envied their sisterhood. Her nomad's life hadn't allowed her to cultivate friendships, but perhaps that was only an excuse and she simply didn't know how to be around the same person for long. She was too restless, fleeing her faults that followed her everywhere as Seneca had said they would.

"Will we have time to visit the fort and the monastery, do you think?" she asked Mani. "I heard the Taklakot monastery has fine paintings and a good library of Buddhist scriptures."

"Taklakot looks peaceful today, doesn't it?" Mani said. "But this morning a body was found on the banks of the Karnali. Tossed down from the fort, most likely."

"Are you sure?" Katherine asked. "Look at those women—they're singing happily."

"The man who was killed worked for the monastery's head lama. It seems he had an argument with the jongpen's men, who manage Taklakot's administrative affairs, and now the lama's people and the jongpen's people are at loggerheads. They'll be more distrustful of visitors than usual, so we will cross the river at night. That way, we can avoid being seen by the jongpen's men, who are quick with their guns."

"A matchlock doesn't allow for quickness."

"It's better if we aren't stopped and interrogated, you agree? The Tibetans may not fling us into the river, but they will ask us to leave. You don't want that, do you? You want to see Lhasa."

"How did you hear about the dead man?"

"The news is all around Taklakot. This is why I talk to people. They can tell you if a landslip has obstructed a path, or if a man-eating tiger has been killed, as we heard in Gunji. The guide you hired when you were here a few years ago, he must have chatted with villagers too."

"Him," Katherine said with a snort. "He was only concerned with making a profit by revealing my identity to a Tibetan official."

Mani didn't reassure her that he was nothing like her previous servant. Instead he directed her to a shaded spot on a declivity of the ridge. Sweat had collected in her armpits and temples, but a moment's rest and the air wicked it dry. At least the gusts here were not as chilly as they had been on the Lipulekh Pass, where ice was likely to glaze over one's eyes if one mistakenly shuttered them for too long.

"You'll wait here?" Mani asked, holding up the empty waterskin he intended to fill.

"Do you feel guilty?" Katherine asked.

"Guilty?"

"You're fooling Tibetans by helping me. And you want to be a monk."

"I wouldn't have helped you if your intention was to attack Lhasa and set up a summer home in the Potala Palace. Tibetans don't want the English here because . . ." Mani seemed afraid to finish the sentence. His fingers tapped the waterskin.

"Because the British government has annexed Sikkim, and parts of Bhutan," she said.

"But you're here as a pilgrim. You want to study Buddhist scriptures. Besides, you're not an Englishwoman. Not really." An image came to Katherine's mind of her first year in England: her governess with a hand over her mouth whispering to a maid that Katherine had the stench of a curry eater. Her expression now must be severe because Mani quickly said, "Forgive me . . . what I mean is . . . of course you are. I must fill the waterskin." His footsteps crunched the gravel.

Katherine took out her journal. It had been a few days since she had last written, and she must record what she remembered before new events smudged the past in her mind. But her hands were shaking. The governess had been a stupid woman. And Mani was ignorant too, a mere boy. Indians were illogical creatures on the whole, in dire need of the steadying hand of the English. Every government official she had ever met, including her father, had said so.

Mani returned eventually with a gift from the women carrying water to the fort: a steamed bread of some kind. "I spoke to a few pilgrims from Garhwal who are going to Mansarovar," he said. "One of them looked familiar. I can't be certain, but it may have been the fellow we saw just before Garbyang. On that morning after the big storm when you got lost."

"I wasn't lost," Katherine said, making sure her tone was even. "He must be going to do the kora." She shoved a piece of bread into her mouth.

Mani set to work smoothing her walking stick with the same knife he used for slicing vegetables and fruit. Not a mile away from them, a man had been killed, but the sun couldn't care less. It was a bright, beautiful day, the sky a soft blue. Ethereal, white cumulus clouds hung so low Katherine felt she could balance a few on her fingertips.

7.

THE MEN WERE DOG-TIRED, BUT COULDN'T SLEEP. THEY SAT around a fire reeking of dung, a fuel that was reluctant to catch flame but offered good heat once it did. With their backs to the tents they had pitched by the black waters of the Sutlej, the bearers drank what Balram realized too late was chhang. No point to confiscating it; the quantity of alcohol was trifling. Ujjal hummed a melancholic love song, the kind he seemed to favor despite his predisposition to play the jester, and Harish and Rana joined in the chorus, their voices by turns passionate and unhappy as the lyrics demanded.

"Keep it down. We don't want to wake the captain," Balram said. Ujjal stopped singing abruptly, *sshhhh, sshhhh,* he said, a finger on his lips, and shifted to make space for Balram to sit. But the others didn't seem keen on his company. "Where did you find the chhang?" Balram asked, wrapping his blanket tight over his coat. "Did you carry it from Mana?"

The bearers said nothing. Passed him the clay pot with the liquor. Balram refused with a shake of his head.

"Let me have it then. This chill is too much for me," Chand said.

"Your feet doing better?" Balram asked.

"Fine. Very fine," Chand said, the last of the alcohol vanishing down his throat. His nose was blackened, and in alarm Balram thought frostbite was slowly rotting every exposed part of his body. But when Chand leaned toward the fire Balram saw it had only been a shadow. The fire blazed in the pupils of Chand's eyes, giving him the appearance of a madman. "Is there anything to eat?" he asked and the men laughed. Jagan said Chand would think about food even when arrows were stuck on his rump. Naga generously passed him a fistful of walnuts, brushing away Chand's thanks with gestures, made uneasy by the attention.

Balram wished he had calmed his own nerves with a swig of the alcohol. Every moment he seemed to be waiting for the earth to crack open and reveal an abyss into which he would have no choice but to fall—an unholy thought to entertain on holy ground. Their camp was near the Toling monastery, its golden spires hidden by hills. But the atmosphere was brooding and sinister. Across the Sutlej loomed cliffs that tricked the eye in the starlit dark, resembling an abandoned fort, the gigantic statue of an old man's scarred face, a demon as tall as the sky. He wished he had Gyan's gift to see into the hearts of rivers and mountains, detect where currents were fast or slow, where deer or snow leopards hid themselves. All Balram could see anywhere was jeopardy.

In the caves something stirred, and the wind brought the sound of these movements to the riverbank and caused the men to gaze up at the cliffs fearful and trembling. These noises were perhaps no more sinister than bats flapping their wings; or it was a snow leopard, or the beast traders had warned Jagan about, a creature neither human nor animal. As the men saw it, to sleep was to be mauled to their deaths.

The captain came out of his tent, a robe tied over his nightclothes, rubbing his inky hands for warmth. Above him, the night sky was sapphire, tessellated with stars that shimmered red, blue, and gold, its colors changing on account of the high altitude. The men hushed, hid the chhang from the captain's sight, and stood up with heads bowed, chins tucked into chests.

"If you don't rest, you'll be too tired to outrun monsters when they come calling," the captain said, and the men began shuffling toward their tent. "Sit, sit," he said, and the bearers did so.

Walking around the men, the captain met Balram's eye and said,

"With logic and science, we can effectively counter superstition. Balram, you know about Herodotus."

"I don't know much," Balram stuttered. He felt the same apprehension his students must feel when he asked them questions.

"Herodotus was a Greek man, the world's first historian. He wrote that beautiful, rare things could be found in countries just outside the inhabited world," the captain said. "Herodotus must have been thinking about Tibet when he wrote those words, India too perhaps. Each one of you must have grown up with stories about treasures in a forest or a desert, guarded by a serpent or a lion."

The darkness quivered with the light of the stars as if it was a living thing. A rock pried itself from the cliff edge and threw itself into the river, and the bearers started. Rana clutched Harish's hand. While the gesture itself was none too peculiar, Balram felt unsettled by the febricity with which they gazed into each other's eyes. He could tell that what was being forged there wasn't friendship. It was none of his business, but the camp was the captain's kingdom, and only a few years ago the English had brought a new law that said men mustn't go against *the order of nature,* whatever that meant. Balram remembered Gyan saying it would be a long while before the English could see what men did in darkness.

Chand shivered and huddled closer to Yogi. "I'm not your wife," Yogi said, shoving him aside. "Listen to the captain when he's speaking. Show some respect."

"In Herodotus's accounts," the captain said, ignoring Yogi, "men fight the enormous ants of Tibet because they want to steal the gold that the ants guard. Isn't that so, Balram?"

"I regret we have to stop here at night," Balram told the bearers, "when I made a promise to you that we wouldn't." Why he felt compelled to offer an apology at such an inopportune moment, he didn't know. "But we must get some sleep, if only for two or three hours. Let's take turns to guard our camp."

The captain cast a disapproving glance at Balram, then pressed his knuckles against his temples as if to dislodge the Hindustani words that had collected sediment-like at the bottom of his mind and wouldn't rise promptly to the surface at his command. "In every mythical story, beasts only attack those who steal from them," he said, his voice holding its own against the wind even if his words came slow. "Am I right, Balram?"

"Yes, sir," Yogi replied enthusiastically before Balram could.

"But we don't seek to steal this country's treasures, not even the gold for which Tibet is famous. We're merely walking along a river, no different from pilgrims," the captain said. "These monsters you fear, the guardians of gold and diamonds, have no reason to attack us."

Doubt flickered across the faces of the bearers. Only Yogi said, "Listen to the captain, he's right."

"Nevertheless, we will be careful," the captain continued. "Balram will arrange a roster for guard duty, and you'll follow it without complaint."

How close the sky seemed from here, Balram thought; in one fell swoop, he could leap from this world to the next. "The wind is too much," he heard Chand say, and he turned to the bearer, who smiled at him. "I must lie down," Chand whispered. Then he collapsed to the ground, shuddered, and moved no more.

THE BEARERS TRIED TO revive Chand long after his soul had left the body. Death couldn't have been an unusual occurrence for them, but here they were in a strange country whose terrain changed every few miles as if it couldn't decide whether it should be a mountain or a plain or a desert, and they were desperate. Their hands pressed down on Chand's chest, and they shook his shoulders and slapped his cheeks to bring him back. Balram smelled the men's fear in the fetid odors emanating from their armpits and feet, and in the foulness of their breath.

"Bad things happen in sets of three," Jagan said.

He's right, Durga said. *Be careful.*

Balram weighted Chand's eyes with the smoothest stones he

could find and pressed them shut. Jagan and Naga rifled through Chand's belongings and brought out his blanket, with which they covered his corpse.

"It's your fault," Yogi told Pawan. "Your food is inedible. That's why Chand was always hungry."

"How dare you say such a thing when you lick your bowl clean every time?" Pawan said.

"Wasn't hungry, Chand, no," Naga said timidly. "I have been giving him raisins and nuts."

"We must hold a proper funeral," the captain said, his manner as brisk and unsentimental as that of a priest at the burning ghats of Calcutta or Varanasi hurrying along weeping mourners. "Let's send him off as your people do, with the correct rites. It's the least we can do."

"Impossible, sir," Balram said. "We can't cremate him. Wood can't be had in Tibet even if you offer to pay for its weight in gold."

"Surely you exaggerate."

"Not in the least. We can't bury him either, because the ground is too hard for us to dig a grave."

"The terrain was the same when I was surveying in Karakoram, but I made sure every single man who died received a decent burial."

Ask him for their names, Gyan said.

In the purple-sheened sky, a million stars glowed bright and fierce. A groan escaped from the corpse swaddled in the blanket, Chand issuing a protest from another world. Startled, the men fell back.

"The body can produce certain noises after death," Balram said. "It's much more common than you think."

But the bearers knew that already. What turned their stomachs was the ease of the man's death, the absence of warning. A frostiness wound its way through Balram, causing his bones to crackle. The men kept watch as the stars turned white and vanished. When the sky began to redden, they edged away from the corpse to examine their own feet in the rags of light. They worried about the purple coin of a bruise on their shin and wondered if the ache in their temples pointed to *something else,* though the nature of the ailment remained unsaid.

The cliffs glowed a grainy yellow, the lines on their visage deepening as the sun advanced across the sky.

The captain stepped out of his tent and Balram said, "We must follow the sensible Tibetan practice of leaving the dead on hilltops." His voice was unsteady. "Corpses will decay with time, and the process will be aided by vultures and other scavengers."

"A sensible practice? It's positively barbarous," the captain said.

"The Parsis do it in Bombay. And they are a famously genteel people."

"It doesn't make it right," the captain said.

"We can set fire to the corpse if we use up all our oil," Balram said. "Hair and skin ought to catch fire. We'll collect the ash for Chand's family to disperse in the Ganga. Does anyone know his family?"

Yogi said he had a wife and two children, a girl around two and a boy who was still a baby.

"But if we try to burn his body the smoke will alert Tibetans to our presence," Balram said. "It would be highly unusual. Most traders leave their dead on the roadside." How plain his words, how cold his tone. As if the corpse in front of him had never been a person.

A lengthy debate followed. By nature the captain was parsimonious, and when Balram reminded him how much they had already spent as taxes at the Tibetan border, he readily changed his mind and agreed they couldn't afford to waste wood and oil on a funeral.

Balram extricated the rings on Chand's rigid fingers and the amulet he wore around his neck for good luck, wrapped these in a rag, and passed the small bundle on to the captain for safekeeping. Chand's wife could have it—in lieu of her husband. In the distance, a silver-gray hare deftly leaped from boulder to boulder as it made its way up a sand-colored mountain, playing some kind of game only the animal knew. The changing patterns of light and shadow sharpened and softened the edges of cliffs. Geese flew squalling across the sky. The Sutlej glittered in the sun, a liquid mirror rippling with the wind. Balram could never decide if the constancy of nature, its disregard really, in the face of death was a comfort or a degradation.

He and Ujjal carried Chand's feet, placing them on their shoulders for ease of carriage. Jagan and Mor held the shoulders. The body was slight, yet in death it had acquired heft. Their knees buckled. Steadying himself, Balram saw himself as a boy, Gyan watching him as he lit his father's funeral pyre, the flames too close and scorching his skin. Now two children somewhere near Dehra would grow up without a father, just as he had.

As they began their trek up a hill, the captain asked Pawan to retrieve his thermometer so that he could measure the boiling point of water.

Their ascent was undignified, the body slipping from their hands often because of its weight and the rocks and wind. Sweat dampened the crooks of their elbows and the backs of their knees, but their fingers turned blue in the chill. Balram saw only the ground at his feet, and the twisted coil of the dusty path that led up to the peak. Sweat hung from his eyelids, mellowing his vision. He didn't mind it. A blurry world could be a merciful world.

By the time they reached the hilltop, Balram's hands had turned to claws and he couldn't remove Chand's clothes. The bearers gasped when Balram told them Tibetans left bodies naked for animals and birds, and cut up corpses into small portions that would easily fit the beaks of vultures. They looked at him as if seeing him for the first time. What could Balram say? He could quote the scriptures: the body was only a container; Chand's soul was already searching for its next form. But his tongue felt like it had been scored with a knife.

Jagan took over the proceedings, chanting Sanskrit verses he had learned from the pilgrims he ferried to temples. His recitation was imperfect, the verses gnarled by his diction. But it had a calming effect, the words sanctifying the air like holy water from the Ganga. The men scattered the flour Pawan had grudgingly given them, as an invitation to vultures, their eyes avoiding the figure in eternal slumber. Balram couldn't glance at Chand's corpse either.

Not a tree or a creature could be seen on the ridges around them. Sculpted over centuries by the wind, the river, and the sea under which the land had once been submerged, the mountains appeared disturbingly alive, capable of movement. In the sun the colors of the landscape changed from dull yellow and gray to vivid orange and red, its magnitude too vast for the eye to perceive. To die in this country where the gods lived, the most sacred land on earth, was also a gift. For the kind of man who sought consolation, such a thought could perhaps offer solace.

On their climb down, the bearers talked about Chand, a new reverence polishing their tones as if they didn't want to anger his ghost. Mor said Chand had agreed to go on the Tibetan expedition only to clear his father's debts. His constant hunger had not been from his stomach but from his mind, which feared—on account of his father, who had once gambled away everything they owned—that his tongue might not taste another morsel of food. Even then, he had wanted to do right by his father. Mor was a stern man, who did what he was told, and Balram believed him. He thought the name Mor was more suited to Harish, who was vain and given to preening like a peacock. Mor never looked into a mirror, it seemed. His beard grew in all directions, even curling upward.

"Chand knew he might die here," Mor said now. "We all do." As if to illustrate his words, he slid down the path but managed to cling to a boulder. "I didn't expect death to come so soon," he said, recovering his footing. Blood dusted a scratch on his hand.

"I wager his death was a real surprise to Chand as well," Ujjal said.

Jagan clicked his tongue. "Not the time for your childish humor," he said.

"The captain will make amends," Balram said, twisting his hands to press his knuckles into his aching shoulder blades. "His family will receive a reward."

Alive we may be worth something to the English, but dead? Gyan said.

"What killed Chand, do you think?" Ujjal asked Balram. "He seemed healthy enough last night, only a bit cold."

"Could have been the beast," Jagan said. "The part-human, part-bear creature. It's a soul eater."

"Tibet's climate, its altitude, it can be too much for some," Balram said, choosing his words carefully so that he wouldn't make the men more anxious. "Did Chand complain of a headache?"

"He only ever complained about being hungry," Ujjal said.

"These things happen," Balram said. The intensity of the wind pushed him down the track and threatened his balance. "I warned you about the dangers before we started our journey. I didn't trick you on that count."

"No one's blaming you, Compass-wallah," Ujjal said, and Balram, furious, ashamed, said, "Don't call me that."

IN HIS TENT THE captain had poured himself a glass of brandy. When Balram entered he offered him a glass too. "Or is it against your religion, to drink while mourning?" the captain asked.

"Must be," Balram said, his brain in knots he couldn't unravel. Water trickled down his neck from his river-washed hair and still he felt tainted. It was as if his own hands had strangled the last breath out of Chand's throat. He had made a series of errors in judgment leading up to this moment. He should have realized Gyan had gone missing instead of imagining him walking along the path of the Tsangpo. When he heard Gyan was imprisoned in Shigatse he should have traveled to Tibet as soon as the snow melted. By himself. Not with the captain, even if his gold coins were essential for a rescue. Not with fourteen men of whom only ten remained in their party now. How many would he lose tomorrow? It wasn't a thought he wanted to think but there it was, no avoiding it.

"I will take that drink, sir, if I may," he said.

"Good man," the captain said.

Balram gulped it too quickly to savor its trail of heat down his throat. The captain poured himself another brandy, but he didn't offer to fill Balram's glass again.

"We must leave soon," Balram said. "The men won't stay here another night."

"What's the name of the hill on which you left Chand's body?"

"I don't know, sir."

The captain drained his glass, wrote something in his notebook, then said, "I took a few bearings with my compass when you were away." He read the words on the page aloud: "*Left of camp is a hill of two hundred meters. Name not ascertained. The Sutlej flows by the camp at a bearing of sixty-seven-and-a-half degrees for about two miles, where it's joined by a stream.*" The captain pointed to his glass, and Balram picked it up to be washed and returned. "Makes for a poor route survey, don't you think?" the captain said. "We have so few native names for hills and mountains."

Balram nodded, unable to fault the captain for fretting about names and numbers while a man lay dead. On their first expedition to Tibet together, Balram and Gyan had been caught in an avalanche, and the snow had buried Balram for nearly five minutes before Gyan managed to claw it away. Gyan put Balram on a docile horse, and took bearings as they rode, and as Balram, frostbitten, breathing ragged, lips and fingers tinted blue, drifted in and out of consciousness. Later Gyan said the survey had kept his mind clear; he didn't worry Balram was going to die. Balram said he understood, though it struck him as a betrayal. In Gyan's place he would have been too anguished to conduct a route survey. But Gyan was a better surveyor than him. Able to tally numbers in his head quicker than Balram. Less prone to daydreaming and brooding. Once he agreed to a job he did it well. The captain had liked telling Balram how gifted Gyan was, and Balram had agreed each time, then secretly kicked a wall.

And now I might be dead, Gyan said.

Outside the captain's tent, Balram found the men shivering as they came out of the river, their bodies elongated so they appeared as tall as the cliffs. Must be the brandy scalding his empty stomach. The river was snow-chilled, but every one of the men had undertaken a dip in its waters, the cleansing of the self after a cremation or its equivalent a ritual prescribed by the gods.

Balram handed the glasses to Yogi, who never complained about performing chores for the captain, and walked over to the shepherds to ask if the animals had been fed. By the river grew clumps of grass, but Rudra said the aridity of the land worried him.

"We'll always be next to a river," Balram said. "I chose this route so the animals wouldn't go hungry." The words lingered in his mouth like a fistful of thorns.

Samarth came up to them, his coat making a surprising racket. He showed them his pockets filled with pebbles. He said he was building a collection.

"A man has died," Rudra said. "Now is not the time."

Samarth's face dimmed. The boy's hair was damp from the river. "Dry yourself properly," Balram told him. "You'll catch a fever otherwise."

"His stones weigh as much as he does," Rudra complained as Samarth staggered away. "It makes him slow. It was a mistake to bring him along. I wish I hadn't."

"Come and eat," Balram said. "Pawan has made . . . what, I don't know."

"What can Kaccha make that I would want to eat?" Rudra said, mouth twisted to form a growl. Seeing Balram's raised brows, he said, "Kaccha is what we're calling Pawan, because everything he cooks is raw. Grass tastes better. But if we eat the grass, the sheep will starve."

THE ROTIS AND LENTILS Pawan served were, as Rudra had predicted, only half-cooked. Balram took a bite and decided he couldn't keep the food down. He had no appetite. The captain, who ate separately from them, beckoned him over with a flick of his spoon. Unwise to flaunt cutlery in this fashion, and Balram had advised against the use of forks and spoons in Tibet, but the captain said he had already given up baths and women, and that was sufficient punishment. "I would have brought along canisters of preserved meat and beans if I knew this"—he lifted his spoon coated with the white starch of lentils—"would be our daily fare."

"You said potted meat was not fit for human consumption."

"And this is?"

"Pawan hasn't learned to change the cooking time according to the altitude."

The captain stirred the dal, his eyes on the river, his hands keeping the rhythm of the blue waves that splashed against rocks.

"I'll put Naga to work in the kitchen alongside Pawan," Balram said. "At least he will stay quiet and not curse the men like Pawan does if they complain about the food."

The captain set down his bowl. "How are the men doing?" he asked.

"They may be thinking of running away, but I doubt they will act on it. They need the money. They're afraid you'll send the police after them."

The captain stroked his beard and winced at the ink that marbled his fingers. Where the beard touched his robe, uneven patches of black spread like mold. The ink wasn't as stubborn as it ought to be. Balram followed the captain to the river, where he washed his hands.

"Many famous explorers died pitiful deaths despite being careful," the captain said. "And this region is becoming more and more dangerous because of the Russian threat. Remember the British agents executed in Bokara twenty-seven years ago for spying? Would they have gone on their missions if they'd had an inkling of the fate that awaited them?"

"My father knew he could die on the pass," Balram said. "Especially in the colder months. And that's exactly what happened."

"I suppose one doesn't undertake an expedition like this without being prepared to meet adversity. Still, it's always a shock, isn't it, when a man dies on your watch?"

"Perhaps asking the bearers to march to Toling after a dust storm was a step too far."

Must you say that, Durga asked.

"You could have chosen hardier fellows."

Balram turned away from the captain to scan the cliffs. The sun was higher now, and it leached the rocks of color. He thought of

Chand's corpse, up on the hill, shadowed by the wings of birds, red slashes blooming across his pale skin, feathers pressing against wounds that no longer troubled him.

"This is not a journey for those who can't master their nerves. You need an iron constitution and will," the captain said.

"The bearers are strong," Balram said.

"In that case we leave the rest to God," the captain said in English. "For he maketh sore, and bindeth up: he woundeth, and his hands make whole."

Yogi brought the captain a glass of tea.

"Not now," the captain said, and Yogi looked crestfallen. "We have to hold on to hope, Balram," the captain continued. "Without it we may as well curl up on the ground and leave our bodies to birds and beasts."

8.

AT TAKLAKOT M— DECIDED that to avoid detection we must march only in the dark. Past midnight we were climbing a hill, a much more dangerous task in Tibet than the reader can imagine, when we heard a suspicious howl. I shouted loudly to discourage wild animals from approaching us and, for some time, my strained voice did have the desired effect. But soon a beast leaped toward us as quick as a bullet, its fur reeking of putrid meat. I fought it off with my walking stick while M— brought out his kitchen knife that was no match for its sharp teeth. In the poor light of my torch I recognized the beast to be a wolf. Worryingly it was not alone; we could hear its pack prowling nearby. I picked up a stone the size of my hand and lobbed it at its head. My aim was excellent. I presume the stone broke the wolf's jaw, for it retreated.

In the brief lull that followed, M— and I managed to run up the hill and take shelter in the grounds of a monastery located at its peak. But the Tibetans would not let us inside. They were worried we had been bitten by corpses reanimated through witchery. They thought we had been rendered contagious! We had to show them that no blood stained our clothes, and that we had not suffered any injuries, before they relented.

After this adventure, I decided that we must travel only in the day. It is hard enough to climb inclines when the sun is shining, and almost impossible to avoid falls at night. But being devoured by wolves is a fate even worse than broken bones.

Though I was displeased with M——'s lack of foresight while planning our journey at night, he has so far been a better servant to me than I expected. In the Orient, lone women travelers seldom have such luck with servants. Only scoundrels usually seek to be employed as their bearers and, in conjunction with the lady's maids, rob the woman once they reach a secluded place.

I have been terribly unlucky with the weather, however. We are close to a depression in the mountains known as the Gurla Pass, which leads to Mansarovar, but frustratingly, a hailstorm has waylaid us. We sought shelter in a cave, and now, late at night as the world sleeps, by a dying fire I write these words smudged with smoke. M—— says gods send storms and other dangers to test us; only those truly seeking to atone will be allowed to reach the holy Mansarovar, and Mount Kailas, which lies to the north of the lake.

~~Ethel, I admit it was a mistake not to be at your side as you lay dying. Forgive me. I regret it so.~~

LIKE THIEVES THEY TIPTOED in the darkness below houses moored to the edges of cliffs. These quaint dwellings, built with no fear of landslips, appeared to be suspended in the air. Katherine was sorry to leave Taklakot without having had the occasion to study the ingenuity of Tibetan architecture, but Mani wouldn't hear of staying behind when the jongpen's men were on the alert.

The weather was mild in comparison to the bitter cold of the pass, but the wind was unpleasant. They entered a temporary settlement called the Bhotia Bazaar, housing merchants visiting from India. Katherine found herself longing for the warmth of mud and stone walls even though these houses had no roofs, only cotton sheets, on account of a Tibetan superstition that slate roofs would confer upon the abodes a permanence that would disturb the spirits who inhabited the earth below. Mani said the sheets, too thin to withstand the winter snow, indicated to the spirits that by the end of the summer, the merchants would finish trading and leave for their homes across the frontier.

Hurrying past the huts, her walking stick barely touching the earth, Katherine couldn't find it in her heart to mock Tibetans for apportioning the land between humans and spirits, she who was trailed by Ethel's shadow thousands of miles and several oceans away from where her sister lay buried.

Up a hill, they came upon the chorten for Zorawar Singh, and Mani stopped to pay his respects. Nearly three decades ago, Singh, the general of a king who ruled over Jammu, had lost his battle with the Tibetans. Katherine had heard that a snowstorm left his men frostbitten and unable to grip swords.

"A ghastly thing, what the Tibetans did to the general," she said. "Displaying his head on a spike in Lhasa." Her voice had grown hoarse from the cold night air. She could have done with a warm bowl of tea, but for such a simple pleasure she would have to wait till dawn, when she expected Mani would call for a rest.

"Tibetans didn't defile General Zorawar Singh Kahluria's body," Mani said as if he had witnessed the battle, though the boy hadn't even been born at that time.

Katherine wondered what it would be like to carry herself with his confidence. Had she been as certain of her place in the world, would she have found it necessary to uproot herself ever so often? Had she not been a stranger at home, would she have spent her life wandering like this so that she would be a stranger in all places and at all times?

"In Kalimpong," she said now, "government officials told me Tibetans hacked Zorawar's corpse and distributed parts of his flesh among themselves—they believed hanging a slice of his body above their front door would make them as brave as the general. His killing is a cautionary tale, told and retold to remind people like me how savage Tibetans can be."

"You can see with your own eyes," Mani said, pointing at the chorten, a circular, three-tiered structure, "that Tibetans treated him with respect. They built a grand monument to house their enemy's bones. An enemy who killed their people."

Katherine looked up at the tomb, and the stars above it that glittered white in the indigo-black sheet that was the sky. Was the savage the general who had attacked another country, or the Tibetan who defeated him and carved up his body as if at a butcher's table? Were the English officials who had their way with native women in their bedrooms and on mountainsides men who surrendered their wits to passion, or men who coerced the weak into submission? Was she, Katherine, a strong-willed woman who had escaped from her mother's cage of shame, or an embarrassment to her sex, a cold and hardened being who had turned her back on her family even as her sister lay on her deathbed?

This battlefield must be beset with ghosts she couldn't see but which passed through her, causing her head to fill with odd questions. She walked quickly into the starlit night, wishing the dead would stop whispering in her ears.

THE WIND CUT KATHERINE's lips and blood seeped into her mouth, the salt burring her tongue such that against the inside of her cheeks it felt like the prickly skin of a rambutan. Clouds moved across the sky, hiding the stars. In the dark they stumbled over boulders. Halfway up a hill that had a monastery at its peak, Mani paused, exhausted perhaps. "Hurry," Katherine said impatiently, and he pressed his index finger against his lips. The insolence of the boy. But in that brief moment when she was silent and the wind eased, pebbles scattered. Mani moved in front of her as if to shield her, facing the direction of the sound. The boy's hands were trembling.

Fear thrummed in her blood. It could be bandits, could be the dead who had come back to life. A gray-white apparition leaped toward them, dust rising behind it like smoke. Her ears boomed with the sound of quickening heartbeats—her own, she realized. Mani was about to die, mauled by a wicked ghost that would then attack her. He snatched her stick from her hands, thrust it toward the spirit, and hissed, "Scream." She saw then that it was no ghost, no corpse that had been brought back to life, but a wolf. She remembered a Scandinavian she had met in Ceylon telling her that one shouldn't run from wolves. She clapped her hands, slippery with sweat. She shouted, cursed, and made herself appear as tall and wide as possible, swaying on the tips of her toes. The wolf snarled, its teeth white and sharp, the rest of it merging with the night. She clawed stones from the ground and flung them at the animal. It howled as if wounded, and retreated. Then, its cries were answered by its pack.

Mani gestured toward the peak. "Monastery," he panted. "People. Better."

But they couldn't outrun a pack of wolves. Sweat streamed down Mani's forehead though the wind had turned icy. Katherine's face too felt like it was on fire. She saw, with an astonishing clarity, the silver-tipped waves of the Karnali marking the river's course below the hill. Above them a dog howled, as if attempting to converse with the wolves. Then what sounded like a child's voice bounded across the dark to ask them who they were. Katherine thought she was going mad or hallucinating, or maybe she was already dead and this was the afterlife.

A gunshot broke the quiet of the night. The wolves scattered; their howls grew fainter.

Birds flew out of the boulders in the hillside, but Katherine couldn't trust her vision, not now. Another gunshot made her jump, fear crawling up her skin cold and viscid like a worm. A flash of bright orange darted toward the bluish night sky, leaving a trail of gray smoke.

"Bandits?" she whispered to Mani.

"Who might you be?" The sweet voice of a child returned to taunt her again.

"We're pilgrims," Mani shouted back. "Did your father fire the gun?"

A plump-cheeked child appeared in front of them, a lantern raised in one hand, his other hand placed atop the head of an enormous black mastiff with a mane that would have put a lion to shame. It barked at them, but the child said something to it and the dog immediately became docile.

"Are you lost?" the child asked.

"You're too young to be wandering alone," Mani said. "There are wolves and all sorts of wild animals here. And what if in our place you had encountered bandits?"

"At the boy's command the dog would have torn you to pieces," said a surly Tibetan man with a blanket pinned across his chest, marching into the small circle of yellow light the boy's lantern threw onto the ground. Through the gap between the folds of his blanket, Katherine saw the muzzle of a gun he held tightly against his heart as if it was a precious thing.

"They're lost," the boy said, and the dog barked in agreement.

A conversation ensued in Tibetan between Mani and the man, who had saved their lives by firing his gun into the sky. Mani expressed gratitude, then regret, that the kind gentleman had had to waste his gunpowder. The Tibetan said they were foolish to be traveling at night, and it was their good fortune that he had been nearby, and Mani slapped his own cheeks to express his remorse. The Tibetan invited them to spend the night at an encampment near the monastery, where other pilgrims had already sought shelter.

"You can sleep without fear of wolves and thieves, because I'll be keeping watch," the child said, his sing-song tone at odds with his air of superiority.

"Shouldn't he be asleep?" Katherine whispered to Mani.

Mani smiled at the child, and followed the man as he led them around the side of the hill toward a vast ground specked with white tents. Guards sat around fires, swords by their sides. After the man and the child left, Mani began to set up her tent.

"We should travel only in the day," Katherine said. "The night wind is too harsh, and the land too dangerous."

"Don't be afraid, mother."

"You could have at least brought your knife out."

"I had rather die than kill a living creature," Mani said.

"And yet you eat meat," Katherine said. The boy was too sancti-monious for his own good. From a neighboring tent a man's voice hissed at her to be quiet.

"We will leave early tomorrow," Mani said. Wolves howled in the distance. Katherine wanted to ask him to be careful, to sleep next to the guards, but stayed silent.

IN HER TENT KATHERINE lay awake for a long time despite her ex-haustion. Her heart had slowed but her mind was traveling quickly after the encounter with the wolf. Half asleep, she heard her mother declare to her father that she was unfit to be a part of their household, and a poor sister to Ethel. Her father protested that Katherine was still a child, and if she retained the mannerisms of an Oriental, it was because she had been in the care of a native ayah for years. "She's not mine, and if she is yours, I don't see it in her face," her mother re-plied. Katherine stood on a chair and examined her reflection in a large mirror upon her mother's dressing table. Her image distorted and snapped like a twig over a fire; she was no longer a child but a woman standing in a dancing hall in Garbyang where girls pirouetted around her, sparks flickering toward their skirts. She felt the heat of flames rising up her cheeks as Chetak entered the room with a pistol in his hands that he aimed at her and fired.

Waking up with a start, Katherine touched her face expecting to find shreds of flesh. It was still dark, but she heard footsteps, then Mani's voice telling her it was time to leave. The words arrived as if through thick ropes of mist. She stumbled outside, the remnants of the dream clinging to her eyes still. Mani set to work dismantling her tent. The metallic taste of blood pooled in her mouth even though the gunshot had been fired in a dream.

How can you be such a fool at fifty, Katherine thought. She found a cloistered nook to make water. As her eyes relearned to identify ob-jects in the darkness, she fretted the child or a wolf would come across her at her most vulnerable. But her fears didn't come to pass.

They set out at dawn along the Karnali River. The wind was still frosty, as it had been at night, and rustled past them toward green cornfields edged by plain, gray hills shaped like the triangular folds of a woollen blanket, their peaks clothed in mist. In the distance they saw a village, prayer flags in five colors representing the elements— blue for the sky, white for air, red for fire, green for water, and yellow for the earth—fluttering on the roofs of houses. On rock walls the Tibetan prayer *Om Mani Padme Hum* was etched. From about half a mile away, she saw a bridge across the river, but on closer examination it proved to be a log placed over the water whose opaqueness the sun's first rays turned to gold.

Mani asked to stop for a few moments so that he could conduct his ablutions.

"Did the wolves return after I went to sleep?" Katherine asked, watching him roll up his sleeves, some prayer as always passing between his lips with his every breath.

"Too many fires, too many men," Mani said. "They're intelligent creatures that know when to stay away."

Katherine stepped barefoot into the river, almost too icy to bear in the first instance of contact. Her feet, pitted with blisters, looked unfit for an expedition that would last ten weeks if not more. A spasm seized her back, causing her to cry out. Mani rushed to her side, but Katherine pushed his hands away. He rummaged through his sack as if it held the exact remedy she required, then offered her a small bottle of oil and suggested she apply it after warming it between her hands. "Go into the fields," he said. "Don't worry about wolves. And no one will see you. The farmers will only be here in an hour or so."

In London, such a suggestion, to disrobe in the open, would have been met with horror. But here, in the brilliant light of the sun that was beginning to dissipate the mist over the hills, the pain so violent it made her acutely aware of her surroundings while simultaneously obscuring the world, she could accept the bottle without protest.

With Mani standing guard, she hid behind stalks of corn that scraped against her bare skin and massaged herself with the oil. Dirt stained her palms black. When had she last washed herself? Mani's medicine brought no relief. Time had worn down her muscles and bones, and there was no cure for it. She could pretend her age had no bearing on her ambitions, but for how long?

Groups of pilgrims began to cross the river, but the narrow log held their attention and they barely looked at her as she came out of the fields.

"Can you carry my things?" Katherine asked Mani, annoyed he hadn't offered already. He took the sack from her, giving her an embarrassed smile.

She balanced her feet on the log, the walking stick stretched across her hands as if she was a rope walker, her eyes on the water below until it seemed to her that she too was moving with the river's tumultuous currents. She looked away, curling her toes so she wouldn't slip. Then she was on the other side of the river. She could only walk slowly, and so Mani slowed down too.

They reached a cheerless place called Baldak dotted with a few tents and flat-roofed hovels outside which vendors sold tea, watched over by the occasional Tibetan soldier carrying a matchlock, its long barrel and forked stand reaching for the sky. By now the sun had risen higher, and its warm rays dusted her forehead with sweat. Mani's oil, or the slackening of muscles in the act of walking, had marginally diminished her pain. She staggered up a hill, Mani carrying the additional load without appearing troubled by it. When they reached the summit he placed the sacks on the ground and stretched his hands toward the sun. "We're now several thousands of feet above the level of the sea," he told her as if he expected her to note it down. "How are you feeling?"

She looked at the wisps of clouds, floating midway over mountains and hills. On the slopes the rain and wind had over centuries sculpted rocks so they resembled the faces of lions or the feet of an elephant, the images changing with the movement of the sun across the sky.

Mani offered her raisins that she refused. She wasn't hungry. "You'll tell me if you're feeling ill?" he asked, and she sighed, exasperated, then noticed the earnest expression on his face. It seemed the world hadn't yet corrupted his heart, and she found his innocence pitiful.

"If I die here, the Almora deputy collector won't send you to prison," she said. "People rather expect a woman of my age to perish in these mountains, of natural causes."

"Don't say such inauspicious things," he said, touching his ears to ward off evil. "Think about your husband and children."

She had forgotten he knew nothing about her. One didn't share such information with servants. Still, she said, "I have no children." Such a confession often made others look at her with pity, as if her barrenness was a great stain on her life. "It's why I can travel, and I like traveling a lot more than I like children," she said. She didn't expect him to understand.

"Our families bring us joy but can be a burden too," he said. "Here in Tibet, notwithstanding wolves and storms, I'm more at peace than in my own home." He clasped his hands behind his head, stretching out his elbows and crackling his knuckles. The skin on his neck had been burnt black by the sun, and she noticed a thin white line where a knife must have drawn blood during a tonsure.

A group of pilgrims and their bearers passed them, hands on their backs, their breaths so loud it sounded to her like the gasps of the dying. Four of the men stopped and rested on rocks, clutching their knees, mouths opened wide. They mumbled words no one could understand. Black-headed birds that resembled seagulls gathered around the pilgrims, who must have scattered crumbs each time they stopped to eat, and the birds now pecked the ground, full of hope.

"How do birds fly at this altitude?" Katherine asked Mani. As if to call attention to the absurdity of these creatures with small lungs wheeling in the air while humans collapsed, a young man started to cough and wheeze. His spit was tinged rose. He blew his nose, and blood stained his fingers. Katherine felt sick. As she watched him, unable to help, he fainted. His bearers quickly picked him up and laid him on a woollen blanket. With each person carrying a corner, they ran with him down the hill, the way they had come.

"I hope they can save him," Mani said, watching the four trotting figures and the swinging blanket. "But it will take them hours to reach a height that's several thousand feet lower than here, and that's the only cure for mountain sickness." The gulls lifted up into the skies. The rest of the group of pilgrims looked stricken. They continued their journey, their steps slow and awkward.

"The sun is too bright here," Mani said. He hoisted the sacks, his own on his back, hers strapped to his chest, managing to stand upright in spite of the weight.

Another group was coming up the hill, but quickly, as if floating through air. One of their members sang at the top of his voice. Behind them trailed sheep carrying small bags of grains or sugar, the bells around their necks jangling, the shepherds whistling and the animals bleating, and all in all they formed a merry group, and Katherine found the earth tilting at the oddities of this world, dark one moment, light in another, like this landscape itself, when she noticed Chetak, his dagger jutting above his hip bone, speaking to a shepherd.

"Look over there," she said to Mani, chin pointing in Chetak's direction.

"Who is it?"

"Isn't that the man you saw at Taklakot? And before that, near Garbyang?"

"Your memory is very good," Mani said. "It's as if the altitude isn't troubling you at all."

"Don't tempt the devil," Katherine said, touching her bonnet for luck.

When Chetak came up to the peak, his forehead was shining with sweat. He saw her and tried to speak, but he was short of breath and settled for a grin instead that creased the skin around his eyes. Sweat plastered the curls that had escaped from his turban against his forehead.

Now she could prove to Chetak that she hadn't been lying about a companion, but she would rather have been alone with him. The wind blew across the hilltop, smelling of snow and grass, and flicking clouds around like marbles.

Up came the sheep in a flurry of bleats and tinkling bells, and they skirted around her like a brook parting at a rock. Each of the men in his group stopped to inquire if Chetak was all right, and slapped him on the back, or tugged at his turban playfully, until it came loose and he stood there with the fabric between his fingers and the wind slipping strands between his lips each time he tried to speak. He told the men he would join them later, and they looked at her and Mani as if curious about the nature of their relationship, but they didn't ask any questions. Katherine saw he had a different way of speaking to men, a roughness to his tone that she hadn't heard before. Still, she envied his easy manner, the way he could strike up friendships with strangers; given half a chance he would find a way to charm a nobleman in Paris.

"I guess this was bound to happen," Chetak said to Katherine, "us meeting. This is the only way to Kailas from Garbyang."

"My son," Katherine said, pointing to Mani.

"No doubt we will meet you again," Mani said, rather curtly, Katherine thought. "But now, mother, we must leave." He began the descent without waiting for her.

"My son is impatient," Katherine said. She was distracted by Chetak's beard, freshly trimmed, an unseemly longing for him twisting through her each time she saw his face. The edges of his mustache twirled appealingly above the corners of his mouth. She hadn't considered that he could be fastidious about his appearance, but there was in him more vanity than she thought likely in a native man of his class (he couldn't hail from nobility with *that* complexion). Feeling unkempt, she raised her hand to smooth her hair, and a flare of pain twisted around her back, distorting her features before she could rearrange them. Chetak's brows furrowed—perhaps from concern, though it was more likely he had caught a whiff of the foul odor rising from her armpit—and she hunched into the folds of her robe.

In the distance Mount Kailas came into view as the white clouds that had enclosed it lifted. Its black-blue, snow-coated, pyramidal summit was easily recognizable from the descriptions Katherine had read, flanked as it was by bare, reddish-brown slopes. This was the mountain that belonged to gods. Only the Buddhist monk Milarepa had reached its peak, and legend had it that he had warned others against following in his footsteps. No man had since scaled the mountain.

"You're very welcome to join our party of two," Katherine heard herself say, her eyes fixed on Mount Kailas. She was being reckless. But if Chetak brought her unease, he also made her feel closer to sixteen than sixty and, on a day like today, was she so wrong to wish to return to a time when her bones didn't rasp and her skin and teeth and hair shimmered, and she trusted her feet to carry her, and her mind was specked with dreams instead of ghosts?

THE LANDSCAPE BECAME MORE and more hallucinatory as they walked toward the Gurla Pass that led to Mansarovar and Kailas. Katherine was stunned by the briskness with which hills and mountains gave way to a plain that had the appearance of a swamp, formed by meltwater from glaciers. Cheerful birds flew above them to perch on small islets created in the middle of brooks by clumps of rock and grass. Mud weighed down the hem of her robe. The twinge in her back slowed her, but it was nothing she couldn't bear.

A few feet ahead, Chetak walked with Mani, attempting to engage him in conversation. Chetak's tone was different when he spoke to Mani; it was more solemn, almost methodical.

At first the boy answered in grunts, the two sacks he carried perhaps exhausting him such that he had no strength left to speak, but Chetak seemed to have a way with words and people, and soon Mani began to tell him stories about the difficult men for whom he had worked.

"Brahmins have impossible rules, worse than kings," Mani said. "They check the caste of those carrying water, those carrying grains, those carrying blankets on which they'll sleep at night. Once I traveled with a man who had brought a priest along to conduct a purifying ritual each time he sipped water, as a precaution, you see, in case the water had been tainted by one of us."

"But Englishmen are worse, don't you agree?" Chetak said. "They make our people walk into the forest beating drums so that the sound will force tigers and boars into the open ground where the sahibs can easily shoot them dead. And this is what they call hunting. And they don't care if we're mauled to death by the animals."

"My friend was part of such a hunt," Mani said. "He felt like he was bait for a tiger."

Chetak sounded to Katherine like one of those rebellious soldiers who had pledged allegiance to the Mughal king during the Sepoy revolt of 1857. But she couldn't imagine Chetak being in thrall of a king either. A man like that wouldn't be bound to anyone.

"Is it any better working for your mother, or is it worse?" Chetak asked, turning to look at her, and she flinched.

"She's a good woman," Mani said, his tone not betraying a trace of irony.

Chetak raised a brow, but luckily his attention was diverted by a bird with gray and chestnut feathers. "Look, the plover has turned up in his colorful summer clothes," he said. "The males have far brighter plumage than females during breeding season."

Mani coughed in disapproval, perhaps because breeding was a subject unfit for polite company.

"It's nature's way, brother," Chetak said. "We can speak honestly now because you're not in the employ of sahibs or Brahmins. Though it must be equally difficult for you to be truthful around your mother." He glanced at Katherine. "I must say, however, that you two look nothing alike."

Not even the hint of a shadow darkened Mani's face. "Are you from Almora?" he asked Chetak.

Katherine's foot struck a stone that went flying toward the islets, unsettling birds that protested with chirps. Her fingers pressed against her walking stick, searching for splinters that she hoped would pierce her skin and jolt her awake. The man who walked in front of her—so close that she could smell the cloves on his breath and this landscape that was part mud and part sand and part stone on his clothes—could reveal her true identity to the highest Tibetan bidder. Why else would he accompany them? She was too old, too hideous, to be found desirable.

Gray clouds thickened in the sky. Darkness abruptly tumbled down slopes, heavy as sodden wool. Mist erased the spurs of the Gurla mountains. Katherine had seen this before, the swiftness with which the weather changed in Tibet. Always a charge in the air, a lit match held over a barrel of gunpowder. Always the possibility that one might be cast into a lake of fire and brimstone. It was thrilling. It was frightening. What could she do but push on? Fear had never stopped her from boarding ships or scaling the Himalaya.

They turned a bend and came across a group of pilgrims, the elderly and infirm among them being ferried on horseback. The sky crackled, and startled horses leaped into the air. An old man, his parchment skin clinging to his bones, slipped from his nervous horse. The sky and the earth merged in a hailstorm that began to pummel the ground. Snow fell as it did in winter, blanketing Katherine's eyelashes quickly. The earth appeared to her as a single shade of white. A great gush of brown water and rocks rolled down a hill, a landslip prompted by the splitting of heavens. All was desolate and yet stunning; sacred, even.

Mani, back stooping because of the sacks, shouted words she couldn't hear over the cacophony of the storm. Chetak's shoulder brushed against her, by mistake perhaps. Her boots sank in the snow that crunched and squelched, and her walking stick slipped from her hands and she found herself clutching Chetak's arm for support.

"We don't see storms like this in Terai, do we?" he said, drawing his elbow, and thus her hand, closer to his chest. He placed his right hand over hers, not in a proprietary manner but gently, as if to comfort her. His palm was hot against her skin. She felt a lightness in her heart though the snowflakes were sharp as daggers on her cheeks. Around her were the blurred, frantic figures of pilgrims, and rivers of muck scything new paths down rocky slopes. The birds and islands of grass vanished under the white counterpane of snow. She heard pilgrims screaming, horses neighing, Mani shouting at her to hurry, and Chetak singing softly—she turned her face toward him in surprise, seeing him framed between her eyelashes laden with snow. "Remember this song?" he said, and his smile took her back to the night in Garbyang when there was dancing and a house floating in the sky and songs about certain movements of the hands or the tongue that men found pleasurable.

"Hush," she said. "The gods on Kailas will hear you."

"Not in this storm," he said, but then the storm stopped as abruptly as it had started. Thick, yellow slabs of sunshine escaped through the clouds. Chetak's hand released hers, and he glanced at his palm as if he had expected his skin to adhere to her fingers just as flesh attached itself to metal when temperatures dipped below freezing point. The snowflakes caught on his beard and mustache glistened in the sun, then began to melt.

"There's a cave ahead," Mani said, retracing his steps and picking up her stick. "We can build a fire."

Inside the cave Mani gathered the twigs and dung that had been left behind by previous visitors. Katherine felt the muscles in her back ache again. In the moment of the storm, Chetak's touch had acted as a balm more effective than Mani's medicinal oil, making her forget all else. Without it her body had returned to its defective form.

She thought the cave extended deep into the mountains, but when Mani coaxed fire from the wood she saw the space was too small to accommodate more than two or three people at a time. Chetak stood by the oval-shaped entrance, neither entering nor leaving, his form a shadow in the light of the sun. Katherine felt unsettled, like the weather. Soot stains trailed down the cave's ceiling. She heard the clucks of tongues as men urged forward the ponies carrying the injured toward Taklakot town, where medicines or bonesetters could be found.

"Come inside," Mani told Chetak, "and dry yourself."

"Give me a moment," Chetak said. He spoke to one or more of the fleeing pilgrims or their agitated bearers. It sounded as if he was attempting to send a message to someone in India, but to whom Katherine couldn't tell. Perhaps it was one of the young women he had serenaded in Garbyang.

"Mother, I mean no disrespect," Mani whispered to her. "But men can have odd notions about those who look like you, and you must not encourage them."

He was an insignificant thing, this boy, with half a brain. Yet his words made her feel she was a child hiding behind jute blinds dampened with water against the summer heat, overhearing punkahwallahs debate whether a greater kindness on her father's part would have been to leave her in an orphanage as most Englishmen did instead of publicly acknowledging her as his daughter.

"In Almora, there's a woman people say is the bastard child of an Englishman and a zamindar's widow," Mani said now, "and her house is always milling with English officers at night."

"How dare you," Katherine said sharply, and Mani raised his palms and said, "No-no, of course you're not like that. But this man, we don't know his intentions."

Katherine remembered her mother saying she should be grateful for her place in their home. In New Orleans quadroon girls were raised to become mistresses of white men, or sold in the slave market, but her father had given her a chance at a different life that she wasted with her immodest conduct. *Look at how you swing your arms as you walk how you stop to gaze into shop windows without fear of seeming countrified how you insist on taking the arm of any gentleman you meet on the street.*

"Mother, be careful," Mani said.

Chetak entered the cave, his body bent in half, and removed his sheepskin coat. The dampness of his shirt outlined the taut muscles across his chest. Must be the mixed blood in her that allowed her to notice his appearance; a good woman would have averted her eyes. Chetak bundled his coat onto a dry patch on the ground and shook his curls, scattering drops of water. The fire hissed and sputtered. He squeezed his turban dry. The flames dabbed russet tones onto his beard.

Katherine remembered the story he had told her about the Englishman and the native woman. Had that been his way of calling her a quadroon? Did he imagine that as a bastard she had no morals? What right did a mere native have to even consider such a spiteful thing?

Chetak shared with them the dried apricots he had purchased from a Ladakhi trader. He spoke to Mani about the deputy collector of Almora, how the Englishman liked going on long walks by himself in the forest and drawing the leaves of plants. Katherine couldn't imagine how or why Chetak would know such particulars. He and Mani talked about a Muslim man who lived in a cave in Mussoorie and had earned a reputation and a vast number of devotees by correctly predicting one's fortunes. "He's now wealthier than a zamindar," Chetak said, "but still lives in the cave like a pauper." Listening to the conversation, Katherine began to think Chetak was just another native; a gossip perhaps, but a simpleton. Nothing special about him.

"I don't even know your names," he said now.

"I'm Tara," Katherine said, stating the name her ayah had given her. The ayah had been convinced that *Katherine* was far too Anglicized for a child whose complexion announced the native blood in her veins. The name had been their secret, until her father heard it and called the ayah a deranged woman, and banished her from uttering it again. Katherine too had cast out the name from her mind—or so she had thought—and yet here it was, promptly on her tongue, as if she had answered to it all her life.

"A holy name," Chetak said, his damp shoulder pressing against hers. She didn't move. The cave smelled musty in spite of the smoke.

"It's the name of the female Bodhisattva," Mani said. "And the Goddess of Wisdom."

"I don't feel very wise," Katherine said. At least that part was the truth. Her character didn't display the traits either of her names should have conferred upon her; no purity in her as warranted by *Katherine,* no wisdom as would have befitted *Tara.*

Mani introduced himself and asked Chetak, "What should we call you?"

As names and surnames in India disclosed not only one's religion and caste but also the region where one was born, Katherine wondered if Mani was attempting to ascertain Chetak's standing in Indian society. Was he an untouchable who turned cowhide to leather, a basket-weaver, or a farmer, disguised now as a man from a less cursed caste?

Chetak introduced himself as Chetak and didn't reveal his surname even when pressed.

"I suppose we are all here to ask the gods to cleanse us of sin," Mani said.

"The boy wants to convert to Buddhism and become a monk," Katherine told Chetak. "Children, I tell you," she said, shaking her head, aware her performance lacked conviction.

"If we repent sincerely, our past transgressions will be forgiven," Mani continued with the solemnity of a parish priest sitting in a confessional. His gaze remained on Chetak as he spoke. "You see, unlike in our temples, here the low caste aren't barred from bathing in Mansarovar or walking around Kailas. You may be a king, you may be a sweeper, it doesn't matter."

"The right country for outcasts then," Chetak said to her, and Katherine felt as if he had looked into her frantic mind and seen every shameful aspect of it. In the warm flush that rose upon her cheeks, she recognized the traces of that morning's dream.

9.

IN THE FOOTSTEPS OF ALEXANDER THE GREAT—
PROPHECIES—A SECRET LIAISON—STALKED BY A
WHISTLE—THE ZEBRA OF THE EAST—ATTACKED

———

THE ENEMY WAS EVERYWHERE AND NOWHERE. THE BEARERS marched in two files, grace in their steps but fear in their eyes. Now they knew they too could drop dead without warning, like Chand. Balram looked up at the cliffs often. The craggy slopes shimmered white in the vicious afternoon light. A gray shape darted across his vision, but then he blinked, and it vanished. Could have been a snow leopard. In Ladakh some called the animal jatpo, the one who stalks. Above them the sky curved bald and smooth, an upturned blue bowl that seemed to have trapped them inside. The men said it felt as if they were tumbling through a void.

To their left loomed a cantilevered bridge trussed with iron chains, built over the Sutlej River. The captain pointed his prayer wheel at it.

"Too many merchants," Balram said before the captain could ask to examine the bridge from close quarters. "At this time of the year, I'm more likely to encounter friends and relatives here in Tibet than in my own home. Might surprise you, how willing my people are to cross a perilous border for a bargain." Half an exaggeration and half a joke, but the captain didn't smile.

"Alexander the Great is believed to have constructed the bridge," the captain said, a belief he had already recorded in his reports of the Tibetan surveys conducted by Balram and Gyan. He moved a bead of his rosary with each step, counting his paces, though Balram and Gyan had surveyed these routes already; the captain would have nothing new to add until after Shigatse, where their previous explorations had ceased. But he needed to confirm their numbers be-cause the native, no matter how proficient, couldn't be trusted. At least he had stopped asking Balram if they could measure the position of the sun or a peak; he understood it was far too risky to bring out the sextant and compass in daylight.

A couple of feet ahead of them, Jagan tapped his left elbow. "Can you hear it? The click-click-click?" he asked Naga, who shied away from him like a dog about to be drenched with a pail of water. "Our expedition will be marked by calamity."

"That man," Balram said to the captain, "will be a pox on us all."

"Talk does no harm."

"Talk slows them down."

"Then do as you must," the captain said. "Remind him of the Swede."

"And the Russians?"

"The Russians too," the captain said. Balram's wry tone must have escaped his attention.

"Jagan," Balram said once he had caught up with the bearers, "your elbow hurts because you have overexerted yourself, or because it's unfamiliar with the Tibetan weather. If you knew this expedition was going to fail—as you should have, since you can apparently foretell the future—why did you come?"

"You won't die in Tibet, Compass-wallah. Fear not. I won't die either," Jagan said.

"I wouldn't be so certain of it," Ujjal said. "I'm tempted to kill you, if only to sew your mouth shut."

Rana snorted, then pretended he had inhaled a pinch of snuff.

"Naturally all of us have been shaken by what happened to Chand," Balram said. "But we'll be more careful. Speak to me at once if you feel ill." If his words made any difference, he couldn't see it in their faces. "No more of this wretched talk, you hear me?" he said to Jagan. "Adversity will be tempted to visit us if you invoke it so often."

"Whatever you say," Jagan said, worrying a callus on his palm.

Harish smirked, and a sneer parted Yogi's lips, and Balram felt as if he was back in his classroom. On some days he despised his students, who could be slothful and belligerent, but perhaps the captain was right and it was his fault that he could guide neither men nor children.

Balram returned to the captain's side. Despite not being weighed down by goods, the captain was slower than the bearers because he took notes to place within his prayer wheel.

"He must have come here after Taxila," the captain said, and it took Balram a moment to realize the captain was still speaking about Alexander the Great. "It's said that philosophers accompanied him on his campaigns. Buddhism must have left a great impression on the minds of those philosophers. Some might disagree, but if you consider it carefully, you'll see that Stoicism and Buddhist philosophy have much in common, particularly on the subject of detachment."

Balram noticed that the captain's tone, clipped and precise in the plains, was beginning to come undone.

"I suppose others must have deemed it to be an eccentricity on the king's part," the captain said.

"What, sir?"

"That he had philosophers accompany him during his battles."

"If you think about it, even the Bhagavad Gita is a book of philosophy," Balram said. "It takes place before a battle, when Arjuna despairs about killing his own relatives and Lord Krishna advises him about the difficult choices he has to make."

"Balram, I have read the Gita."

"Of course. Perhaps anyone with a conscience requires a philosopher on the battlefield to convince them it's just and right, even necessary, to take another's life."

"Why, aren't you quite the philosopher yourself," the captain said.

THEY FOLLOWED THE SUTLEJ until the river itself changed direction as if it had wearied of pursuing the same route to the sea year after year. Balram considered the parched riverbed under his feet, scaled like the skin of a fish and as brittle as an old man's teeth.

What had caused the river to drift from its course? Perhaps the ground itself had shifted, earthquakes being far from unusual occurrences in these parts. Perhaps the sediment that had collected on the banks had nudged the Sutlej farther to the right.

"It's as if the river doesn't want us to chart its path," Balram said to the captain.

"Don't be foolish," the captain said.

They crossed the riverbed, bags on their backs and boots in their hands, dust sputtering as their feet breached the dried mud. Then the river itself, gnashing around their ankles. On the other side, the terrain was empty save for a row of ancient chortens in the distance, dismembered by inclement weather. Dust whirled between the ruins, thick as swallows. They set up tents by a sheep pen Tibetan farmers must have erected a long time ago, edged with some kind of leathery shrub, the stones lopsided and the walls haphazard, but it was a solid thing, wearing moss like a proud flag as if to declare that it had withstood rain and snow and things men hadn't seen yet. The light was softening and golden, the sky a silky red to the west. Samarth splashed around in the water. "Boy, you won't stop until you catch a fever," Balram shouted at him, half-wishing he had seen Inder play with such joy at least once. Samarth trudged up to the sandy bank, a smooth pink pebble in his hands that he had picked up from the riverbed.

"Compass-wallah." Jagan called Balram over to where he stood apart from the other bearers, cleaning his boots with a fistful of grass.

"If this is about your elbow—" Balram started to say.

"Isn't it dangerous to follow the route Gyan must have taken? If what people are saying is true—"

"Which people?"

"The traders at Mana—"

"Those traders," Balram said, "they spend days waiting for the pass to open and the skies to clear. They gossip to while away their time, it's what they do. You didn't meet any beasts in Toling, did you?"

"We don't know what killed Chand."

"Wasn't a bear."

"I didn't tell you earlier, but the traders, when they warned me about the bears, they also said a spy from Dehra had been caught near Shigatse. He was charged with treason and sold into slavery. Could be our Gyan."

"Yes, and Gyan is now owned by a lama who's cruel and corrupt," Balram said, a fresh panic burning his skin. It was the first time he had taken Gyan's name in a long while. It hurt him to say it; there was a knot in his chest, a crack in his voice. He saw Gyan writhing beneath the boots of a Tibetan lama who was also a feudal overlord. He heard Gyan offer a lesson in arithmetic or science for an hour in the sun. He saw Gyan swap his prisoner's garb for a monk's clothes, and this was easier to imagine, Gyan with his shaved head bowed in a dark hall, reciting scriptures, gold-brocaded tapestries hanging from the ceiling brushing against his face each time someone opened a door and a breeze covertly entered the room.

Me, a monk? Gyan said.

"Compass-wallah?" Jagan said.

"I heard the same stories. So have Gyan's parents."

"Is it wise then? Real traders take the well-traveled road to Gartok, but we are here, among ruins. Won't Tibetans find it suspicious?"

"You're a good man, Jagan," Balram said. "But your words, they frighten the men for no good reason."

"You said my words remind you to be careful."

Anger flashed in his mind like lightning. Balram couldn't tell why. Was it that these men expected him to offer conversation and consolation as if he was a sage? What he liked most about traveling was the cocoon of silence that surrounded him, the warble of a river or even the hiss of the wind so metrical it didn't upset the cadences in his head. But now his ears echoed with his own hollow words, the shouts of bearers, the noises of animals, and the certainty in the captain's voice.

"I didn't mean to upset you, Compass-wallah," Jagan said, and Balram wondered what ferocious expression the man had seen on his face.

"Don't call me Compass-wallah," Balram said. "If anyone overhears it, they'll be suspicious."

In the camp, the bearers clustered around a fire, shivering into their blankets. The serrated outlines of cliffs and mountains darkened against the sky.

"Gyan started calling me Compass-wallah," Balram said. "But the compass I used belonged to the Survey. I didn't have my own, like the captain does."

"You must have been good at using it."

"No more than others. It requires no skill, no particular knowledge. But Gyan didn't need a compass. He could tell the direction blindfolded, measure angles with his eyes. When he called me Compass-wallah he wasn't praising me, he was making fun of me for my reliance on the contraption." Balram smiled at the memory of his friend's gentle ribbing; at the time it had irritated him, the childhood rivalry between them bristling still. Now that Gyan was missing, it seemed he could be unconstrained in dispensing praise. "Gyan's work was remarkably proficient. He was a better surveyor than any English officer," he said.

"Maybe they'll name a mountain after him."

"Now there's a prophecy I can assure you will never come true."

Jagan laughed, then tried to gather up his frizzed hair on the crown of his head. The parched skin on his wrists had the texture of bark. "I'll watch my tongue," he said.

A COLD DRAFT WOKE Balram from his sleep that night. A bearer tormented by his bowels must have gone out of the tent and forgotten to secure the folds. Balram waited for the man to return, but his shivers became more pronounced and still he heard no footsteps. On the ground he sensed an emptiness where bodies otherwise lay packed as tightly as feathers on a bird's wing. With his blanket wrapped around his shoulders, he got up.

Tibet at night was brighter than a forest at noon, each star in the sky the burning wick of a lantern. He had no trouble seeing where he was going. Around a fire that was nearly dead, the shepherds, and Ujjal and Naga, meant to keep watch, slept. Balram nudged Ujjal awake.

"If even one animal is missing in the morning, the captain will make a pouch out of your skin to stuff his maps," he said. The threat revived Ujjal, who in turn woke Naga and the shepherds. Naga made tea over the fire and gave the men almonds stored in his pockets that were as swollen as a squirrel's cheeks.

Balram, stomach full of the tea that he should have refused, warmed his hands. Then he walked some distance from the bearers to find a solitary place to make water. He didn't want to piss in sight of the chortens. Ruins they might be, but they were sacred, never mind how he felt about gods. In the starlight the rock faces appeared strangely human. A silvery shape flashed in the distance, gone so soon he couldn't be certain he had seen it. He ought to have brought a lantern or a flame torch—what he took to be the impression of a snow leopard's paw on the ground, on closer examination, turned out to be a footprint, belonging to one of the bearers perhaps.

In his nearly four decades on earth, Balram had seen a snow leopard only twice. When he was a boy he had traveled to Leh with an uncle in winter, and a snow leopard had wandered close to a sheep pen, but Balram hadn't noticed it when he pissed in the morning, steam rising from the snow where the piss hit, and all the while the snow leopard watching him from a rooftop, meeting his eye as he wiped his freezing hands against his coat, a wry look on its snow-crusted face. The second time too he had missed the animal's presence; in Ladakh with the Swede, he had been calculating the height of a hill and, pointing a spyglass toward it after a whole afternoon of taking measurements, seen the leopard toward its base, not a whisker moving or eye blinking, perched like a king on a throne as a rose dusk spilled out of the sky onto the earth below. Balram remembered his heart jumping under his chest, full of awe, not so much fear, but perhaps he was misremembering things and he had only been afraid.

Now he loosened his clothes and did his business. The wind brought to him the odor of piss, not his own but a stench that was acrid and sweet, a smell he related to the snow leopard from his previous travels. The animal marked its territory along ridges and streams by digging up earth, and by lifting its tail and spraying urine on rocks. A pulsing anxiety edged Balram's white breath. There was no movement in the landscape except for the swirls of dust that rose and fell with the wind. No undergrowth either in which an animal could observe its prey. But a snow leopard knew how to hide itself. The snow leopard was always going to spot him first.

Guttural sounds pierced the air in quick, brief flashes. Balram had the peculiar sensation of being at sea once more, as if he was riding the crest of a wave on a ship with creaking masts. The land mimicked the swells of the sea, full of peaks and troughs.

A voice in his head—was it Durga's voice, was it Gyan's?—admonished him for not returning swiftly to the tent where the air might be as repugnant as at a fish market from the men's sweat and gaseous expulsions but where his safety was more assured than here. He ought to ask the bearers to investigate the sounds. But he was their leader. Not much of a leader admittedly. Still, he couldn't push them into the path of a snow leopard that skulked behind rocks.

Against his instinct he marched toward the source of the sounds. Lacking weapons, he picked up a stone to fling at any animal he came across. Judging by the noises it made, he surmised it was in pain. A wounded leopard was as dangerous as an able-bodied one, and liable to attack those it perceived as meek.

He climbed up a low hill, his feet moving behind the trail of his own white breath, and below, he saw as clearly as the light of day two men engaged in sodomy. Mercifully their heads were turned away from him. Balram quietly made his way back, feeling as surprised as he had when he first encountered statues of fornicating gods on a temple wall.

The fire was brighter on his return, and sparks leaped out of it into the air. Next to it, Samarth slept folded over a sheep that he cradled in his arms, for warmth perhaps. Catching sight of Balram, Rudra clouted the boy on his head. Samarth jumped up with a yell. "Moti," he said, clutching the sheep to his chest as if it was his pet. To grow fond of an animal on a dangerous journey was unwise, but what did a child know?

"Let the boy sleep," Balram said, and Samarth promptly lay his head on the sheep named Moti that served as his pillow. Ujjal, still in a state of half-stupor, smiled at Balram, the upturned corners of his mouth painted red by the rising flames.

Harish and Rana must have sneaked out of the tent earlier, when the bearers on guard duty had been sleeping. The two would return when the sky was only moments away from being lightened by the sun, the hour at which the guards were most likely to have succumbed to the demands of sleep yet again.

Smoke gathered in his throat. The pious white canopy of the captain's tent appeared to him to be an omen of sorts, but what did it portend? Balram scratched his arms furiously, as if some meaning would emerge from the pain. Men died, men fornicated, and sometimes men fornicated after a death to remind themselves they were alive.

What do you know of desire, Durga whispered in his ears. Years ago, when he returned home after a surveying expedition to Tibet, there was some gossip in the neighborhood that a man had been seen entering his house in his absence. But Balram had never asked Durga about it, knowing full well their neighbors blamed her for giving birth to a child like Inder and were eager to tarnish her name further. And what right did he have to complain even if the rumors were true?

Not that he had even dreamed of touching another woman since they married, but when it was just him and Gyan somewhere away from home, he was content to sit next to Gyan, sipping tea or bland gruel, by a fire the wind wanted to put out, wolves watching them from a distance, eyes glittering like stars. They didn't have to speak and sometimes it was hard for Balram to speak because he was afraid of what he would say, mind made pliable and soft by the altitude. They could fall asleep on the other's shoulder or with their backs pressed against each other for warmth, and these small gestures made Balram feel his birth was no great tragedy after all, that he could be rooted to the earth instead of floating over it like an apparition. For all the clamor of his wants, he also knew how to exercise restraint; he might have learned it as a child when there was no mother or father to hold him after he fell down and spilled blood and salty tears made their way to his tongue, no finger but his own to dab them away. But it might not have been enough for Gyan, who with a sly grin had slapped Balram on the back when his marriage was fixed, had called Durga his sister from the moment he met her, had carried their children on his back when they were small. He never asked more of Balram, though their lives had been spent in the knowledge that the other, if not traveling, was no more than a mile away. Only once, at the beginning of a tour, after Balram had a nightmare, had Gyan held him for long to ease his shakes. Then Gyan had slipped his hand under Balram's chuba, an afflicted look on his face. Balram had sat up hurriedly, and if Gyan had been hurt, he hadn't shown it. Instead, he had told Balram to go back to sleep.

Balram thought now that he would have to keep the bearers' secret. He felt exhausted. He had too many secrets of his own already.

THE NEXT MORNING THEY reached a spot where the path forked into two like a snake's tongue. To the left was the Daba monastery, built on a cliff a few hundred feet above a village as if to encourage monks to hold themselves above earthly pleasures. Behind the monastery, the narrow dwellings that housed the monks tilted on the edges of rocks, delicate like birds' nests. Prayer flags fluttered on the hills. Golden barley fields surrounded the village, their stalks weighed down by seeds, drooping toward the ground ready for harvest.

They turned right, and Balram stepped over a pit in the ground where a snow leopard seemed to have scooped out the earth to mark its presence. The animal must be watching them, but from which direction? He heard the distant, pleasing chimes of bells and the intonations of cymbals struck together in prayer at the monastery.

"If only we had a barometer or a theodolite," the captain said, pointing to a ridge with his prayer wheel, "we could have calculated heights accurately. Tonight we must find an isolated spot to camp so that we can measure the latitude."

"Certainly, sir," Balram said.

"I have no doubt that the Survey will have finished printing and distributing my maps before the Swede disembarks at Gothenburg," the captain said. "At best his calculations will serve to verify my work." He picked at a scab that had formed on his knuckle, a consequence of frostbite perhaps, to expose the shiny pink skin underneath.

Balram had forgotten the Swede. Fortunately the steepness of the path barred the captain from continuing the conversation. Their feet dislodged stones that hit the men who walked ahead. Apologies were shouted, curses muttered under breath. Balram listened to the chimes from the monastery. These sounds shouldn't have traveled so far. Could be the bells that shepherds tied around the necks of sheep, or yaks, but Balram saw no flock nearby except for their own, and these animals had no such paraphernalia, only the bags of grains on their backs.

His ears must be deceiving him. No one else spoke of the sounds. The bearers marched silently for once, their postures defiant; they carried their loads as if their flesh was made of steel and their bones cut from marble.

They reached a plain watered by a narrow stream. Around them hills looked burnt in the harsh light of the sun. The white clouds floating over the blue sky planted fleeting shadows on the slopes. Whorls of dust hid and revealed strange forms in the distance that Balram took first to be bandits, then pilgrims. Again he heard the infernal noise. Now it sounded less like a bell and more like a whistle.

"Should we shoot them for meat?" the captain asked.

The spectral shapes were wild asses that the Tibetans called kiang.

"Gunshots may alarm villagers," Balram said. "We don't want them asking questions."

"I'll never understand why Tibetan Buddhists won't kill animals themselves," the captain said, "when they willingly eat the meat of yaks and sheep that Muslims slaughter for them. Mighty hypocritical, don't you think?"

"Very little grows at this altitude, sir. They don't have much choice."

The kiang sprinted closer, playful and friendly, ears cocked. In winter their coats were tinted chestnut, but now their fur was reddish brown. Balram advised the bearers to keep their distance; the animals were temperamental.

"A specimen of the kiang was brought to Calcutta over two decades ago," the captain said. "It took a fancy to a pony and followed it everywhere. I read about it in the journal of the Asiatic Society. Apparently no one could examine him because he would bite any stranger that dared to get close."

"What happened to the animal?" Balram asked, wondering why the English couldn't leave good enough alone. "I can't imagine it fared well in the heat and rain of Calcutta."

"He was sent to England—but since he would only eat and drink in the company of the pony, the pony too was dispatched with him. I don't know if they survived the voyage."

An unsatisfactory, if expected, conclusion. The kiang in front of them rolled on the ground with their feet in the air, then sprang up almost immediately and shook off the dust on their coats. Balram heard the whistle again. "What's that sound, you think?" he asked.

"This animal is quite similar to the zebra, even though it doesn't have stripes," the captain said. "Mind you, I have never been to Africa, but this is how they appear in sketches."

IN THE EVENING THE sky turned scarlet, then a luminous shade of blue, and the hills on either side of the camp glowed like embers, as if holding within themselves the light of the sun. The temperature fell by several points. The bearers who had removed their coats to set up tents, and provisional sheep pens with stones, shivered in their sweat-stained clothes. The ground rustled with the quick movements of nocturnal creatures the eye couldn't grasp.

Pawan, who had always claimed to dislike cooking, seemed fright-fully bothered by Naga, who kneaded flour and rolled out rotis with-out as much as a crease on his forehead. "Your wife must be sleeping with your brothers," Pawan said to Naga, thrusting his hips back-ward and forward. "Your balls will shrivel to the size of the kishmish in your pocket." He demonstrated by pinching two of his fingers to-gether and holding them up. "Your crotch will be infested with fleas." He scratched his manhood over his coat. Naga fussed over the fire, quiet as a butterfly. "Your wife is a whore," Pawan said. "Don't have one," Naga said, at last forced to speak. The other bearers found Pawan's performance, and Naga's dignified response, hilarious, and the mood in the camp was cheery.

Harish and Rana whispered to each other, no spark in their eyes to suggest they were lovers. Then Harish spoke loudly: "We Rajputs are never afraid." Rana playfully hit his arm.

"But you said yesterday that you're descended from the Mara-thas," Mor pointed out to Harish. "We mustn't lie in the land of gods."

Harish pretended not to hear him.

"What are you saying, crazy fellow?" Rana asked Mor. "I can't understand you because your beard seems to be growing out of your tongue."

Balram turned his gaze toward the shepherds. The pony nearly took off Rudra's chin as he repaired its shoes.

For a while Balram studied the men closely, wondering why he knew them not at all and, proving himself right, managed to miss the exact moment a container of chhang was brought out of its hiding place, wrapped in a rag, and passed around from one eager hand to another. A generous swig of the liquor caused each man to thump his chest and point to the sky and utter Chand's name. "Hope you're doing well up there, friend," Mor said. "Hope the gods are taking good care of you." Ujjal burst into song, tapping his hands on an upturned bowl as if it was a drum. Rana shared his snuffbox, and some of the men sneezed exaggeratedly after inhaling a pinch. The captain ordered the bearers to keep their voices down, and they did so at once, shoulders drooping, eyes downcast. The captain asked Balram to walk some distance with a lantern; its light standing in for the horizon would allow the captain to calculate the angle of the North Star, and thus the latitude of their camp.

Balram called Ujjal and set out. Ujjal sniffed the air for the scent of dal. He was worried others would feast on the meal before they got back and leave nothing for him. Naga had whispered he wouldn't serve anything raw, Ujjal said—an easy promise if you thought about it, but impossible for Pawan to keep. "Then it's going to take a while," Balram said. He looked around for the source of the preternatural whistling sound he had heard in the day, but didn't encounter a figure, human, animal, or spectral, in the half-darkness. He stood still for a long while, hoping the yellow light of the lantern would serve as a baseline for the captain's calculations. Above him constellations of stars formed the shapes of bears and hunters and sages.

When they returned to the camp, the bearers were eating. Ujjal rushed to join his friends, calling them bastards and bellowing at them to leave some food for him.

"The latitude appears to be 31° 27' north," the captain said, a bowl of dal in one hand and his notes in the other, "but I might be wrong."

"Calculating latitude by stargazing is always difficult," Balram said.

"But a more pleasurable activity could hardly be found."

Balram glanced at the men, who were finding joy in snuff and chhang and the company of each other.

"My interests must seem obscure to the men," the captain said. "Even to you. A man my age must have a wife and children, and a fortune, not a compass and sextant, you must think."

"A family can be a burden."

Is that so, Durga said.

"Remember never to say that in your wife's presence," the captain said, and waved at him to leave. "Go eat."

Balram joined the men, who thanked Naga for cooking them simple but delicious food. Naga barely looked up from his bowl, and he winced each time his name was mentioned. Pawan said mosquitoes would always pick blood over wine, and the bearers hooted with laughter. "Kaccha cries like a baby," they said. Balram cautioned the men against indulging in too much chhang and snuff at such a high altitude. Harish boasted that on account of the royal Gupta blood in his veins, his lungs were unnaturally powerful, and, as if to demonstrate it, sang a few bawdy rhymes with great vigor, accompanied by Ujjal. "You said you were a Rajput less than an hour ago," Mor told Harish. Balram was exhausted by the alertness the day had demanded from him, and these tunes that encouraged others to dance made his eyes heavy. Eventually someone helped him up to his feet and guided him to the tent, where he lay on a sheet that didn't stop the icy ground from sending chills up his spine.

He heard Durga's bangles clink as she pressed a cool palm against his forehead. Thunder roared outside, and a vicious downpour followed. In horror he realized that his head had widened and his body had shrunk. Floodwaters surged around him, and the force of the currents impelled him down a river whose waves mocked him for trying to remember its name. Rain fell from the sky into his wide-open eyes. In the periphery of his vision, he saw his arms and legs separate and float away.

Balram woke up, his shirt damp. *I am drowning,* he thought, before recognizing it was a dream. He heard shouts, and his mind went to Harish and Rana. He looked around and didn't see the two of them.

A boisterous wind thrashed the tent. The sounds woke the bearers, who asked if the sheep were being attacked by beasts. Their voices, dulled by alcohol, were listless. A few pulled their blankets over their heads as if hoping to disappear, so that they wouldn't be required to investigate the sounds.

Balram's movements were slow too; he realized it, but he couldn't make himself be any quicker. In his mind he was still floating down a river in spate. Then he heard the whistle that had haunted him. At last now he knew what it was: a signal. For a moment he sat still, blood pulsing against his temples with the might of a hammer splintering rock.

BALRAM STUMBLED OUTSIDE INTO the cold Tibetan night. Shooting stars arced across the sky. Yogi and Mor, the two bearers meant to keep watch at that hour, threw dung into the fire and Yogi barked, "Who's there? Who's there?" The fire cackled. They heard feet thumping, hooves clattering, a low droning sound like a thousand bees humming. Rudra stood behind them, shouting into the dark, calling for Samarth. Balram attempted to speak but found his tongue was affixed to the roof of his mouth.

You're better than this, Gyan said.

The sheep were frantic. Their small bodies knocked against the rocks that confined them. The pony strained against the rope around its neck, neighing and kicking. Through the darkness ghostly lanterns inched toward the camp and, in their swinging lights, disembodied hands and legs resolved into the shapes of men. Behind them were murky figures on horseback, hands holding flaming torches. Hooves kicked up dust that distorted the vision. The hills that enclosed the camp appeared to be drawing near, as if to smother them.

Balram understood that during the day these bandits had lurked in the grooves of hills, passing notes on their movement through the sounds he had heard. He ought to have voiced his suspicions, warned the men. Now they would be slaughtered, and only he was to blame. *Let it be quick,* he thought. This too was the siren call of the abyss.

Pick up a stone at least, you fool, Gyan said.

"What should we do?" Yogi asked, twisting Balram's elbow as if to shake him out of his stupor, and Balram pushed his hand away; he wanted to be alone, he wanted to think before he spoke, only there was no time, there was too much chaos. The ground itself seemed to be trembling. Mor started to run, but the bandits had encircled their camp and he had to turn back.

"Good Lord, deliver us," Balram heard the captain exclaim. He emerged from his tent with his clothes askew, but his posture was of a man in command. "Guns, in the trunks, take them out," he shouted at Balram who, at last roused into action, tottered toward the captain's tent, Yogi behind him.

By now the sheep had climbed over the boulders. The animals scattered in all directions, perhaps to avoid the horses on which the bandits rode, and the bags slung on the backs of the sheep brushed against Balram's knees. The wind hissed through rocks. As the sound of hooves grew louder, terrified men ran out of the tent, screaming. The captain shouted orders that Balram couldn't hear. Dust scratched his eyes, and his chest tightened. Some of the robbers seemed to be crawling on all fours, leopard-like and deliberate, toward the camp. Perhaps they had heard the captain shout the word *guns.* These thieves could most likely see the camp, but their figures were still indistinct to Balram.

He ran into the captain's tent, where the trunks were stacked in a corner. Without the light of a lantern, he couldn't easily find the one in whose secret compartment the rifle had been hidden. The captain, exasperated, urged him to be quicker in the name of God, Queen, and country.

Quick-quicker-quickest, Gyan taunted him.

The cries of animals and the squawks of bandits curdled the blood. Balram's trembling hands grasped the Snider-Enfield rifle just as the captain asked, in English, "What's taking you so long?" Then Balram extracted a case of cartridges from the trunk but, as he tried to open it, his fingers cramped. The captain clucked in annoyance and shook his rifle as if he wished to slam its barrel into Balram's chest. Balram managed to pry the buckles of the case open and felt the metal coat of a cartridge beneath his fingers, its coolness in sharp contrast to the hot sweat that made his palms slick. He passed it to the captain.

Now the bandits were close to the tent. Everything was tinted a deep orange by the torches that blazed toward the sky.

"At the very least we must put up a fight," the captain said as he lifted his gun, pressed the cartridge into the barrel, and closed the breech. Through the fabric of the tent Balram saw the wicked glints of swords that cut the ropes holding up the tent and, before he could warn the captain, before they could run out, the canvas fell like a heavy curtain over their faces, blinding them.

BALRAM CREPT OUT OF the collapsed tent. In the torchlight, the dust was iridescent. The captain had eight bearers and two shepherds, and the bandits numbered forty or more. Their voices were loud, but Balram couldn't understand a word. Terror dried his mouth. Stars flickering in the sky, knives glinting below on earth. Balram felt as if he was floating underwater. Spectral figures drifted around him like the remains of a sunken ship. The captain barked at the bearers crouching in the shadows. Balram's fingers trembled as he cupped his mouth to scream *don't resist, let them take what they want.*

Really, Gyan said.

In the orange light Balram saw the felt boots of a bandit, dyed red and black, embroidered with delicate white flowers. The bandit stepped closer to him, and Balram thought this must be what it felt like in a battlefield to thrust your bayonet into another man. So close you were like brothers and might as well have been reaching for an embrace. But he had no weapons and he was going to die.

The bandit must be eighteen or nineteen, eyes red and a sharp nose that had been broken and healed back crooked, but otherwise his face looked unmarked by this ruthless life. The gleam of a silver knife pierced the dust as his hand impelled it toward Balram's thigh as if to incapacitate but not kill him. Balram heard the boy's breaths, smelled the yak butter in his clothes. In the few moments the knife would take to tear his skin, time slowed so that Balram could not only see but also count the number of light and dark lines forged on the blade. A turquoise jewel beamed at its hilt.

"Watch out," a voice warned just as Balram leaped back to dodge the knife, then a rifle cracked and the hand vanished. A slit in his coat, a scratch on his skin. The ringing in his ears was so loud it hurt like a fist to the face.

Balram had fallen to his knees without realizing it, and now he stood up shivering, a rope twisting around his heart. He turned his body toward the direction of the gun and stumbled over the inert shape of a man—was it the bandit who had been about to kill him? Blood flowed from the dead man's wound, a viscous river of sparkling rubies. Balram guided his foot slowly, right, then left, over the corpse. Bright light seeped into his eyes and he thought he must be dead, but when he blinked he saw the captain's tent had been set on fire. Someone dragged him by his arm. "You're alive," he heard the captain say, no particular relief lacing his words. He shook a casing still emitting vapor out of his rifle and extended his palm toward Yogi for another cartridge. "Save my papers," the captain said, his voice hoarse from the smoke and dust. "*Now!*"

His gun kept the bandits from approaching the tent. He had drawn himself to his full height and he moved without hesitation and he was as calm as a lion certain of his superiority facing an advancing herd of buffaloes. But a lion might yet be trampled underfoot.

Balram set to work with the man next to him, who he now saw was Ujjal. There was no time to ask after the others. His pants were damp; sweat or piss, he didn't care to check. With Ujjal, he rolled up the side of the canvas where the fire hadn't yet reached. From under it, they pulled out the trunks that held the precious gold coins that could convince a turnkey to set Gyan free—but first Balram himself had to survive the night.

The heat of the hissing flames scalded his skin. Sweat poured down his forehead and clung to his eyelashes. Gunshots punctured the night, the echo nearly indistinguishable from their source. But it seemed the captain was the one firing and the bandits had no matchlocks, only a few swords and butchers' knives and bejewelled knives and hoes and sickles, as if they had been working in the fields all day and had set out to loot at night. Balram willed himself not to listen to the screams. What could he achieve with his bare hands? He couldn't fight and he wanted to kill no one, not even in this moment.

Coward, Gyan said.

Think of our children, Durga said.

Gyan would have snatched a knife from Pawan and blindly slashed thieving men; he never did like parting with his belongings. But the best Balram could do now was to save the gold. In the sooty light of the flames, he saw the arrogant sparkle of the captain's compass and pocketed it when Ujjal's head was turned. He would have thrown Herodotus into the fire, but the teacher in him chided him for harboring such a disgraceful thought. The wind grew fierce, toying with the flames. Other hands now helped them transfer the captain's belongings. Balram glimpsed the prayer wheel on a blanket, then it was gone. The frequency of the captain's gunshots went up, as did the howls of men and the cries of animals. Balram wondered if he should ask the captain to fall back; it wouldn't do to have a dead white man on his hands. He should have thought of that before embarking on this blighted expedition. Maybe none of them would survive this night.

Then the torches began to retreat, and the sounds of hooves grew fainter, and the dust settled. Someone cheered, someone cursed, Pawan perhaps: "Go to hell, you sons of whores." Ujjal clutched Balram and said, "We're alive. Can you believe it?" He bent down and prostrated in front of a god only he could see, touching his forehead to the earth, but didn't get up, exhausted.

The camp was silent except for the bleating of sheep and the crackle of the fire that was burning the captain's tent down to ash. Balram wanted to tell the bearers to gather water from the stream and put it out. But who should he call for, what names could he take, who among them was alive, who was dead? Before he could speak, the men extinguished the flames with blankets, in this instance the bleakness of the land and the coldness of the wind a blessing that sapped the fire's strength. Like a ghost the captain stepped out of the smoke, gun held at shoulder height until he saw the trembling forms of the bearers and brought it down.

IN THE FRAIL MORNING light they counted the dead with their bloodshot eyes. The corpses of bandits, numbering two, were easy to recognize on account of the thickness of their sheepskin chubas and the superior make of their boots. One man's face was shattered and the white fragments of his skull embedded in the ground, but his hands clutched a matchlock that marked him as a brigand. He mustn't have had a chance to light the fuse and fire a shot, the mechanism of his gun slow, unlike the captain's modern rifle. Perhaps the bandit's gun was only an object intended for display, to frighten pilgrims into parting with their possessions.

Balram's nostrils twitched from the stench in the air, of shit and burnt flesh and metal and smoke and gunpowder. Silhouettes of birds flew out of hard-edged clouds that drifted over hills. Rudra wandered across the plain, picking up the sheep that seemed too stunned to move and returning these animals to what remained of the pen. Samarth, Harish, Rana, Naga, the pony, and God only knew how many sheep were missing.

On their path lay a dead horse that belonged to the bandits, its beautiful black coat stained by the blood that had gushed out of a bullet wound. Mor spewed out a yellow, congealed mess of half-digested dal and roti. Jagan cursed him. "Like you haven't seen a dead horse before," he said, but then he himself started to tremble. Twisted legs poked out from beneath the horse's torso: the legs of a bearer, wrapped in puttee. Mustn't have had the time to pull on his boots.

Six of them worked together to lift the horse before they saw Naga had been trapped beneath it. His cheek had a gristly wound in the shape of a hoof through which the wind prodded his broken teeth. In the moments before it died the horse must have kicked Naga with such force that he tripped, then the horse itself had collapsed on him before he could escape. The men squatted around Naga, saying his tongue was taken from him even in death. Made no sense to Balram, but he had an inkling they must feel they were going mad. He felt that way too.

He encouraged them to look for Samarth: "The boy will also die if we don't find him now." But they didn't budge, not even Rudra. Their hands straightened Naga's clothes like he was a groom being readied before the wedding. Candied nuts spilled from his pockets to the ground, which the men returned as if he would require sustenance in the afterlife.

The clouds in the eastern sky glowed a fierce red. Two figures approached the camp. Now the men jumped to their feet, shouting. The captain, who had shifted to the bearers' tent, dashed out with his rifle raised to his waist. Yogi scuttered behind him, a cartridge bag slung over his chest and the captain's coat folded across his hands. But the stragglers were only Harish and Rana, claiming they had wandered too far at night in an attempt to piss away from the stream, not wanting to defile their drinking water and suchlike, only to be barred from returning by the arrival of bandits. They hadn't seen Samarth. Was this Naga? Was he dead?

Don't just stand there, Gyan hissed in Balram's ear.

He clapped his hands to get the men's attention. He said the brigands would return to exact their revenge, most likely at night. "We must leave as soon as we find Samarth," he said. "We will take the road to Mansarovar favored by traders and pilgrims. Easiest way for us to follow. Less risk of being attacked." He remembered the men they had met on the Mana Pass who had asked if they could travel together to deter bandits. How quickly he had rejected their offer. He had not wanted to believe his plan to rescue Gyan was flawed. Now he could see it clearly, but he couldn't turn back.

The captain gave no sign that he approved or disapproved of Balram's decision to walk with hundreds of other pilgrims, taken without his permission.

Jagan grunted, lifting the primitive silence that cloaked the group as if they were men before language. "Should have done it earlier," he said, and since he was the group's prophet, most of the bearers

nodded. "Even if a crowd means the captain has to be more careful."
He rubbed his left elbow, holding Balram's gaze.

"What about Naga?" Ujjal asked, directing his question at Jagan.
"He's dead and so we should forget him?"

Balram knew they were too exhausted to carry a body up a hill
and then march at a pace that would allow them to escape the scrutiny of bandits.

"Naga's death is a great blow to us," the captain said, "and I can
only imagine how much more difficult it will be for his family to learn
he's not coming back. But we should continue our expedition so that
his death wasn't in vain."

"But sir—" Ujjal said.

"If you stay here, you'll be killed. Is that what you want?" the
captain asked.

A snort caused them to look up. The pony trotted toward them,
dirt braiding its mane, its manner unusually timid but its body by all
appearances intact. In spite of themselves the bearers greeted the
animal as if it was a long-lost friend, their spirits raised by its unexpected appearance. When they attempted to stroke its neck, it kicked
its hind legs to express its displeasure.

"All right, Colonel," Ujjal said. "We'll salute you from afar." He
raised the edge of his palm to his forehead exactly an inch above his
eye, with his thumb close to his forefinger: a soldier's salute.

The captain handed his rifle to Yogi, who held it like it was a fragile crown resting on a velvet cushion. With a click of his fingers, the
captain gestured that Balram should walk with him. Yogi followed
them two steps behind.

"We're not leaving before we find Sam," the captain said, scratch-
ing his nose and transferring the soot stains on his fingers to his face.

"Of course not, sir," Balram said. A tightness in his chest told him
he would see nothing good. Why look then? He asked the bearers to
salvage the remnants of the captain's belongings from the fire, and
reminded them to collect any empty casings they came across so that
the bandits, should they return, wouldn't speculate about the make of
the captain's gun.

From the pockets of his robe the captain produced a spyglass with which he surveyed his surroundings. How had he not yet discovered his compass was missing, and maybe his prayer wheel too? But there were more pressing questions at hand. By the stream, too shallow for a boy to drown, they found carcasses of sheep that had been hit by stray bullets and had dragged themselves to the water to die. Balram called Pawan and Mor and told them to skin the animals and pack the meat. He made Mor responsible for filling goatskins, and asked him to collect water far from the corpses of animals, and Mor began to object about being a bhisti, just as Naga had. "Do it in Naga's memory," the captain said. "Remember how quietly he went about his work." Mor said, "Yes, sir," and chewed on the dry skin hanging from his cracked upper lip. The sun broke through the clouds and the hills shone silver. Balram thought he saw Naga on the peak of a hill, raising a hand in farewell, but maybe it was a shadow or a snow leopard or a dream. He didn't know Naga at all; no reason for his spirit to show itself to him. Maybe it was Samarth. Must have wandered there chasing after sheep.

Balram forded the stream with the captain and Yogi. Frost sparkled on the grass. The air was chilly, but the sun was now bright enough for Balram to see that what he had taken to be the shadow of a boulder was in fact a small human, body crumpled into a ball, a sheep barely able to breathe clasped to the chest.

"Samarth," he said, waking the boy, who held his sheep closer as his eyes adjusted to the light. "You're all right then?"

"I hid before they could get me," Samarth said.

"You did well," the captain said, squeezing the boy's shoulder. "Even saved Moti. You're a bigger man than most men I know."

Samarth grinned, but his expression changed as they walked toward the camp. The treeless plain was the color of cinnamon and strewn with the fleece of dead sheep and wounded sheep and the still-glossy coats of dead horses, dense tails bedecked with tassels. The captain shielded the boy's eyes and told him to grip his elbow because the sights were too gory. Always a surprise to Balram to see the captain's kindness toward the boy. He could comfort Samarth while Balram didn't even know how to speak to his own son.

The bearers had wrapped Naga in his blanket, as if that could save him from the mouths of hungry beasts. Above his head they had placed a lamp fashioned from a bowl half-filled with oil. A twisted rag served as the wick, the flame protected from the wind with rocks piled high around the bowl. As Balram bowed his head to pay his respects, the wind snuffed out the flame, or perhaps the gods did, affronted by his presence. Pawan picked up the bowl and cast off the half-burnt rag. To the men who watched him in surprise, he said, "No sense in wasting good oil. The bandits stole most of our provisions."

"We have to be careful with our money," the captain agreed.

10.

ON THE SHORES OF Mansarovar I encountered a great
crowd. It was a shock to the senses. Still, the scenery—a vast
blue expanse of water surrounded by lavender hills and snow-
capped mountains—is striking, if sullied by the presence of
several caravans of donkeys, sheep, and ponies, and the traders and pilgrims whom these pack animals serve.

Hindus believe the lake (sarovar) was first formed in the
mind (manasa) of their God of Creation, Brahma. They say
the lake is sacred, and a dip will cleanse one of all sin, similar
to our own practice of baptism. ~~But no water is so holy it can
cleanse my impure blood.~~ But even this sacred place has its
troubles. M— tells me the hills here are infested with bandits.
Travelers do not seem to be particularly worried about being
attacked. Pilgrims are awestruck by what they cannot see—
the gods on Mount Kailas, the elusive golden swans that are
meant to live on Mansarovar, or the miraculous properties of
the lake's waters. Point out to them a gang of brigands on
horseback, and I promise you they will be unimpressed.

Lhasa is nine weeks away, if my calculations are correct,
and if we cover twelve miles a day.

WHEN THEY REACHED MANSAROVAR it was nearly night, but the
shores of the lake had the appearance of a fairground. Traders and
pilgrims chattered as their cooks stirred cauldrons of rice and tea,
and their servants smeared linseed oil on their callused feet. Plumes

of smoke rose from the fires, smothering the tents in gray. In the monasteries embedded into the hills around Mansarovar, drums pounded, reminding monks it was time for prayer. The lake itself seemed untouched by the appetites and devotion of men, and shimmered silver and purple in the twilight, its waves so serene they resembled folds of silk.

Mani and Chetak asked Katherine to keep an eye on their belongings, and left to find a suitable camping place for the night. Katherine couldn't stop herself from untying the knots of Chetak's bundle. Her hands trembled such that it took her twice as long, and she sweated in spite of the wind because she was afraid she might be seen. She found nothing of note, only a few items of personal grooming, rations, twigs wrapped in cloth, a folded tent, a blanket and a waterproof sheet, all the fabrics coiled so tightly she couldn't tell shirts from trousers or turbans. Afterward she felt like a thief though she had stolen nothing. She kept glancing at her fingers, half-expecting them to rot. Why had she sneakily examined a native man's belongings?

A pika emerged from a hole in the ground to nibble at a wildflower. Chetak and Mani returned. She felt a strange cheer in her heart, and wondered when or how solitude had become less appealing to her.

"The wind is a terrible thing here in Tibet," Chetak said as he picked up his sack, "but at least we don't have to fear mosquitoes or snakes."

"Come, mother," Mani said. "We found a cave."

Set in a hollow in a red-tinted, rocky hill, the cave was hidden behind a mound of stones previous inhabitants must have gathered to deter the worst of the winds from breaching its entrance. For good fortune someone had balanced yak skulls on top. Knots of fur still clung to the horns but the eye sockets were cracked and empty. Mani wouldn't hear of Katherine removing them, as that constituted blasphemy.

The dead, always watching her.

Mani set up her tent near the cave and Chetak pitched his own nearby. After a quick meal of tsampa, they decided to turn in for the night, the men exhausted by the long march and the cold. Katherine told Mani to sleep in the tent, as if to prove he was indeed her son. He said he would sleep in the cave, but she wouldn't budge. Chetak watched them, looking amused. When he went to sleep, Katherine entered the cave. Troubled intermittently by a spasm in her back, the wind rifling through the gilt-edged waves, and the moonlight that neither concealed nor revealed the landscape, its blue sheen leaking into her dreams, Katherine slept poorly.

In the morning she woke up before Mani and Chetak. A soft mist hung over the lake, its color a deeper blue than the sky, and tinged with gold where the sun's rising orb flared in its waters. Hunching against the wind, she walked half a mile, around a promontory that hid her from the tents. Gulls darted into the lake and scooped up fish that thrashed between their mandibles. Katherine removed her boots and clothes, and walked into the water wearing only her chemise and drawers. She was moving as if propelled forward by invisible strings. Rusty orange ducks perched on the floating nests they had made with dried grass. Her flesh and mind turned numb in the icy water, but it wasn't a disagreeable sensation. A moment underwater, then she came up for breath. The cold was so pronounced everything around her seemed to hush, and her breath turned into crystals above her upper lip. She waded to the shore, and her bare feet sank deep into the sand that glinted on her bruised skin.

Clenching her teeth, she sat shivering, waiting for the wind to dry her, her limbs awkward no matter where she placed them, bent like the branches of a dying tree. A cairn at the edge of the lake collapsed. She was the one who should have died, she who had no children, no love, no home. She was the one who courted death on these inadvisable expeditions to forbidden kingdoms. If God wanted blood, He ought to have picked her, not Ethel. Had their mother been alive, she would have said so too. In the pinpricks of wind that pierced her skin she felt the sharpness of her mother's censure.

Katherine dressed herself even though her underclothes were still damp. She wrung her hair dry and tied it into a loose knot. A group

of noisy Tibetan children entered tufts of tall reeds, perhaps to empty
their bowels. Behind them was a black tent Katherine hadn't noticed
before, its canopy only a few feet above the ground, almost flat.
White bead necklaces, and clothes, hung from ropes secured to the
pegs that steadied the tent. A Tibetan woman stirred a cauldron of
tea or water over a fire. Katherine approached her with as much clatter as possible so she wouldn't be startled, with the intention of asking if she could warm herself by the flames.

The woman's black hair was braided with turquoise and amber
gemstones, and her lustrous brown skin reddened toward the cheekbones as if brushed with rouge. Before Katherine could speak, she
greeted Katherine with a friendly smile and without any questions
gave her a bowl of tea, and pulled a rug close to the fire and invited
her to sit. The tea was salty and made of yak milk and Katherine liked
its unusual flavor, though in Kalimpong she had learned that for most
outsiders it was an acquired taste. The fire's warmth was welcome
and she sat cross-legged on the rug and the Tibetan woman broke
off a white bead from one of the necklaces hanging on the tent rope
and offered it to her. Katherine tried to say no, then realized the beads
were cubes of yak cheese. She gestured to ask if the yaks were out
to pasture already, and the woman replied in Tibetan but Katherine
couldn't understand what she was saying. The woman ladled more
tea into her bowl, and Katherine began to feel guilty about drinking
milk that ought to be for the children who were now returning to
the tent after washing at the lake. It was astonishing, the generosity displayed by those who had so few possessions; Katherine had
encountered it again and again in the East. She cared not at all for
children, but the woman's three boys were sweet and shy, and she
made faces at them as they drank their tea, making them laugh, tea
sputtering out of their mouths. A dog came down a cliff to lie by their
side, and they started tickling his belly. They tired of that pastime
quickly and turned toward Katherine as if for amusement, and she
crossed her eyes and stuck out her tongue and pulled her own cheeks,
which made the children hoot in mirth. They were easily pleased,

these boys who looked to be between five and eight years of age. Behind them she saw Chetak's tall form and attempted to rearrange her features, but the surprise on his face told her she was too late.

"There you are," he said to her. "Your son is looking for you everywhere."

He greeted the Tibetan woman with an exaggerated bow and without fanfare or preamble gifted the boys dried fruit, which made them gasp with joy. He pressed a cluster of sugared almonds into the hands of the Tibetan woman, and her cheeks reddened further. The children tugged at the hem of Chetak's coat, asking for more, and the dog began to bark, and the mother scolded the boys and the animal and they hushed. The woman went into her tent and returned with a plate laden with three pieces of steamed bread, circular and soft and shaped like flowers. Chetak tore a piece in half, and shared the bread with Katherine. He pointed at the beads in the woman's hair and told her they suited her, and she couldn't have understood his Hindustani, but she blushed, her face turning coy as if she had only then noticed he was handsome. Even after a night in the tent, his appearance was so neat one would think he had a maid to press his clothes and powder his nose. Katherine had seen how tightly his clothes had been wound in his sack, and yet they didn't look crumpled at all.

The morning light was a familiar blue but it seemed to her now that it wasn't a melancholic blue; more a soothing color that was sweet if a little tart, like a berry on her tongue. Chetak whistled at the dog, and praised the woman's cooking—"The bread is delicious," he said, his tone sweet as honey—and she looked pleased. Watching Chetak, Katherine thought he was a man charmed by every woman he met, but what did she care? She wasn't looking for a husband or a lover. All she wanted was to reach Lhasa.

After serving them more tea, the woman ordered her children to fetch water from the lake, and the dog ran after them. Chetak leaned toward Katherine and flicked off the crumbs of bread that had spilled from her mouth onto her lap, and she was astounded that he would dare to touch her—her robe—in this fashion. She watched the movements of his fingers as if mesmerized, a corresponding heat flickering on her skin below her thick clothes. The heat of the fire caused steam to rise from the damp fabric that clung to her body, but now it looked like an embarrassing admission of her desire.

Chetak brought his hand toward the back of her neck, and she worried he would feel the hastiness of her pulse thumping below her ears. "Why have you tied your hair when it's still wet?" he asked in the frank manner typical of natives. He brazenly loosened the knot and her hair tumbled frizzy and gray over her shoulders. The Tibetan woman folding the clothes hanging on the tent ropes smiled at her as if she hadn't seen anything amiss. Katherine met Chetak's eyes, and the color of his iris that wasn't black or brown or blue or green, and might in fact be colorless, unnerved her. He was here next to her and not at all, something remote in him that she couldn't reach. His fingers touched her cheek and lingered there for a moment that passed too soon, and then the Tibetan woman was approaching him with a necklace of cheese, insisting he accept it. He rummaged in his pockets for coins, whatever there had been between Katherine and him vanishing like a once-purple wound that had healed without a suture or scar.

THEY PACKED THEIR CAMP. Once Chetak was out of earshot Mani said they would have to do the parikrama if Chetak didn't leave. He believed them to be pilgrims.

"The Dolma Pass on the path around Kailas is very steep," Mani said. "Difficult to climb. It's nothing to me, but is that what you want?"

"What do you expect me to do?" Katherine asked. She would add a few more days to her journey; climb a mountain pass so high the sky itself would appear below her like a cliff ledge. She recognized her foolishness but felt incapable of changing her own mind.

They set out, Chetak watching every pilgrim carefully as if the proximity of these strangers made him uncomfortable. He must be an outcaste as Mani suspected, forbidden in India from even stepping on the path to a temple, or wearing a shirt, dogs set on him if his eyes

met those of an upper-caste man. Perhaps his bluster hid his disquiet
at being around so many Brahmins, whom Katherine saw now with
the recognizable sacred thread looped over their shoulder, chanting
Sanskrit verses, knee-deep and shivering in the waters of Mansarovar. She almost felt sorry for Chetak. But perhaps he was no different from men anywhere else. Frederick's booming voice, which you
could hear two doors down, did nothing except prove that the man
was less proficient in the bedroom than he imagined. (His cousin
might disagree, and she was welcome to him.)

The wind whipped Katherine's clothes dry, but patches of damp
persisted, prickling her skin, sending messages from another world.
At least her back no longer ached. She carried her own sack, though
Mani had transferred most of her belongings from it, including the
blanket.

A ribbon of white sand encircled the lake. Bright yellow gorse
bloomed near it, chewed on by ponies. Pikas darted past them with
such frequency Katherine had to be mindful not to step on one. On
the lake, ducks bobbed with the waves rather inelegantly while flocks
of geese and cranes glided onto the water from the sky with the grace
of ballet dancers, sunlight glinting at the tips of their wings. Tibetan
pilgrims prostrated in the direction of Kailas, the five points of their
bodies—hands, knees, forehead—touching the ground. Then they
got up and prostrated again.

"To do the parikrama like them, all the way around Mount Kailas,
it will take three weeks," Mani said to Chetak. "Buddhists have strong
hearts. That's why they can do it so easily." He said Buddhist prin-
ciples appealed to him more than the Hindu religion to which he had
been born. He didn't want to marry, he didn't want to be bound to
earthly pleasures, he said. Chetak glanced at her, but didn't ask what
she, Mani's mother, thought of it. Instead he told Mani that he too
found the institution of marriage abhorrent; a wife and children were
shackles. "I will have no freedom to do what I want, go where I
want," he said. "People said I would change my mind once I grew
older, but I'm the oldest I have ever been and I feel no different." To
Katherine it sounded as if these words were edged with truth as

nothing he had said before. The three of them couldn't have been more different from each other, and yet they wished for *freedom* even if their definition of the word didn't match. (No Englishman would admit to sharing such traits with a native, but she had been tainted at birth; she recognized it to be a poor excuse, maybe even a desperate one.)

A string of ponies unencumbered by saddles and the whips of bearers, all reddish-brown manes and white legs, raced down a slope.

"They're kiang, wild asses. We'll see wild yaks too," Mani said.

"Doesn't this remind you of being on the Grand Trunk Road?" Chetak asked. "There are as many people and donkeys and caravans here as on the highway, if not more."

The sapphire hues of the lake tinted Chetak's face such that he appeared to belong to the pantheon of the blue-skinned Hindu gods whose images Katherine had seen in paintings. He dabbed at his forehead with a red cloth that he then twisted around his head like a turban, but inattentively, so that long strands of hair escaped through its loops to brush against his beard and neck. Katherine's right hand lifted to push his hair behind his ears but she stopped herself midmovement.

When they halted for lunch, Chetak insisted he would cook with his provisions—lentils and wheat flour—which were princely in comparison to the tsampa Mani would have served.

"It's a good day today," she said to Chetak and, in the silence that followed, worried he had misconstrued her comment. "I have been able to enjoy a feast. First the Tibetan bread, now this."

For some reason Chetak's simple fare of dal and roti brought to Katherine's mind the first and only formal dinner party she had attended after Ethel's death. Then she had found the chatter and tinkling glasses of wine and sliced beef forked into mouths so repulsive that she had to excuse herself. Now, however, she had no qualms about easing her hunger. How could she explain such madness? Why was she despondent in some moments but not others?

"I wish we could get some respite from the rain," Chetak said, and Katherine, looking up at the horizon, saw storm clouds gathering as if a great witch had loosened her curls, black tendrils tumbling down from the sky into the lake's waters. She felt the ache returning to her spine and thought, *this is only right*. She would never see Lhasa because she didn't deserve to. Here were the gods reminding her that even the holy waters of Mansarovar couldn't wash away her sins.

THE STORM THREATENED TO be a beast; the clouds that darkened the sky looked as solid as stone. When the wind arrived, carrying with it the sweet scent of rain and the sharp, burnt smell of lightning, the lake's surface rippled as if it was an enormous skirt sewn out of silvery fish scales. Katherine checked that the straps of her bonnet were tied firmly around her chin, aware it did her appearance no favors but grateful for the warmth it assured. In spite of the weather, Chetak inquired after her bonnet as if he was asking about an elderly parent. "It's unusual," he said, a child's mischievous expression on his face. Katherine lied that she had found the bonnet by the side of a road in Almora. Mani, hearing this story for the first time, said Tibetans believed it was bad luck for owners to come across the hats they had lost. "This was never mine," Katherine said. Mani didn't look convinced.

The lake emptied of birds. Pikas scurried back into their burrows. The poles to which pilgrims had tied prayer flags tipped dangerously toward the ground. Swollen with rain, the sky pressed against the earth and erased the horizon; the landscape, which had until then appeared vast and spacious, constricted to form an impenetrable shadow.

Rain washed over the hills and drenched them in seconds. They took shelter in a cave formed by an overhang whose depth barely accommodated their figures. Chetak extracted his waterproof sheet from his sack. With Mani holding up the sheet from one side, and Chetak on the other, they managed to create a barrier between themselves and the rain. The three of them stood in a row, Katherine flanked by the two men, the water from their clothes dripping onto her feet. She should have been uncomfortable, or fearful. Instead she was pleased to be standing so close to Chetak. Elated even. It was silly. She forced herself to think of Virgil's *Aeneid,* Juno contriving a thunderstorm so that Aeneas and Dido would seek refuge in the same cave. What had her love for Aeneas brought Dido? Only death, then a reunion with her true love in the underworld. But no one awaited Katherine there—*except Ethel.*

She edged her faithful stick toward the top corner of the sheet where it had curled down toward Chetak's tiring hand, and tried to push it up, her shoulder pressing against his. She was only partly successful. She could hear waves heaving toward the shore of the lake, Chetak's rough breaths, and the sound of his coat crinkling under the pressure of her touch. Below Chetak's right ear was a narrow, silver-white scar, raised and knitted together as if with a needle, and she wanted to touch it and ask him how he had acquired it.

From the distance came the shouts of men and the cries of sheep. The rain lightened and the men no longer had to hold up the sheet that had served as their umbrella. Like a fragment of a dream, a white pony flashed past them, plump goatskins hanging from its saddle-bow. "Was it . . . ?" Katherine asked and Chetak said, "Its owner must be upset."

Mani asked Katherine to wait while he investigated the shouts, which had grown louder. Chetak moved away from her to swing the waterproof sheet in the air so that it would dry, and Katherine imagined a depression in her skin where it had pressed against his coat, a patch that was barren and fetid but also sacred like a yak skull. He rolled up the sheet and leaned it against a rock. She fiddled with the straps of her sack for want of something to do. The left side of his body, exposed to the rain, was wet and dripping. He tried to squeeze his clothes dry, but they were too tight and he would have to take them off and dry them by a fire and he wasn't going to do that in her presence.

Birds she couldn't see squawked. The waves lapped against the shore in a steady, soothing rhythm now. But every few moments, voices called out to each other in the distance, tearing the quiet of the rain-softened landscape. She removed her bonnet and let down her hair, glad it veiled half of her face.

"Where is the boy?" she said, attempting to sound irritated even though she was glad Mani hadn't returned. As if she was a young girl wishing away the chaperone at a dance.

"I thought you liked my company," Chetak said. She knew it meant nothing—he would have said this to any woman.

The rain had chilled the air and she shivered as a breeze drifted in from the lake, leaving a flickering trail across her skin. She pressed the bonnet between her fingers, the fleece dislodging under the pressure of her nails. Chetak moved closer to her and clasped her wrist and drew her toward him and waited a moment as if to allow her to protest. She closed her eyes, afraid and eager, and felt the warmth of his mouth against her lips. His mustache and beard were not at all bristly as she had expected them to be, but soft, and fragrant too. Perhaps he smoothed them every morning with scented oil as the Arabs did. She felt his teeth on her lower lip, sharp and pleasing in their insistence, and his fingers in her hair, unexpectedly tender. Her hands were around his shoulders, his wet clothes misting her fingertips, but she continued to clutch her bonnet too, the texture of it between her fingers reminding her that this moment, like all other moments, was fleeting, and already he was pulling away from her even though she wished he wouldn't. He wiped his lips with the back of his hand without meeting her eye, and she wondered if he regretted the kiss. She was about to ask him when Mani returned to say they should resume their journey; he said a ragged group of men were chasing after their unruly flock of sheep.

"Listen to them screaming," Mani said. "I thought someone had died."

Katherine retied her bonnet over her hair and watched Chetak slide his sheet into his sack even though it was still damp. They began to walk, boots pressing into the mud, and Chetak spoke to Mani but not to her. She wondered if her mouth stank of decay or if he had been repelled by the rope-like coarseness of her hair. Then she remembered he was only a native. Why should she care about how a low-caste, dark-skinned man perceived her? In her head her mother said she had seen this day coming right from Katherine's childhood. The only surprise was that it had taken so long.

Around her the summer afternoon now resembled a winter evening, white mist rising from the blue lake like the spirits of the dead and floating toward desolate hills. Through its ghostliness, tentative shapes emerged that in due course became sheep with bags strung across their backs, became bearers whose shoulders drooped on account of their heavy, rain-soaked clothes and sacks and trunks.

A man wearing a dry felt hat attempted to guide the sheep away from the direction of the hills. Running around him was a mud-stained urchin who comically fell on his knees several times on account of his unbridled enthusiasm. The man, thin but not slight, helped the boy up and spoke to him in a voice that was both resolute and affectionate. He was close enough for her to see that he had a sharp nose below which a well-trimmed mustache formed a neat triangle with his full lips, and a broad forehead with two deep lines etched into the skin where his eyebrows nearly met in the middle. His posture didn't suffer on account of his damp clothes, and his gait was so methodical and precise it reminded her of the movement of the hands of a well-oiled clock.

Chetak gestured that they should go ahead, that he would catch up with them. "Are you sure?" Katherine asked, and there must have been a pleading note in her voice, because Mani looked at her sharply. She collected herself and said, "All right then."

Katherine lifted the sodden hem of her robe that was gathering grass and mud and surveyed the disorderly group of men and sheep with an indifferent eye. Mani whispered to her that Chetak's departure was welcome. "If we walk quickly he may not find us again," he said. His hastiness irritated her. "We can be on our way to Lhasa without going around Kailas," he said.

Then her eyes alighted on a figure shrouded in mist, his hands flailing in the air to encourage the sheep to move, his manner that of a drowning man thrashing his limbs in the water. Behind his sideburns, his ears fanned out wide like an elephant's as he urged the men to make haste in a language that didn't suit his tongue.

The light was faint and yet for Katherine there was no mistaking the single line of black ink that traveled down the man's forehead to the tip of his nose before vanishing into the overgrown thicket of mustache and beard that concealed his lips and neck. She glanced at him again, hoping she was wrong. His skin and hair were an unnatural color. Pressing her stick into the mud, she hurried away, afraid he would look in her direction and see her for who she was as clearly as she saw him.

11.

CAMP BY THE SACRED LAKE—
BONES RAIN FROM THE SKY—THE CAPTAIN'S DOUBTS—
A QUARREL AND A REALIZATION

———

AT MANSAROVAR JAGAN COMPLAINED OF HIS ELBOW ACHING. Soon enough they encountered a great storm that passed almost as quickly as it arrived. But the rain scattered the sheep, and the pony. Samarth ran after the animals, falling down often until Balram helped the boy. The captain shouted orders that the soft earth hushed. His dye was leaking. The lake had vanished in the storm, erased by cloud. Now it reappeared in front of Balram, blue and smooth.

Pilgrims emerged out of the drabness to file past them, but in the dim light the captain's faltering disguise wouldn't have been evident to them. None made an impression on Balram, apart from a young man who arrived to ask if they wanted help with the sheep. He said he was a pilgrim, traveling with his elderly mother. Balram sent him away, careful to obstruct his view of the captain. Moments later Balram saw him with his mother, a woman with a fur-lined cap perched upon her silver hair like a rat. Her right hand clutched a long stick as if it was a spear. She was tall and stately and walked with the sprightliness of a younger person, though the color of her hair suggested her advanced years.

Mother and son quickly became specks in the distance, but a passerby stopped to make conversation with Ujjal. Afterward Ujjal said the man could have been a pilgrim, or a trader, or neither of these, or both of these, a strange man whose eyes were green, or gray like a snow leopard's, not that he had ever seen the animal, but he had seen

a tiger, had Balram seen one? Balram asked him to start setting up the
bearers' tent, which now belonged to the captain. They would camp
here for the night. Jagan found the pony and tethered it to a pole a
Tibetan shepherd must have erected by the water.

The captain shuffled toward the holy lake for a dip; no strangers
around now to observe his sins and dye being washed away. Mud
squelched under his feet, rising up to his ankles. Irrationally it seemed
to Balram that the gods he didn't believe in would set fire to the water
and punish the captain. Then the captain immersed himself and
emerged shivering but unharmed, the running dye giving him the
appearance of a striped animal. Balram asked Yogi to bring the captain a fresh set of clothes.

THEY TURNED IN FOR the night, only a blanket as a shield against
the elements. The dampness of the earth seeped into their clothes.
They couldn't light a fire. They had exhausted their last reserves of
fuel that evening. Without Naga's intervention, Pawan's food had
yet again been inedible. The men huddled together, stomachs growling, mouths cursing loudly as if that would keep them warm. Ujjal
sang about lovers eloping to a forest. Harish and Rana clapped their
hands to the rhythm of the song; not the weather for music, but
maybe it kept the men from thinking of frostbite and bandits and the
rotting corpses of Chand and Naga, feathers of vultures fluttering
against their ribs.

The singing must have been loud because the captain came out of
his tent and ordered them to be quiet. "It's freezing here," Balram
said. "And we can't drink chhang for warmth because we don't have
any and also we are next to the sacred Mansarovar."

He sounded more forceful than he intended. He expected the captain to scold him, but the captain called him inside. "Buy a new tent
tomorrow," he told Balram. "I have been looking through the route
surveys around the Tsangpo that you and Gyan conducted before."

The captain sat down on a rug in one corner, and showed Balram
his sketches and maps in the light of a lantern. His pencil followed the

Tsangpo's path through white space. Here the river curved and there it meandered and here it wound around imagined hills. Balram thought of how the Tibetans revered the Tsangpo; the river was holy to them; the river was their mother and father. But what did the river mean to the captain, who didn't depend on its moods and swells and tides for sustenance? Did he imagine it to be a kiang that could be tamed and directed where he wished? Did it occur to him that rivers had hearts and souls, that anyone who listened carefully could hear their whispers and songs?

If Balram preferred surveying to teaching and fatherhood, it was because he liked hearing the murmurs of the landscape. Walking alone under clouds silvered by the sun, past fields yellow with rapeseed and pewter mountains striated with snow, he felt his heart beat to the rhythms of the world: the lapping of the waves of a river, the wind whistling down hills, even the snorts of a yak or the rustle of grass as a startled hare leaped toward its hiding place. Only in those moments did he feel wholly himself and also one with the world. Gyan had said something similar; that he saw himself most clearly in the blue waters of Tibet's rivers and lakes. Could give you a fright if you weren't prepared, but could be a consolation too.

The lantern's yellow light exaggerated the paleness of the captain's face. Balram thought he could see the outline of the captain's skull beneath his skin.

"All our troubles notwithstanding," the captain said now, "our journey hasn't departed much from your original plan. If we continue at this pace, we will be able to reach the Tsangpo earlier than scheduled."

"God willing," Balram said, in spite of himself.

"When you buy provisions tomorrow, can you get a prayer wheel too?" the captain asked. He tugged at a single long hair that curled down to his eyelid from his brow. "I racked my brain about this, but which one of our men would steal a prayer wheel? My compass, I understand. It will fetch a good price."

"The wheel must have got lost in the fire," Balram said, suddenly feeling the compass in his pocket as if it was an ailment in the bones announcing itself through a sharp pain. "Our bearers aren't thieves. They believe the eyes of the gods are on them at all times."

"And what do you believe?"

"That I must do my duty," Balram said. But he couldn't tell if his duty was toward the bearers, his wife and children, or Gyan. Already two men had died as the captain searched for the mouth of a river and Balram searched for his missing friend. Was the ambition, or life, of one man more valuable than the lives of a dozen others? If only Lord Krishna would appear in the guise of a commoner to advise him; if only philosophers accompanied their party to help him sift right from wrong. In his ears Durga tut-tutted at his wrongheadedness. He pressed his nails into his wrist so that the pain would be more acute than her voice.

"I can't replace your compass," Balram told the captain. "But I'll find you a new prayer wheel tomorrow."

"When our bearers have lost their lives, to fret about an object— however valuable it was to me—seems inconsiderate. Some may even call it just punishment for my actions."

Ink was still dripping from the captain's hair onto his forehead. In the ghastly light he looked like a fallen man.

"How dreadfully young they were, the bandits I shot. I won't forget their faces in a hurry," he said. He scratched his beard with the tip of his pencil. "*And he that killeth a man, he shall be put to death.* Leviticus 24:21. I had good reason to kill another, of course. Why do I still worry about God's punishment?"

"A dip in Mansarovar is said to cleanse men of all sin," Balram said for want of something to say. "But the lake doesn't feature in the Bible, I suppose."

"The walnut juice has proved less durable than promised," the captain said, turning his wrists and examining them with a frown. "Even without a bath I would have had to reapply it."

AT SUNRISE, THE CAPTAIN stained his skin and hair, and the men stepped into the water. Bone-cold and shuddering, they prayed for salvation. Mor, Yogi, and Samarth tonsured their whole heads in the memory of those who had passed from this life to the next: their loved ones perhaps; Chand and Naga perhaps. As they dried themselves in the bitter wind, Balram heard them whisper about misfortune. They saw the wrath of the gods in the shapes of clouds, or when a foot struck a pebble and caused a heap of prayer stones to collapse. Everywhere they looked, all these bad omens.

Yogi fanned the captain to help the colors dry faster. Balram said it was unnecessary. The wind would do the work.

"Where must the Swede have reached by now?" the captain asked Balram, taking him by surprise. The captain had a contradictory mind that rivaled his own, one moment full of repentance, eager to atone in his sage's costume, and the next moment a giddy conqueror willing to sack villages to extend the borders of his empire. Always two people hidden in his skin.

You know what that's like, Gyan said.

The bearers bustled about reorganizing their belongings and provisions, tallying their losses, reminding Balram of what he should buy before they set forth toward the Tsangpo. The captain warned them to be judicious in their demands; he wouldn't indulge any unnecessary expenditure. They had begun the journey at the village of Mana with twelve bearers, of whom only seven remained. A great saving of money in his eyes perhaps.

Fingertips stained by ink, the captain proceeded to conduct a survey for a route map, Yogi trailing him obediently. Balram asked Ujjal to follow them. With his usual lack of tact, Ujjal said he would eavesdrop on the captain. "If he or Yogi complains about you, you'll know by evening," he said, his chest puffed up like a ridiculous bird. "I'll keep him away from crowds too—freshly painted, the captain stands out even more. He doesn't realize he will fool no one."

Balram took Mor, Jagan, and Pawan with him to the markets around the lake where Tibetans sold precious stones and sacred jewelry and tsampa and dried fruits. In front of a woman selling painted yak skulls was a muscular man of Balram's height, wearing a ragged chuba, thick, black hair left uncombed such that strands rose into the air like trails of smoke. The man stood with his hands on his hips, haggling with the woman tersely, then offered her a flower he must have plucked from a shrub. It made her smile. His broad shoulders, and the easy way in which he moved, made Balram think it was Gyan. Something like happiness flooded his body and lifted his soles from the ground. "Gyan," he said, clutching the man's shoulder, and the man turned around, and of course it wasn't his friend. Balram apologized, wondering how he could have made such a mistake.

The men didn't ask him any questions. Even Pawan was quiet. They bought provisions, wood, and a sturdy yak-hair tent from a nomad at a price that would meet with the captain's approval. They shared almonds and remembered Naga, and Chand, who had consumed most of Naga's private supply. "For a few moments when I wake up in the morning everything feels fine," Mor said, "but then I remember Naga and Chand have died."

Back at the camp, Pawan started cooking lunch and Balram went on a long walk along Mansarovar by himself. Even now each pace of Balram's was thirty-one-and-a-half inches, as if his feet weren't his own and he was just a contraption made by a white man. Gyan too walked the same way. But could he even walk now, or were his feet shackled?

The sky was bright. The lake's waters were turquoise where the sun's rays slanted down toward its surface, and sapphire in the shadows.

A mile from the camp, Balram encountered a monk of indeterminate age, carrying an empty pot and a prayer wheel. Transfixed by the sight of the prayer wheel, Balram attempted to make conversation with the monk before realizing the man couldn't speak or hear. He accompanied the monk to the lake, skirting flocks of bar-headed geese whose yellow-orange beaks pecked the grass, and pilgrims who chanted prayers, rudraksha bead necklaces threaded through shivering fingers.

Perhaps noticing that Balram's eyes were on the wheel, the monk offered it to him. He refused the coins Balram attempted to place on his palm with a furious shake of his head. Balram insisted he be allowed to carry the pot, nearly snatching it from the monk's hands, and filled it with the lake's holy water. The monk pointed to one of the many monasteries up on the hills. *Too difficult for you,* he gestured. Balram smiled.

The pot was lighter than his sack, and he had no trouble climbing the winding path up the hill, but the monk cast him a look of disapproval. He had a firm manner that suggested more than a passing acquaintance with solitude, and he didn't care to make himself agreeable to Balram.

The monastery was bare save for the elaborate murals on the walls. In the darkness of the prayer hall, the figures in the paintings weren't immediately evident, but Balram recognized the images of goddess Tara, and the Buddha under the bodhi tree where he had attained enlightenment. Monks chanted prayers by the altar, and their deep, throaty voices calmed his disorderly mind. What would it be like to ask for clemency here, to plead for forgiveness, to implore that he be allowed to stay within these walls for the rest of his life? The Buddha had left his family behind. Could he too leave Gyan and Durga and his children? The monk tapped him on his shoulder and pointed to the floor, a silent request he place the pot there.

Scampering down the hill afterward, Balram turned the prayer wheel in his hands. It would have been easier to return to the captain the compass he had pocketed, to make amends, but he couldn't bring himself to do it. Would the gods punish him for stealing? He remembered Samarth's babble and the captain's sketches. The scurry of mice in the Survey office. The shouts of his students as they darted out of the classroom. The voices of his daughters rising and falling as they mastered a song, and Inder striking a drum out of tune and Durga scolding him. He remembered the lightning jolt on his skin when Gyan's wrist brushed against his as they marched forward, feet bound together as if undertaking a strange marriage ritual. Then sunlight blinded his eyes and the landscape turned gray. Breathless, he collapsed into the hot earth. He heard Gyan's voice, felt his friend's hands on his shoulders. "Sit up," Gyan said, and so he did.

They were waiting at the Tibetan border for officials to inspect their papers. The frontier camp bustled with ponies and sheep, and Gyan pressed his leg against his to reassure him about something.

"You never talk about your daughters," Gyan said to him.

"They cause me no trouble," Balram said. "One day Durga will find them good husbands, and they'll leave home. But Inder—even Durga's parents tell her we should have drowned him when he was younger. They tell her we mustn't let the devil live among us."

As he spoke, Balram recognized he was in a trance. *Wake up, wake up,* he urged his dream self, but he had been plunged into another world and could see no path to escape.

"How can they call such a sweet child the devil?" Gyan asked. "Of all your children, he looks the most like you."

Gyan's words slowed down and the space between each letter became infinite. Balram saw their faces and bodies changing; it was no longer him and Gyan but Harish and Rana. Then a cold splash of water hauled him out of the world without shadows. An unfamiliar voice asked him if he needed a physician.

"There are no doctors here," Balram said, pressing his palms into the stones on the ground, grateful for the twinges that awakened his limbs. The prayer wheel lay by his knees, mercifully unbroken, and he picked it up now and blew on it to remove the dust caught between the etchings.

"I have heard Tibetan medicine men can perform magic that English doctors can't," the voice said.

Balram looked up and saw a bearded face, a man whose dark complexion and features suggested he hailed from the plains watered by the Ganga, a low-caste man in all likelihood, an ironsmith or a mason, but his eyes were a peculiar green or gray. Was this the pilgrim who had spoken to Ujjal earlier? Balram saw why Ujjal had mentioned a snow leopard; the man was furtive, wily, dangerous. His movements had the stealth of a great hunter.

"I found you unconscious," the man said, squatting down to the ground so that his strange eyes aligned with Balram's face. A turban the gaudy red of a rooster's comb was tied around his head. "These heights—we often forget the danger they pose to those of us not from here."

In appearance and build Balram was closer to Tibetans than this man who couldn't possibly tell a yak from a dzo. Still, Balram only said, "I'm grateful the gods sent you to find me."

"Let me take you to your camp," the stranger said, extending a hand to lift him up. "You look weak."

Balram demonstrated he didn't need help by walking at a quick pace. The man followed, attempting to make conversation, his manner friendly. *Have you seen Mount Kailas yet? Doesn't the lake seem so placid now, when it was as stormy as the sea just yesterday? Do you plan to travel to Gartok for the horse races or do you intend to trade at Gyanema?* Balram thought of how Gyan had been a perfect companion on his travels. The two of them had seen clouds skimming peaks and deer tangling their antlers and delicate cups of blue poppies and said nothing because they understood that to be in the presence of such beauty was sufficient; it was a gift, this private conversation they could have with the landscape.

Now Balram looked back, as if Gyan might have leaped through a tear in his dream to follow him onto the shores of Mansarovar. But he didn't even know what Gyan looked like now, if his skin had turned sallow from hunger or if it was dark and leathery from hours of toil in the sun. Each time Balram returned home after a long journey, he was surprised to see his children were taller, empty spaces in their mouths where once there had been teeth, or a new tooth that stuck out of the front lip much to Durga's chagrin. His daughters favored expressions he hadn't heard before, and the changes in their bodies frightened him. Gyan too must have become someone else— but who? Durga said Balram himself had changed after Gyan's disappearance; he had grown so sullen and withdrawn, anyone would think he had sent Gyan to the gallows.

The stranger didn't seem to mind Balram's silence. He spoke of the golden swans that could be spotted on the lake, though Balram had never seen one himself. Fortunately for him, Samarth with his bald head and an artless grin the size of the Himalaya crossed their path.

"I won't impose on your goodwill any longer," Balram said, placing his hand on Samarth's shoulder.

The man smiled, a tight smile, eyes empty. Beneath the shawl wrapped diagonally over his shirt Balram saw the shape of a knife that hung from a girdle. He had the odd, inexplicable feeling that he knew the stranger, had met him before, but was it in a dream or a market in Mussoorie, he couldn't tell. Behind him Mansarovar beamed in the light of the sun, its waves sparkling like silver scrolls carrying the words of gods.

THE NEXT MORNING THEY set off toward the Tsangpo. The path they had followed to Mansarovar had rippled with traders and pilgrims, but now the trail was quiet. The bright sun turned the land white. When they came across a stream Mor made a fuss about collecting water, and the bearers said Naga had been quiet even when he grumbled. They said it was strange they noticed his absence. One could miss a voice—"I sometimes hear my grandmother call out to me even though she died two years ago," Ujjal said—yet here they were missing a silence, and what could account for such an odd thing? Ghosts, the men decided. Naga and Chand were walking with them as ghosts.

Pawan wished the plague on bandits. Jagan said he ought to be cursing zamindars instead. They stole their tenants' crops and took their money when it was the tenants who tilled and watered and plowed the land. "If the world robs you of everything, nothing you can do but become a thief yourself," Jagan said.

"Just like you to feel sorry for murderers," Ujjal told Jagan.

"Few men become bandits for the pleasure of it," Balram found himself saying. He was explaining a difficult subject as if he was in his classroom. He greeted a group of Tibetan women carrying lunch to their husbands or brothers in the fields, baskets and babies slung around their backs, the turquoise beads in their braids shining in the sunlight. Yogi let out a low whistle and Harish clouted him on the head.

"Jagan is right. The young Tibetans who attacked our camp were most likely farmers whose crops failed," Balram said. "The monasteries overseeing their villages must have levied high taxes. When they couldn't pay, they became bandits."

"So the monks in Tibet are like our zamindars?" Jagan said.

Balram wished the world held those certainties, clear lines as in a map to divide the good from the bad. He looked at the Tibetan landscape around him and thought he couldn't even describe it correctly or evoke its colors in a sketch or a dream or memory; like life, it seemed to change its aspect with each glance—joyful, desolate, bright, dark, purple, pewter, friend, foe, which was it, he didn't know.

"A few high lamas may want to wear fine silks," Balram said, "but the Buddha advised his followers to wish for nothing. Most monks take that to heart." He looked at the captain, who was still measuring his pace with his rosary. He took notes every few minutes and deposited these scraps in his coat pockets because his new prayer wheel had no secret compartment.

Soon the men quieted, and Balram thought the day's march would pass without incident. Almost that very second a spray of bones fell from the sky. The bearers ran around haphazardly as the bones clattered against stones. They called on the gods to save them. A lammergeier was dropping bones from a height to shatter them and expose the marrow within. The bird swooped down with its hooded beak and sharp, prehensile claws, its legs feathered as if it had stepped into pantaloons, making a peculiar noise that caused the men to cower. It gathered the broken bones and flew up, only to drop them again.

"What if these are Naga's bones?" Jagan asked. "Or Chand's?"

"Tibetans believe vultures guide us through reincarnations," Balram said. "They won't attack us."

"Not when we're alive," the captain said. Balram wondered if the lammergeier had perceived on their flesh the odor of carrion. "The Swede must be somewhere near Mount Kailas, looking for the source of the Tsangpo," the captain continued. "Shouldn't we find it before he does?"

His question, unsuitable for this moment, brought to Balram's mind a vivid image of Inder. His son had the distressing habit of repeating the same sound—a grunt or a whimper or a scream—that made Durga press her hands over her ears and his daughters flee to the market. But the boy was a simpleton, a fault beneath his skull that no one could see, or the devil residing between the strands of his hair, obliging him to be difficult even when he didn't intend to be so. How often had Balram looked at Inder's face and thought all the child wanted was for his father to be able to read his thoughts? Instead, Balram chose to indulge the whims of white men who kept up a fiction that entire parts of the world would remain unnamed if their own tongues didn't christen them, and uncivilized if not appended to their list of conquests. With that end in mind the captain asked the same question again and again, through deaths and hauntings and rain and snow, and Balram was courteous in his replies each time, a courtesy he didn't extend to his own son.

"We agreed upon this, sir, before we set out from Mana," Balram said now. "Your objective is to chart the route of the Tsangpo all the way to the sea, to confirm it becomes the Brahmaputra, and so, for the purposes of this mission, its source is unimportant." He scratched the skin beneath the sleeves of his coat, and noted his nails needed pruning. He wished he could reach Shigatse quickly so that he could look for the monastery where Gyan was being held.

"What do you propose then?" the captain asked.

"Our best chance lies east. Once we cross the Mayum Pass, we will come across the Tsangpo, a week from now if we allow the sheep less time for grazing."

"I wish I could consult my compass," the captain said.

Balram shifted his gaze to the land, mostly dust and stone, blanched by the sun but with the occasional green fabric of a meadow overlaid upon the stark terrain. The compass was in his coat pocket and once again he felt its shape against his skin, the metal scalding hot for a moment as it branded him through the fabric.

"The Bible says there's nothing new in this world," the captain said. "*It hath been already of old time, which was before us.* What do you think of that, Balram? Here I am, looking for a river that passes through gorges no human eye has seen, but it bears repetition that God has seen its path. However difficult it appears today, God will guide us."

Balram couldn't tell why the captain was quoting the Bible instead of Herodotus. Perhaps the men he had killed and the men who had died serving him had disturbed him more than he indicated. Perhaps he knew Balram had stolen the compass.

"This monk's robe that I wear is causing me to muse on the nature of our undertaking," the captain said, as if he had read Balram's mind. "No doubt some will criticize the disguise I have adopted. They will say a man can't call himself a good Christian while pretending to belong to another religion. But I do this in good faith. God sees my conscience even if others can't."

The captain was thinking of how his disguise would appear to his god, but not to Balram or the bearers. Unlike Balram, who couldn't slough off his brown skin, the captain could have a bath and return to a privileged life Balram would never know.

Around him the men wondered if their journey was cursed. Balram asked Ujjal to sing, and he was out of breath and rattled, but he agreed. In time Ujjal's voice, hoarse as it was, calmed the men, whose pace matched the rhythms of the song.

THAT NIGHT, BALRAM SAT with the captain in his tent to discuss the particulars of the route they had followed. A commotion caused the captain to set down his pencil. The lantern's feeble flame flickered, and the glass darkened at the top of the globe. "What is it now?" the captain asked, looking weary.

Outside, the shepherds and the bearers had gathered in a circle by one of the two fires they had built. In their midst stood the light-eyed stranger who had attempted to befriend Balram, now holding a sheep in his hands.

Jatpo, Balram thought, *the one who stalks.*

"Moti is dead," Samarth said through tears that drew two lines on his grimy cheeks.

"Not yet," the stranger said kindly. "Don't lose heart."

Balram wondered what authority he had to speak up among men he didn't know.

"Moti hasn't been eating properly the last few days," Rudra said. "Do you see the froth around its mouth?"

"What are you doing here?" Balram asked the stranger.

The stranger placed Moti on the ground. "It's grown weak," he told Rudra. The animal was breathing quickly, its eyes staring at the sky.

"No point keeping it alive," Rudra said. Samarth tugged at the sleeves of Rudra's coat, sobbing. "Listen to me, boy," Rudra said, bringing out a knife. "This is an act of mercy."

Moti began to convulse frantically at their feet, a last gasp as the glint of the knife shone in its unseeing eyes. Samarth buried his face in his hands.

Unmindful of the chaos in the camp, and the hour, flocks of geese gossiped happily by springs of water that emerged mysteriously from the ground. On the toothed, rocky hills that ringed their tents, yaks rested on the grass, their forms melding with the blackness that curtained the slopes. The sounds at Balram's feet, the sheep's thrashing and its rapid, stertorous breathing, ceased.

"Moti didn't suffer—much," Rudra told Samarth, his knife slick with blood. "Be grateful for it."

Samarth wept. Balram looked at him with envy. Inder couldn't sense another's pain; when he hit Durga and his sisters and they winced or cried, he was indifferent.

Under Jagan's direction, the men buried the sheep away from the springs, in a shallow ditch they covered with stones. The stranger joined the men as if he too was part of their group. Balram left them to perform their rituals, intended perhaps for their dead peers and not the animal. A sharp wind chilled the compass in his pocket, and it speared his skin like an icicle. The geese flew away, black smudges against a violet sky.

Ujjal broke from the group and came to Balram with news of the stranger. "He told us his name is Chetak, after the blue horse that saved his majesty Maharana Pratap's life during a battle," he said with a dramatic flourish, as if announcing the king's entry into the royal hall.

"A man can't be named after a horse," Balram said.

"Chetak is a symbol of courage, he says," Ujjal said.

"He can't find out about the captain."

"None of us have said a word about the captain, or our mission." Ujjal turned to look at the man and said, "I don't think he has even seen the captain. He's been asking us about our villages, how our women manage when we are away, whether our parents have enough to eat."

"What if they don't? Is he going to take sacks of wheat to every village?"

"Why are you so angry with him?"

"Send him away," Balram said. "We can't have him here. Too dangerous for the captain."

Over a fire Pawan began to cook the skinned, salted, and dried slabs of flesh that belonged to the sheep the captain had inadvertently shot during the bandit raid. Now that he didn't have to worry about sharing his cook's responsibilities with Naga, Pawan seemed more at ease. The smell of roasting meat caused Samarth to retch.

Someone brought out a small goatskin bag and told the boy to take a sip. Samarth spat it out—must be chhang, Balram thought. The bearers chortled, asked the boy to toughen up, drank from the goatskin themselves, pinched snuff from Rana's box while Rana's hand drew circles on Harish's thigh. Pawan unwisely raked red embers with a ladle. In the distance the thick snow that clad the mountain peaks was a startling white against the darkening expanse of the sky. The stranger named Chetak said he would pray for Moti's soul, and he didn't do it in a way that suggested he was making fun of

Samarth. He said he understood the bond men could have with animals; they were loyal friends, sometimes more so than two-legged creatures, he said.

Balram called Samarth over. "I have an important job for you. Go to the captain's tent and tell him not to come out. Tell him I said that."

The bearers sat in a circle around the fire, the alcohol diminishing their fears and magnifying their voices, which ricocheted in the dark. Balram thought they took to Chetak easily as they never had to him. Chetak told them about the summer market in Dehra where vendors sold yak tails and tiger claws and dancing bears, and the commotion last year when a memsahib sent a man to buy a bear cub and the evening ended with two bears loose, one even taking a ride on a palanquin. He spoke about the rains that swelled rivers until they left their imprints on the roofs of houses, and the painted ladies who huddled behind the barracks at sunset. Yogi said that in the darkness the whores charged much more than their faces were worth, and Rana said he had promised his wife he would remain faithful to her, and Harish said a promise was an admirable thing, but men had wants women couldn't understand. After all these long days and wakeful nights, the bearers seemed glad to speak of a subject unrelated to omens and curses, and this man Chetak, he was a charming fellow, Balram could see, and with his stories he put the men at ease. He was clever too; he didn't drink and instead watched the men lose their inhibitions like a predator patiently waiting for its prey to tire. Or was Balram imagining it because he was afraid the captain would be discovered, which would jeopardize his goal of finding Gyan?

From the depths of the darkness an animal cried. Wings fluttered. A creature scrambled behind rocks, its feet scattering pebbles. The bearers looked up, fear yet again flushing their faces.

Balram made use of the interruption to say, "Well, Chetak, Chetak it is, isn't it? Your companions must be wondering where you are."

"He's traveling alone," Jagan said.

"Is that wise?" Balram asked.

"There isn't enough flesh on me to tempt a wolf," Chetak said, slapping his arms, "and since I have no belongings, I'm invisible to bandits."

"If not for bandits," Mor said, "we would have been as wealthy as kings."

Ujjal hissed at him to be quiet.

"Our kings are hardly wealthy," Chetak said. "Most of them no longer have kingdoms or riches because the English have stolen their land and diamonds." His face was a mask even if his words were perfidious. "But you're right, I must return to my tent."

Chetak stood up and patted Balram on the shoulder as if consoling a child. Then his thumb pressed down on the edge of Balram's clavicle with such force that it would have crumbled had it not been for the thickness of his coat. Balram tried to shove Chetak's hand away but couldn't; though leaner than Balram, the man had twice his strength. Then Chetak loosened his hold, picked up a blade of grass that had pinned itself against the collar of Balram's coat, and blew on it ceremoniously. His breath smelled of cloves, not at all sour like that of the bearers. He smiled, his teeth white as snow. "You have good men here," he said. "I heard two of them died on this journey—such a pity. You must make sure it doesn't happen again."

"I don't control the skies and the fates of men," Balram said. "You seem to have mistaken me for a god."

"But you brought along a child," Chetak said. "It's a big responsibility. You can't ignore that."

Pawan sharpened a knife against a stone, wincing as sparks flickered and discordant clanks rent the air.

"People think it's nothing," Chetak continued, "to lead men through dangerous marches in a country such as this because they want to make money, or win the favor of their gods, or because like the English they want the thrill of an expedition or a hunt. But if a man dies on your watch, his death will trouble your conscience for the rest of your life. It's not worth it. Take it from me." He spoke as if he was an oracle or the noble leader of a great nation, or a rebel.

"I would have asked you to join us for a meal, but we're tired and need to rest," Balram said. He told Pawan to wrap up slices of meat for the visitor to take away with him. It was a pointed farewell.

"No doubt our paths will cross sooner than we think," Chetak said.

The threat implicit in those words couldn't have been an accident. Chetak walked into the dark, claiming his tent was here or there, only a yard or a mile away, to the east or the west. He refused the bearers' offer of a torch. The man's eyes were like a snow leopard's, and perhaps he could see just as well as the animal that hunted at night.

Around the fire the bearers wondered if Chetak was a deranged pilgrim, or a god in the guise of a human, or a demon.

"He seems like a good man," Jagan said, pushing his hair behind his ears. "Unhappy with our English masters, certainly, but that's not unusual, is it? God knows I hate how they support the cold-blooded zamindars who flatter them."

"We know better than to share our true feelings with strangers," Ujjal said. "For instance, Jagan, I wouldn't dream of mentioning in Chetak's presence what it's like to sleep next to you. All those noises from your stomach I have to hear when I'm trying to sleep, and the terrible smells that follow me into my dreams—your stinking feet, and your farting, friend, the farting especially is out of control. You should—"

A fist curved around leaping red flames to slam into Ujjal's nose. Howling, Ujjal covered his face with his cupped palms.

"I apologize," Jagan said, but curtly, holding a rag toward Ujjal so he could staunch the blood spilling out of his nose. Ujjal, his face lifted to the sky, ignored him. Jagan shook his left arm, and Balram heard his elbow crackling.

Over his coat Balram traced the shape of the compass. They were all behaving badly, and he couldn't tell why. Mor handed Ujjal a dampened rag, and Ujjal pressed it against his nose. After he had cleaned up, Balram encouraged Jagan and Ujjal to shake hands like

Englishmen, much to the amusement of the others, and the bitterness of their mood receded. Talk returned to Chetak.

"The horrible way he was speaking against the English, he could have been part of the Sepoy Mutiny. Maybe he was one of the soldiers who fought for that idiot Mughal king, don't you think, Compass-wallah?" Yogi asked, and the appellation startled Balram as if Yogi had accused him of theft. But an opposing thought uncoiled in him too: at last he deserved the title of Compass-wallah on account of the object he now possessed.

"In Dehra I heard about a bandit who helped rebel soldiers," Mor said.

"I heard that too," Jagan said. "A bandit who raids only wealthy zamindars, then shares his loot with people like us. Everyone lies to the police for him. If he flees east, people tell the police he has gone west."

"But why would he be in Tibet? It's not like he can fight the English from here," Harish said.

"Whoever this man Chetak is, I hope you remembered to be discreet in front of him," Balram said. "You can't talk to anyone about the captain."

"Of course not," Yogi said. "We aren't stupid."

Chetak knows, Gyan said. *Why else would he be here?*

Balram took the captain's food and cutlery to his tent. Samarth, his cheeks tearstained but eyes dry, told Balram that he and the captain had calculated they were now at an altitude of thirteen thousand feet.

"Well done," Balram said. "Pawan has a bowl of tsampa for you." At the sight of the meat on the captain's plate, Samarth rushed out.

"Poor boy," the captain said. "He said his pet sheep died?"

"Remember at the Survey office there was talk about someone called the Robin Hood of Terai?" Balram asked the captain. "Was he ever caught?"

"I don't think so," the captain said. "Why do you ask?"

"Bandits have been on my mind."

"And who can blame you?"

The captain prodded the meat with the edge of his knife. For an Englishman he was adept at eating without a chair and table, even if he couldn't do without his cutlery. He pointed in the direction of his bottle of brandy, and Balram dutifully served it in a glass.

"Just before we left for Mana," the captain said, "a policeman came to the office with a drawing of the bandit you speak of. He asked us to keep an eye out for him during our surveys in the jungle. Did you not see that sketch?"

"I must have," Balram said.

The captain gulped down the brandy as if it was water. "The sketch was most certainly a poor likeness," he said. "Drawn with the aid of descriptions gathered from peasants, who must have lied through their teeth to protect their savior. I heard the police shot dead many of his associates, but he himself escaped to the Deccan."

"A better place to hide than Tibet," Balram said.

"Plenty warmer than this godforsaken country." The captain picked up a slice of meat with his fork and shook his head. "Tastes only of dung."

Balram now knew why Chetak's face had appeared familiar to him, even if it bore almost no resemblance to the sketch that had been passed around the Survey office, the lines fading into the folds of the paper, baldness punctuated with the odd prickle of hair, a tooth curving out of the mouth to rest against the lower lip like the crooked tusk of an elephant. Still, the artist who drew Chetak must have been gifted, because from these false stories he had managed to catch the man's likeness in his eyes, the abyss within the rim, eerie and tempting and still, and at the center, the pupil, black and smooth as a river stone glowing in the sun.

"I'll stand guard with the men tonight," Balram told the captain. "We won't survive another bandit raid."

12.

....

THE BLANK PAGES IN this journal are a disgrace, but the
events of the past few days have disconcerted me. M— has
been ill, and I now find myself in the untenable position of
being his guardian. He encourages me to leave him and make
my own way, a dastardly notion I could never entertain. We
are miles from any settlement, in a gorge that sees no travelers or pilgrims. M— chose this path on account of its isolation, and now we are paying dearly for our desire for
anonymity. We are running out of fuel and food. Yesterday I
cut my hair to feed the fire, and the odor was so foul I had to
carry M— out of the cave that has been our dwelling place
through his sickness. The days are strange and the nights are
long and windy and cold ~~and the dead arrive in droves to tell~~
~~me their grievances.~~ If these be the last words I ever write,
I should have wisdom to dispense. But in moments of utter
desperation, I find that I am occupied solely by questions
about food, water, and fuel. I now have much in common
with our ancestors whose primary form of expression was
drawing simple figures of humans and animals on cave walls.
Words cannot warm or nourish me. The exhausted mind
cannot dress sentences so that they will appear smooth and
pleasant.

———

THEY CLIMBED UP AND down hills the color of ash, following a path to Lhasa that no one else seemed to frequent. Chetak would never find her now. Along with sadness, Katherine felt some relief too when she remembered how his eyes had turned flinty after the kiss.

Night arrived without warning. Above her the sky hung in tatters. Where the wind had ripped through its thick folds a few stars stepped out warily. Katherine had the unnerving sensation of being enfolded by a giant bird's wings, the darkness bristly like feathers against her skin.

Mani hadn't mentioned the white man she had seen by the lake, disguised as a Hindustani, a pretense that echoed her own, except that the man's skin carried all the evidence of having been burnt by the sun while her own complexion (which had caused her mother no end of displeasure) was in its natural state the shade of almonds (which her mother had equated to the color of decay). Perhaps Mani hadn't seen the foreigner, though it was unlikely; the boy said little, but he missed not even the presence of an ant.

In any other land, meeting a fellow explorer would have been an occasion for excitement. Once, on a journey to Canton, when her ship had berthed at Victoria, an excessively kind German man had offered to protect her from the natives even though the port was under the jurisdiction of the British government and the Chinese themselves didn't betray any curiosity about her. Still, after several months of exploration, she had welcomed the opportunity to speak without restraint to a fellow traveler from the West about the odd habits of natives, and trade advice on what one ought to wear and eat. Someone else in her position would have also pressed letters into the hands of the traveler who was homeward bound, but in those days before Ethel had fallen ill, Katherine had felt no compulsion to inform her sister of her whereabouts.

They reached a narrow gorge that appeared to stretch toward the horizon. It must have been the path of a river or a stream at one time, but it was now dry. Above its steep walls, the sky appeared as a black sash, causing Katherine's mind to fill with apprehensions she couldn't name.

Mani pointed to a depression in the rocks, described it as a cave, and said they would camp there for the night. His voice sounded hoarse, perhaps from speaking too much.

The cave's roof was low. To enter, they had to bend their knees and hunch their shoulders. A cursory inspection revealed no signs of animal presence. The air, though musty, wasn't foul with the odor of piss and dung.

"I'll not stay here. It's too small and suffocating," Katherine said, and crawled outside.

"Mother, you can't even see where you're going," Mani said. "Let me at least light a torch."

Annoyed, Katherine deployed her walking stick to tap his hands. Unwittingly, she struck him with more force than she intended to, and he leaped back, letting out a sharp cry as he did so. He collapsed to the ground.

"Are you hurt?" she asked.

"I don't think so," he said.

"Try to get up."

But he couldn't. Katherine propped him up with the weight of his body concentrated upon her arms, neglecting the ache in her own spine. Leaning against her, Mani hopped on one foot.

"I don't remember our terms of agreement stating that I would be your bearer," she said.

"A good night's rest and I'll be fine."

Katherine had no choice but to camp in the cave she despised. Mani seemed to have twisted his ankle. After laying him down, she lit a fire by the entrance, to allow the smoke to escape, and to deter four-legged visitors.

"There's nothing your tea can't cure," Mani told her as she offered him a bowl of warm water into which she had stirred their dwindling rations of barley flour. He sipped the soupy mixture without complaint, using his fingers to crumble the lumps of tsampa floating in the liquid. Beads of sweat speckled his forehead. Katherine pressed her hand against his cheek and detected the beginnings of a fever. She didn't know where they were. God forbid, but if Mani didn't recover, how would she survive in the wilderness? (And why did she always have such bad luck with servants?)

After finishing the tea, Mani tried to sleep, but the smoke made him cough. Katherine let the fire die, then fanned the air with a rag to push the smoke out of the cave. From Mani's sack, she extricated one of his medicinal oils and rubbed it on his ankle, and the boy thanked her and said it was as if they were in truth mother and son. She smeared the oil on her aching back and tried to make herself comfortable and failed. It was going to be a long and difficult night.

IN THE MORNING KATHERINE walked to the end of the gorge and discovered it opened into a plateau dusted with glittering frost. Slung over her shoulders was a bundle with the goatskins Mani used to store water, nearly empty now. She had slept fitfully. What madness had seized her to believe she could walk across Tibet at her age? Why had she chosen (*chosen!*) this life of discomfort? The wind felt like salt against the blains on her skin.

She came across a patch of grass that had sprouted around a small pool of water. She scooped up the water into a goatskin bag, felt its iciness travel down her throat and gullet, and thought she should have boiled it first.

It was a clear day, the sky blue and soft, white clouds hanging low, the sun so bright the eyes ached. Until now Katherine had trusted Mani to find provisions and good camping grounds, and she had neglected to be attentive to the route they followed. She knew Lhasa lay to the northeast, and the position of the sun could guide her to the Forbidden City, but what if hordes of bandits, wolves, or raging rivers conspired to stop her? And what of Mani?

She walked to the end of the plateau, where the land dipped down a rugged precipice to rise again as if it was a wave of the sea. The dust-colored hills around her ripened to a yellow in the sunshine; not a cheery yellow but the palette of sickness.

Katherine returned to the pool to tug at the grass, which would serve as kindling. Their roots clung to the earth and she couldn't pull them out easily and she had to settle for breaking the blades in half.

As far as she could see, only her figure cast a shadow on the ground. Such a secluded place, of imagined safety, had been her secret, a refuge in the mind where she could hide while attempting to fit into a London society that considered her a curiosity, a half-savage. But this land didn't care if Katherine lived or died; it would endure in some shape or form long after all beings perished.

In the cave, Katherine built a fire with great difficulty, eyes burning and lungs constricting because of the smoke. She stirred a mere spoonful of the tsampa into the water to make the meager amount of flour that remained last longer.

Mani looked pitiable. A yellowish substance half-sealed his eyelids. He insisted he was fine and attempted to stand without success. "I'll be better tomorrow," he said.

BY THAT AFTERNOON MANI'S fever was so high, the boy was rambling deliriously. First he told Katherine the gods were punishing him, then he called out to the gods themselves. "Are you angry I helped an Englishwoman?" he mumbled. "But she isn't English, not really. You know this better than I do."

She tried to feed him tsampa and mopped up the food that dribbled down the corners of his mouth. She hadn't been at Ethel's bedside, but was now taking care of a native servant she barely knew. She told him stories about her travels to help him sleep, and rubbed oil on his feet, hoping these small gestures, through their repetition, would calm her mind (and his too) like a prayer. Those early days of her tour when she had balked at the notion of sharing a tent with him seemed to belong to another lifetime.

The sunlight began to dim. Mani gripped her hand, his fingers damp with sweat, and stuttered, "If this be my fate, I accept it. But it need not be yours."

Katherine pushed his hand away.

"Mother," Mani said. "Mother."

"Are you thirsty?" Katherine asked.

"Mother," he said again.

She understood now that he wasn't calling out to her, but to the woman who had given birth to him, who must be at this moment cooking, or cleaning their home in Almora. Would she sense her son was in distress? Would she curse the Englishwoman who had promised him riches and spirited him away to a forbidden kingdom? She would have known what to do, which poultice to press against Mani's forehead, the right oil to smear on his chest. Katherine knew nothing that would prove useful to another human. A lack in her that her own mother would have attributed to her self-absorption. Now she heard her mother's voice with such clarity that she looked around and saw two ghostly white figures in the darkest part of the cavern.

Mother and Ethel drifted toward her, their skin occasionally turning translucent to merge with the blackness of the cave.

"Your selfishness knew no bounds even when you were a child," Mother told Katherine. "Wicked as you are, you didn't even visit Ethel on her deathbed."

Ethel smiled at Katherine, a wide, red-toothed smile. Blood spilled from the corners of her mouth. "I wanted you there," she said, "because I was so very afraid."

The wind's beats were hasty yet steady. From which well of darkness in her had these deranged images sprung out? Katherine tightened her robe and stepped out of the cave into the gorge, where the crisp air reawakened the faculties of the mind. The figures vanished.

But she was six again and new to England. Their house thronged with visitors asking if little Katie had taken to the English weather yet, what a change winter must be after the Indian summer, and Mother all the while claiming Katherine's brown complexion was a shame, a consequence of the unwise hours she had spent in the tropical sun. Soon she would be fair, Mother said.

Standing now in the Tibetan cold, Katherine felt the brisk hands of maids applying copious amounts of violet powder onto her skin at Mother's behest, then Mother's fingers, soft as butter and sharp as talons, pinching her cheeks without affection while noting the powder hadn't whitened her skin at all. "I'm trying," Mother would tell Katherine's father, but Katherine wasn't hers, Katherine's complexion was an affront to the masquerade that was her marriage, Katherine had poor manners that a lifetime in a manor wouldn't rectify, and a temper that could have only come from her real mother, who was a whore. "Not a whore," her father would say, and Mother would retort, "A nautch girl then." Once Katherine had interrupted them to say she had been gifted to Father by God. Such was her fear that she might be labeled a savage that she had never allowed herself to feel any curiosity about the woman who had given birth to her.

Mother did keep her word to Father; she *tried*. She did her best to teach Katherine how to be a good woman and a good wife; she never raised her hand against Katherine or starved her or dressed her in Ethel's old clothes, instead swaddling her in expensive silk dresses and even silk stockings and bonnets. Only her tongue betrayed her inability to love the bastard child her husband had foisted on her. So in her own home Katherine had always remained an outsider. She had left at the first opportunity. Her departure wasn't an act of abandonment but restitution. She would always choose flight if it was imperative to her survival.

THE NEXT DAY KATHERINE followed the crests and troughs of the land at a quick pace despite the aches in her bones. For miles she spotted nothing but bare hills and bare earth and bare skies, not even the thin breath of God manifesting as a wisp of white cloud to sully the blue. Like a warped mirror the heat distorted the earth, its sheen oppressive. In the air hung her odor, the pungent smell of an animal being led to slaughter. Somewhere in the distance was Lhasa and the crenellations of ridges that rose behind the red-and-white walls of the Potala Palace, snow feathering the saw-edged mountains, all of which she would never see if she allowed even a splinter of guilt to lodge in her heart.

Sweat pasted her coat onto her skin. Her sack was twice as heavy as it had been on account of her folded tent and vessels, which Mani had carried before. Lost in sleep, he hadn't noted her departure. She had left a dying man behind to save her own life.

Four summers ago a mountaineer who was part of the first ever group to reach the summit of the Matterhorn, and his guides, had been accused of cutting the rope that linked the members during their descent. The mountaineer and his guides lived; their companions died. *Murder,* some had called it. But who could tell what had really happened up there? Even if they had cut the rope it would have been to survive, and those actions that seemed so vile in London were often the only sensible approach in the wilderness.

Katherine heard Mother's voice, reprimanding her for her *moral decrepitude,* and Katherine was twelve again and couldn't fathom the meaning of those two words but knew without doubt that an evil thing resided in her, a brute that crawled through her veins owing to the injudicious mixing of blood (as Mother had been heard to say). She looked at her arms now and her skin appeared to pucker as if in her veins a serpent was making its way toward its quarry. She clasped the walking stick Mani had obtained for her, and it scalded her palm.

In the distance a marmot stood on its hind legs on a rock. Katherine considered laying a trap to catch it, but she had no implements except for her stick, lacked hunting skills, and Mani would have told her the marmot was invested with sacredness, that killing it would invite the wrath of gods, or that its meat was unfit for human consumption. Then the sunlight creased and the marmot disappeared.

Around her, the angular hills, and the snowy peaks that rose behind them, began to acquire a golden, divine luminescence. Dusk. She hadn't realized it was so late. Hunger tightened her stomach. She uttered Seneca's words as Mani would chant prayers before a

particularly difficult ascent: "*To what end do we toil, and labor . . . ?*
We may enlarge our fortunes, but we cannot our bodies; so that it does but
spill and run over, whatsoever we take more than we can hold."

The setting sun now painted the sky an incandescent violet. *I have*
taken on more than I can hold, Katherine thought.

IN THE LIGHT OF the stars she walked back to the cave and built a
fire that sputtered and threatened to die. Through the smoke she saw
Mani sipping from the goatskin bag she had left by his side.

"You seem better," she said.

"I thought you had left."

"Preposterous."

"Who will it serve if we both perish here?"

"There's opportunity for that yet. I found nothing to eat. You
said there were settlements, but none that I could spot today. Maybe
tomorrow. Do Tibetans eat marmots?"

"You ate a marmot?"

"Tibetans believe marmots are related to humans, don't they? I
remember hearing that in Kalimpong. Maybe in Burma."

"In desperate circumstances, people will eat other people to survive."

"There's no situation in which I would prefer cannibalism to star-
vation."

"A relief to know, mother," Mani said, and Katherine smiled. He
took a deep breath and continued, "I apologize I have to bring this to
your attention now, but my family . . . my father—he left us when I
was small. My sisters and my mother are dependent on me. With the
advance you paid me, we cleared a few of our debts, but there are
more, too many. Now that my return looks difficult—"

"Why does it look difficult?"

"If I don't survive, would you mind paying a part of my wages? I
know I don't deserve them, but whatever amount you think appropriate, if you can give it to the Almora deputy collector, he'll seek
out my family."

"Nonsense. You'll give them the money yourself."

"You don't understand," Mani said, forcing himself to sit upright with great effort. "I would have become a monk as a child if I didn't have to help my mother."

By the entrance of the cave the fire burned down to embers that emitted an orange light. Mani coughed up sputum that he spat into a corner of the cave, cleared his throat, and said, "I was seven when I first entered Tibet. I was a bearer for a trader who traveled to the Gyanema market every summer to sell wheat. I have been working ever since then. I couldn't become a monk and let my family starve."

"Listen to me now," Katherine said, adopting her mother's formal, mistress-of-the-house tone. "I'll go to Mansarovar tomorrow, hire a porter and a pony, and return here with them, then we can continue to Lhasa. The pony will ferry you. Our journey will be slow, but I'm in no hurry. We're certain to find a doctor in Lhasa. Your ankle will heal in no time."

In the silence that followed she realized she didn't mean everything she said. She would retrace her steps to Mansarovar—to find a new guide. The day's wanderings, when she hadn't come across a Tibetan or even a source of water, had made it evident that she couldn't reach Lhasa on her own. But she wouldn't leave Mani to die. She would hire a man with a pony to keep him company, and to take him to the border once he was well enough.

"Mother, you can go to Lhasa another time," Mani said. "Walk back to Mansarovar the way we came, and there will be many pilgrims returning to Hindustan. Join them, and you'll get back to Almora safely."

His breathing became ragged. The change in Mani was swift, and unexpected. Katherine's fears swelled as his wheezing grew louder. She ought to make him something to eat, but they had consumed the last of the tsampa the previous night. She stared at her walking stick and wondered if it might be edible, or if she ought to burn it for warmth. She leaned against the wall of the cave, too exhausted to move.

When she opened her eyes it was morning, and outside the light was blue and opaque. A figure at the entrance of the cave that she took to be a wolf caused a scream to rise up her throat, but the wind shifted and it vanished. She stepped over the cold ashes of the fire and went out into the empty gorge to piss. As she lifted her robe and squatted, she had the overwhelming sensation that someone was watching her. Chetak, she thought, leaping up in fear, smoothing her robe down and stepping away from the water trickling between her feet. How humiliating for her that he should see her like this. But all was still. Only the wind, always chattering in Tibet, always in a rush, scoured her skin. Katherine studied the slopes, but there was no movement. Her heart, which couldn't accept that she would never see Chetak again, was playing tricks on her. She touched her lips, dry and rough as a stone, and pulled the dead skin apart. Blood moistened her tongue. She didn't mind the taste of salt.

She headed to the pool to fetch water. The sun rose higher, its rays already scorching. Marmots came out of holes to stare into the horizon as if they were philosophers lost in thought, attempting to decipher the meaning of life. Below a mountain whose peak the wind had chiseled into the shape of a lion's head, antelopes kicked up dust, the V-shaped horns revealing to Katherine the males in the group. This landscape that had earlier appeared barren to her thrummed with life she had failed to glimpse. She was reminded of the Buddhist texts the monks in Kalimpong had taught her, each one of which broached the illusory nature of what the mind deemed real. *You think it's a snake in a room, but in the light of a lantern you realize it's only a sash.* Or was it *You think it's a sash, but it's a snake in the room?*

Walking back to the cave, from the corner of her eye she saw a movement on the rocky walls of the gorge. The brightness of the sun dimmed her vision. She reached the cave and looked up. A boulder moved. Couldn't be. She looked again. It wasn't a boulder but an animal, its domed forehead and thick tail surfacing and disappearing as it walked—glided, it seemed to her—along the ridge. Katherine blinked. No, there was no mistaking it. How long it had been watching them or whether it had marked them for prey, she didn't know, and she had the urge to run and escape, but Mani could barely walk and she could never outpace a wild animal, certainly not a snow leopard.

In the cave she kindled a fire and waited a while. Mani dozed. It must be noon. She put the fire out and looked around. No sign of any predator. She packed their belongings and told Mani they would walk back to Mansarovar, where they would find food and medicine. He protested he was too frail. She said they would starve if they waited for his ankle to heal. "I'm paying your wages, and you have to listen to me," she said. Outwardly she was calm, though she felt as if each movement she made was not hers but that of a proxy. Her mouth tasted of ashes and a dull ache pooled behind her eyes.

She forced Mani to stand, lending him her walking stick, and like a scarecrow the boy draped himself over it, his skin hanging loose from his bones, his chin resting on its edge.

"We can't just sit here and wait for death," she said.

"Death comes when it chooses. We can't hurry or delay it," he said as she tried to carry all of their belongings at once and her spine screamed in protest. He extended his hand, leaning forward on the stick and nearly losing his footing, and still she had no choice but to return his sack to him.

Katherine thought she should have hired a group of servants, like the white man at Mansarovar, even if a caravan of animals and a dozen bearers would have attracted unwarranted attention. Now they were about to be killed by a snow leopard and no one would notice their absence. The animal might sense Mani's weakness and attack him first, giving her time to escape. What a mean thought. To make amends she asked Mani to place his hand on her shoulder so that he wouldn't have to put too much weight on his injured foot. They limped out of the gorge, Katherine expecting the snow leopard to leap on them. But the ridge was empty.

Only the strength of his mind allowed Mani to walk. Occasionally a chill overtook him, and its passing left him drenched in sweat. His skin shimmered in the sun as if the gods were beautifying the offering of his body before snuffing out his life. Blue veins were sprinkled around his eyes, and his cheeks were bristly and yellow.

Katherine was startled each time the scree, loosened by their boots, clattered. "Tayata Om Bekandze . . . " Mani chanted the prayer to the Medicine Buddha, eyes half-closed such that he stumbled often. Maybe she was mad to think she could save the boy, but his death would haunt her forever if she were to leave him behind. As Ethel haunted her. Even now she could hear Ethel rasp in her ears. *Look at how you care for a stranger, when you didn't even visit me on my deathbed.* Katherine sipped water from a goatskin bag. Her mouth remained parched.

Mani leaned forward and retched, the blisters on his lips gaping like knife wounds, yellow mucus drying around his nostrils. A small rock bounced down a hill in the periphery of Katherine's vision. Turning her head, she saw a hare vanishing behind boulders. Such calm. She wondered if she had hallucinated the shape of a snow leopard. While light-headed and hungry, had she taken a sash for a snake? But in her memories there were also moments when danger had approached after sounding a loud warning and she had failed to listen. Once, when Katherine had been a girl of eleven or twelve, her mother had made her work with the cook as a punishment for some perceived slight, and she had been unable to move her fingers out of the way even as she knew the cold knife she held would slice her dirt-colored flesh and not the stubborn turnip trembling in her grip.

They staggered forward. Mani clutched her hand so ferociously her skin turned red. Katherine couldn't ask him if they were on the right path; his eyelids were almost knitted together by a crusty secretion. They would die of thirst or hunger or sickness, and their flesh would be picked apart by vultures, and their white bones would gleam in the sunlight. She could see well-wishers grasping Frederick's hand to offer condolences and recriminations: *she shouldn't have, she was too old, whoever heard of Tibet, where is it, my God, the end of the earth, whatever possessed her to go to such a place?* Mani said, "Save yourself. My life is worth nothing." And she wondered how he had the clarity to formulate such statements when delirious.

An hour or so later, she spotted bar-headed geese standing in a circle in a field of grass. The birds were almost always in the proximity of water. Then a lake became visible as a sheet of blue, its exact shade varying according to the angle at which the late-afternoon sun fell on the water.

"Did we pass this lake on our way to the gorge?" Katherine asked, and Mani said, "Maybe." They stopped to rest, lying down on the grass with their sacks serving as pillows, Katherine hoping a snow leopard wouldn't attack them on a plain and trying to keep her eyes open. Then it was dark; she didn't know how it happened except that she must have fallen asleep without meaning to. She woke Mani and said they should move. They might be on the path of animals for whom the lake must serve as a watering place at night. Clouds drifted over the weathered faces of hills and mountains.

Where to set up the tent? Mani was shuddering and was of no help. She was annoyed with him and wished he could stop being ill. She started to hammer a tent peg into the ground with a stone twice the size of her fist. It slipped from her hands. *Oh, she was useless.* Mani, half-dead, pried it out of her cold hands, and sat on the grass with his legs stretched on the ground to erect the tent.

Once inside, Mani promptly fell into a deep, loud sleep. Through the fabric of the tent Katherine saw the light of a torch and heard the clatter of horses. Were these passersby pilgrims or bandits?

She made her way outside. The air felt thinner than before, a sharpness to it so that every breath inhaled and exhaled cut through the lungs like a scimitar. She stumbled but broke her fall with her hands, stones wedging themselves into the skin of her palms. On all fours, she saw two men on horseback, their features hidden by rags wrapped over their faces such that only their eyes were visible. They were conversing with a pedestrian holding in his hand a torch whose flames cast a golden glow over his face. With a start she saw that it was Chetak, and almost called out to him but stopped herself. She must be mistaken.

Katherine stood up and rubbed the exhaustion out of her eyes. It was him. There was an urgency to his gestures as he passed letters, or a wad of currency, to one of the men on horseback. They bowed their heads as if he was not only their trusted friend but also their master, then cluck-clucked their tongues in a signal to the horses to move. Chetak raised his hand to bid them farewell. The dust kicked up by the animals sparkled in the light of his torch, and he looked like an ethereal figure, conjured by her imagination and hunger and want. His head turned toward her just then, and she stared at him, waiting for his image to dissipate.

She was aware of his torch moving toward her. Her mouth tasted of cloves and rain as in the moment he had kissed her after the storm. Then the flames were so close to her face she had to draw back from their scalding heat.

"It's you," he said, sounding as surprised as she was.

"Who were those men?" she asked. "What are you doing here? Where were you? Why did you disappear after we . . . ?" Or perhaps she said nothing.

He moved the torch to his left hand and, with his right, touched the edges of her broken lips crusted with dried blood. Her hair, matted with sweat and grime, pressed against her cheeks. Up in the sky a star twinkled before a cloud raced to smother its defiance. "What happened to you?" he asked.

"Mani is unwell," she said, drawing back from him quickly, but he held her hand and clasped it to his chest before letting go. Whether he did this out of pity or affection, she couldn't tell. It couldn't be prompted by desire. She must look frightful.

Chetak asked her to hold the torch as he examined Mani with the certainty of a doctor, holding the boy's wrist to check his pulse, pressing his ears against Mani's chest where his shirt was damp with sweat and pulling down his lower eyelids to ascertain if the whites of his eyes had turned yellow. Sparks flitted too close to Mani, who winced but acquiesced to Chetak's prodding without question, only asking for his mother through chattering teeth, and Katherine said, "I'm here, right next to you."

"You must eat," Chetak said. He dug a pit and made a fire with the twigs in his sack, which as she had discovered held a vast array of items, not only his clothes and fuel but also food.

Even the smoke couldn't weaken the sour, putrid smell of sickness that hovered around Mani. Chetak roasted meat on a pan, his sleeves rolled up, the hair on his arms golden in the orange light.

"Is it a marmot?" Katherine asked.

"Mutton. Well cured with salt, you'll find," Chetak said.

"Were you sending messages to people at home with those men on horseback?" she asked. "You seemed to know them well."

"I do know them, yes." He seemed hesitant to say more, and she was reluctant to ask because she didn't want to hear about a lover or children. Even now, starving and every bone in her body aching, she could see how beautiful he looked, his hair black and glistening in the light of the flames, his eyes wild and his manner majestic like a stag. She wished she could acquire him just as Englishmen on a battlefield returned home with whatever caught their fancy, ivory armchairs and diamonds and even deposed young Indian princes and princesses.

Chetak put down the skewer to prop up Mani against a rock and made him drink milk from a bowl. A rosy warmth spread across the boy's pallid cheeks.

"This will taste awful, but it will cure your illness in a night," Chetak told Mani, and asked him to sip from a brown bottle. Mani stuck out his tongue and flicked a few drops into his mouth so that his lips wouldn't touch the rim of the bottle, his expression sour on account of the bitterness of the medicine. He coughed, but didn't spit it out. Katherine saw from the black letters printed on the white label that it was Warburg's tincture, a remedy given to English soldiers, and she couldn't imagine when or how Chetak could have procured it. He offered them cubes of browned meat that they ate with their fingers. Katherine found it rich and unpleasant after the meager diet on which they had subsisted for days.

"I saw a snow leopard earlier," she said, listening to the wind flittering through the hills.

"Is that why you decided to leave the cave?" Mani asked. "You could have told me."

"What cave?" Chetak asked.

"Not far from here," Katherine said.

"It's good fortune to see a snow leopard," Chetak said.

"Tibetans believe they're sacred," Mani said, the meat or medicine restoring in him a level of alertness Katherine would have deemed impossible only a few moments ago. "They believe snow leopards guard mountains."

"How could you get lost on your way to Mount Kailas?" Chetak asked him. "It's a straight route from the lake."

"He has been ill," Katherine said. "Where were you? You disappeared after the storm."

Chetak had the grace to look embarrassed then. "I ran into a few acquaintances by the lake," he said as he served them tea, dun-colored on account of his generosity with milk.

Mani said he needed to sleep, and Katherine helped him into the tent. He asked her for a story, as if he was only a child, and she told him about a vulture that took care of an orphan girl by bringing the little girl the food it stole from the homes of the wealthy. Her ayah had told Katherine this tale when she was three or four and she had never forgotten it. She expected Mani to say it was a foolish story, but he fell asleep quickly.

When she came outside she saw Chetak had set up a tent nearby. A fire sputtered outside it, and he sat with his hands held up against the flames.

"It was good of you to share your food, and medicine, with us," she said.

"I have to leave at dawn tomorrow," he said, as if clarifying that he couldn't be her provider or savior. She wanted him to be neither, but on this night she would have liked him to clasp her to his chest so that the sound of his heartbeat beneath her ear would silence the words of the dead. An animal grunted in the distance, a yak perhaps, its hooves thumping against rock.

"There is comfort," he said, "in this wilderness, I find. No one around for miles. I prefer it to cities, where there's always a drunkard shouting at the moon and a soldier threatening to shoot him."

"I don't mind cities," Katherine said. "I like Calcutta, even though the last time I was there people couldn't stop talking about a cyclone that had destroyed everything. Killed over twelve thousand people. Tore ships apart, over a hundred of them." She was nervous and speaking too much. "But I agree, I prefer the sound of the wind to the babble of men and women."

Chetak was staring at her. She didn't want him to look at her too closely, she who had been visited by ghosts. But he had already glimpsed the granite in her bones, the thickness of native blood in her veins, the mahogany tint to her skin, the self she attempted to disguise as he too did for reasons she didn't know. He drew her close to him and she noticed the strength of his arms from a lifetime of work under the sun, then the faint scent of meat lingering in his beard. She unfastened his turban and ran her fingers through his hair, enviously silky even in this ungracious Tibetan weather, then kissed the scar below his ear, heart quickening such that it hurt.

HE WOKE HER UP, his face barely visible in the darkness. She had fallen asleep in his arms, and the fire had died. A chaste night, but what else could have happened? Mani was ill and nearby, she was pretending to be a Hindu pilgrim, and Chetak was—who was he? She still didn't know.

"We'll get frostbite," he said. But she held him for a moment more, inhaling the scent of earth and sweat on his skin. "I suppose it's time for you to leave," she said.

"We will meet again," he said, but it wasn't a promise, and already there was a restlessness in him that she could sense at her fingertips.

The sky was lightening in the east. The black shapes of a herd of yak moved slowly across a distant slope. Chetak packed the tent in which he hadn't slept. He placed slabs of cooked meat wrapped in cloth next to her and asked her for a bowl, into which he poured a few

drops of the tincture. He told her to administer it to Mani twice during the day. "It may have a purgative effect," he said with a smile.
Then he gave her directions to Mansarovar and advised her to consider returning home, as Mani would likely be too weak to walk
around Kailas. She was miserable, but tried not to show it. Chetak
kissed her forehead, his lips soft as if he had smeared them with butter, and then he was gone.

13.

———

IT WAS ALMOST DUSK WHEN BALRAM CAUGHT THE FIRST GLIMPSE of the Horse River. The water was quiet and clear. On the riverbed stones glistened round and smooth. Balram knelt on the sandy bank and let the river run through his hands and felt in its frostiness the memory of the glacier where it had been born, the pulse of snow falling on mountain peaks. To him it sounded like a heartbeat, a confirmation that the river wasn't a blue spiral on a map but a living thing, a creature capable of renewal. It emptied itself into the sea and recast itself every few months. He wished he could do the same.

Small, black silhouettes darted in the water—fish the length and breadth of his index finger. Balram was about to plunge his hand to touch a fleeting shape when the saffron of the captain's robe edged his vision.

"Are you certain this is the upper reach of the Tsangpo?" the captain asked. "What the Tibetans call the Horse River?" Behind his beard, a robust black on account of fresh dye, his lips were stern.

"Wherever a river flows, on its banks you'll find fields and villages," Balram said. "We will come across these soon enough. You can direct your questions to the villagers."

Did you have to say that, Durga asked.

Balram no longer felt the need to hide his disapprobation from the captain (*but why?*). The compass was the beginning of something (*but what?*).

His defiance provoked no anger from the captain. "Isn't it

something?" he said, and inhaled the air as if it was scented with incense, then sat down in a comfortable nook between rocks with his pencil and notebook.

Yogi and Mor examined the reflections of their bald heads in the water, and agreed, out of the captain's earshot, that his receding hairline left his scalp smoother. The tonsure had caused their heads to be red and bristly. Jagan said it wasn't the time to rest; his elbow was hurting. The men groaned. "Not that again," Ujjal said.

Samarth approached the captain with a story about a stone he had picked up, and the captain indulged his prattle. He gave the boy a pencil and a piece of paper, and taught him how to sketch a depression in a nearby slope that took the form of a puckered mouth, wrinkles radiating from it like sunbeams. Across the river a yak chased a hare that leaped into a crevice between rocks and vanished. The yak didn't seem disappointed; it scratched an itch in its neck against a boulder.

Loud, guttural sounds tore through the placid air. Balram jumped up, but his limbs had fallen asleep, and he would have plunged into the river if Ujjal hadn't grabbed his arm. The clamor, which came from a hilltop, was distorted by echoes and clouds. In the silence between grunts, Balram heard the thrashing of wings.

"I told you," Jagan said.

"Why are these damned birds following us?" the captain asked.

"A sky burial," Balram said. "But it's late and the vultures will leave for their nests soon. I doubt they know about us."

Distinctly human voices overtook the sounds of birds. Trooping down the hill toward the river were Tibetans, a few cloaked in monk's robes, others carrying mallets and butcher's implements for grinding bones and dicing flesh. These men, the low-caste Ragyabpas, must have attended to the corpse that had drawn the vultures. Balram stood in front of the captain, hiding his notebook and discomfiture. The captain jabbed Balram in the back with a pencil and gesticulated toward the Tibetans, now performing their ablutions at the river. One wore a coat that was ragged but distinctly European.

"I must find out who gave him that coat," the captain said,

stepping around Balram, and Balram had to hold him back by grabbing his elbow. "Let me," Balram said.

Above them, the sky abruptly turned black. The river emptied of
light. Thunder crackled in the distance. The vultures, flesh spilling
from their full beaks, flew toward their homes.

Balram greeted the Tibetans as a trader might. The monks' pleas-
antries took the form of warnings—*a storm is coming; the danger of
flooding in the event of rain is far too great to justify making camp on a
riverbank; grain prices are rising; go to the trading mart and sell your
stocks quickly.* Balram thanked them for their advice and pointed to
the foreign article of clothing. "Where might I purchase a similar
coat?" he asked. The atmosphere turned dank. The wearer pushed
his hands into the pockets of the coat and sallied away toward the
hills, between which a looping path must lead to a village.

"The coat belonged to the man who is now in the bardo," a Tibetan monk told Balram, the briskness in his voice suggesting any
further inquiry wouldn't be welcome. "On his death his clothes were
distributed to his kin."

"A white man must have come this way, I suppose," Balram said.
"Perhaps the man who died helped him, and the white man gifted
him the coat to show his gratitude."

"Perhaps," the monk said.

"Was it a long time ago, or was it now?"

"I wouldn't know."

Lightning scarred the horizon, and the Tibetans bid Balram a
hasty farewell. As soon as they departed, the captain began to fret
about the Swede. Only the Swede could have passed this way, he
said; only he would trade a coat for grains, foolishly believing Scan-
dinavians could withstand the cold better than Tibetans. Balram suggested the coat might have been gifted by a Jesuit missionary who
had visited Shigatse years ago.

Pawan served them food. The lentils were raw and everyone
called him Kaccha again and told him to stop living up to his name.
After the meal, Harish and Rana slipped into the darkness of the hills.

All these wants in the men, which even the propinquity of death couldn't tame.

Balram remembered one sunny December morning when he and Gyan had skipped their lessons at school to walk six miles or so to a waterfall, where Gyan had tiptoed on the gushing water and dangled one foot over the edge. He stood there for what felt like hours but could have been seconds, swaying and grinning as the currents jostled him toward the bed. Balram had thought Gyan would die, with the sun gilding his hair and the shadows of his lashes on his cheeks, and he had wanted to kiss Gyan and kill him for subjecting him to such terror. On another day, watching a corpse burn, Balram had clasped Gyan's hand tightly, seeing in the distorted, wavering light above the flames the brevity of their lives. But that had been it. Balram wasn't like Harish and Rana. He didn't act on his every desire the moment it shimmered in his vision.

Now he offered to keep the first watch alone, and the bearers protested, but he waved them toward their tent. The storm the sky promised hadn't come to pass, and the sounds of thunder remained distant. No floods tonight. No stars to count either. He thought he saw a curved form slip between the rocks leading to the river but, on getting up to investigate in the solitary flame of a torch, detected nothing suspicious. The tips of his boots pressed into a heap of softness—the shit of a snow leopard or a fox, barely distinguishable from stones if not for its texture that he had determined on account of his misstep. Too stiff to be new, too yielding to be ancient. Where was the animal? The fur of snow leopards allowed them to disappear into the Tibetan landscape, but the sheep and the pony ought to smell a predator now that the wind was still, and raise an alarm.

Balram scraped his boots clean against a rock. Why did it feel as if a snow leopard stalked them, stalked *him*? He thought of Chetak. At Mansarovar the bandit must have seen the captain, with the dye running over his face, and recognized him as an Englishman, his enemy. The captain couldn't vanish into the Tibetan landscape as the snow leopard could.

Harish and Rana returned to the camp, breathless, sweat shining their faces wherever the dim light of the torch erased the shadows.

Makes you wonder, doesn't it, Gyan said.

"Unsafe to wander at this hour," Balram told the two men.

"We . . ." Harish said.

"We went for a piss away from the river," Rana said.

"I know what you were doing," Balram said.

"We weren't . . . we were . . ." Harish said.

"It's none of his business," Rana said, glowering at Balram. He held Harish's hand in a proprietorial fashion and dragged him toward the tent.

A drizzle began and, in moments, thickened into a heavy downpour that silenced the fires. The shepherds, who had taken to sleeping in the sheep pen, bolted past Balram into the bearers' tent, blankets drawn over their heads. A flash of lightning painted everything white and revealed sleeping forms. Balram pulled off his boots and nudged Yogi awake.

"What sense does it make for me to stand in the rain?" Yogi asked. "I won't be able to see anything."

WHEN BALRAM WOKE UP the tent was empty. Outside there was a great bustle. The men were gathered around the sheep pen. White mist hovered above the river like smoke. A dreadful foreboding coursed through Balram's veins. Misery was a tedious thing, a revenant that clung to him and loosened and tightened its grip around his neck. The sun painted careless, broad strokes of gold across the gray sky. Balram wanted to keep his gaze on the heavens so that he wouldn't have to look at the carnage around him. But there was no avoiding it. Dead sheep everywhere. Bloodied fur coating the ground. Pink entrails spilling out of lacerated bellies. Grains caught on tufts of grass. Samarth wailed and Rudra smacked him on the head and ordered him to be quiet. The bearers were silent. What was there to say except that they were cursed, and hadn't they said it too many times already?

A group of Tibetan women who must have walked down to the river to gather water chanted prayers, to ward off the evil they sensed in the air perhaps. Their red coral necklaces clattered as they brought their hands together and bowed before the mountains.

"How could you let this happen?" the captain said, turning to Balram, his eyes vicious. His beard was matted with ice, engendered by the humidity of his breath, warmed at night by a blanket pulled over his face. His nose and forehead were red and blistered, the skin peeling from the intensity of the sun.

"You were standing guard when I went to sleep," Balram said, turning to Yogi.

"It was pitch-dark, because it was raining, and so I couldn't see very well, but don't you think I would have heard something? How could so many animals be killed without a sound? And what is that?"

Balram's eyes followed the direction in which Yogi pointed his finger. In the pen the rib cage of a sheep moved with the wind as if still alive. No animal or bird could have picked a skeleton so clean of flesh in one night when it took the sun and the wind years, if not centuries.

"Is Colonel missing?" Balram asked Rudra, unable to see the pony's flesh and bones in the graveyard for animals that was their camp. Rudra nodded.

Balram approached the women and asked if snow leopards had attacked the sheep and yaks in their village. The women said they let their mastiffs out at night to deter bandits and wolves, but in recent months the nights had been quiet and there had been no intrusions. Tonight, however, they would take turns to keep watch, because the creature that had massacred the sheep was a malevolent one, the ro-lang, or maybe a snow leopard; only they would kill twenty sheep when two would sate their hunger.

"What did they say?" the captain asked afterward.

Balram considered lying, but it was too much of an exertion. "Ro-lang," he said. "They think it's ro-lang or a snow leopard."

"A *rolling*? Never heard of it," the captain said.

"Corpses woken up by an evil spirit," Balram said.

"We have lost everything," Jagan said. He pointed to the rib cage of the sheep, yellow seeping into its terrifying whiteness in the first rays of the sun. "We can't continue."

"We're so close to Shigatse," Balram said. The captain was watching him with narrowed eyes. "We can't let the captain down now."

"Sheep, grains, tea, ponies, even cooks and porters, can be purchased," the captain said, his fingers circling an ink stain on his left wrist. "I'll not pretend to be unmoved by the killings of these poor animals"—he glanced at Samarth—"it's frightful. It will cost us a great deal of money to replace them, but it must be done for our mission to be a success, and it will be a success." Then, in a whisper that was delivered with the authority of an order, he spoke to Samarth. "Come with me, boy. I have some measurements to confirm. You can help me."

THE MEN TOOK DOWN the tents and packed their belongings, but they wouldn't gather the bones of sheep. Balram piled up the dead animals and lit the bodies on fire—no man wanted to eat the meat tainted by the poisoned teeth of ro-lang. His eyes watered from the smell of burning fur and flesh, and his nails were red. The fire died quickly. In his attempt to expunge all trace of the calamity, he had only created more of a mess. The bearers coughed because of the foul smoke, but made no attempt to move away from the direction of the wind.

Balram asked Rudra to look for the pony, but Rudra pretended not to hear him. Without the pony the men would have to carry the goatskins themselves, and given their diminished numbers, the additional weight would be too much of a burden. Balram set out to search for the animal.

As he walked, the blurred outlines in the distance crystallized into the jagged edges of hills and mountains. He saw the captain teach Samarth the right way to place his foot on the ground to count paces. The boy was clumsy, but the captain was patient.

"Sir, you haven't seen the pony, have you?" Balram asked.

"The bearers are anxious, understandably so," the captain said, shaking his head either to express concern about the men or as an answer to Balram's question. "I wager they're about to turn on me, or each other. We ought to have been better prepared to withstand the attacks of beasts and bandits. I thought we were. What went wrong?"

"Visibility was poor yesterday because of the storm."

"The sheep aren't mute."

"But snow leopards are sly," Balram said. Samarth was watching his face closely as if afraid to miss even a word. "And last night the skies were loud."

"It's not two animals we lost but nearly the entirety of our pack. Their distress should have been more pronounced than thunder."

"Our work is very tiring, and the advantage, and disadvantage, of the exhaustion we feel is that we can sleep through fire and flood. Yogi must have fallen asleep too—he just doesn't want to admit it."

"That's all very well, but we have to acknowledge that our position is going from bad to worse."

Balram attempted to steady his expression. It appeared even the captain's faith had turned brittle. If he decided to abandon the expedition, Gyan wouldn't be rescued. Wasn't that just the way of the world? A man could formulate all the plans he wanted, and there was no telling if the gods would allow it. Balram could build a house with the sturdiest stones so that it would outlive him, and still find it crumbling in a tremor so mild even the fine webs spiders spun between trees remained unbroken.

"Let's forget this river and go home," Balram said, making a wild guess that such a statement would prompt the captain to disagree with him.

Behind the captain, wings gathered in the sky—vultures returning to break their night's fast on a hill.

"I don't mean we give up. Far from it," the captain said, as Balram had expected. "But we have to reassess."

"It's best to do that once we reach Shigatse," Balram said. "It will take us three weeks. Maybe four. No more than that."

"Shigatse is nearly four hundred miles from here, according to your previous route surveys," the captain said.

"Yes, sir. But now that we have so few sheep we should be able to cover that distance quicker. And once we reach Shigatse we can purchase more goods and animals. Or, if you want to leave Tibet, south of Shigatse are passes to the kingdom of Sikkim, and Nepal."

"I didn't tell you about the time I was very ill, did I, Balram?"

"No, sir. As I was saying, Shigatse——"

The captain stopped him with a raised hand.

"I was thrown off a horse at the age of eight. I was so badly injured I couldn't leave my bed. Doctors said I might not walk again, but I decided my dreams wouldn't be constrained by disease. I plotted a life of adventure for myself. A childish thing to do, no doubt, yet one that restored my spirits. You hear me, Sam? There's a lesson in it for you, too. You have seen many horrors at such a young age. But remember, if I had allowed myself the bitter pleasures of self-pity, of enumerating my disappointments, I wouldn't have climbed mountains. My feet wouldn't have touched Tibetan soil."

On the riverbank, a piece of driftwood shaped like the prow of a ship caught a sunbeam that lent its damp coat a bright, oily sheen. A marmot sidled out of a crevice and climbed onto the driftwood and surveyed the world from its edge, as if it were the captain of a ship. Above them more vultures flew toward the hilltop, the opposite poles of life and death contained within the span of their soaring wings.

"*Be strong and of good courage,* the Bible tells us, and this is how we must be," the captain said in English. "And that's how we will defeat the Swede."

"Very good, sir," Balram said.

"I imagine you feel compelled to fulfill our mission to honor Gyan's memory."

"Gyan isn't dead," Balram said. He scratched his elbows with nails reddened by the blood of sheep.

"I hope you're right," the captain said. "He was——he is——our best surveyor. You won't mind me saying so."

"Of course not," Balram said. The captain had always praised

Gyan's work more. At the Survey he talked of recommending Gyan for the Royal Geographical Society's Patron's Medal once it was safe for his identity to be revealed, after his retirement. Not once had the captain mentioned putting forward Balram's name for a medal. Might be a petty rivalry, like between the captain and the Swede, but it stung Balram, even now.

You're no longer a child, and I might be dead, Gyan said.

BALRAM WAS LOOKING FOR Colonel on a trail that wound around hills when he heard a gunshot. He stumbled, touching his coat above his heart to feel for blood. No one had shot at him. He crouched close to the ground, though there was no boulder to shield him from bullets. The hills loomed above him, stained purple by shadow and green by moss. Vultures rose growling into the air. A yak came racing down the slope and Balram leaped out of its path just in time. It darted past him to crest another hill, its form dwindling to a dot. Above him the wind forced partitions through thick rolls of white and gray cloud, revealing in the apertures the vivid blue of the Tibetan sky. Balram heard the clatter of hooves. Must be bandits.

Then he saw Colonel sauntering down the slope. A man held the pony's lead and clicked his tongue in encouragement each time the animal hesitated. Quelling the wave of fear that rose within him, Balram waved his hands like a madman and yelled in Tibetan, "Shoot me if you want, you bastard, but that's my animal you're stealing." Cold air rushed into his throat. His gums ached. A vulture circled above him, dropping down levels. "Colonel, come here," he shouted again, as if the pony knew obedience, or order. His words were met with a laugh. By now the man had climbed down close enough for Balram to distinguish his features.

"What are you doing with our pony?" Balram asked.

"Found him wandering," Chetak said, a look of amusement or contempt flitting across his eyes as he handed over the reins. "I was bringing him back to you—I thought you must be camped nearby. A mistake to buy such a bad-tempered animal. How much did he cost?"

"Why did you shoot the yak?" Balram asked. He saw no pistol on Chetak's person, but it could be hidden in his pockets or tucked into his boots.

"I only meant to frighten it," Chetak said. "It was following me."

Balram led the pony back on the path toward their camp. A hare watched them from a burrow, eager to graze on moss but constrained by their presence. There was only one reason for Chetak to be curious about their group: he wanted to point out the captain to a Tibetan soldier and claim a reward. He could also steal their gold coins, then live like a king in Lhasa until the English forgot him. But Balram needed the gold to rescue Gyan; it was the sole reason he had agreed to the captain traveling with him on this ill-fated trip. If the captain wouldn't part with the money willingly to save his best surveyor Gyan's life, Balram would do what was needed. The compass in his pocket proved he could.

"Everything well?" Chetak asked, only a step behind Balram.

"Why shouldn't it be?" Balram said. He thought of the rib cage he had hidden behind a boulder near the camp, as if shoving it out of sight would erase it from his memory. He turned to look at Chetak, who was unwinding his turban for no reason. Long hair spilled down his shoulders. On this cloudy morning, when the light was dim, his hair and teeth gleamed, their luster determined not by the sun but by the bright blood in his veins. A robust man, neat for a traveler, no mud encrusting his boots, no stains on his clothes. He walked silently, his feet seemingly never touching the ground.

"You suspect I'm a scoundrel," Chetak said, "but I'm a far better man than the crook in your party who swaddles himself in saffron."

Balram stopped. The pony strained against the rope, and Balram hissed at the animal to be quiet.

"I heard the men call you Compass-wallah," Chetak said. "You're one of those people who help the English draw maps. I may have come across a surveyor or two before." He stepped forward to gently scratch between the pony's ears, and the pony, wistful and subservient, moved its head toward his chest. "What's in it for you? No money, not much of it anyway, no honor either. All the glory is the white man's, all the worry is yours. How do you estimate it to be a fair trade?"

"If you inform Tibetan soldiers of his presence, it's not the white man alone who will suffer. We'll be sent to prison too, or worse, killed."

"You exaggerate."

"I know Tibet well, and I'm familiar with the ways of its people." Balram found his lips widening into a most inappropriate smile as he spoke, and he couldn't tell if his brain had erroneously imagined such an expression would appear threatening. "Do you think our shepherd who's only a child should be fed to vultures? You're a better man than that."

"You seem quite certain about a number of things you have no way of knowing."

"But I do know," Balram said, lowering his tone as if he regretted having to speak. "You're a bandit, a thief, a wanted man in Hindustan."

"Say that I am—what does it matter? In this land I am as free as you are. Freer, since you're in a white man's shackles."

"They say you gifted slices of melon to an English officer who was delirious and starving after having been on your trail for weeks. You don't kill the men who hunt you, you leave them tied to a tree. That's why the English call you the Gentleman Bandit, and a gentleman wouldn't want our group to die."

"On that count you're doing quite well with no help from me."

Balram felt in his pockets for the captain's compass. "Here, keep this," he said. It was not much of a bribe, but he held Chetak's hand as if he were a new bride and placed the compass on his cool palm. "It shows you where east and west is," Balram said. In that moment when the pony's lead was unmanned, the animal decided to take flight, and he threw himself after it, nearly collapsing to the ground. The rope cut a diagonal, stinging line on his right palm, which was slick with sweat. The hare that had deemed them harmless to gnaw at a moss-coated stone dashed back into its burrow. Balram blew on his palm and cursed the pony under his breath.

Raising the compass to the sun, Chetak squinted at it with one eye shut. "The compass can direct our feet east, but the universe can still send us west," Chetak said.

"You can trade it for a few maunds of tsampa on a lean day," Balram said.

Chetak slipped the compass back into Balram's coat pocket. It was a familiar gesture, an intimate one too, as if they knew each other well.

"Everything is not what it seems," Balram said. "We have a common enemy—the English."

"I have seen you with the Englishman," Chetak said. "You respect him, and not because you have to."

"A friend of mine traveled to this country on Survey business three years ago. But he was revealed to be a spy, and he's being held prisoner at a monastery in Shigatse. I'm searching for him."

"And you're traveling with the white man to find your friend?"

"When my friend didn't return," Balram said, "the captain asked me to carry out his mission. I was planning to look for him once I entered Tibet. Unfortunately, the captain decided to accompany me. But my plan remains unchanged. The captain doesn't know. No one does. Only you."

"Easier for you to speak the truth to a stranger than your master."

"You won't be hanged in this country," Balram said. "The Tibetans care even less for the English than you do." He hesitated, touched the compass, then continued, "I know people who can help you start anew, live a good life, in this beautiful country. My uncles have been trading with Tibetans for decades—they have many friends in the Tsangpo valley and even Kham."

"Why is the white man here?"

"What do white men want? To measure the height of a mountain, to note down the color of the mucus spat out by Tibetans and calculate the length of their stools."

The pony flared its nostrils.

"And Shigatse is the white man's destination?" Chetak asked.

"Lhasa, if we don't suffer any more setbacks," Balram said,

wondering why he couldn't be truthful. Perhaps Chetak had been right and he did respect the captain. Perhaps after years of being yoked he didn't know how to be free, like a homing pigeon that forsook the sky for a cage.

"You imagine your captain will let you rescue your friend?" Chetak asked now. "And how will you free him when you have a white man in your party? You just said Tibetans don't take kindly to foreigners and their helpers."

Balram tugged at the lead to encourage the pony to stay still.

"You don't have a plan, only a vague notion," Chetak said, and Balram felt as if Gyan was speaking to him in Chetak's voice. "Listen to me, I can help. Let me help."

"What can you do?" Balram asked, incredulous. "And you want to help me, a stranger? Why?"

"Not just you," Chetak said, "but the men, and that child, all of whom you brought along knowing full well they could die."

"I may be slow," Balram said, "but even I'm not dull-witted enough to believe the words of a thief."

14.

2 SEPTEMBER 1869
....

Dear Ethel,

I HAVE ADDRESSED YOU often enough in my dreams, but words come slowly to me now that I have permitted myself to write to you. No pigeons, horsemen, or ships can ferry my message to you who died on this very day four years ago, news of which I received several weeks later, thereby imprinting on my mind two different times of your passing: one that your husband recorded in his letter (at which moment, you, still alive in my mind, were admiring the lace collars of your eldest daughter's dress, seasoning a slice of cold beef with anchovies, and asking your doctor if a more effective treatment for your illness couldn't be contrived), and the other when I read the letter in Calcutta, your husband's words traveling like splinters under my skin, the blood that gushed out of your mouth with your last breath lapping the edges of the paper. Not having witnessed your death, I was at a disadvantage; you stubbornly remained alive in my mind. I wished your husband's letter had never reached me. On some days, I pretended it hadn't. At last, when I visited your grave, I heard you speak to me, and I welcomed the haunting. I was guilty. I ought to be punished.

What is this grief that afflicts me so? Beyond childhood, we spent so little time together that I ought not to perceive your absence. But I think of you every day.

I remember you as a child, delicate and pretty, with blue

eyes and hair so golden it shone like the sun even on those days the sky was heavy with snow. I wished I looked like you. When I was ten I kept up a fast for thirty days, forsaking those dishes dear to my palate, pleading with God that on the thirty-first of that month my features should dissolve and rearrange to resemble yours; how bitterly disappointed I was at the end of that exercise.

We weren't always well behaved with each other. I remember Mother pinching my forearm in the mistaken belief that I had pushed you in the garden and caused you to fall, even though you had tripped over a root or a shovel and I had been reading in the library. That day you did not correct Mother, perhaps because our father had praised my intellect the previous evening, having found me perusing volumes of the *Asiatic Journal* (already I was curious about the country to which half of me belonged even though I was not ready to admit it), and you, in a fit of jealousy perhaps, sought consolation by causing me distress. But on other occasions you persuaded Mother to be less severe with me.

I told you little about my travels (I, who cannot stop speaking to you now even though you are dead). Do you remember that soon after I married, I visited Crete and Constantinople? In that short time, Mother collected stories about Frederick's infidelities from maids and neighbors. In all these stories, there appeared to be a familiar figure of a distant cousin of Frederick's who facilitated the upkeep of the house in my absence. You lowered your eyes as Mother questioned his conduct and listed my failings. I imagined you were repulsed by my lack of attachment to my own husband or to any of you. When I inquired about your health after you buried your stillborn son, you said I was fortunate to have no children who required my attention; having never learned to love, I would never have to fear loss. I didn't tell you this, but it was painful to hear those words then and, as you can see now, it was untrue.

I am grateful we grew closer after Mother's death, and your illness, two ships forced to collide by the intensity of passing storms. Will you stay with her, your husband asked me when your disease was deemed incurable. Perhaps he thought that I, a childless woman of a certain age, had no prospects other than directing the emptying of your chamber pot.

My refusal to return required an explanation. I did not offer one then, but I can do so now.

To look after you, I would have had to give up my life, which others saw as wasteful. What could I possibly lose if I did not spend another year with Buddhist monks? But in your mortality I saw my own time on earth diminishing. The future where all things were possible and stretched toward the horizon was suddenly curtailed to the distance of an arm's length. A woman with children can hope to see her dreams fulfilled by her progeny; she continues to live in her children after her death—as you do, Ethel, as you do—but what would be my achievement, my legacy? Would it be my letters to you about traveling through Tibet, which brought me my own share of fame even if they could not rival the fanciful stories of male explorers who confronted such danger—polar ice, savages, cannibals, dragons, storms—that their return home was seen as a miracle? Would it be my novel that only a few read?

Perhaps my greatest achievement would have been to stay at your side—tending to your sores, wiping your sweat-stained forehead, placing roses by your bedside to alleviate the sour smell of sickness. Instead I chose to continue my travels, my writing. I wanted my name to be remembered. (I forgot that those of my gender ought not to share in the aspirations of men.)

I did not understand then that our best selves need not be shown to, or appreciated by, others. Those who serve silently, at home as in the battlefield, without desire for fame, without plaques engraved with their names, are no less worthy of praise than a general whose chest is decorated with medals or the adventurer after whom mountains, rivers, or islands are named.

As I write this letter, M—— asks if his name appears in my journal. I do not say this, but I am inclined to believe that I only want to write about you. As if by writing and rewriting, however incoherent the sentences or the sentiments expressed, I might forgive myself, and find a way to earn your forgiveness too.

(I don't imagine this letter will be printed. But I shall not cross out these words as I have before. Dearest Ethel, on the anniversary of your death, in lieu of flowers at your grave, I offer you these measly words.)

AFTER A FEW DAYS of rest, they resumed their journey toward Lhasa. The wind nudged them forward, but they didn't walk as much as limp, Katherine troubled by her moody spine and Mani by his bruised ankle despite the support of the walking stick that she had lent him. She wondered why the aches in her had stilled in Chetak's presence, though she didn't dwell on it.

They crossed a valley bounded by grass-covered hills and a small lake whose waters turned out to be brackish and unfit for human consumption. The sun was sharp in her eyes, and burned the exposed skin on her hands. "Sometimes I feel this land wants to kill us," Katherine said.

"In that unlikely event, I hope you'll be liberated from the cycle of births and rebirths," Mani said, rephrasing the words of a Tibetan prayer Katherine had heard in the monasteries of Kalimpong.

"One can never win an argument against Buddhists," Katherine said, "because they consider all things in the world, even the argument itself, impermanent."

"There's comfort in it, don't you think? It's good if you can accept that nothing lasts forever. I have never understood why this knowledge makes men nervous."

Katherine couldn't tell if Mani's words were intended to rebuke her, she who wanted to leave a legacy and refused to vanish without a trace. Most unbecoming, for a woman to harbor such ambitions, but was there a person on earth who didn't tend to a garden or their children or their paintings, however inelegant or lacking their creations, in the hope they would outlast them? Still, she didn't want to argue with Mani. They were marching toward Lhasa, the sacred city was only a few weeks away even at their slow pace, and after everything they had been through, wasn't that in itself some kind of a miracle?

THEY REACHED THE TOP of a hill and a settlement came into view, ghostly and cracked, like the worn shell of a long-dead animal. The houses looked empty and yet Katherine could have sworn faces crowded the windows, the wan faces of spirits.

Mani began climbing down the hill, wincing each time his injured foot struck the ground more forcefully than he intended. Her walking stick offered him support, but it was insufficient to steady his gait.

"Let's stop for a while," she said.

"And spend the night here? Where will we even camp?"

His monk's equanimity was waning. He must be in more pain than he was willing to admit. Katherine felt sorry for him, but she wished he could bear it like a man and show no outward signs of discomfort.

The houses in the settlement were decrepit, doors loosening from hinges, the wind hissing through broken windows, scorpions and other symbols painted on the walls for protection fading in the sun.

"Nomads must use these houses in the summer," Mani said to her. All places in Tibet appeared to be as familiar to him as the rooms of his own home, where he must be able to find a bowl or a purse filled with cowries without stumbling in the dark. Whereas Katherine hadn't stayed in one house long enough for her feet to know where the carpet was liable to be worn or for her nose to tell her where the wainscotting had moldered.

Toward the end of the ghost settlement was a house with diamond-shaped, dried yak-dung cakes stacked neatly around its flat roof. Prayer flags tied to twigs were planted in its four corners. Katherine approached the boundary wall around the house and saw two Tibetan mastiffs in the courtyard. Registering her presence in the same instant, they let out a series of terrifying barks.

A middle-aged man rushed out of the house holding a butcher's knife. Mani bowed deeply, speaking in Tibetan. His words seemed to reassure the man, who calmed the dogs and opened the gate to invite them inside. Perhaps he took Mani for a monk, a misconception Mani must not have tried to correct.

Katherine pulled up the collars of her robe and pushed her bonnet as far down as her eyes, and hoped no one would pay her any attention. Gray hair yellowing in the sun, hands and feet and mouth blistered so that she was more blood than skin, she was becoming unrecognizable even to herself. She didn't imagine anyone could now spot the English half of her degraded form.

Like the house in which they had stayed in Garbyang, the red, wooden front door here too opened into a stable for yaks, and dzos and dzomos, the Tibetan names for the progeny of cows and yaks, cooped up as closely as chickens in a crate. Attacks by wolves or snow leopards must be commonplace here, else the family would have kept the animals outside.

A short staircase led up to the floor where the business of life was being attended to with as much bustle as could be imagined, the man's family numbering four or seven; no sooner had Katherine learned the features of one face than another one appeared. Four daughters, the farmer told Mani, the girls prone to chatter and laughter. Their mother was a quiet woman who stirred a pot of tsampa over the fire, her expression unvarying as her mother-in-law issued a stream of instructions about the pace at which the ladle ought to move and the amount of yak butter to be added. Katherine tried to rest her back against the wall and knocked against one of the many pails of water the women must have fetched from a stream or a lake.

Mani told the family's fortunes, seeing their future in the loops that the smoke drew in the stale air, which appeared to impress the Tibetans, even the mother-in-law, who became more subdued the longer he spoke. Unable to keep pace with the rapidness of his Tibetan, Katherine studied the faces of the daughters. Their hair was plaited into several thin braids and threaded with turquoise and orange gemstones and green strings. Their silver and copper necklaces, shimmering when they caught the light of the fire, clinked as they leaned forward, eager not to miss any of Mani's words. On occasion their elbows nudged each other, and feet tucked under skirts were brought out to kick a shin if a smile appeared when other faces remained grave. Katherine found herself tumbling back into the past; she was seated at the dinner table with Mother upbraiding her for picking up a slice of carrot in the gravy soup with her fingers, and Ethel mimicking her action in jest or solidarity, much to their mother's chagrin.

Now Katherine looked at Mani through the eyes of the Tibetan girls, and thought they might find him handsome. He had lost a considerable amount of weight, and appeared gaunt to her, but others perceiving his sharp cheekbones might see in their prominence a sign of high breeding or royal blood. He hadn't shaved his head in weeks and his hair had grown thick and black, retaining an unnatural gleam. The hem of Mani's robe was stiff with mud, yet he had an air of distinction. Her own appearance was so disheveled that none of the Tibetans exhibited any curiosity about her and accepted her without question as Mani's mother.

"The seasons, days and nights, the waxing and waning moons," Mani said, "they remind us everything is impermanent. Death is always with us."

He pointed at a yak skull above a trunk, the Tibetan prayer *Om*

Mani Padme Hum written in black letters in a single column across what must once have been the animal's face. Its presence reminded Katherine of the Egyptian practice of bringing out a skeleton in the middle of a feast to remind guests of death, which Montaigne had written about in one of his essays.

Even the giddy daughters looked somber by the time Mani finished speaking. A meal was then served. The farmer's wife, who proved to be a remarkably strong woman, capable of lifting the cauldron of tsampa with barely a crease on her forehead, said it was difficult to purchase meat, the marketplace in the nearest town being some distance away. Though the family owned yaks, and hare and other small game could be easily caught, like most Tibetans they must have balked at the thought of slaughtering animals with their own hands. The woman apologized to Mani for the simple fare, and Mani said they were grateful for the food and shelter.

Afterward they were taken to a small room where blankets, flour, and what appeared to be foul-smelling cheese made from yak milk were stored. Katherine was offered two sacks spread out on the floor, while Mani secured a much more comfortable-looking mattress comprised of several blankets arranged one on top of the other, a bed suitable for a monk.

When the rattle of vessels and jewelry had hushed and coughs had given way to snores, Mani offered his bed to Katherine. But she declined it. "Is your foot still troubling you?" she asked.

"Only a little," he said. "We have been lucky, in spite of everything. I could have died, but I didn't. The gods want me to live so that I can be a monk. As soon as we return home—"

"If anything, we have had terrible luck."

"I received English medicine in the middle of nowhere, thanks to your friend."

"Why, is he not your friend too?" Katherine asked, her tone as impassive as she could manage.

"Let's not pretend I'm a child who can't understand what he's seeing."

Katherine wanted to protest, then decided against it.

"To have come across this family in a deserted village," Mani said, "that's good fortune too."

"Village? You said this is a summer settlement for nomads."

"Mother, were you not listening when they spoke?"

Katherine, too embarrassed to admit to her superficial knowledge of Tibetan, remained silent. The smell of yak cheese flavored the air and gave it the consistency of haze. Now Mani could see that she was far from the learned woman she professed to be. She wasn't a scholar of Tibetan language or Buddhist scriptures or the works of the Stoic philosophers whose words she used to bolster herself in times of distress. Her knowledge of all philosophies and religions and languages was rudimentary. Why, she only had the barest understanding of how she ought to conduct herself in her home and outside, all these matters that came to others naturally but for her required much deliberation.

Through the cracks in the windows gusts of cold wind slipped into the room, lightening the odor of cheese and causing the stacks of blankets to sigh and floorboards to creak.

"They asked me to exorcize the ghosts in their village," Mani said. His voice was small, as if he expected her to ridicule him, but Katherine thought of the ghosts at the windows, thought, *I didn't know others could see them too.*

In the story Mani went on to tell her, the village had once been prosperous, or as prosperous as a Tibetan village could be, rich in barley, yaks, sheep, and goats. Unexpectedly a bandit raid had left them poorer. Just as they were beginning to pay off their debts, they were attacked again. This time, the villagers were prepared for a battle, unlike the first instance when their only option had been surrender. But the bandits had guns and swords and the villagers only had sticks and sickles. The battle ended in an easy victory for the invaders. Deaths were many.

The village fell into a deep mourning. Vultures flocked to the hills in such great numbers to feed on the dead they blocked the sun. Grief encased the houses like clay, stifling breaths and hope. Those who survived began to see dead children stealing yak butter from pots. Dead husbands scribbled messages to their wives in the soot that stained the bottoms of pans. Mothers who had hurled themselves in front of their children to save them from bullets trailed fresh blood around the house. Driven mad by these visions, the remaining villagers fled their homes, flinging open doors and windows for ghosts.

"The farmer who lives here lost two sons," Mani said. "He says he can't leave because their ghosts are trapped here."

"And he requested you to perform an exorcism?"

"On the one hand he wants his sons' souls to be freed, but on the other he encourages his family to stay in this house even though it's most unsuitable for them, being so isolated, because he believes the departed are here with them. Unlike most people, the farmer finds the presence of ghosts comforting. Even if he won't admit it." Mani sipped water from a bowl the Tibetans had left for him; his voice was weak from having spoken too much. "His sons had terrible deaths," he said, "which is why they wander the earth as ghosts. The farmer should have organized the correct rites for the passage of their spirits a long time ago. I told him so. It's futile to hold on to those who are gone."

"Easy for you to say," Katherine said, then realized she had spoken with more malice than she intended.

THE NEXT MORNING THEY set off in the solid darkness of the hours before dawn. The women of the house were milking the yaks that had already fed their babies. The daughters urged Mani to stay for tea, eyes averted from his face, their smiles shy in the golden light of lanterns. Mani demurred politely.

Away from the settlement he stumbled and would have fallen if not for Katherine grabbing his robe, nearly tearing it. "You're still weak," she said. "We should have rested for another day."

"This journey has changed you," he said. "You're behaving like my mother, saying what she would have."

"Don't be a fool. It will be difficult for me to secure a new servant, and to train him."

Mani didn't look offended. Katherine disliked these discussions, so common in the East, about duty and responsibility and sacrifice for one's family.

They walked past fields that had grown wild, the ears of barley tinted brass. In other villages there must be harvest festivals, and the sounds of drums and prayers and men cheering at a horse race, but here there was only the wind fussing around the ripening grain, and heavy stalks bowing contritely. Dark skeins of geese flew above them, scribbling the letter V in the sky, a parting gift on their way home.

"The Tibetan family didn't suspect you," Mani said. He paused to rest his injured foot on a boulder. "You look like us, you're now one of us."

In that moment Katherine was six once again and on the ship from Calcutta to Portsmouth that was carrying indigo, ivory, silk, and pepper, all more valuable than her. She had wandered away from the family with whom she had been sent off, onto a deck where she wasn't meant to be, and a pale, yellow-haired woman had shrieked and called on the crew to remove her, as if Katherine's complexion was as contagious as eruptive fever. How clearly she could hear those screams even today; how vividly she remembered the colors—the blue of the sea, the marbled waves, the white light of the sun.

"Did you know your mother?" Mani asked her now.

"Why wouldn't I know her?"

"Your father married your mother?" Mani said. "I suppose this was not uncommon at one time."

The boy meant no disrespect, Katherine could tell, though he could have just as well tainted her with a tar brush. Wasn't that what they said in England of people like her? The only surprise was that a servant had the temerity to raise the subject, but whatever boundaries there had been between her and natives had vanished on this tour, perhaps because Ethel's death had left her deranged.

"My father never told me who she was, and now he has been dead for over thirty years," Katherine said, deciding there was no reason to lie any more to Mani. She didn't care if he mentioned it to the Almora deputy collector; she could always refute it, call Mani a liar, and no one would believe a native's words over an Englishwoman's, even one of dubious parentage like her.

"It could have been someone you knew well," Mani said. "The woman in Almora I told you about, the one with an unfortunate reputation, she thought she was English. But just before her marriage, she found out that the ayah who had cared for her was in fact her mother. And then the man she was meant to marry—he was an officer in the Infantry—he broke off their engagement."

Katherine had never thought her ayah could be her mother. Impossible. The woman who gave birth to her couldn't have lived in the same house as her father, even as a servant. It would have caused the wildest rumors to spread. It was too much of a risk. Katherine couldn't remember her father speaking to the ayah differently or treating her with affection.

Time had all but erased the ayah's features from Katherine's memory. She was *ayah*, without a name, more a shape than a person; rough fingers that had brought a spoonful of soup to her mouth when she had been ill; a voice that had whispered, "Tara, look at the sky" as a rainbow hurriedly scribbled over gray cloud; a shadow sneaking the rich Indian sweets Katherine liked from the market into her room at night. There was something else: a tearstained kiss on her cheeks on the banks of the Hooghly before Katherine was taken to the ship sailing to England, a whisper in her ears: *goodbye, my daughter, don't forget me.* Or perhaps the ayah had said *beti* as an endearment and now Katherine's imagination was fashioning a blood tie.

Waiting for her in England was her mother, who had visited her husband in India twice in the six years of Katherine's life. "Your sister is home," she had stiffly told Ethel, and Ethel, only eight years old at the time, had taken her hand and said Katherine was too small to have been without their mother all this while, and with Father always traveling. Now that Katherine was in London, she would no longer be alone, and Katherine had said, "I wasn't alone, I had ayah." Perhaps Mother had grimaced then, perhaps that was the exact moment Mother decided she didn't have the goodness of heart to love a bastard child, but it had made Ethel tender toward Katherine in those early days before Father joined them, when it was just the three of them by the fire in the evening, words crackling under her fingers as Katherine hunched in front of a book and Ethel chattered about dolls and dresses. If Katherine hadn't missed her ayah, hadn't been scalded by Mother's glowering looks, it was because even as a child she had recognized Ethel's love for her as sisterly, edged with distrust and envy on some days perhaps, but generous and honest too in its own way. Who would ever love her like that again?

The ayah must be long dead. On Katherine's return to Calcutta at nineteen, she had inquired after her, only to be told the ayah had left for her village in the Punjab or the Himalaya, or the plains by the Ganga. The ayah had vanished as if she had never existed.

"I'm being ill-mannered," Mani said now, drawing her out of her reverie. "No one would dare ask such questions of their owner."

"You're a free man."

"My mother and sisters would disagree," he said, no bitterness in his tone, only affection. "They think they own me."

They set out again and, as they walked, she tried, and failed, to remember the ayah's face. The topography of the land made it difficult to think. Their feet sank into sand—the mountains had bewilderingly given way to a desert. Their footprints unsettled the rippling patterns the wind had drawn on the white knolls. The sand was pristine, with the appearance of silk, but it scratched her eyes and tongue, spilled into her boots, and clawed at her blisters. It was as if the land was reminding her of its ability to transmogrify. What appeared solid was in fact water.

Mani, with his sore ankle, had to crawl up on all fours, the walking stick proving to be more hindrance than help. Katherine held his elbow. Clutching each other for support, they managed to clamber up and down mounds. Tears streamed from her eyes, not only from the wind and the sand but also from the ache in her spine. How was this possible? There were snowy peaks in the distance, and sand below their feet. Farther ahead sparkled a sheet of blue-green water that Mani told her was the Horse River, the upper stream of a river

Tibetans called by different names, though mostly they referred to it as the Tsangpo, the River.

"All this sand is from the Tsangpo?" Katherine asked.

"In winter when the water level falls, the wind carries the sand away from its banks and deposits it here," Mani said.

They slowly made it to the river. Antelopes grazed in a green pasture on the other side.

"We're near the path to Lhasa now," Mani said. "Rather than march with traders, we will walk on trails that run parallel to it. We'll meet fewer travelers, but we'll be close to the main route. You'll be able to find help quickly if something goes wrong."

"Very good," Katherine said. She shut her eyes, exhausted. Imprinted behind her eyelids were the triangular hills of Tibet, white clouds smudging their peaks, sand and dust and pebbles scattering at her feet, the ground shifting, the earth itself in perpetual motion such that her destination hobbled away from her each time it seemed to be within her reach.

IN THE EVENING, AS Katherine wrote in her notebook, she realized that Ethel had died on this very date four years ago. How could she have forgotten it? (The date she had scribbled atop the day's journal entry might not be correct, but Ethel had died in the beginning of September, something that hadn't occurred to Katherine until now.) She would write to Ethel tonight, say what she hadn't said all these years. The wind taunted the flames of the fire that Mani had kindled such that her sentences, like her thoughts, were always half in shadow. At this hour the words arrived on the page with the intensity of a riptide.

"Do I find a mention in your book?" Mani asked.

"You won't be in any danger because of me. I have not taken your name."

"That's not why I asked."

"I have acknowledged your help without revealing your identity.

I'm aware I wouldn't have got this far without you. I'm grateful the Almora deputy collector recommended you to me."

"He's a good man, but I'd rather work for a woman."

"That's considerate of you."

"A learned woman like you, is what I meant. Once I accompanied an old woman from Jaipur to Kailas and she spent the whole journey talking about how wealthy she was, how wealthy her sons were, and how wealthy her grandchildren would be, and I had to tell her that if she didn't stop speaking, word of her wealth would reach bandits, and we would be attacked. But even that wasn't sufficient warning. She continued to whisper to me about her riches. Imagine traveling to this sacred land and thinking only of holding on to your diamonds or kingdoms."

Katherine's bones ached. The temperature had dropped rapidly, and she could smell autumn in the threat of snow advancing through the cold air. She had previously witnessed how winter arrived in Tibet, one night the air crisp and biting, and the next morning a blanket of snow announcing the change of seasons, the bleak wind like an axe reaping the hillsides.

As if he had sensed her fears, Mani said, "It won't snow for at least another month."

"Did you read it in the smoke?" she asked.

"Time for us to sleep, I think. We're both tired."

Mani curled up under a blanket by the fire. She wondered if she had offended him by mocking his predictions. It had seemed to her that she had remade herself in this journey, but perhaps these changes in her were so small as to be invisible.

The night sky rippled as if a stone had been cast at its center. Each concentric circle radiating from the core was a mesmeric shade of pink, purple, or blue. Katherine lay down to sleep. Through a thin gap between the flaps of her tent she saw stars tumbling toward the earth. The wind rocked the tent. She sat up to pin the entrance folds together, and outside she saw standing across from her tent and observing her with blue eyes an apparition in gray and white.

A decade from now the weight of her guilt might become easier to carry; just as the muscles strengthened each time one lifted a pail of water, rendering the task easier in due course, the mind too could become accustomed to sorrow. But Katherine saw now that there was no possibility of erasure, neither of guilt nor ghosts. Until she joined them, the dead would pay her daily visits. Like the farmer in the cursed village, she too ought to welcome the haunting. She ought to be glad that unlike her ayah's, Ethel's face was still clear to her. She wanted Ethel to remain in her for as long as she was alive, Ethel's golden curls casting dappled shadows on her skin as a tree might trace its patterns onto the earth in the sunlight.

"Ethel," she whispered, shifting to the side to make space for her sister inside the tent. "I'm glad to see you."

15.

CAMP AT SHIGATSE—A RECONNAISSANCE—
THE MONASTERY UP A HILL—A SHOCKING DEATH—
A WAKEFUL NIGHT—DEPARTURES

———

THEY WERE AT LAST IN SHIGATSE, BUT TIME WARPED SUCH THAT it seemed to Balram that they had been marching forever and had only left Mana yesterday. Must have been the beginning of summer when he bid farewell to Durga and the children, the days warm, sunlight stretching to the darkest corners of every room, wildflowers blossoming in the cracks on slate roofs, and the wind fragrant with the scent of ripening fruit that split open as they plunged from trees to the ground. Now it was a cold September morning, the sky low and gray, a sharp wind scattering dust that stung like bees. Pebbles of ice, separated from floes upstream, lapped the banks of the Tsangpo, a notice of the unfavorable weather awaiting them.

Gyan was here, but where? Atop every hill loomed a monastery where he could be found. Balram couldn't release his friend's name into the wind and expect a trail to flash past him like an arrow. The world now seemed too big to him, and the town bigger, even though he knew the alleys where the best bargains for chhang and yak meat could be had, or where the monks gathered for butter tea in the afternoons. As a child, he had traveled with his uncles to the markets in Shigatse and seen manacled prisoners being made to beg. Later, as a spy, he had watched Tibetans welcome envoys from Kashmir with khatas, the white scarves draped around the necks of visitors and gifted as offerings at monasteries. But now Balram felt as if he was seeing Shigatse for the first time.

The captain walked up and down the river, calculating the

altitude, or the depth and width of the Tsangpo. With no Tibetan settlement nearby he could move freely. "I would like to visit the Tashi Lhunpo monastery," he said to Balram.

"But sir——"

"It's not pertinent to our expedition, I'm aware."

The captain turned his gaze toward the town. From where they stood, they could see the Shigatse dzong, painted in red and white like the Potala Palace, embedded into a dust-colored hill. Somewhere below this fort was the Tashi Lhunpo, around whose cobbled alleys traders sold tsampa and meat and fabrics, the wares becoming less earthly and more mystical the closer the merchants were to the monastery. At its gates the streets smelled of incense and the yak butter used to light lamps, which pilgrims bought as offerings. Balram remembered those scents from past visits and had no intention of revisiting them.

"A century ago, the Panchen Lama granted George Bogle an audience at the monastery," the captain said. The wind moved through the river and pieces of ice clinked against rocks, and the captain pushed his rosary and prayer wheel into the pockets of his coat. "You must have heard about Bogle?" he continued in the doubtful tone of a teacher who thought his students were dull. "Bogle was Warren Hastings's private secretary, and Hastings was India's first governor general."

"Wasn't Hastings impeached for corruption?" Balram asked.

"Acquitted. A clever man, a real diplomat is what he was. He dispatched Bogle to Shigatse, and the Panchen Lama welcomed him. Shows you the Tibetans were once friendly to my people."

"Now that they can see how the kingdom of Sikkim and the Dooars have changed under the English, they don't want that for their country."

"You speak as if you disapprove of us."

"Of course not, sir."

"In any case, our man Bogle, twenty-eight years old at the time, stayed in Shigatse for much longer than his mission warranted. He wrote in his journal that his time there was like a *fairy dream, a perfect illusion.* He wrote, *I could not bid adieu to the lama without a heavy heart.* Now, tell me, Balram, does that sound to you like a man saying farewell to a learned monk? Or a man who can't bear to leave a lover behind?" The captain paused for Balram to answer and, when he didn't, said, "Bogle is believed to have had a Tibetan wife. Forbidden love has its own appeal, I suppose."

Balram's eyes flitted to Harish and Rana, sitting side by side, leaning close to each other and whispering, the temptations they didn't decline so obvious he wondered why others hadn't commented on it. He thought of Gyan, the words unspoken between the two of them, and Durga, always Durga on his mind too, the scent of the flowers with which she washed her hair floating toward him now like a spirit seething at his unfaithful musings.

"I don't think it's a good idea for you to come with me to the market," Balram told the captain. "I'll purchase sheep and provisions from a merchant I trust—it will be a quiet transaction. Your presence will raise questions, alert spies. You don't want to be captured, sir, not after two men died for you."

The captain looked startled, as if he had forgotten Chand and Naga, but he regained his poise quickly. "More important than trust is the price the merchant quotes for the sheep and food. We're facing an unexpectedly large expense."

"I'll strike a bargain," Balram said, and was surprised by the ease with which he could lie. He felt for the compass in the pockets of his coat and its coldness seeped into his blood through layers of fabric like a leech's mouth fastened to his skin.

He pulled off his boots and woollen socks. In front of him, the Tsangpo split into slender blue-gray threads, separated by rose-colored, sandy islands. By a bend in the mountains half a mile away, the threads merged again. At the camp Ujjal began to sing, with Harish and Rana beating accompaniment to his song on upturned bowls that served as drums, ladles for mallets. The men looked thin, mere outlines of their former selves. Terrified, and yet awaiting the next calamity with a pinch of snuff, song, and dance.

Boots in hand, Balram forded the river, its icy currents causing him to gasp in shock. In the distance, Shigatse was enveloped in a coppery light.

Once on the other side of the river, Balram turned back to glance at the camp, and he wished the bearers would abscond before he returned so that he wouldn't be held accountable for their fortunes. Black granite mountains rose behind their tents, wads of gray clouds skimming the peaks. The clouds seemed to be animated by more than vapor, assuming the shapes of dragons, serpents, and demons. They cast drifting shadows on the slopes, which flickered in his vision. For an uncanny moment, he felt as if he was the one moving while all else was still. Then he blinked and the world resumed its normal course.

THE RIVER'S SANDY BANKS gave way to inclines. Around the hills Tibetans had painted short white ladders that the dead could climb to reach a higher realm. Balram thumped his forehead against a boulder. Its rough edges stabbed his skin. What course could he take? He would have to betray the men and the captain, or Gyan yet again.

Maybe you won't find me, Gyan said.

On the river's eddies, coracles spun wildly as they ferried grain from fields to markets. Wild geese, beaks half-open, gray feathers almost black against the ashen morning sky, trailed the boats. Their lack of fear was justified by the tepid response from the oarsmen, who hissed when the birds swooped toward the sacks but didn't swing an oar at them, perhaps guided by their Buddhist belief that one mustn't cause harm to others.

In the foothills nestled houses with yak skulls nailed above red wooden doors. On the dung cakes pressed into the walls were the imprints of the fingers that had shaped them into circles. Through half-open doors that led into courtyards Balram saw women pounding barley, watched by dogs and goats. He asked them if they had heard about a merchant from Mana who had vanished near Shigatse. Perhaps the man had exhibited an interest in the Tsangpo. Perhaps he had studied its currents like a lunatic intent on committing the quicksilver movements of ripples to memory. He asked the questions methodically, but his heart beat uneven rhythms and he felt light-headed. The women were gentle and smiling, and offered him yak butter tea and dried strips of yak meat. They told him nothing of note.

The sky darkened. Through a gap in the clouds crepuscular rays tumbled toward the earth. Balram passed barley fields where farmers tilled the land with horses, and they too greeted him kindly, in the hospitable way of Tibetans, but they had no news of Gyan. Two men came down a mountain with their flock of sheep and a dog that expertly rounded up strays. They listened to Balram's questions with interest, named all the monasteries in the hills around them. They hadn't heard of anyone being imprisoned either.

For the next few hours, Balram climbed up hills and knocked on the doors of monasteries and bowed before the statues of the Buddha in prayer halls and admired murals and thangkas and visited the quarters of monks. He found no trace of Gyan. Walking down a hill from the fifth monastery, Balram thought he could comb the villages in Shigatse for Gyan for another day or two while claiming to the captain that he was yet to find a good price for grains and sheep. But then the captain would fret about the Swede. Balram would no longer be able to delay their march to the Tsangpo gorge, a near impenetrable whorl of rocks and rapids that spelled death to visitors. Perhaps there was some cruel comfort to be found in knowing that the fate of the bearers, whether left to his fancy or the whims of the captain, were unlikely to diverge.

Balram reached the foot of yet another hill. As he inspected his surroundings, a group of dogs barked at him viciously. He jumped up on a boulder. "Quiet, quiet," he shouted at them. A lone guard standing outside a circle of watchtowers whistled at the dogs and they dashed toward him. Balram used the distraction to scamper up the hill. Stones were laid haphazardly on the track for ease of passage, which suggested the trail led to either a monastery or the ancestral house of a high-ranking Lhasa official.

Two small boys dressed in mud-crusted woollens, their cheeks as red as apples, hopped down the steps. A Tibetan mastiff followed them, friendly in their presence though in size the animal reached the top of their heads. It sniffed Balram's boots and turned up its nose as if it sensed his feet were still damp from the river crossing. Balram asked the boys where they lived, and if they had met any traders and pilgrims from Garhwal or Kumaon. They chatted with him easily, asking him questions instead of replying to his queries.

"Where are you from?"

"Are you here to trade coral?"

"What about turquoise beads?"

"Sugar?"

"You want to buy a horse?"

Their lack of shyness made Balram think of Inder, who had never as much as uttered a word in its entirety. *Why can't Inder be like these boys,* he thought, and shame branded his skin at once. Inder hadn't chosen to be this way; his imperfections weren't his fault but that of the gods, or Balram himself.

Preoccupied by these thoughts, he barely paid attention when the boys told him that a man who looked like him was imprisoned in a monastery up the hill. He was alerted to the import of these words only because the dog licked his hands, jolting him into the present.

"The man you speak of, did you see him by the river?" Balram asked.

"Do you have the sea where you live?"

It took a while for Balram to gather from the boys that their village had had an unusual visitor, two years ago, three years ago, or maybe it was before they were born—on this count they quarreled, the mastiff punctuating their raised voices with its barks. When it quieted, they said the man had the peculiar habit of carving messages onto logs, or ladles, and dropping these into the river. Later the man was revealed to be a spy. Soldiers were about to shoot him dead but the Old Man Lama with a stoop, from the monastery up the hill on which they stood, said the spy should be imprisoned, not killed. Then the dog chased after a hare and the children darted down the steps after it.

A drizzle had begun by the time Balram reached the monastery, a modest dwelling set in a nook on the hill, made of stone. Green mountains, half concealed by clouds, loomed behind it. A gate opened into the monastery's courtyard, in the middle of which a pole stood tall and upright, prayer flags tied around it with saffron ribbons. Next to it, juniper incense burned in a cylinder, raindrops flattening the tendrils of scented gray smoke. Two small outbuildings flanked the monastery, housing the monks perhaps, burrowing into the hillside so that there seemed to be no separation between boulder and brick. Narrow stairs, near-vertical like trees, led up to the prayer hall, its entrance watched over by statues of snow lions installed above the door and protector deities painted on the walls.

Rain soaked the prayer flags, and it was beginning to saturate Balram's coat too. Something like hope soared in his veins, but he tried to pin it down as if it was a dead butterfly inside a bell jar, its existence solely for the purpose of ornamentation.

A monk wearing a maroon robe and a pronounced stoop came out of the tenement to Balram's right. His skin was without wrinkles and his face was youthful, but he could walk only because two young monks gripped his elbows on either side, acting as his crutches. Rain soldered their clothes to their skin.

In Balram's imagination Gyan's rescue had entailed soldiers and pitched battles and fires, screams and blood and tears. Instead there was only this, the steadiness of the rain, the water like a cold snake crawling down his neck, his clothes sticking to his skin that burned with a feverish warmth, these odd, contrasting sensations that could only be caused by fear swarming his brain.

Balram told the monks he had traveled from Mana. The elderly lama paused, black eyes scrutinizing his face as if he could see Gyan in him, the Gyan who lived in his head. "Come along," the lama said, or something similar; Balram couldn't hear him clearly in the rain. Two more monks joined them, no older than Samarth or Inder, and between them they managed to drag and push the lama over the steep steps to the prayer hall. No elegance or dignity to it, but the lama laughed. *So this is the enemy,* Balram thought, shame carving his cheeks.

They entered the prayer hall lined with rows of red-cushioned wooden seats. The windows were high up on the walls and the light was murky, but the gloom was dispelled at the altar by the tall, gilded statue of the Shakyamuni Buddha, and the quivering flames of butter lamps that revealed divine figures on either side of the statue. The altar itself held incense and offerings, ears of barley, and bowls filled to the brim with water, tea, and tsampa. The murals on the walls, of the Buddha and Bodhisattvas, dissolved into the black paint, mere outlines hinting at the stories they once told.

The lama seemed to have entered the hall to inspect the barley that farmers had deposited in a corner as tax or offering. Cold drafts of air wandered in through the door. Balram directed his glances into the shadows. No Gyan.

After the monk finished his inspection, Balram set down a fistful of coins at the altar as an offering and asked if he could tour the monastery.

"You're not ready to admit the true purpose of your visit," the lama said, and his mysterious words sounded to Balram like one of the voices in his head.

A young monk said he would show Balram around. In a clockwise direction, they circled dark rooms with statues of the Buddha in his various forms, chortens that held the remains of dead high lamas, and a library with ancient manuscripts. Rows of golden flames flickered in enormous lamps that looked like vats. With spatulas monks removed excess wax so that the wicks wouldn't drown in the melted yak butter.

Up a stairway, the monk led Balram to one of the two outbuildings in whose rooms monks went to die. The rain cracked its whip against the walls. A raging wind slammed doors shut. In the darkness Balram could barely see his companion. The small squares of grilled windows on the walls stopped not only intruders but also sunlight. The monk lit a lamp and, in the snatches of flickering light, Balram saw broken steps that led up to a room with a heavy wooden door padlocked from the outside. The curve of the stairs and the shadows crisscrossing it lent the room the appearance of being suspended in air. Balram knew it was an illusion, a consequence of the room being carved out of the hillside. He would have turned away, he almost did, but he was arrested by an inexplicable conviction that Gyan was on the other side of the door. The monk said the tour was over. Balram slowly climbed up the steps, listening for Gyan's voice. Nothing to see there, the monk said. Balram felt foolish.

Months after his father had died, Balram had heard his voice addressing him as if they were in the same room. He had believed his father's soul had delayed its departure to the next life, distrustful that his only child would study, or feed sheep, without instruction. Enmeshed in him was his father's blood, his character, his restlessness, and even now Balram's reflection in the water sometimes startled him because the image that scrutinized him dryly was that of his father. His father had died when he was a child, and he had also never died at all, his presence evident in the shape of Balram's nose, the lines on his forehead, the ache in his heart that could only be relieved by mountains and rivers and solitude. And now the same instinct that had asked him to listen because his father was speaking told him Gyan was here. He felt the heaviness, the certainty, of the knowledge in his body as an animal might sense the earth was about to convulse and flee its cave for the open meadow.

Though the sounds of the rain and the wind made it difficult, Balram inquired about the locked room as loudly as he could. Ignoring the monk's request that they now retrace their steps to the hall, he narrated a story about people who lived in caves in China. These structures carved out of the hillside were more comfortable than the manors white men built, he said. He had a friend named Gyan who, after spending many nights sleeping under the stars during his travels, would dislike life in these caves from which one couldn't see the sky.

Balram hoped his voice would carry across the door, and it must have, because he heard chains rattle and a low wail that could have been a chant or a cry for help. He would have recognized that voice anywhere, in hell or heaven, but maintaining his composure, he asked if he could meet the person in the cave. Was it a monk who had chosen to retire from the world? He attempted to speak in league with the wind, timing his words to coincide with its pauses and completing his sentences before it returned.

The young monk said the man locked behind the door wasn't a lama but a dangerous spy; only those who brought him food had the key to open the door.

Standing on those stairs, listening to the floor creaking in the wind, Balram wondered why he was incapable of action. In his place, the captain—why, any white man—would have freed Gyan by overpowering the monk, who was no more than a scraggy boy, cheeks sprinkled with red pustules and eyes as gentle as a doe's. The captain would have slung Gyan over his shoulder, should he be too frail to run, and dashed out of the monastery and down the steps of the hill, a gun in his hand to deter assailants.

But how could Balram raise his hand against a monk? Faithless, godless he might be, yet he hadn't as much as clouted one of his students who infuriated him. At most he spoke harshly to his son, who didn't deserve his anger. He wasn't the kind of man who would pick up a sword to defend his home from the English, a lack in him that the likes of Chetak would condemn—but he could no more change his traits than the moon could cast its light in the day.

Balram asked to speak to the elderly lama. A monk who had argued against the execution of a spy would listen to reason; he might barter a man's life for coins that would gild the monastery's bare roof.

"I'll come back soon," he said as loudly as he could to reassure Gyan. *Let it be Gyan,* he thought.

BALRAM HURRIED BACK TO the camp. The rain dissolved the world around him as if it was made of clay, but he didn't mind. A miracle had occurred in his life that knew no miracles. Not only had he found Gyan—the particulars the elderly lama shared had confirmed it to him—but he had also negotiated Gyan's release. A portion of the silver and gold coins the captain stored in the hidden compartments of his trunks would buy his friend's freedom. But would the captain part with his money? Would Balram have to lead a mutiny? (And what after that?) He remembered Chetak's words: *You don't have a plan, only a vague notion.*

In the rain the Tsangpo had risen higher than he anticipated, and its waters had submerged the small islands he had seen that morning. Boots held high above his head, Balram stepped into the mud-colored, frothing water. Its arctic sharpness scored his knees, rose to his waist; without warning, shards of ice coalesced as a blade against his neck. He tried to spit out the water that wanted to choke him. The currents wrenched him downstream and he wondered if he should surrender, let the river prize his body apart as in his dream on the night of the bandit raid. He hadn't fought to save his friend's life and had instead arranged a barter—a life for a purse of stolen gold. The river was juror and judge, turnkey and executioner. He welcomed the punishment. The waves, now opaque and as black as the sky, spun him around.

But then the currents pardoned him, pushed him to the shore, and he stood up and tried to comport himself with as much dignity as a man soaked to the bone could muster. A great sorrow he couldn't place lay tangled up in his chest; a hurt in his throat, the thrill of finding Gyan vanishing like light, like warmth. Why did he feel this way now?

In the tent the bearers had assembled in a circle around what could only be a corpse shrouded in a white sheet, the fabric tainted red by the blood seeping into it from the body it enclosed.

I drowned in the river, Balram thought, *and now I am a ghost looking at my own lifeless body.* He clawed at his skin, and blood dusted his nails. The captain knelt by the corpse, hands clasped together in front of his chest as if seeking forgiveness.

"What happened?" Balram asked, his own voice unfamiliar to his ears. The bearers turned toward him. So they could hear him, and so he must be alive. The corpse admonished him with its stillness.

Ujjal and Jagan took Balram aside, acting in tandem as if they were friends. Their voices were preternaturally calm, but they looked pale and their hands shook, and blood and mud stained their coats and boots.

"When it started raining heavily the captain asked us to move the tents away from the river," Jagan said. "Yogi took us to the base of the mountains, to show us a spot he had found for the camp."

"That's when we heard grunts, growls, a rumbling kind of noise," Ujjal said. "We couldn't see very well. Because of the rain. I thought it was"—he uttered something incomprehensible—"but I must have been mistaken."

"He saw a snow leopard," Jagan said.

"Could have been a cloud," Ujjal said. "There was a movement, of a kind, then a boulder came crashing down the mountain. I shouted at everyone to get out of its way, but my warning came too late for Yogi. He tripped as he tried to run. The boulder crushed him."

"Whatever curse stalks us," Jagan said to Balram, "it won't rest until it has snuffed out all our lives. I feel it in my bones." He tapped his elbow. "Compass-wallah, you must convince the captain to turn back. It must be evident, even to him, that this land doesn't want us here— it bucks like a horse to throw us off. And how far is the Tsangpo gorge from here? A month's walk, two months' walk at least, and we have to cross it in winter? Do you think any of us will survive?"

As if he had heard Jagan, the captain turned toward them. Balram squatted next to him, the river in his clothes pooling at his feet.

"We must, funeral, hold for Yogi," the captain said, his Hindustani flustering perhaps under the strain of the day.

"Impossible, sir," Balram said and realized that they had had the same conversation before.

"When Chand died," the captain said, "Yogi asked me not to leave his body to vultures if he was to meet with a similar fate. His family would be aghast, he said."

Outside, the rain changed direction with the wind, falling slanted on the tent. Balram could hear the angry river, the waters hurrying to convey an urgent message to the sea. Inside the tent it felt like they were trapped within the rib cage of a gigantic animal not long dead; in his eyes flashed the image of the sheep whose bones had been licked clean by a snow leopard or a ro-lang, as if by the long tongue of time itself.

The captain stood up.

"We can't, sir," Balram said. He was tired. He didn't want to repeat his objections again.

"Then I will have to pray Yogi forgives me," the captain said.

Balram followed him out of the tent. First the captain stopped by
the makeshift pen where the pony slept and Samarth sat hunched
under a waterproof sheet. The boy's shoulders juddered and his
mouth was open. He looked like he was about to scream, though no
sound came out of his throat. Rudra should have tried to calm him,
but perhaps Rudra didn't feel calm himself. The captain pulled Samarth up to his feet and guided him to his tent, where he offered the
boy a thimbleful of brandy. Samarth sipped it, his face blank as if the
bitter liquid didn't scorch his tongue.

"Is it best if we return now, do you think?" Balram said.

"Preposterous," the captain said. "Three of our men have died,
and this is what you have to say?" He smoothed the heap of blankets
and sheepskins that served as his bed. "I'm saddened that those under
my care have come to depart the world in such a foul way, but I also
know that we have to continue our journey to honor their names. I
don't expect the bearers to understand, but you—you know why this
mission is important to me and the Empire. I can't return home
empty-handed."

Balram admired the captain's resolve; he despised it too. Picking
up Samarth's tumbler, he poured himself a good glug of brandy. He
waited for the captain to censure him—he shouldn't have touched a
white man's possessions without his permission, but these niceties
were long forgotten. The compass was in his pocket, after all.

"Men have achieved great things by faith alone," the captain said.
Whether it was faith in God, or themselves, he didn't say.

NO ONE COULD SLEEP. Outside, the rain swelled the river. How
quiet it had been in the morning; how it roared now, wild and black,
as if reminding Balram of its strength.

And you thought you could pin it down on a map?

Whose voice was that? Not Gyan or Durga; perhaps the gods.

The men sat in a semicircle around the corpse. When alive Yogi had cast a cloud over them with his devotion toward the captain, and now that he was dead they were uneasy because they could only mourn him with the formality one expressed toward a distant colleague. And yet they had spent weeks in such close quarters they knew his secret vices—he scratched his balls and thrust his unclean, fetid fingers into the sugar jar when he thought no one was watching and he claimed to be repulsed by Tibetan women who bathed only once a year, and yet, when they had camped near Mansarovar, they had caught him pleasuring himself behind rocks, watching nomad women gather water. At the holy lake of all places! He must have angered the gods there. The bearers shared these stories without malice and almost with wonder that a man so alive yesterday was today mere gristle and pulverized bone.

"There were twelve bearers at the village of Mana," Jagan said. "And now we are six. The gods are cutting us down."

Even Ujjal didn't dispute his words. The hours ticked past. Mountains creaked. The river wrangled with rocks. Exhaustion caused some of the men to drift toward sleep, but footsteps approached the tent and they sprang up. "Who is it?" they asked each other. They had no weapons apart from Pawan's knives, which the fool refused to take out of his sack. Outside, the sound of slipping feet, a man cursing.

"Must be bandits," Ujjal said.

Balram got up to investigate, only the dim light of a lantern guiding him. The night was a morbid black, but he could tell the river had risen dangerously. On a boulder in front of the tent, water lapping at his feet, stood the figure of a man Balram recognized, though he was sheathed in darkness.

Chetak tended to appear at the most inopportune moment, as if he spent his hours observing their every move. Had he seen Yogi die? Had he come to rescue the men from this disastrous expedition, from Balram? Did he want to steal the captain's gold after pointing him out to Tibetans?

"Took me a while to find you," Chetak said. "Other matters to attend to, unexpected things. I was hoping not to lose sight of your captain—I have a feeling he can help me."

"He'd rather put a bullet through your heart, I suspect."

"We will see who shoots first." No menace in his tone, which was friendly. "Your friend, you found him?"

The lantern's flame died in the wind. "Come inside," Balram said. Better to have a beast in plain sight than in hiding.

The bearers greeted Chetak with relief. Simultaneously Chetak's lips twisted in surprise at the sight of the body. "Someone was killed?" he asked.

"Yogi. You met him," Ujjal said, patting the ground in an invitation to the bandit to join their watch.

"I wish he could have been buried before sundown," Chetak said.

"We don't bury our dead," Ujjal said, looking puzzled.

"Yes, but you can't find wood here," Chetak said. He looked uncomfortable. Balram wondered why.

Chetak dried himself with a shirt he produced from his sack. He said, "It is foolish to follow a white man." He said it matter-of-factly, removing strands of hair from the shirt in his hands. The men gasped, widened their eyes, nudged each other. "Look, you don't have to worry about me," Chetak said. "I knew he was an Englishman the moment I saw him near Mansarovar. I'm not interested in setting Tibetan soldiers after you. If anything, I'm concerned about all of you. And there is a child in your group—where is he?"

"The boy is fine," Balram said. "He's here with his uncle."

To Balram's surprise Mor started to cry, silent tears streaming down his cheeks. Jagan drew circles on his back as if to calm him down.

"It's the captain's fault," Jagan said.

"Not yours," Ujjal said.

"There is no reason for you to be penalized for an Englishman's ambitions," Chetak said. "Look at how they loot our kingdoms. They have taken everything we own. They don't deserve our loyalty."

"Maybe not," Ujjal said.

What was bewildering, and admirable, about Chetak was his ability to assume the accents and gestures of those around him in such a skillful manner that now, looking at him, a stranger would fail to identify him as a visitor to their tent. It was as if he had traveled with their group all along. His expression was grievous when the men stated their fears. Wildness flashed in his eyes that reflected their anxieties. He agreed the men ought to go back to their wives and children. He claimed to know Mor's cousin, and the holy man who lived in Ujjal's village to whom all the children were expected to donate a portion of their sweets and fruits. He spoke about deaths, ghosts, and miracles. The men looked upon him as a friend. They told him the captain's motivations for exploring Tibet were misguided.

"The gods created the highest mountains on earth for a purpose—to keep Englishmen out of this country," Chetak said. "Your captain doesn't seem to understand that only thieves enter houses after the door is shut." He shot a sly glance at Balram, perhaps to acknowledge the irony of his statement.

Harish, whose head rested on Rana's shoulder and whose fingers were interlaced with Rana's, said, "We could have avoided these accidents had we followed the path of traders."

"I would have run away," Mor said, "except the captain said he would punish our families if we abandoned him."

Balram worried the bearers would mention the true nature of their expedition, which would lay bare his lie to Chetak that the captain was keen to see Lhasa. He was about to intervene, but it struck him that Yogi's death, unfortunate as it had been, presented an opportunity. This too was fate; perhaps the gods that had extinguished a man's life were offering him a way to save others.

Stepping outside to piss in the rain, Balram stopped when he saw Chetak following him.

"You didn't answer my question," Chetak said. "Did you find your friend?"

Balram listed the hills he had climbed, the number of people he had spoken to, the elderly lama who needed money so badly he would let a prisoner go. It was a relief to speak the truth.

The bandit embraced him as if his own brother had been found. "We will free him," Chetak said. "And we will return to Terai."

BEFORE DAWN CHETAK TOLD the half-asleep bearers, "I don't want to disturb you when you bid your final farewell to the dead. We will speak later." Then he vanished as mysteriously as he had arrived.

In the first light of the sun, Balram, with the rest of the men, took Yogi's corpse up a hill and divested it of clothes and rings. After marching for weeks, Yogi, like all of them, had become gaunt. His clothes billowed around his rigid frame; his rings were loose and slipped off easily. The rain cast such a pall over the landscape that it appeared the sun had never risen. The men chanted no verses. Their mouths expelled clouds of white breath as they walked down the hill to the river, where they sprinkled water on their faces. The weather was too cold and pneumonia was assured if they attempted to bathe and purify themselves. What would have seemed unimaginable at the time of Chand's death was now ordinary, not worthy of a second thought.

Afterward in the bearers' tent Pawan built a small fire under the canopy to cook tsampa. The men squatted on the damp ground. Balram saw a resolve in their eyes that had been empty only hours before.

Balram couldn't eat. The men who died scribbled ghostly words on his skin. *Murderer, traitor, fool.* He thought of Gyan locked up in a grotto, a punishment that he, Balram, ought to have suffered. The flames swerved with the wind, and the tent, already full of smoke, darkened further. At the entrance stood Chetak. He must have known Yogi's last rites had been performed; he must have been watching them all this while. It was an unsettling thought. The bearers invited him inside and pressed a bowl of tea into his hands.

"You stay here. Let the captain say what he wants," Ujjal said, but nervously.

"Where are you headed now?" Balram asked.

"I will go with you to meet your friend."

"Which friend?" Ujjal asked.

"Gyan," Jagan said. "You found him?"

"He isn't dead?" Pawan said.

"He lives in Shigatse?" Ujjal said.

"What does he do?" Harish asked. "Does he have a wife here?"

"Many wives, must be," Pawan said.

"I'll help you," Chetak said to Balram. "You can't free him by yourself."

"He's a prisoner?" Jagan said. "So the rumors I heard at Mana are true."

"What rumors?" Ujjal asked.

"That a bad lama has made Gyan his slave," Jagan said.

"I don't need anyone's help," Balram said.

"Your captain won't let you free him," Chetak said.

"That's between me and the captain."

"What is?" the captain asked as he entered the tent with Samarth, noticing Chetak only when it was too late for him to turn back. Frantically he hunched into the coat he wore over his saffron robe. The rain had washed out much of the ink on his hair and beard. Without his gauze frame, the green tint of his eyes was evident.

The fire buckled in the wind. The captain dashed out of the tent. Balram followed him, the river perilously close, ice snapping at the heels of his boots. Only a brushstroke of saffron hinted the captain was a foot or two ahead of him. The rain had made a blank canvas of the earth.

In the captain's tent, the floor, covered with waterproof sheets, was clean and dry. He ceremoniously took off his boots and wiped his feet on a mat at the entrance.

"Why is that man following us everywhere?" he asked. He toweled his face, then flinched at the smudges of ink darkening the fabric.

Balram remained at the entrance. He didn't want to defile the captain's space. Like the man and his maps, every corner of his tent was neatly ordered.

"I don't know any more than you, sir," Balram said. "He's of no concern to us. But in the market yesterday I heard Gyan has been imprisoned in a monastery here in Shigatse. I was rushing back to tell you, only—"

"You seem to have misunderstood the purpose of our expedition. You were meant to purchase livestock, not ask about your friend. And let me make it clear to you, we will not be stopping for any man, alive or dead."

"One day—that's all it will take."

"How might we save him? Do you reckon we should send our artillery regiment ahead?"

"The head lama of the monastery where Gyan is being held, he's more than willing to free Gyan for a price you can afford."

"Listen to yourself. Why would the Tibetans hold a spy, a British subject, in a monastery of all places?"

"It's remarkable that Gyan is alive, sir. His mother has prayed for nothing other than the return of her son. She is a good woman. She was a mother to me too when I was a child." Balram took off his damp coat and folded it across his arm. "Yesterday I visited the monastery where they're holding Gyan." How reckless it felt to say his friend's name aloud so many times, almost as if he was declaring his love, or his decision to organize a mutiny.

"Instead of buying sheep."

"I had to find out for myself."

"I have heard that Tibetan lamas are corrupt, and charge high taxes from farmers, but it beggars belief that they have taken to kidnapping people to demand a ransom."

"The monks saved Gyan's life. Without their intervention, soldiers would have executed him, because they correctly deduced he was a spy." A weariness seized Balram's limbs, but he persisted. "The monastery is poor, and the money they're asking for Gyan will keep them from starving this winter. I should have told you all this yesterday, and I would have if not for Yogi."

"The money I have is not mine. It belongs to the British government. How will it look if I fritter away the entirety of the amount the Survey advanced me on securing your friend's release, with no new knowledge gained? My name will be disgraced. I'll serve as a cautionary tale for all British explorers. I'll be put on trial for corruption."

"Sir, it's our duty to protect the men who work for us."

"If Tibetans learn of my identity—and they will if you persist with this foolishness—they won't show me the kindness of imprisonment, but will introduce me to the beaks of vultures. The danger of this has already been magnified because of this man, the stranger in the bearer's tent, whom you have brought into our fold. What's wrong with you, Balram? Do you wish to see me dead?"

"The stranger is nobody. He's traveling by himself. He's lonely. If he wanted to tell the Tibetans about you, he would have done so a while ago."

"A man seeking company will find it on the road to Lhasa, which is popular with traders and pilgrims alike." Balram saw a glimmer of dread in the captain's eyes. "I'm not suggesting we forget Gyan—far from it. As soon as we're back in Hindustan, I'll secure his release. But I can't rescue him now and jeopardize my life and my mission."

"Sir, you told Gyan that you would station surveyors along the Dihang, the Siang, the Brahmaputra, all those rivers that could be the very same as the Tsangpo. You told him surveyors would watch the waters for messages from him. I believe he was sending a message when Tibetans caught him."

"We didn't receive any messages from him."

"That's not his fault."

"I would be careful of what I say to my superior if I were you," the captain said, his tone cold, the misshapen stripes on his face offering a fleeting glimpse of a ghost, a malevolent being, a demon, hidden beneath his skin. "Get rid of that stranger, offer him money if it will keep him quiet—more than what he'll get from Tibetans if he informs them of a foreigner's whereabouts—and tell the bearers we will leave at dawn tomorrow, come what may, flood or fire, rain or snow."

THAT NIGHT, WHEN BALRAM heard the bearers slip away on the tips of their toes, he didn't open his eyes. Chetak must be waiting somewhere nearby, ready to offer them guidance. Ujjal touched his feet as if seeking the blessing of an elder, and whispered that he ought to join them.

"Remember to take the boy, Samarth, with you," Balram said, sitting up in the dark. "Stay away from Survey offices, soldiers, and policemen." He didn't know if the men could make it back home on their own, and all at once he became aware of the dangers he ought to have cautioned them against, but now there was no time. Quickly he told Ujjal that in Shigatse town he would find traders returning to Leh or Kalimpong or Mana. "Don't cross a mountain pass on your own—you'll lose your way," he said. "Join a trader's caravan. As long as you don't impose on their rations, they won't mind your accompanying them. Take whatever food is left in our camp."

"Why don't you come with us?"

"If something happens to the captain, none of us will know peace in our lifetimes. I have to return him to the Survey, alive."

"Then I'll stay with you."

"Easier for me to convince the captain to give up on this expedition if none of you are around. Leave, now. God willing, we will meet again."

Ujjal looked as if he was about to cry.

"Ford the river in daylight, and only after you find a shallow spot," Balram said.

"You've been a good leader to us," Ujjal said.

"Yogi will disagree. And so will Chand and Naga."

"Wasn't your fault."

Balram patted Ujjal on the shoulder, then nudged him out of the tent.

"We could tell the captain you didn't stop the deserters," Rana said. He and Harish had chosen to stay behind. "Why, we could wake up the captain right now."

"You won't do any such thing," Balram said. He didn't mean it as a threat, but it sounded like one. If they returned to Badrinath, or Mussoorie, the two men wouldn't be able to spend time together as they did now, and they were risking death for these brief moments of pleasure. He should feel sorry for them. He understood them well.

After Rana fell asleep, Balram took the compass out of his coat. In the mellow light of the lantern he saw that its needle no longer moved; like this expedition, it too was dead.

16.

KATHERINE AND MANI FOLLOWED THE TSANGPO EAST. THE RIVER wound around hills that were sometimes bare and sometimes carved into terraced fields. At this time of the year the last of the barley had been reaped and arranged in conical haystacks, their yellow softening the sharpness of the inclines.

They passed farmers eating the food their wives had brought to the fields, brothers or neighbors sitting with them in a circle, yaks grazing not too far away, a scene of simple contentment of the kind Katherine would never know. Sometimes the farmers gifted the two of them strips of dried yak meat that they chewed as they walked, pain tapping the same rhythms on Katherine's spine, blisters darkening her feet and fingers, dread burbling in her mind that these impaired appendages would begin to putrefy and poison the blood. Always these fears that she wouldn't reach Lhasa. She tried not to dwell on them. She could also feel the land strengthening her muscles, allowing her to walk for longer. Though she was possibly risking scurvy on account of the lack of fruit and vegetables in her diet, she suffered no visible consequences as yet.

The path they took veered above the river, and sometimes onto its banks where villagers gathered water, and children played in the sand, smiling when Mani waved at them, leaning on the walking stick that had more or less become his now. One afternoon they came across two women herding sheep, armed with slings that they employed skillfully to cast a pebble so that it landed at the hoof of a wayward animal and encouraged it to return to the flock. The women gifted them dried apricots, which Katherine accepted with gratitude even though the apricots were turning brown.

Mostly the path was empty, just her and Mani, not much conversation between them except to inquire about the state of each other's feet. When the wind hushed, Katherine heard the hooves of mules carrying sugar or wheat or textiles to Lhasa. At night, voices of drunk traders or bearers drifted over the hills. Only miles between her and these men, but they could have been in another country.

When she couldn't sleep she didn't want to think of Chetak and could only think of him. Weeks had passed since she spent the night with him by a small lake. Still, she felt as if their parting hadn't been final. Perhaps it was no different from how even now her eyes perceived Ethel everywhere, as if Ethel wasn't truly gone, as if one day Ethel would sit beside her and they would have tea and cake together. So now there were these two figures in her mind, both lost to her and yet their presence tangible like sunlight falling on her skin.

She had all this time for contemplation because their march was without incident. The weather held. No wolves or bandits crossed their path. They skirted the city of Shigatse and its famed Tashi Lhunpo monastery, thus avoiding its crowds, which suited her but left her unable to describe the sights. She worried her journal would be dull in comparison to the accounts written by male explorers who battled natives, hunted bears, waded through mud in malarial swamps, and sacrificed their flesh to lions and tigers and mosquitoes only to prevail over whatever calamity befell them. The male explorer never had a quiet day like she did. He allowed himself the indulgence of a siesta or a game of cards only when the sun shone so bright to be in its presence was to court heatstroke. Without such romance, which she understood to be half-pretense, how could one tell a story that readers would consider worth the price of the book?

At least now she was at the threshold of Lhasa, a city she had been trying to reach for over ten years—ten years in which the world, her own and that around her, had changed. Ethel had died; wars had been fought and won, far away in America, and next to her in the Dooars, where the British Empire had defeated Bhutan; a railway had been built under the ground in London, where a woman had started practicing medicine, and who could tell which surprised people more. But Lhasa was still a forbidden world, unseen by Europeans apart from the Jesuit missionaries who had passed through the city in the seventeenth and eighteenth centuries, their accounts sparse and dull, illuminating little of the Tibetan way of life. The English scholar Thomas Manning was said to have had an audience with the Dalai Lama in the early years of this century, but he had published nothing about his trip.

Katherine's only competition was the poorly disguised Englishman she had glimpsed near Mansarovar. She didn't worry about him; Lhasa couldn't be his goal. Men were always chasing the unseen peaks of mountains, or crossing oceans to reach islands where treasures awaited discovery. Even if the Englishman was headed to Lhasa, she would still be the first European woman to reach the city. Her book, once published, would secure her an invitation to address the male fellows of the Royal Geographical Society.

Look at her, head inflated by possibility. She ought to be ashamed.

To Mani, Lhasa was the Place of Gods, a city of prayer where the rich and the poor alike were expected to renounce their possessions, be they rags or yards of silk, a lock of hair that belonged to a departed child, or a wedding ring. Fame and wealth wouldn't even be on a true pilgrim's mind. But as much as she sought deliverance, and repented, Katherine couldn't be like Mani. She was too impure. It was what her mother would have said about her.

WHERE THE TSANGPO CLEAVED into two, its tributary advancing northward toward Lhasa, Katherine and Mani met with a great storm. They sought refuge at a monastery, where the monks took them for mendicants and confined them to the entrance hall by the gate, its walls lined with gilded, cylindrical prayer wheels that Mani spun clockwise, seeking blessings. The rain didn't stop all afternoon. At last something to write about, Katherine thought, but the recurring nature of these events would strike her readers as dull. How many storms had she seen already? An encounter with the mythical snow lion would have been more exciting.

The monks served them gruel. They finished their meal and dusk swooped down and the monks closed their doors after asking a farmer to offer them a place to sleep. The farmer was less generous than others they had met, or didn't have room to spare, and cast them into his stable with yaks and goats. They slept poorly. The animals snorted and plopped dung onto the floor, where it hissed, hot and fetid, eager flies buzzing around the shit. All night the rain thumped against the stone walls of the stable, like a drunk demanding to be let inside. No sooner had Katherine drifted to sleep than its insistence woke her up again.

In the morning the rain continued. The farmer seemed anxious. Mani whispered to her that if the rain ruined the grains he had stored to be traded at marts, he would lose money.

They set out on the path to Lhasa, Katherine's bonnet yet again proving to be a poor shield. The sky spread itself above them like a black tablecloth. They met a man carrying a heavy basket over his head. He paused to warn Mani that the river had breached its boundaries and was flooding the fields.

"There's no good time for a flood," Mani told the man, "but we must be thankful it's happening now, after the harvest."

The man bowed, perhaps mistaking Mani for a monk as others had.

Afterward Katherine told Mani, "How can you say we should be thankful it's raining *now*? We're so close to Lhasa, and our plans will be ruined if we're caught in a flood."

"Mother, it serves us well to think first about those who call this country their home."

Katherine was reminded of all the times her mother had similarly censured her, though less tactfully than Mani. Before every journey she made, her mother had exclaimed at her self-absorption: *what of her family wasn't her cousin getting married did she not want to meet her nieces hadn't her uncle just died what of Frederick what kind of wife neglects her husband when she knows he might be snatched by another woman.* Katherine now shuddered in the rain that sank its teeth into her shoulders. Mani called a halt to their march and suggested they wait until the sky cleared. Rather than beg a farmer to offer them a place to sleep, he found a secluded spot on an elevation to raise her tent and told her there was a cave nearby in which he could sleep. She asked him to stay, but feebly. When he left, she was glad to be alone.

From inside her shelter, Katherine looked out at the rain-washed blur that was the landscape, illuminated by strands of lightning. She could glimpse the outline of the Lhasa River, flowing briskly. How far she had come, how close she was to achieving her dream. It was possible on a night like this to believe that each time she traveled she jettisoned aspects of herself that no longer served her; that she had become stronger and wiser. But her mother's words pounded in her ears with every beat of the heart. Katherine realized no part of her could be cast afresh even in this new world, because all parts of her were imprinted with the port wine stains of her past.

THE RAIN SLOWED TO a drizzle the next morning. White clouds nestled in the furrows of mountains, like birds that had found comfortable branches to perch on and were reluctant to leave. Katherine wondered if they were marching the march of the condemned, then felt embarrassed by the constancy with which doubts plagued her mind. The monks in Kalimpong had tried to teach her composure; they liked to say that her hands could shape clay into an exquisite sculpture, but it was a futile exercise to wonder if she would find an admirer eager to purchase it, or if the artifact would shatter in the wind. Ultimately no aspect of life could be changed by hope or effort alone. Always there was the unknown: the death of a sister; the evidence of a husband's betrayal in an infant he brought home; and the fury of the gods in the floodwaters lapping at one's feet. And if the unknown couldn't be mapped the way surveyors charted rivers and countries, why waste hours agonizing over what might or might not be?

The Lhasa River, its texture made coarse by silt, swirled with the remnants of all that the water had pried from the land: stalks of barley, a frayed blanket, a shiny pot, the furry corpse of a goat, a woman's turquoise bead necklace. The water rose above the lines of prayer flags Tibetans had strung over it. Katherine felt she was like the river, calm for many miles, furious for several others, the color of her skin changing as the river waters did according to the season and the weather, stillness a trait unknown, only constant movement making it possible for her to be a part of this earth.

Hard to believe that only a river crossing and a few miles stood between her and Lhasa. The sun was shining now, but the river was still surging from the storm. They found no place suitable for fording.

Then they met a boatsman who offered them a passage to Lhasa in his coracle, on the condition that Mani discard his walking stick, too long and unwieldy to be ferried. Mani cut the stick into small pieces to serve as fuel.

As soon as Katherine lowered herself into the coracle, she became aware of its flimsiness. Yak skin had been stretched over a timber frame shaped like ribs; to sit in it was to invite the sensation of drowning. Perhaps a watery grave awaited her. She would float down this river like a dead goat, her passing unremarked and ignored by the world at large. She imagined the pages of her journal dispersing in the water, the erasure of her words and the erasure of the self.

"It's safe," Mani said. His voice could have been the voice of God reprimanding her. Rivers meandered but ultimately emptied into the sea; vapor returned to earth as rain and snow, and swelled rivers again. To track the mouths and sources of rivers as male explorers did across the world was perhaps to search for the meaning of life itself, forgetting that one's path, even if rambling in appearance, was in truth cyclical. *Unto the place from whence the rivers come, thither they return again.* These words were from the Bible, but who wanted to accept that life began and ended at the same place for all? Not even her, pursuing a legacy so fragile it could dissipate with a coracle in the Lhasa River.

Another passenger joined them, a tradesman from Nepal. The boatsman disappeared behind a boulder and returned with the fourth passenger, his pet goat, carrying his belongings in two saddlebags on its frail back. They arranged themselves in the coracle such that their weight was equally distributed, then set off, the boatsman attempting to steady the vessel, which, unmindful of his paddle, spun like a top in the currents. In the space of a moment, the sun was to their west, east, and north.

The goat bleated, the tradesman hissed, the river growled. Katherine allowed herself the indulgence of a gasp. Only Mani looked composed. Even the boatsman's eyebrows were raised. The goat defecated without care, the droppings rolling into every nook and corner with each swift turn of the coracle. Then the animal began to chew the sleeve of Katherine's robe. She pushed its head away. Around them the river roared, its waves white-tipped as if they belonged to the sea. Katherine pressed her hand down to steady herself and felt the softness of a pellet of dung stick to her fingers. She didn't dare lean forward and wash her hands in the river, and instead sat as still as she could, the sun bright and the wind hasty, the Nepali trader not even glancing at her, in part because of the imminent danger of drowning that painted red threads in the whites of his eyes, and in part because he must see her as a pilgrim. The goat licked her fingers and she turned away, repulsed. Wouldn't Chetak laugh if he were to see her now? (But why was she thinking of him?)

The coracle turned with the river, almost crashing into a boulder. A high-pitched sound buzzed in her ears, which she realized was the sound of her fear. The river was growing increasingly furious, hurrying past rocky cliffs and sandy banks. Katherine tasted bile on her tongue and knew she would vomit. Her clothes were damp from the river spray. The brown, frothing currents seemed to be above her, below her, swirling in her throat and eyes, but it also felt like she was flying in a storm, the wind tearing her apart.

With some difficulty, the boatsman steered the coracle to the shore and asked them to step out. Katherine's robe dragged through the water and the sand. She retched, but her mouth was dry. She sat down on a boulder, waiting for the world to stop spinning. The goat stayed at her heel, apparently having made up its mind to devour her boots. Mani touched her shoulder briefly and offered her a root that looked like the sliced tail of a rodent and still had dirt on its light-brown skin.

"Ginseng," he said. "Very expensive. The Nepali asked me to give it to you." She nodded her thanks at the trader, who seemed to be chewing the same root. It was bitter but quelled her nausea. The river's currents were quick and noisy. She turned away from the water to look at the mountains, above which clouds moved as if possessed by a mystical spirit.

"How long before we see the Potala Palace?" she asked Mani.

"We haven't reached Lhasa," he said. "We were asked to disembark because the river is too dangerous."

To be so close to Lhasa was thrilling and disappointing. She felt she couldn't wait another moment. "What now?" she asked Mani.

The boatsman tied his paddle to the coracle and lifted it over his head as if it was an umbrella. He gestured they should follow him, and they did, Katherine wondering if this strange procession of men, woman, and goat would proceed on land to Lhasa. Each obstacle the gods placed in front of her only made her more determined, erasing all other thoughts from her mind. After a mile the boatsman deemed the river serviceable again and they returned to its currents, the coracle twirling, the paddle spattering them with water, and Mani holding the goat's hind legs as it had moved on to chewing Katherine's talisman, her bonnet. Lhasa must be ten miles away, and it felt like ten thousand.

As they entered smoother waters, the air became pleated with dust. Katherine closed her eyes in the vain hope of deterring the nausea that the waters provoked in her yet again. The irony of it. She, a hardy traveler who had spent as many as six months at a stretch on a ship, had met her match in a lowly coracle. The Nepali trader began to utter prayers.

"Fear not, we have arrived," she heard the boatsman say. They were now in the shallow part of the river by the shore, but beyond that, all was dust.

LHASA, AT LAST!

But where was it? Katherine could see nothing in the haze, which had the consistency of wood shavings and the tint of dried apricot.

Though dust scraped her nose and throat, she said, "What else will the gods send to stop us?"

Mani brought down the rag he had wrapped over his nose and mouth and said, "A dust storm affords us the best opportunity to enter Lhasa unnoticed."

The Nepali trader was a mere shadow in the dull light. While a cloak of invisibility was no doubt beneficial, she hoped the heavy curtains of dust would lift at least briefly to allow for a first glimpse of the city or the Potala Palace. Now she was unable to see her own feet.

They walked a mile or so, orange dust freely thumbing through her hair, grit drawing tears from her eyes and blood from her cracked lips. Then she heard the clanking of bells, the sound of horses galloping toward her at full speed. Dazed, she stopped in the middle of the track. Mani wrenched her to the edge and asked her to prostrate. "Pay your respects," he said urgently. It was the Tibetan custom when convoys of officials or soldiers passed by. Katherine knelt and touched her forehead to the earth, ignoring the blaze of pain in her spine. The horses raced past without slowing down. When she looked up she saw brief flashes of color, the muddy brown of the coats worn by soldiers, the yellow of their hats, and the white of the flags scribbled with prayers and affixed to their matchlocks.

"We're seeing more soldiers because we're close to Lhasa, I suppose," Katherine said.

"High-ranking officials always travel with a cavalcade," Mani said. "But I'm surprised they didn't delay their business, given the dust."

They came upon a high stone wall inscribed with the Tibetan prayer *Om Mani Padme Hum*, behind which stood yet another band of soldiers, matchlocks slung over their shoulders. One of them, a young man with a thin, sharp mustache powdered with dust, shouted at Mani to identify himself. "Mother and son," Mani said. The dust had formed a second skin under her robe, and caulked her ears and nostrils. Mani's voice sounded muzzled. The soldiers didn't dispute his characterization of their relationship.

"They seem to be preparing for war," Mani said once the soldiers had let them pass. "But who would attack Lhasa?" He looked at her anxiously. "Is it the English, mother? Have you kept from me the truth of why you're traveling to Lhasa?"

The dust storm at once quieted; Mani's words could have been a spell to make it hush. "It grieves me to see you suspect me of wrong-doing," she said as calmly as she could. "But it's the English officers in Calcutta who will find your accusation even more damning—those great men reduced to such a sorry state that they have to seek the help of a woman to enter Tibet. And what will I do for them? Translate their English into Tibetan and ask people to surrender?"

"I apologize," Mani said quickly. "Forgive me. I must be weary."

Katherine noticed his limp had become more pronounced, or per-haps it was that he had employed her walking stick with such dexter-ity he had concealed his pain from her. Now, without the stick, he couldn't do so any longer. She asked him to hold her hand for sup-port, but he declined.

They turned a bend in the path and were immediately surrounded by a third group of soldiers on horseback, who asked them to furnish papers to indicate they were who they purported to be.

"Why," Mani asked them, "are you conducting these checks? I have been to Lhasa many times and never seen so many soldiers."

"We have received information that foreigners are attempting to enter our sacred city," a soldier said. His eyes were reddened by dust and smoldered like cinders.

Mani took a step back. Katherine thought of the white man in disguise; were they looking for him, or her?

"What papers can we show you?" Mani said. "We're pilgrims. We come here every year. No one has asked us for anything."

He shouldn't have said that, because it made the soldier angry. He jumped off his horse and stood in front of Katherine with his hands on his hips, the matchlock looming over his shoulder like a serpent head. Katherine heard her heart pounding, the beats trebling each moment and causing a darkness to spread behind her eyes. It was as if she was climbing the highest part of a mountain pass and the altitude had wrung all the air out of her lungs. She tried to smile. The soldier scowled at her.

He must be only sixteen at most, gaunt, with smooth skin, and long black hair tied back in a pigtail and tinted brown by the dust. Yellowing stains of tsampa and tea specked his black Tibetan coat. Dried dung coated his boots. He chewed on something, tobacco maybe, twig or ginseng maybe, and spat it out, not quite missing her feet.

She understood she was in peril; the sweat that dampened her armpits told her so. But she didn't want to believe it. The dust clouds had stilled, and a blue sky had become visible. The path shimmered in the sun. The soldiers' horses, magnificent mares with black or brown coats gleaming in sharp contrast to their haggard riders, were quiet and friendly. She had escaped detection for months; it seemed inconceivable that these soldiers could come between her and her destination now.

The soldier boy smiled at her, but it was a sarcastic smile. He snatched the bonnet from her head, its strings cutting into her chin, and she yelped without meaning to. She snatched it back from him, glaring, not caring what happened to her. Two of the soldiers on horseback laughed.

Boy soldier looked disappointed by her gray hair. A drop of blood dusted her fingertips when she touched her chin. He audaciously walked around her, so close she could smell his reeking breath. She couldn't speak to him, or Mani, because she feared (there it was, the fear she had been expecting) that he would recognize her accent as alien.

Another soldier asked Boy to check their bags, which he did. Mani looked at her anxiously. Boy asked them to remove their boots. One of the soldiers at the back protested. He was a middle-aged man, the oldest of the soldiers, and had until then watched the proceedings with disinterest, his silence broken only by his persistent chewing, and spitting, of tobacco. "Why must you earn the wrath of pilgrims?" he asked. Boy's cheeks flushed. Everyone was quiet for a moment.

Then Boy pointed to Katherine's boots and gestured that she should take them off.

Katherine heard the ocean in her ears—fear lashing against her skin like waves in a storm. "My mother is too old to be troubled like this," Mani said, and she smiled at him sadly. The horses stamped their feet. Mani was trembling. How had she forgotten how young he was? A chill passed through her, as if Ethel was chastising her for her ambitions that had caused her to neglect her sister and jeopardize a boy's life.

Extracting her boots from her swollen legs proved to be a more arduous task than she, or the soldiers, had estimated. She had to sit down and stretch her feet. Everything around her was sharp and glittering and silent. Boy noticed a protuberance in her blanket, its pockets where her journals, wrapped in oilskin, were secreted. He attempted to cut it open with a knife, and she resisted with a scream, carelessly placing her hands in harm's way. The scene would have turned remarkably bloody had the middle-aged soldier not asked Boy to stop. Undeterred still, he pressed his hands on the blanket, and hooted as the shapes beneath the fabric became apparent to him. Mani's face was now ashen. Katherine felt as if she had stepped out of her body and was watching a simulacrum of herself clothed in dust.

The soldiers conferred among themselves. Katherine stood up, not without difficulty, blood seeping into the rags she had tied over the wounds in her feet in the fashion of a sepoy, dust lodging in the gaps between its folds and causing her skin to feel as if a match had been lit underneath. She pulled on her boots. Boy extracted from the blanket her notebooks, pencils, and pouches with coins, the latter insufficient on their own to elicit suspicion, the value of coins being much less than what might be found on a trader, though admittedly higher than what would be considered a reasonable amount for a beggar to carry. But there was no disputing the English words on the pages of her journal, the letters so small they could have been rows of black ants, comprehensible to none but herself, and yet their foreignness evident to these soldiers who might have been illiterate.

With unexpected swiftness, the middle-aged soldier swung down from his horse to inspect the book. Turquoise jewels glinted in his ears in the sunshine that edged toward the earth through the dust. He asked Mani if they were English spies, and Mani shook his head. In broken Tibetan—grammar and fluency having deserted her in her hour of need—Katherine said she was a pilgrim traveling with her son; that she had been taught to read and write English by a memsahib. Was that such a crime? The soldier said he had never before met a woman who could read and write. He asked her what she had written in the book. "Only a few thoughts of mine," Katherine said truthfully, and the men burst into laughter. Who had a thought valuable enough to set down on paper? Was she a female Bodhisattva whose every teaching had to be recorded?

Katherine wondered what would become of her. It would be a year, maybe two, before Frederick even thought to notify the viceroy in Calcutta (he couldn't be blamed; such was the nature of the expedition she had undertaken), and by the time the viceroy sent messengers to the Tibetan border, she could be dead.

The soldiers chattered among themselves, not at all anxious that she and Mani might try to escape. Mani had by now found his tongue, as if being caught had somehow freed him or he had accepted their new fate as a Buddhist ought to quickly. He joined in the confabulations, testily making a few declarations about her knowledge of Tibetan scriptures and claiming she was hoping for an audience with the Dalai Lama, being equally well versed in Tibetan, Hindustani, and English. The middle-aged man turned the pages of her journal over and over, as if in the act the words would suddenly become decipherable to him.

One of the soldiers rode away in the direction of the city. Katherine's mouth was parched and she reached for a goatskin water-bag and Boy snatched it from her hands and was promptly reprimanded by his senior, who bowed as he returned it to her. The water she drank spilled from her mouth onto the front of her robe, and the dust that had collected on the folds of her neck trickled down as rivulets of dirt.

After a while, the soldier who had departed for the city returned with a man wearing a fine sheepskin coat and elaborate jewelry. His demeanor was that of a high-ranking official, or perhaps he was a messenger of the lamas who ruled Tibet, the monastery being more powerful than any garrison. He buzzed about like a fly, looking at her journal, bending it in the middle as if to test its mettle, slapping it against his palm, then issuing commands she couldn't understand.

At length the soldiers mounted their horses again, and asked them to march, but away from Lhasa; perhaps they would now be taken atop a hill and shot, and their corpses would lie where they fell, easily accessible to birds of prey without any effort on the part of these men. *Ethel, here I am, receiving the punishment I deserve,* she thought. Mani continued speaking with the soldiers, but in a low voice. His Tibetan was too colloquial for her to follow.

The official in the sheepskin coat left. "They'll not kill us," Mani whispered to her. "But they don't want us to enter Lhasa."

"They'll have to kill us to ensure we don't enter Lhasa, won't they?" she asked. How calmly she said these words, as if to be shot was nothing. No one cared if she lived or died. But Mani didn't deserve that fate. *Selfish,* her mother had called her. "Will they let you go?" Katherine asked. "They won't kill Indians, will they?"

Boy clicked his tongue and placed his finger on his mouth, asking her to shut up. Mani hobbled. The wind rose and fell again. Lhasa was at a lower altitude than the mountains she had crossed to reach the city, yet it felt colder here. They walked for several miles, the soldiers surrounding them on horseback. Mani chanted Buddhist prayers, as if to convince the soldiers the two of them were indeed pilgrims, but he might only have been calming his own mind. The soldiers didn't seem impressed.

"I'm sorry I couldn't help you reach Lhasa," Mani said to her. Boy pointed his matchlock at them and pretended to fire a shot, and laughed as they jumped in panic, their nerves frayed.

Katherine felt compelled to turn back toward Lhasa, as if to bid farewell to a dream she had cherished so much she had risked her life for it—not once but three times. She couldn't be faulted for her lack of diligence or courage. But her journal, with all her impressions, was in the pocket of a soldier's coat, where she imagined his sweat had already begun to efface her words. And without her words, who would know of her trials?

At first the dust, then the hills between them and the city, had intercepted any possibility of glimpsing the Potala Palace, but now, perhaps because Katherine was at an elevation, she saw, beyond the rust-colored Lhasa River, the grand structure with over a thousand rooms and a thousand windows atop Lhasa's Red Mountain, the White Palace at the bottom, the Red Palace and its radiant golden roof at the very top, and the clouds above the palaces, glowing, infused with a touch of rose, as if they couldn't believe their good fortune to have manifested themselves above this holy structure. Those with keener vision would have perhaps seen the servants readying the rooms for the Dalai Lama to take up his winter residence. For all its solidity, in keeping with Buddhist beliefs, the Potala Palace had a quality of transience to it, as if poised to disappear into the clouds above it at the whim of the gods. Boy leaned from his horse to nudge her with the tip of his muzzle, but so glorious was the image of the palace that a strange calm descended over her like a pall of soft mist. A herd of antelopes leaped across the path, chased by a majestic brown bear. Boy seemed to want to fire his gun, and took out what looked like a tinderbox, but the middle-aged soldier warned him not to shoot; these bears were rare, he said. Boy said it was only for defense, in case the bear attacked. The animal, perhaps deeming them to be insufficiently delectable for its supper, vanished into the hills after the antelopes. Katherine thought God was speaking to her through what she had witnessed, the Potala Palace and the boy with his bloodlust, the sacred and the profane within mere moments of each other, reminding her yet again that life was cyclical. It might be unchristian to believe that every creature's time on earth consisted of a series of births and rebirths, but she believed it nevertheless. If she were to die tonight, perhaps she would return tomorrow as a vulture circling the Potala Palace, a hungry bear scampering after nimble antelopes, an antelope jumping so high that it seemed to be flying, or perhaps she would be reborn as a Tibetan soldier, a servant of the Dalai Lama, or a child living next door to her nieces and, in that new life, she would one day visit her neighbor's home and find a portrait of Ethel and pause to pick it up, wondering why the face in the drawing appeared so familiar to her.

17.

AFTER WHAT FELT LIKE A MOMENT'S SLEEP, IT WAS TIME FOR Balram to wake. The morning was misty, but sunlight seeped in through the warp and weft of clouds. In the billowing currents of the Tsangpo floated dubious things from which he averted his gaze, aware that on a hilltop nearby was Yogi's corpse, his dead eyes being plucked by birds, his blood-tipped fingers dangling from the mouths of snow leopards.

Inside his tent, the captain slept peacefully, rosary wrapped around his wrist like an amulet for protection. Balram's eyes took a while to adjust to the darkness, and he saw—too late—Samarth sleeping on a rug, under a light blanket that couldn't have kept him warm. Rudra, and the bearers, mustn't have wanted to risk capture by sneaking around the captain's tent at night to take Samarth with them. Or they thought the noisy boy would be a liability, or that he was safer with Balram.

Shaking the captain awake, Balram said, "They're gone. The men. Only Harish and Rana are left."

In his muddled state the captain took a while to understand Balram's words. His movements were slow and unsteady as he touched the Herodotus and the rosary and prayer wheel. He asked for his compass and Balram reminded him it was lost, a lie he uttered with one trembling hand against its lid. The river was loud, drunk on the ice that the deluge had loosened from mountains and glaciers.

Balram waited for the captain's outburst. Harish and Rana joined him, shivering in their coats. On the hill where they had left Yogi, vultures gathered, their feathers lustrous in the first rays of the sun. Samarth staggered out of the tent, cheeks blotched and eyes rheumy and sweat dusting his forehead. Balram placed his palm on Samarth's forehead. It was as warm as a blacksmith's forge.

"What happened to the sheep?" the boy asked, shivering with panic or the fever. "Were they attacked again?"

Balram explained that the men and the sheep were gone. Samarth cried when he heard Rudra had left him behind but had remembered to collect the pony.

"Maybe he forgot you in his hurry," Harish told Samarth, his tone suggesting he was offering consolation, but his words only caused the boy's sobs to grow louder.

The captain stomped out of his tent, his rifle between his hands. "Tell me the truth," he said, the muzzle grazing Balram's chest. "You saw them leave and you didn't think to wake me?"

"I saw them leave," Balram said, aware he was reciting the captain's words back to him and yet unable to stop himself, "and I didn't think to wake you."

Harish and Rana stepped back. The river sputtered. On the hilltop vultures hissed. The captain raised the gun and its barrel scratched Balram's chin.

"If it goes off by mistake," Balram said, his voice sounding surprisingly calm to his own ears, "your fate will be to die in Tibet. Only I can lead you back to Dehra."

"Watch your tongue," the captain snapped, flecks of spittle leaving his mouth along with his words.

"Sir," Balram said, lowering the captain's gun with his hands and meeting no resistance, "listen to me, please. If not yesterday, the bearers would have deserted us tomorrow. We've faced too many accidents, lost too many people. The men were convinced we were cursed, and I couldn't change their minds."

"*You* couldn't change their minds. It was a mistake to put you in charge."

"If you had seen them leave last night, sir, what would you have done? Shot them?" Balram asked. "What good is a wounded or a dead man to us?"

"The deserters are cowards," Harish said. "But we are not. We will walk with you along this river, captain, sir, all the way to the sea."

"We don't care how long it takes," Rana said.

"I have Rajput blood in me—and we Rajputs are famous for our courage and loyalty," Harish said.

"You won't survive an hour in the Tsangpo gorge by yourself," Balram said.

"How do you know?" Rana asked. "Have you been there before?"

"No," Balram had to admit. "Even Tibetans don't visit, because the terrain is impossible."

Samarth coughed, body bent in two. He spat yellow phlegm tinged with a worrying green onto the rocks.

"Might you be able to give the boy some English medicine?" Balram asked the captain, who looked like he wanted to smash his fist into Balram's face. Instead he slung his rifle over his shoulder and led Samarth back to his tent.

Clouds parted above mountains, their peaks gasping in the sun like pearl fishers surfacing from underwater.

"What now?" Harish asked Balram.

BALRAM FOUND THE CAPTAIN by the river, gazing into its depths as if seeking answers from his own reflection. But the water, brown and dense with silt, was no mirror.

Without his gun, and the anger that had reddened his face, the captain looked pale and infirm. His hairline had been retreating since they began their journey, and it caused his forehead to seem wider and more prominent than before.

"How many years have passed since I left home," the captain said, startling Balram, who had thought the captain hadn't noticed his presence. "When I count the sacrifices I made, and what I gained in return, it's difficult not to feel disheartened." His nails scratched the rock on which he sat, as if he wanted to carve his initials into stone. "You know, Balram, I learned of my mother's passing only three months after she died. I can name every hill in Kashmir, but I have forgotten the names of my nieces and nephews. The woman I loved is married to another. She said she couldn't be with a man who risked his life to draw maps. Was she right? Perhaps. I have come close to death often enough during these travels, but what do I have to show for my daring? Only a passing mention of my name in a few journals that geographers read. Do you realize, Balram, how intolerable it is, how humiliating, to have faced hazards in vain? I graduated from the military academy with the medal for the most distinguished cadet, a young man poised to change the world. But look at me now. I am no different from others, nothing but flesh for these vultures"—he pointed his skinned fingertips at the sky even as his gaze remained on the water—"and yet I want to keep marching across lands that will devour me whole, climb mountains that will do their best to push me off an incline. What is this thing in me that won't let me stop? Is this what they call madness?"

Balram flinched. It did him no good to witness a white man's shame. In Mussoorie an English officer had had his manservant whipped until his flesh parted because the servant had the temerity to smile when the officer, in attempting to shake off a wad of hay that clung to the toe of his boot, nearly slipped. But why think of that now? Balram had overseen a mutiny, and only force of habit had him reverting to old patterns of thought.

"You have seen more of Tibet than most white men, sir. It's no insignificant achievement," he said. In the river the currents carried a dead bird encircled by feathers that moved in tandem with the corpse, like an elaborate funeral procession.

"The glory I seek will be the Swede's."

"We don't know if he's here."

"I suppose I could leave Tibet to the Swede and the Russians, go home, take a wife, manage the family estate. But even now, when I have been abandoned by my right-hand man, I can't tell myself to give up."

"I haven't abandoned you."

"But you intend to rescue Gyan. Isn't that why you encouraged the bearers to leave?"

"I didn't encourage them."

"You should have stopped them. It was your duty, Balram, your duty. You'll be punished for neglecting your responsibilities."

"All I ask for is a short detour. Once Gyan is freed, we can continue your expedition."

"Do you take me for a fool?"

A crazed look shone in the captain's eyes, framed by brows thick as pelts. "Without men and sheep we will travel less comfortably," Balram said, "but we can make do with fewer resources. I surveyed Tibet for you with very little money, I found work when I had to, begged for alms if needed. I can do it again. You won't go hungry, I assure you. You'll sleep in your tent as you do now. You'll be able to conduct your surveys and—"

"Gyan was imprisoned for being a spy and, as his friend, you too must have appeared suspicious to the monks. Why did they let you leave?"

"They need the money. I promised them Gyan would return to Hindustan at once. Don't you want him to be freed?"

"He was—*he is*—my best surveyor."

"And you can have him back at the Survey." Balram spoke more gruffly than he intended. It shamed him that he was still no better than the boy he used to be, that he could draw a line from the hour envy had sprouted in his heart to the moment Gyan was caught by the Tibetans and shoved into a cell; his own hand had all but orchestrated the imprisonment.

"I told the monks that Gyan is a trader, not a spy," Balram said. "An eccentric trader, I said, and they seemed to believe me. In any case, for a certain sum of money, you'll find that people will swear anything is true, that the sun is in fact the moon or that a goat is a bull. This monastery I speak of doesn't have the wealth of Tashi Lhunpo. Winter is almost here, and it will be a cold and dark one for them without this unexpected windfall."

"If you're determined to be simpleminded about this, tell me why they would let Gyan find his way back to Hindustan by himself," the captain said. "At the very least they'll escort him to the border as they have been known to do. Won't my identity be revealed in the commotion?"

"I'll secure Gyan's release," a voice Balram by now recognized as Chetak's said. "The Englishman can stay right here—no one needs to find out about him."

The bandit spoke as if he had been part of their conversation all along. Drops of water clung to his beard, glossy black punctuated with the odd strand of white. How did this man move through the world so silently, like a wisp of cirrus cloud across a blue sky?

"Why is he here?" the captain barked at Balram, standing up.

"We don't need your help," Balram told Chetak.

"I believe you do."

"Do you know Tibetan?" Balram asked.

Chetak shook his head.

"You can't even speak to the monks then."

"The language of money is the same across the world," Chetak said, impertinently stepping in front of Balram to address the captain. "I can put your fears to rest. If the monks are as poor as your man claims, they won't inform officials that they traded a spy for gold. They'll say he died."

"Your assumption is that I'll part with my funds to aid your cause," the captain said, no fright or alarm in his voice. "But you're wrong. I'll not be disbursing the money under any circumstances. It's not in my power to do so."

"Your assumption is that you have a choice in this matter," Chetak said in a quiet, unobtrusive manner that held the menace of a snow leopard sneaking up on its prey.

"Tell me plainly," the captain said to Balram. "Is this man doing your bidding? Do you intend to have me killed?"

"I don't take orders from others," Chetak said. He parted his coat as if to insolently display his manhood to the captain, but he wore a tunic underneath and a shawl over it, the latter held in place with a narrow sash across his hips from which hung charms and a dagger placed in a leather sheath.

The captain turned toward his tent, but Chetak stood in his path. "Out of my way," the captain said, his voice echoing upon the mountains.

"If you're going to fetch your guns," Chetak said, "let me save you the trouble. When you were doing your business behind the rocks, I threw them away."

The captain laughed as if the bandit could only be lying, but then his eyes turned to Balram.

"I didn't see," Balram said. "I didn't ask him to—I don't even know this man."

"How you hurt my feelings with your callous words," Chetak said to Balram, his palm pressed against his heart. "You have always known I'm a wanted man."

The captain's mouth opened in surprise, then he muttered, "Of course, of course he is." Edging closer to Balram, he slapped him on the arm, a friendly gesture made belligerent by the intensity with which he performed the action. "You knew who he was all along," he said, now clutching Balram's shoulders and shaking him, his voice high-pitched with anger. "You asked me about the Robin Hood of Terai—this is him, yes? You arranged for a scoundrel to join our group? Was the bandit raid on our camp also your doing? Did you have our sheep killed? What is it that you hope to achieve with your deceit?" Before Balram could answer he continued, "Do you realize you have proved my critics right? All those who told me natives couldn't be trained to follow the methods of scientists and geographers? They said savages can't be civilized. I resisted, but how wrong I was, how wrong."

"Sir, you're smelling a conspiracy without reason," Balram said, his voice rattling as the captain pushed him backward and forward, as if he was made of straw, no bones or flesh to augment his frame. The captain might be despondent and weary, but he was stronger than he looked. Balram tried to extricate himself from the captain's grip, the tightness of which caused his frayed coat to give up wool.

"This man, Chetak, he met our group by chance, recognized you as an Englishman, and was curious about your intentions," Balram said. "He's famous for annoying the English. You have heard the stories, sir. When the Dehra magistrate went on a hunt, he stole all his cartridges and the magistrate had to return without having fired a single shot." The captain's eyes were as wide as melons. "But Chetak won't hurt anyone. The English officers call him the Gentleman Bandit, sir, you know this. I told him to keep your truth from Tibetans, and he has. He won't endanger a boy like Samarth or men like Harish and Rana, whom the Tibetans will punish for helping you."

The captain let go of Balram's coat only to grasp his throat, and his two thumbs pressed into Balram's windpipe a lot more firmly than they ought to. The world grayed. Black crows flew across his eyes. Balram was dimly aware of Chetak intervening on his behalf, prying the captain's hands away from his throat, raising a fist toward the captain's face, or was it his ribs, then the clack of bone against bone. Feet slipped, the metallic scent of blood rose up to his nostrils, Gyan whispered to him that envy was a terrible thing, Durga told him his children needed their father, vultures hissed, the river grumbled, a blade of light pierced his eyes. Then, darkness.

When he came to, the captain and Chetak were two shadows locked together like the sky and the earth on a stormy day, no distinct line that was the horizon to tell one from the other. Their movements seemed unnaturally slow to Balram, perhaps because of the lack of air in his blood. His jaw was locked, he couldn't call out to them to stop, or shout for Harish and Rana, where were they anyway. Then, like a bird falling from the sky, the captain slipped backward and crashed into the river, his lips forming a circle but no scream coming out of his throat or perhaps it was Balram who could no longer hear. Chetak dusted his hands as if he had been plucking weeds. The

captain spun with the currents, his coat, saturated with water, clinging to his body but his saffron robe floating around him like a shoal
of colorful fish.

Balram waited for the captain to swim to the shore. The currents,
giddy with the memory of the rain's abundance, turned into knots
around the captain's limbs and pulled him down to their churning
depths. Sunbeams lit his wretched face, which seemed to Balram to
be the last glimmers of death. Somewhere the arm of a clock turned,
but time was still, time was swift, a moment was as long as a lifetime
and a lifetime was as brief as a moment. Balram attempted to stand,
but his knees were like putty. Before he could find his bearings, a
small figure dashed past him and Chetak to dive into the river, arms
outstretched, fingers pinned together like a kingfisher's beak.

Samarth was no match for the river's turbulence. Before he could
reach the captain, the water swept him away, hurling him toward the
rocks on the shore. Chetak cussed and dashed down the riverbank,
apparently at the same pace as the currents, because he was where the
boy was in the blink of an eye, pulling his coat off his shoulders, kicking off his shoes, rolling up his trousers, and wading into the water to
throw his hands around Samarth, whom the currents spirited away
even as Chetak tried to apprehend him. A tussle ensued, between
Chetak and the river, and Chetak and Samarth, the boy like an animal
ignorant of what was good for its survival, insisting on swimming
toward the captain—*the captain!*—Balram had forgotten him. He
had drifted toward the other side of the bank and only his forehead
could be seen above the surface of the water, then he vanished, he
had drowned. Balram had let him die. But he appeared again, his
neck barely above the water, and Balram felt such relief that he knew
at once what he had to do.

The currents exhorted Balram to submit, at first gently ferrying
him downstream and, when he attempted to resist, turning spiteful,
submerging his head beneath the water like a bully. The cold speared
his skin. Flailing against the river's might, he tried to rise to the surface. Above the water the sun looked murky, a lantern held up in
black fog. Water rushed into his mouth and silt lined his tongue and

nostrils. His limbs were weak after the captain's throttling, and his lungs burned as if a fire was consuming them. He ought to stop struggling. Let the river carry him wherever it wanted.

Don't you dare, Durga said.

Coward, Gyan said.

Balram thrashed his legs and strained against the currents until his hands found purchase on the captain's coat. He held on to it as tightly as he could, taking long, lusty gulps of the chilly air. Slowly his vision cleared.

He put all his strength into hauling the captain's not inconsiderable bulk toward the riverbank, where he saw in the periphery of his vision Harish and Rana waving, their mouths opening and closing to form words of encouragement perhaps. The wind and the river lopped off their voices before they reached him. His own body felt to Balram as heavy as a mountain. The spiteful river wanted to drag him down to its depths. He feared he could no longer hold on to the captain owing to the agony that tore every muscle in his arms apart.

Under his feet shorn of boots—he must have cast them off before entering the water though he had no recollection of the act—he felt the sharpness of the stones on the riverbed. The pain came as a relief to him because they were out of danger at last. He allowed his mind to relax and all at once the water jostled against his chest with the force of a giant mallet. He lost his balance and yet again he was drowning and the captain too was sinking with him.

Then hands pulled him out of the water, pressed against his chest until he coughed up mud. Slaps stung his cheeks.

"Thank the gods you're alive," a voice said. Balram opened his eyes, and the sun seemed too bright to him, but his limbs must have been numb or frozen because he couldn't raise his hands to shade his face.

"The captain," he managed to whisper.

"Built like the devil," Rana said. "Nothing can kill him, not this river, not even snow leopards or the ro-lang."

"He'll live, just about," Balram heard Chetak say. The bandit was carrying Samarth on his back. He put the boy down next to Balram and removed the pebbles Samarth stored in the pockets of his tunic, the weight of which must have hastened his near-drowning. Samarth wheezed. His face was white, his lips blue.

UNDERWATER BALRAM'S MIND MUST have become as permeable as air. Thoughts drifted in and out. He fell asleep. He gained consciousness. He overheard others whispering about him, and the captain swearing at the bandit.

"You tried to kill me," the captain said, "but what else can one expect from a thief?"

"It was an accident," Chetak said. "I had to stop you—you were about to kill your guide."

The captain's silence seemed to acknowledge that the bandit's statement was true.

"A lesser man would have asked his servants to tie me up," Chetak said either by way of an apology or in an attempt at reconciliation, "though the fact remains that they wouldn't have been able to overpower me."

Harish and Rana grunted derisively, but didn't challenge him.

The sun crisped Balram's shirt and warmed his blood and brought feeling back to his limbs. Harish helped Balram sit and fed him spoonfuls of brandy that dribbled out of his mouth and onto his chin. In the periphery of his vision, Balram saw their coats, weighed down with stones, laid out on rocks to dry. Above him, white clouds moved swiftly in the wind. The coughing fits from the captain's tent reminded him that he ought to check on Samarth. He had every intention of getting up, but his body refused to listen to his mind.

Chetak sat next to Balram for a while. When the captain was out of earshot, he offered to steal his money. Englishmen always concealed their gold coins in their coats or trunks, Chetak said.

"Do you agree?" Chetak asked. "Trust me. I'll not run off. I'm a man of my word. I'll save your friend."

When Chetak moved away, Balram closed his eyes. He was home again, and Durga was lying next to him. He could smell the familiar

scents, of sesame oil on her skin, clay and smoke under her finger-
nails, the sweat that glistened in the nape of her neck where soft
strands of hair curled around his fingers as he pulled her toward him
at night after the children were asleep. He sat up, filled with want;
then Gyan came to his mind, Gyan chained in a dark cave, Gyan
whose words must have shrunk to grunts, Gyan whose eyes must
have forgotten the patterns the sun's rays could draw on the floor. An
unfamiliar pain kneaded Balram's hands and shoulders, reminding
him of the threat the river had posed to his life.

Atop a peak a few vultures could be seen confabulating like
guards at the entrance of a fort, a companionship blossoming among
them now that their hunger had been sated. Below the mountains, a
similar fellowship seemed to have sprung up between Harish, Rana,
and Chetak. They chatted by the bearers' tent, which was in a state of
near collapse. Harish and Rana had begun the process of dismantling
it before Chetak pushed the captain into the river. For some reason
they were in no hurry to put it back together. How odd these days
were, how strange their pared group—a child; a bandit; an Englishman; two bearers willing to risk death for their love or lust as if they
were Laila and Majnu; and then Balram himself.

Pulling his half-damp coat over his shoulders, Balram hobbled
toward the captain's tent, outside which he sat reading Herodotus.
Around the captain's left eye glowed a purple-red bruise that must
hurt each time he blinked.

"How is Samarth?" Balram asked.

"No different," the captain said.

"I'll ask Chetak to leave," Balram said.

"What if he reports us to the Tibetans? Better to have him in our
sights. He has my guns—I'm certain he didn't fling them into the
river. I had left them outside. My mistake. But at least it means he
didn't search the trunks and find the money."

"Our expedition has gone poorly, sir, for which I can only apologize. But once Gyan is released, we can give the bandit a little money
and—"

"What's stopping him from taking my money now?"

"He says he wants to help Gyan. I believe it's the truth. He rescues goats and buffaloes from the traps English hunters set because he has a kind heart. He fights for those without——"

"Nonsense."

"What's important is that the rescue of Gyan needn't spell the end of our expedition."

"I can't let the boy die," the captain said.

"Is Samarth——"

"He won't survive a march over the gorge."

"He can go home with Gyan. To survey this river, we don't need anyone else. Not even Harish and Rana. I can guide you."

How easily Balram lied. He knew the Tibetans would force him, and everyone in the group, to leave with Gyan—if they didn't spot a white man in their midst. And if they did, who knew what punishment awaited them? The rock on which his feet rested was hot. He looked around for his boots.

"Harish washed your boots because they tipped into the mud," the captain said, a finger massaging the temple above his bruise. "Fur doesn't dry easily. Give it a day."

A pack of kiang raced down a mountain slope toward the river, dust clouds lashed to their hooves. These animals spotted their motley party, but not having had reason to be afraid of humans yet, quenched their thirst at the river and scrutinized the ground for grass. Balram wondered if their unsuspecting tongues would chance upon a bloodied feather or a severed limb. These entrails in the river were inside him too now. A just punishment, all things considered. Let his sins discolor his blood; let the world know him as a cannibal. He had set out to assist a white man as he mapped a river, and the river, angry at being surveyed without its permission, had called Balram to account. Remembering the compass only now, he looked for it in the pockets of his coat and found it gone—the river must have claimed it, rightly so.

"What if you were to go into Shigatse town?" the captain asked. "Perhaps you'll run into the bearers?"

"There's no telling how they'll react."

"Ask them to take Samarth with them. Rudra owes the boy that much."

Balram's breath whistled loudly between his teeth. "Can't make it across the river today," he said. "Maybe tomorrow."

"Who knows where they'll be tomorrow," the captain said. Samarth coughed vigorously. "What if they send Tibetan officials after me?" the captain continued. "Should we make camp elsewhere?"

"The bearers can't give you up without implicating themselves. Easier for them to pretend they served a trader who dismissed them midway to avoid paying their wages. Happens often enough."

"I was surprised you saved my life," the captain said.

"I didn't do much."

"You're right on that count."

BY EVENING BALRAM'S HEARTBEATS were steadier, but Samarth was feeble. The captain gave him sips of brandy and swaddled him in his thickest blankets. Chetak devised from the meager provisions in his sack a simple meal of dal and roti that they ate quickly.

Around them the mountains were quiet save for the wind. The vultures flew home, but dusk lingered in the sky in defiant crimson smudges.

"I keep hearing Ujjal and Jagan bicker," Harish said.

"Food doesn't go down my throat without a good sprinkling of Kaccha's curses," Rana said, the smooth shine of his empty bowl betraying his words. "But I'm glad I won't have to hear about Jagan's elbow again."

Chetak smiled. In Hindustan the police would offer a handsome reward to those who had information about the bandit's whereabouts, but here in Tibet the captain was the wanted man. This inverted world, so precise and yet dreamlike, had an unreal quality to it.

After his meal, the captain whispered to Balram that he should stay in the tent with Samarth and keep an eye on his belongings while he performed his nightly ablutions, guarded by Harish and Rana. Samarth looked frightful. Phlegm stained his pillow. Balram boiled water in the dying sputters of the fire—they had exhausted the last of the wood and dung—and took the steaming pot to Samarth. He told the boy to inhale the steam, and placed a blanket over his head and shoulders to trap the warm vapor. It struck him that he had never looked after Inder this way; Durga cared for the boy in his fevers and chills.

Quiet as a shadow, Chetak slipped into the tent, held Balram's gaze, then pressed a finger against his lips. The bandit rifled through the captain's coat, robe, and blankets, finding nothing but scraps of paper and pencils. Then he padded to the corner of the tent where the captain's trunks were heaped. Balram nearly called out to him to stop.

Chetak set aside the first trunk that had held the rifle and pistol, then opened the one below it. Balram looked away, as if that would absolve him of blame. The steam seeping out of the woollen blanket stung his eyes. Around his forearms he saw the contusions he had suffered on account of the captain and the river, swelling now in the light of the lanterns in the tent, the flames casting a yellow tinge over the black and purple patches on his skin embossed with the stark redness of broken capillaries. The captain's fingers on his throat must have left similar bruises. Samarth inhaled, coughed, then blew his nose on a rag that Balram pressed into his hands through the folds of the blanket. Balram's shoulders ached when he leaned forward. He heard the wind and the river, then voices drawing near. He looked up to see the bandit close the trunk. "Hurry," Balram hissed.

Samarth almost cast his blanket aside, but Balram pulled it down. "Inhale with all your strength," he said, and Samarth duly obeyed him as Inder never did.

Chetak slipped out. Balram's head ached.

Samarth shrugged off his blanket. Sweat glistened on his wan face and snot crusted his nostrils. His eyes were red and swollen, and on his lips blood thickened on blisters like sap on the bark of a tree. The captain entered the tent, sat down beside Samarth, and placed in the boy's hand a pebble as smooth as a plum, tinted an iridescent black. Samarth's eyes sparkled before the phlegm lodged in his lungs caused him to cough. The captain rubbed his back and said, "Slowly, slowly." His eyes flicked to Balram's, and Balram's chest tightened with fear.

THE WIND'S GREAT CACOPHONY woke Balram the next morning. Chetak was missing, but Harish and Rana presumed the bandit was taking inordinately long to conduct his morning business. It was no surprise, they said. This altitude twisted one's bowels, they said.

As their fuel rations had run out, they couldn't light a fire to cook a meal. For breakfast, Balram suggested they mix roasted barley flour with cold water, resulting in a meal that had the texture of gum and tasted of sand. Along with the river water they ingested all that had lived and died in the currents, and the captain said cholera or dysentery was bound to follow.

Only a moment later did Rana notice that Chetak's sack too had disappeared. The captain turned pale, and dashed to his tent. By the time Balram entered, the contents of the captain's trunks were strewn about on the floor, and the captain was shaking his notebooks as if his pouches of gold coins would miraculously fall out of their pages. "Where is he?" he shouted, and Balram's hands went up to his throat, where he could still feel the shape of the captain's fingers.

"Let me go to the monastery where Gyan is locked up," Balram said. "I'm certain I'll find Chetak there."

The bruise around the captain's eye was darker and yet almost lustrous on this gray morning. Stepping over his belongings, he walked out of the tent and shouted at Harish and Rana to pack up the camp.

"Where are we going, sir?" Rana asked.

"To recover what has been stolen from me," the captain said. "And you," he said, turning to Balram, "you're nothing more than a common criminal. You put the bandit up to this, didn't you? This was always your plan. You never intended for me to map the Tsangpo."

Samarth shook under a mass of blankets, weak and feverish. Balram helped him gather his belongings, a task made difficult by his refusal to part with his pebbles. The captain reapplied what was left of his dye onto his hair and beard. Their journey was drawing to a close—Balram sensed it in the quickening pulse of the wind, the low grunts of vultures on the hilltop, and the long, rippling shadows the mountains cast on the Tsangpo. They would either free Gyan or be captured themselves. Balram would either return to his school or be hoisted up the gallows for betraying the Empire. Exhilaration, then dread, surged in his heart. These feelings were perhaps no different from what mountaineers experienced on summiting a peak, a madness settling in their brains deprived of air, the terror of descent darkening the joy of reaching the peak.

At the fording place where the river shallowed, Balram hoisted Samarth over his shoulders and began to cross. His limbs ached, and he felt as if his legs had been hooked to fishing tackles that reeled him backward. They made it to the other side. Harish and Rana said the captain couldn't show himself to Tibetans, their eyes sending each other messages Balram couldn't comprehend. The wind was now threatening and icy. The captain shivered. When Balram suggested he stay behind with the bearers, he snapped at Balram to be quiet. He carried a trunk, but despite him lending them a hand, they had had to leave behind most of his sheepskin rugs and blankets and glasses, their numbers being insufficient to ferry all of his possessions.

In the villages they passed, their ramshackle group earned them the curious stares of Tibetans, some of whom recognized Balram from the day he had inquired about Gyan. They stopped him to ask if he had found his friend. Balram said he hadn't. He volunteered the additional information that their camp had suffered a misfortune, but claimed falsely that it was on account of a snow leopard attack, which caused the villagers to shrink from him as if he carried the pox.

They climbed the hill on which the monastery stood, the captain overruling Balram's protests.

"I don't trust you to bury me right," the captain said. "And I know better than to show myself to the Tibetans—I'll stand at a safe distance from the monastery. You tell the monks Chetak is a crook, get the government funds back, then we leave."

His tone didn't suggest he believed his own words. He must know that his journey was over.

In the distance was Shigatse town, shrouded in a blue light. The captain scratched a dye stain on his thumb.

Samarth shuddered as Balram put him down. He leaned the boy against a boulder and wiped the sweat off the boy's hot forehead with a rag. When Samarth didn't stand up after a while, Harish and Rana pulled him to his feet. His body was so limp they had to drag him with their hands hooked under his armpits. None of them commented on the ferocious redness that cobwebbed the whites of his eyes or the damp patch on the crotch of his trousers that they spotted whenever the two bearers unwittingly caused his coat to rise. Samarth muttered about his favorite Moti, dead now for weeks, and Colonel, the pony, whom the bearers must be chasing somewhere in the alleys of Shigatse town.

Monks stood outside the monastery's main entrance, rosaries around their necks, their right arms bare against the whipping wind, their robes bunched onto the other shoulder.

"Let me find out if Chetak is here," Balram told the captain. "Please, sir, the Tibetans must not see you."

"Don't try to trick me," the captain warned, but he spoke haltingly, as if he knew he was at their mercy, an odd position for an Englishman.

From the monks' animated chatter, Balram understood that a man had arrived at their doorstep with gold coins that would see them through three winters. Such an exchange, a spy for gold, was a matter to be approached with caution, they said. Alms could be received, and blessings offered in return. This much was moral. But could one set an enemy free and not risk damnation?

Balram slipped past the monks. Inside the prayer hall Chetak and the elderly lama Balram had met on his first visit were engaged in a fluent conversation conducted entirely through gestures.

Though light beamed from the Buddha's golden face, the hall was steeped in darkness. The door was open and the wind tumbled around like a mischievous child, snuffing out the wicks of lamps. Doubt jabbed Balram's mind. He hadn't set eyes on the prisoner. What if it wasn't Gyan? On this journey, all his calculations had been wrong, and his recklessness had cost the lives of men. Perhaps the gods, having noted his maggot-ridden heart, had brought him to the monastery to serve justice.

A monk closed the door and relit a few lamps. The air grew stuffy with the sweet scent of incense. Chetak spotted Balram and hurried toward him.

"Come on, brother," Chetak said and thumped Balram on his shoulder, still raw from the previous day's scuffle with the river.

Balram's vision wavered. The lamps blinked and the figures in the murals leaped out of the walls. A thangka depicting the White Tara swung from a pillar like the pendulum of a clock, as if measuring the hours he had left behind on earth.

"The monastery has set generous terms," Chetak told Balram. "They will let your friend go, but they seek an assurance from us that he will return to the border immediately. I have taken the liberty of giving them that assurance."

"Without a word of Tibetan?"

"I have been told my face is quite expressive."

"Is it my friend they hold as prisoner?"

"Why are you asking me this now?" Chetak said, his voice rising in disbelief. "Didn't you confirm it was him? You didn't ask to speak to him first?"

"This doesn't concern you," Balram said. But he felt ashamed. The captain was right; he was a poor leader. He couldn't do anything right. All he wanted was to be left alone, by his students, his bearers, his children, even Durga. Only Gyan had understood the nature of the silence he required.

"It does sound like a Survey man," Chetak said now, kindly. "And I guess since only one such man is missing, it stands to reason it's your friend who's imprisoned here."

Balram thought that in another life, the Gentleman Bandit must have been a benevolent king who shared his wealth with his subjects; something of this past life seeped into him even now in the way he held his head high but at an angle, in the authoritative tone in his voice, and in the kindness he showed unasked to strangers despite his chosen profession as a plunderer.

A monk stepped out of the darkness, holding a lamp high, his expression so mournful he could have been conducting a corpse to the forlorn heights where vultures gathered. Behind him stood a hunchbacked figure, mangled, filthy, and reeking of rot and piss and sweat and vomit.

"Gyan?" Balram said.

"So it is your friend," Chetak said. "What a relief."

The figure drew back from Balram in alarm, as if he had intended to strike him. "Gyan, it's me, Balram," he said. The monk with the lamp encouraged Gyan to step forward with a wave-like movement of his hands that caused the light to illuminate a patch of the cob-webbed ceiling, then the cracked red floor.

Balram's heart beat so fast he couldn't breathe. He blinked back tears; pretended he had an Englishman's reserve. He moved closer to Gyan and rolled up the sleeves of his chuba; lined with lamb's wool and fashioned out of sheepskin, they extended all the way to his ankles.

"You're going home," Balram whispered, wishing he could clasp Gyan to his chest even as the vicious stink almost caused him to retch. "Your mother has been waiting for you for so long. She never gave up hope." The chuba's sleeves were stiff with dirt, and simultane-ously claggy with snot or drool.

Gyan's lips moved, but no words emerged. Who had it been, speaking assuredly in his ear all this time? Gyan's gaze was affixed to the ground, and his expression was remote. Balram wondered if his mind had atrophied in the swells of darkness he must have shared with mice and fleas.

All this while Gyan's absence had been palpable in him, like an empty socket in his skull where an eye should have been. In the early days of Gyan's disappearance, Balram hadn't even been able to eat; how could he, when Gyan might be starving? How could he laugh when Gyan was in prison? How could he dream when his friend might be sleepless? Then one afternoon at school, separating boys pulling each other's hair, Balram had heard Gyan speaking to him and, if it had been startling at first, it had soothed him over time.

Now he had Gyan in his sights and he ought to feel mended and whole; younger, lighter. But he didn't even feel relief. Perhaps it was that the Gyan who stood in front of him wasn't the Gyan he had known, the man with hefty muscles plainly distinguishable below his tunic, and sharp eyes that accurately measured the height of a mountain without the help of instruments. His limbs shook like those of a drunk always sipping chhang, and his skin was sprinkled with ash-colored blotches that resembled the lichen growing on dead trees.

Balram tucked Gyan's matted hair behind his ears. The filth in his hair was thick like grease and coated Balram's fingers, but he felt such tenderness that his thumbs lingered on Gyan's cheeks until Gyan slapped him away. Gyan's nails were long and sharp, and clamped into the web of skin between Balram's fingers. The pain was piercing and concentrated.

Balram thanked the monks. He put his hand around Gyan's shoulders and guided him toward the door. He sensed fleas in Gyan's chuba, lice crawling in his hair. It began to rain, and the light in the prayer hall dimmed even more. Had Gyan lost a tooth or two, or was it a shadow? Balram couldn't tell. His friend's cheeks were gaunt, hollows edged by bones sharp as knives. The chuba slipped down his shoulders as if waiting for another form to enter his body and fill his clothes.

Gyan clutched his hand, and Balram remembered the two of them at thirteen swimming in the river and collapsing on the soft sand afterward as parrots chirped and trees swayed in the wind and sunlight strained to breach the thick green canopies. Gyan took a step forward, and Balram remembered a night they had spent on the rooftop of a dak bungalow smoking opium until the stars in the sky appeared mismatched, a few green and red and the others violet, everything hazy and upsetting and the world not at all pleasant and soft as they had hoped. Gyan felt the sting of the rain-bearing wind against his face and winced, and Balram remembered slipping into a crevasse, its blue throat enticingly wide open, its white, glassy teeth glued to his cheeks, and Gyan hauling him out. Gyan stopped, and Balram remembered the captain asking him to trace the path of the Tsangpo, a journey that was delayed because Inder was ill, but even after his boy recovered, Balram had concocted excuses to avoid the trip; months before, he had petitioned the captain for a grant of land in recognition of the services he had offered the Empire, and the captain had denied his request, but said yet again that he would recommend Gyan's name for a medal at the Royal Geographical Society. Then Gyan had offered to travel in his stead, and Balram hadn't said *I'm protesting by not traveling.* He hadn't said *We deserve a plot of land and a pension from the English.* He hadn't said *I deserve a medal too.* Even now he couldn't say *The English pit Hindu against Musalman, neighbor against neighbor, and friend against friend, and make fools of us all.* Each time the captain said "Gyan is my best surveyor," it had only spurred Balram to do more, take risks he wouldn't have otherwise. He touched the calluses on Gyan's fingers and wondered how he could have been so foolish.

A monk no older than eight or nine darted past Balram into the prayer hall. Jumping up and down in excitement, the boy said to the elderly lama that a white man in disguise was part of Balram's rank and file.

"I hope this winter won't be harsh," Balram said to the lama.

"Foreigner," the boy monk said, pointing an accusatory finger at Balram.

The lama asked Balram to wait. Chetak cupped his hands over the flame of a lamp with such tenderness he might as well have been attending to an injured bird. He didn't seem worried about this turn of events. Perhaps this was what he had wanted to witness all along: the vanquishing of an Englishman. Balram wished he could escape with Gyan; in this moment he didn't care about anyone else. He thought of Samarth and decided the boy would be well looked after at the monastery. Rudra must have made a similar calculation before setting off without him at night. An orphan's cursed life, Balram thought. It had been his life too, and he had been fortunate to have Gyan in it.

Young monks ushered the captain into the hall, along with Harish and Rana, who were still holding Samarth up. The lama gazed in wonderment at the captain dressed in his saffron robe stained by dye and rain and sweat. The captain didn't seem to notice Gyan and Balram.

"The boy looks very ill," Chetak said to Harish and Rana. "He needs medicine."

"He does," Harish said, flinching as he glanced at Gyan, as if worried the filth on Gyan could malign his polished person. "Is this . . . him?" And Balram thought of how the Gyan at his side was so frail he was almost vapor. Chetak whispered to the elderly lama, whose knees must be aching, because he cautiously lowered himself onto a cushion seat. Lacking Tibetan, Chetak gestured furiously. The captain recoiled from the monks who crowded around him, not with anger or menace but wonder—he must be the first white man they had ever seen.

One of the monks removed the captain's wire glasses and put them on, and the others clapped and laughed as if a great trick had been performed. Even in the dim light of the prayer hall's lamps, the captain's green irises had the lurid brilliance of pond scum against his weather-beaten, sun-browned, peeling skin and the fraudulent blackness of his beard. His bruise shone brightly.

The captain blinked frequently, as if the world would reorder itself around him once he could see it more clearly. Red blood seemed to spill out of the mouths of the demonic deities in the murals on the walls. The edges of their teeth curved sharp and eager.

Gyan fled toward the grainy darkness that lay beyond the light of the lamps. The monks stopped him. He held his wrists together and extended his hands toward them, asking to be cuffed and returned to his cell. "Gyan, don't you recognize me?" Balram pleaded, but Gyan wouldn't even look at him. A searing pain began in his heart, no different from the ache he had felt when he first heard the stories of Gyan being held prisoner.

Samarth fainted. Fortunately he didn't hit the floor because of the crush around them. Rana slapped the boy's face, rather harshly, to wake him up.

The elderly monk called for order. Balram and the other visitors—barring Chetak—were guided to a room near where Gyan had been immured. Lanterns were lit, but the cell was more of a grotto than a room, without even a crack for a window. Here Gyan seemed more at ease while Harish and Rana gasped for air; after all these months in the wilderness, to them it must feel like the walls were smothering them. In the confined space Balram could smell the filth on the men's skin and hear their chests rise and fall, their breaths loud and erratic from fear.

"How well your plan to save Gyan has worked," Rana said. "Was it worth it? Three of our friends are dead, and we're prisoners ourselves. While this man—this friend of yours—he's happy here, he doesn't even want to leave."

Balram's mind was in tangles, swiftly moving from one fear to another. He glanced at Gyan, sitting away from them in a corner, disappearing into the darkness as the outline of a hawk might fuse with the clouds. He looked at the captain, his restless fingers worrying the beads of his rosary, his eyes fixed on the ground. Exhaustion buckled Balram's knees. His shoulders and arms were weak and sore, as if the river was still attempting to drown him. He slumped to the ground, rested his back against a wall. Then someone shook him awake. For how long had he passed out? Two monks had brought them water and tsampa. Balram refused the food, and begged them to grant him an audience with the elderly monk. "Look," he said, forcing them to turn to Samarth, wheezing and tearful. "You're killing a child."

I'm killing a child, he thought.

The monks left.

Gyan crawled forward to eat from the bowl, using his fingers to scoop out the flour. He drank the water quickly, streams dribbling down his chin. The captain was trembling, the lantern's flame flickering in his eyes, teeth clenched and veins bulging in his forehead as he studied Gyan as if he was a wounded animal that could hurt him. His *best surveyor*, and he hadn't even said a word to Gyan. He seemed full of fright. Anyone would think they had conspired to push him underwater, and maybe they had. A day before, Balram would have attempted to reassure the captain—*the lama seems like a good man, a true Buddhist who won't sanction killings*—but their relationship was now broken.

When Gyan retreated to a corner, Balram spoke to him softly, hoping his voice could lift Gyan out of whatever hell he had descended to.

Remember how, after you lost a toe to frostbite, the captain suggested slicing off one of my toes too so that our gaits would be the same?

Remember the time we went on a survey to Kumaon and met a memsahib looking for her lost dog? You told her it must have been eaten by a panther, and at first she threatened to shoot you, then she cried.

Remember how we were chased by bandits in Turkestan? We had to run from them, then return, because we still had to record our paces.

Gyan used his long nails to extricate the food caught between his teeth. "Where are you, my dear friend?" Balram said, and gods, why did it feel like he was a bird flying with the clouds and Gyan was an ant scurrying through grass; this vast space between them that couldn't be crossed on foot or horseback, like all the gaps in his life that he could sense but didn't know how to fill, between his thoughts and actions, between him and Inder, between him and Durga on those days she saw how he couldn't be a father to their children, or between him and his students as he told them that al-Khwarizmi, a mathematician who had lived in Baghdad, was the founder of algebra and they gazed bleary-eyed out of the windows. Balram was a surveyor who couldn't bridge these great distances, not with maps or equations or words.

A monk creaked the door open to say they had been summoned outside.

"By whom?" Balram asked. He didn't receive an answer. They were led out of the grotto, their steps echoing in the corridor. Gyan didn't want to leave, and he had to be dragged forward by monks who seemed to find his intractability amusing.

Outside the monastery, the rain had stopped. Waxen clouds converged above their heads. Balram heard the hooves of horses being led up the hill and realized that an entire regiment was about to arrive.

The captain attempted to smooth the creases in his robe, determined to hold on to his dignity no matter how hopeless his fate. Lavender shadows meandered across his forehead. The crosshatch of wrinkles embedded in the thin, dark skin below his eyes and within his bruise grew more prominent. "I will plead your case," Balram said, feeling sorry for the captain, and the captain snapped, "You have done enough."

Chetak stood with a group of young monks, smiling benevolently at Balram every once in a while. Blue light gleamed in the bandit's animal eyes. Balram couldn't tell how Chetak had managed to avoid scrutiny without a word of Tibetan. Was it by giving up the captain?

Samarth lay down on the ground, shivering in the cold, mucus encrusting his nostrils. Gyan's brows curled as if the dwindling sunlight troubled his sight, and he buried his face in his hands. Balram had the uncanny sense that he had been in this moment before, everything ending, his own life a mere curlicue of white breath about to be erased by the wind. He was four and had at last understood that he didn't have a mother like other children. He was seven, and his aunts, weeping, whispered to him that his father had died on his way home from Tibet. He was twenty-eight and a crowd stopped him in the market to say his son—Inder was three then—was possessed by the devil and would be shunned. He was twenty-nine and a neighbor told him his baby had come out of Durga's womb already dead and blue. Now, all these years later, the parts of him that had become disjointed in those moments ached as if wounded anew.

A light rain had begun by the time the Tibetan regiment reached the hilltop. The edges of the hillside crumbled under the unexpected weight of horses and soldiers; rocks loosened and rolled down the slopes, and some must have fallen on roofs or on people, because there were shouts and screams from the villages below.

The approaching soldiers, young men wearing conical hats and ragged tunics, white flags tied to their matchlocks, the fabric darkening in the rain, pointed at the captain in surprise. The captain stood straight, defiant, but his hands were shaking.

Two officials whose fine coats suggested their high rank spoke to the elderly monk, who seemed to be standing with great difficulty. Villagers came up the track behind the horses to find out the reason for the commotion. The apple-cheeked children who had told Balram about Gyan visited with their mastiff and a gaggle of boys and girls and dogs. The ruffians among them brandished slings as if they were guns.

One of the older boys raised his sling and shot a stone in the direction of the captain. Balram shouted at the captain to duck, and he did, but the stone missed the captain anyway and struck Harish instead. Blood gushed out of the cut into the bearer's eyes, blinding him. He shouted in panic. Balram held his elbows down and asked him to tilt his neck toward the sky. The lama chastised the boys and a monk quickly fetched a bowl of water and a rag to clean the wound.

The elderly lama beckoned Balram over, and the soldiers pushed him forward though they had no reason to, causing him to stumble. Berry-red smears left by Harish's blood punctuated the black dirt under his nails. The lama explained to Balram that regretfully the captain's crime was deserving of the death penalty, while the rest of their group, including the sick child, would likely face imprisonment.

As he was speaking, soldiers bound the captain's wrists behind his back, and tied his ankles together so that he would trip if he tried to run. The captain protested loudly, threatening punishment in English as if the soldiers were his serfs, as if the untethered Tibetan landscape too was smudged with the red of the British Empire.

The captain's outcry prompted laughter from the children, who seemed to think he was putting on an act for their amusement. Gyan cowered close to the ground, the sleeve of his filthy chuba pressed against his eyes, and Rana dabbed with a rag at the blood that refused to congeal around Harish's wound. A soldier rifled through their sacks and the captain's trunks, so thoroughly that he found the secret compartments with the survey notes and sketches and maps.

"If you escort us to the border, the British government will pay you a considerable sum to free the white man," Balram said to the high-ranking officials. "Hold him at the border until one of us returns with the money."

The officials conferred with each other, then with the monks. They asked the villagers to disperse. Samarth, slumped on the ground, shuddered violently. The fever was beginning to cause his eyes to protrude from the sockets. Just as Balram asked a monk if he could spare medicine for the boy, convulsions wracked his body. The monk pressed a rag into his mouth, but when the fit passed, Balram saw that Samarth had bitten down on his tongue. Blood spilled out of his mouth. Someone fetched a foul-smelling bottle and poured its contents—a black, oily liquid—into Samarth's mouth, causing the boy to scream as if his tongue had been set on fire.

"Please, let us leave, and we will never return," Balram pleaded with the elderly lama and the generals. "Think of the child—he doesn't deserve a life in prison. He'll not survive it." Chetak agreed, his brisk gestures indicating that the natives ought not to be punished for the whims of a white man.

The rain stopped, but the light was still patchy. Around them the implacable wind screeched, and mastiffs whined, and the sky grew white as bone. Gyan attempted to run back into the monastery, the hem of his chuba raising dust. The Tibetan soldiers restrained him.

Samarth's wheezes became longer and louder. In the air was the bite of snow.

The officials questioned Balram about the captain's maps, if copies had been made, if the captain had drawn them with intentions of conquest.

"He's an honorable man," Balram said. "He likes to draw what he sees on his travels. The Russians are worse—now they would like to annex Tibet, wouldn't they?"

"No Russians here," one of the officials said.

"Of course not," Balram said. He looked up at the sky, and there was a solidity to it that seemed impenetrable, the color of it reminding him of white knuckles in fists curled too tight. Without warning, grains of snow drifted to the earth. On contact with his skin the snow melted, and he wiped off a drop on his forehead with the side of his thumb.

His white breath moved like a crooked finger through the air. A few monks retreated to the monastery, urging the elderly lama and the officials to seek shelter indoors. A watchful group of soldiers circled the captain and the bearers, the wind flicking snow into their eyes. For want of gloves, their hands shuddered.

A preternatural change came over the animals. The horses strained against their harnesses, ears pricked on account of a threat Balram couldn't hear. Tails arched across their backs, eyes whitened by fear, they stamped the ground. Dogs growled, retreating from the hillside. The time of judgment had come—Balram felt certain. The cold wind scored on his skin the withering remarks of others: *you lead men to their deaths; you're a poor leader; sinners don't deserve deliverance.* It was right that he should perish, like Chand and Naga and Yogi, and the Gyan he once knew but who no longer inhabited the body of his friend.

The air shifted yet again and Balram searched for his cap in the pockets of his coat. It was missing; he must have lost it in the jostle while being taken prisoner. The wind brought with it an odd, pungent smell, so robust it clawed at his nostrils. He looked at the sky, wondering what fresh misfortune the gods were about to hurl in his direction. Then he heard the clatter of scree loosened by feet, sensed a movement on the precipice, where the air, thick with cloud and snow, was opaque and ribbed like a seashell. A phantom shape moved in the periphery of his vision; a kiang or a fox, he thought, but when he turned there was nothing. He couldn't tell light from shadow, and he felt that in these few moments he had aged years. Then he was looking into the frosty eyes of a snow leopard that stood on the edge of the cliff. But it couldn't be—he was hallucinating. He pointed at the magnificent creature and turned to the others. *Do you see it? Is it not a—? Can it be? But how can it be?*

Balram scratched his skin to wake himself, but the snow leopard, far from disappearing, placed its forelegs on a boulder as if to take stock. Black rosettes bloomed on its pale gray coat, and its thick tail curved like a sickle. Balram now knew that the pungent odor was the scent of the animal, or its piss, with which it marked its presence, always invisible yet tangible. He ought to be afraid; he ought to run into the grotto of the monastery where the animal's paws couldn't reach him, but he was arrested by its gaze. It seemed to him that he was looking into a part of himself that he had always known existed but had never acknowledged.

The blue undertones in the animal's eyes were the same blue found in the depths of a crevasse, or the abyss into which Balram often imagined he would fall, the prospect of descent into another world as thrilling as it was frightening. The wind blew again, whitened by snow that gathered like a cloud over the hill and obscured the leopard.

"Where did it go?" he asked Chetak, who gripped Balram's shoulder and shook him, as if to wake him from a deep sleep. Balram pushed him away, turned to monks and soldiers, and insisted, "You saw the snow leopard, didn't you?" They said *I did* and *I did not,* and these were perhaps not two distinct answers but one and the same. His questions made them uneasy, and these feelings of disquiet seemed to be amplified by the sudden appearance of two vultures that hovered watchfully above the monastery. The dogs scattered, howling, and a few horses managed to escape. Soldiers ran after them, shouting at them to halt.

"Do you practice black magic?" a monk asked Balram. He turned away and rushed to the precipice, Tibetan soldiers and Chetak a step behind him. No sign of movement, no tracks on the earth. But emanating from a rock below his feet was the odor of urine so strong it masked the freshness of snow.

"Do you smell it?" Balram asked, and Chetak replied, "Must be the dogs." He expected the bandit and the soldiers to mock him, but their expressions were somber. Even if they hadn't seen the snow leopard—and perhaps he had fashioned the animal out of the cold and the weakness in his bones—they too sensed peril in the white wind, the vultures, the cries of the distressed animals. The soldiers looked at him with suspicion. A few of the monks chanted prayers, their fingers counting the beads of their japa malas. In tighter circles, the birds flew right above the captain, seemingly grasping that he would soon be carrion. The captain hunched his shoulders and bent his spine, shrinking his form as if he wanted to disappear into the earth that would not only survive him but also change its features so that it would be unrecognizable in the maps he had drawn. Other men would come after him and, in time, they too would be subdued by gods.

As a child Balram had learned to contain the longings in his heart, the desire to see those he had lost. He had accepted the presence of death in his life as if it was no more extraordinary than a flower tucked into a woman's hair or a thread of rudraksha beads around a holy man's neck. One day—perhaps today—he too would lose his form. One day—perhaps a year or two from now—Gyan and Durga and his children would wake up unable to remember his face or the timbre of his voice. One day he would be a ghost wandering the streets of Dehra and the corridors of the Survey. But he had trudged across this land for so long that somewhere his foot must have pressed against a still-forming rock, and one day, three years or three centuries later, a snow leopard passing that way might come across the nebulous imprint he had left on earth and sense his soul in the hollow of the rock. That would be his legacy as a surveyor, not a medal in his name or his statue in market squares, but it seemed to him now that it was more than enough.

EPILOGUE

KATHERINE LISTENED TO THE WIND SOUGHING IN THE BRANCHES of a species of willow that was more shrub than tree. The Tibetan soldiers guarding her and Mani had decided to make camp that evening in Gyantse, a trading town with an ancient monastery and a red-tipped fort zigzagging across jagged hills stained yellow by the evening sun. A tributary of the Tsangpo parceled the land it glided past into small islands. Poplars swayed in the evening breeze. Pigeons flocked to puddles to slake their thirst, and from distant houses came the sounds of mothers calling to their children to return home.

"A pretty picture," she told Mani. "No storms, no wolves. The land is happy we're leaving."

"It looks different because you don't have to hide who you are anymore," Mani said. He pressed the bones of his foot, which seemed to be troubling him still though he never complained. "The realization of our worst fears can be a form of freedom too."

"Must be exhausting to be a monk," Katherine said. "You have to find meaning even when you had rather cry."

"This journey has been difficult, but we have to accept that suffering is a part of our lives. It's not unexpected. It's not an anomaly."

"I could do without it, on the whole," she said, smiling, though the truth was that his serenity had made an impression on her—how could it not? Here was a young man who practiced what the Buddha preached every day, and accepted life's disappointments without anger. In this journey, he had been her guide and servant, monk and mendicant, son and teacher.

"You'll be glad to hear," Mani said now, "that the soldiers are

considering returning your book to you at the border. I told them
you're a scholar, that your words won't harm others."

If someone else were to turn the pages of her journal, smudged
with dirt, soot, and rain, they couldn't tell (as she could) that the
shape of certain letters had been dictated by the temperature, the pace
of the wind, and the extent of numbness in her fingers. They wouldn't
recognize the falsehoods she had chosen to animate, the creatures and
strangers she had concocted solely for purposes of entertainment.
The words she had scrawled under the frank gaze of the sun and the
moon had meaning only for her, and wouldn't survive without her
revisions and amendments. But, even if her journal was lost forever,
she ought to learn from the Buddhist monks who created intricate
paintings called mandalas out of colorful, crushed stone to represent
the universe. It was a delicate process that took weeks, despite which
they destroyed their beautiful creations upon completion, to illustrate the transitory nature of life. Her journal, like the mandala, was
impermanent; that was all there was to it.

Better to conquer grief than deceive it, Seneca had written, words
she had found so objectionable she had stubbornly closed her mind
to them until now, seeking in her restlessness a cure that couldn't be
secured.

She told Mani she was heading to the river. The soldiers didn't
seem to care if she wandered alone by the camp. In part it must
be because there were no female guards to keep an eye on her while
she washed or pissed. Mostly, they seemed confident she wouldn't
be able to find her way over the mountains without Mani, and hence
wouldn't flee without him. All these months of travel later, she could
accept that they were right.

The current group of soldiers who watched them were cordial but
aloof, and they asked no questions now as she passed them. The soldiers at Lhasa had deposited her and Mani at an army encampment,
as if it was a stage stop, and there they had become the responsibility
of a new group of matchlock-carrying soldiers. In this manner, they
had journeyed from Lhasa to Gyantse, and would continue thus until

they reached the border, where she and Mani would be freed, no doubt with strict warnings not to return.

Under a deep blue sky that was slowly turning red, Katherine ambled through a poplar grove, her steps guided by the river's babble. The last of the sunlight illuminated the ridges and hollows on the slopes in the distance. A voice uttered an Islamic prayer whose words Katherine recognized from her travels through Alexandria or a port frequented by lascars (or was this a memory from her childhood, when she had heard prayers from mosques as she accompanied her ayah on an errand?).

Through a gap in the trees, Katherine saw Chetak kneeling and touching his forehead to the ground, offering prayers in what must be the direction of Mecca. She waited, standing as still as she could, glad she had been afforded a few moments to compose herself. The mere sight of him had caused her heart to lift.

After she had caught her breath it occurred to her that he hadn't introduced himself as a Muslim. There was no need, certainly, but why hide it? What would prompt a Muslim to visit a land sacred to Hindus and Buddhists? And wasn't Chetak a Hindu name?

Dogs growled in a village across the river, and birds chittered as they returned to their nests. She thought she heard gunshots in the distance, but she must be mistaken; Tibetan Buddhists didn't hunt, and the soldiers who guarded them had rusted matchlocks that Mani had told her wouldn't fire.

When Chetak finished his prayers, Katherine stepped toward him and said, "Have you been following us?" But he looked surprised. In the evening light his eyes seemed to be a different color.

He asked her if she was headed to Kalimpong, and she confessed that she and her son—"My servant, really," she said now—were being held prisoner. He didn't seem surprised to learn she was half-caste, a fact she related as if she was talking about the weather, though it was the first time in her life that she had referred to herself as such to another. But he was perplexed that the Tibetans had correctly identified her as an interloper.

"They received intelligence that a foreigner was bound for Lhasa," Katherine said, and saw what could have been shame curl his features, but the sky was now darkening and she couldn't be certain of it. Had he been the one to warn them? How could that be when neither she nor Mani had mentioned Lhasa to him? "You called this a sacred country. You behaved like a Hindu pilgrim," she said, hurriedly, fear rising in her throat, but it wasn't because of his deception. She was worried Tibetan soldiers would call her back, and her time with this man would be, as always, curtailed.

"You of all people should understand why pretense is sometimes necessary," he said, though his tone was far from accusatory. She remembered their last night together and she wished she could once again fold herself neatly into his arms, and press her forehead against the sturdiness of his chest. But soon she would return to London and visit Edinburgh to lay flowers at Ethel's grave and meet her nieces. With time, this journey, like all journeys, would acquire the quality of a dream. Had it been her at twenty touching the trunk of an elephant in Ceylon? Had it been her dining with a handsome captain near Canton, smiling encouragingly as he stroked her wrist so that he would let her stay in a cabin whose fare was far more than what she could afford? Had it been her shuddering one winter night on a palanquin by the Ganges, only the light of a torch to show bearers the way and frighten beasts? Those experiences seemed almost preposterous to her now, as if she had merely imagined them. In a few more years her memories of Tibet too would soften like the veins of a leaf yellowing with time. This man, solid now in front of her, his clove-smelling breath on her face, would become an ethereal figure.

"I'm Sulaiman," he said.

She wanted an explanation, and was too stubborn to ask for it. Besides, what did it matter? He must have never heard of Seneca or Shakespeare, eaten with a fork and a knife, or hailed a hansom cab, and yet he was a kindred spirit; she detected in him a restlessness that was familiar to her, except that he embodied it with an equanimity she lacked, she who belonged in neither mountains nor cities, she who was neither white nor brown, she who wanted both adoration and seclusion.

"You must have heard about me," he said, and she laughed and said, "Why, because you're really the Black Prince of Perthshire, fleeing Elveden Hall?"

"Prince who?"

"Maharaja Duleep Singh. He now lives in . . . never mind."

"The English call me—what is it that they call me? A gentleman? Terai's Robin Hood? They have many names for me," he said in a rather brazen tone, as if he was informing her that he was indeed the Perthshire prince. "But I'm not dangerous, trust me. The English are afraid of me only because I side with those who have nothing."

Katherine touched her lips; she wished she hadn't kissed him, thought it thrilling too. Who would have imagined she would have such an intoxicating experience at the age of fifty? "I have met bandits before," she said. It felt true to her, though those bandits had only been men who had fallen on hard times, sailors stranded in ports, drunks and gamblers and thieves with an itch at their fingertips.

"Not many people know my real name," he said. He looked at her as if she might be an unworthy recipient of such a secret.

"Do you think a woman in my position can tell others about a bandit? I'll be ostracized."

"I'm not a common thief," he said. "And we can all agree that no one steals more than the English. They snatched the Koh-i-noor from the king—this prince you spoke about, Maharaja Duleep Singh, when he was just a child."

"I haven't given it much thought," Katherine said. He was no longer charming and playful like a snow leopard cub. Now he was the snow leopard with a bloodied mouth and a torn carcass at its feet. All that anger in him, a tightness between his ribs that she could sense. How well people hid their real selves, but perhaps that real self was a muddy river even to them, its depths obscure.

"The Tibetans are treating you well, I hope," he said, his expression kind once again.

"There's not much to eat," she said, "and they can't cook as well as you can."

"You should join us," he said, as if he was inviting her for tea. He explained that he was accompanying a group of Tibetan soldiers also headed to the border with yet another English prisoner, an explorer of sorts who had wished to follow the Tsangpo all the way to the sea. "There are many of you here," Chetak said, and she remembered the white man she had seen at Mansarovar. "I'll ask if both companies can be merged. Makes sense, doesn't it, as we're all headed to the border?"

"Mani will be pleased to see you," Katherine said. "He wants to thank you for your medicine, which cured his fever."

She headed toward the river. He walked with her, and turned his head away for the sake of her modesty as she washed her hands and legs and face. The river was calm and expansive, flowing between purple-brown hills. A light bloomed in every window of a house that clung to the incline of a distant mountain and, above it, stars glimmered in the ultramarine sky. She sat down on a boulder, her feet splashing the cold water of the river, and she couldn't tell if the sudden rush of sadness she felt in her heart was because soon she would have to leave Tibet behind, or bid farewell to this man, a thief who spoke and acted like a nobleman.

"Why are you accompanying Tibetan soldiers?" she asked.

"Tibetans and I share a common enemy, the English."

"The English are an honorable and just people. The Maharaja Duleep Singh lives lavishly in England, paid for by Her Gracious Majesty, Queen Victoria."

"The Koh-i-noor costs a lot more."

"I consider myself to be English," Katherine said, but it sounded as false as it had when, at ten, she had told her mother that her hair too would one day turn golden like Ethel's. Always Katherine had believed that at an indeterminate point in the future she would become who was she was meant to be, yet fifty years on earth had brought her no clarity. She was English and she wasn't, she had loved Ethel and she hadn't, she loathed Mother and Frederick and she didn't, she wanted to escape into the forests of India with this outlaw and she didn't.

As the earth turned so did she, certain emotions recurring in her in daylight only to disappear at sunset. Sometimes a concealed thought would be revealed under a dark sky like the pocked face of the moon. All she knew for certain was that she still inhabited this earth, and Ethel didn't—these seconds and hours Ethel hadn't been allotted but would have eagerly grasped with trembling fingers. Katherine, who had only ever been restless, thought she would be glad if the clocks paused and the wind ceased and the tides neither ebbed nor rose, and she had a moment of stillness in this grove with this dangerous stranger by her side.

SEVERAL MILES FROM SHIGATSE, Balram walked below a blue sky that seemed as smooth and round as a bead of glass. He hunched his back as Gyan did, illogically afraid if he straightened his spine his head would graze the curve of the cloudless sky and cause it to shatter.

They had marched past villages where children ran behind them, gawping at the soldiers and the white man they guarded with matchlocks; up and down hills that were barren except for the occasional tangle of shrub or tufts of grass and along the tributaries of the Tsangpo whose waters were the color of mud on cloudy days and a sparkling blue on warm days. They had climbed mountain passes swathed in green, the dampness of clouds rifling through their bones, ducking under prayer flags strung across paths, and cautiously adding mani stones to the heaps that other travelers had stacked by the bends in the tracks for good fortune. Balram could walk without counting paces, but for the captain it seemed difficult; he stopped every few minutes and touched his pockets as if hoping to find a piece of paper on which he could record his notes.

At night the fifteen Tibetan soldiers tasked with accompanying them to the border tied their arms and legs with rope, and watched them as they slept under a violet-blue sky thick with stars. Now their hours had a rhythm to which their limbs responded without the threat of force and, as a rooster might crow in the morning at the first suggestion of the sun's luminescence in the east, the men too extended their wrists to their captors when it was time for them to sleep. The soldiers were stern but not unkind, and their behavior toward the captain was no harsher than it was toward Balram or the others. Every Tibetan then didn't turn savage at the sight of the white man, yet the tales white explorers told of Tibet were of a violent land and a violent people.

Maps too were full of such false stories. Which map showed nomads threading colorful wool into the ears of their sheep, the pilgrim who prostrated and brought his forehead to the earth with each step as he circled tall mountains to pray for the health of all sentient beings, or the snow leopards that wore their tails like scarves when the nights were cold? Balram wanted maps that indicated these lives or he wanted no maps at all, and it seemed to him—now that he was likely headed to the gallows—that he had wasted too many years on false pursuits.

Perhaps even looting was more honest than surveying; no pretense in it at least. Balram thought of Chetak, who had struck an agreement with the Tibetans to walk with them until the frontier. His accomplices must be waiting on the mountain pass where the English claimed their Empire began, to spirit him away into the forests. Chetak had said Balram could flee with him and escape the captain's punishment. "You can see your children again at night or in disguise," he had said, "but not if you're hanged."

A life as a fugitive didn't appeal to Balram, and yet he ought to consider it if he wanted to live.

For now, having earned the trust of the guards, Chetak walked as a free man; no ropes bound him at night, and no questions were asked if he disappeared for many hours, as he often did. Somehow, just as a bar-headed goose knew the direction of its nest no matter how many thousands of miles it had flown from home, he too found their group however slowly or briskly they marched. He was inscrutable, this man who called himself Chetak, his real name a secret. Balram admired the bandit's reserve. He wished his own tongue wouldn't be so keen to express his every thought and truth. It was a sort of freedom too, to retain a self that the world—and the English masters—could never grasp.

When he looked around their group now, he saw that Chetak was missing again. Samarth's pace faltered. They had been walking without rest since morning, and the boy seemed weary, fever clinging to his blood still. "Almost there," Balram said to encourage him.

They passed a small settlement near Gyantse, and though the sun hadn't retreated beyond the mountains in the west, the villagers had already set their mastiffs free and the dogs were prowling the alleys to frighten ro-lang or bandits or wolves. The mastiffs saw their group and charged toward them, all bared teeth and growls and bristling black and brown fur. Balram and the bearers tried to forestall the creatures with shouts and furious swings of their sacks, and the Tibetan soldiers loaded their matchlocks, but it took too long—the wind snuffed out matches as soon as they were lit. Eventually one of the soldiers managed to fire his gun, and the dogs fled. Luckily, no man or animal appeared to have been injured.

Afterward, the villagers who owned the dogs, contrite and perhaps fearful of the soldiers, arrived at their camp with gifts of yak milk and butter, tsampa and chhang. As darkness descended, the alcohol mellowed the severe expressions of the soldiers, and their grips around their matchlocks loosened. Balram saw how young they were, how sparse their beards, and how robust their faith in the order of things. He envied them their innocence.

The soldiers praised the villagers for brewing the chhang well—just the right balance of sweet and sour, they said. When the villagers sang songs about love and work, the soldiers joined the chorus. Their voices weren't melodious and the verses were harsh. "If a master isn't kind, he's an ass in the skin of a leopard," they sang happily.

Balram glanced at the captain, whose beard sank into his chest as his fingers drew sketches on the ground. The captain no longer spoke to Balram or Gyan. One afternoon when Gyan slipped, the captain had glared at Balram as if Gyan's clumsiness made him an unworthy candidate for rescue. When Samarth approached the captain for a story, the captain had told the boy, rather sadly, that he wanted to be left alone.

After the villagers left, the soldiers grew quieter. One of them bound the captain, but he spared Balram and others the indignity and discomfort of shackles for the night, and the novelty of it caused them to sit utterly still around the fire long after it died down, afraid any movement would cause the soldiers to query the generosity of feeling—induced by chhang and a full belly—toward their prisoners.

Soon Harish and Rana fell asleep, and the captain closed his eyes. The Tibetans had let him live for a fee they would claim at the border, a decision precipitated by the uncanny appearance of snow, vultures, and the snow leopard at the monastery in Shigatse, all of which had suggested to the monks that some higher power wanted them to survive. A miracle, the gods intervening on Balram's behalf for once. Still, the captain had the appearance of a man who had lost everything—even hope. The Tibetans had confiscated not only his Herodotus and sketches, but also the dead bearers' belongings, and now they were returning home without even the men's ashes or bones for their families to pour into the Ganga. But the captain, the captain had his life, and his account of this journey even without a route map or measurements would likely win him the Founder's Medal from the Royal Geographical Society. He must know this and still seemed unhappy.

Balram made Samarth imbibe a spoonful of the black medicinal liquid a monk at Shigatse had offered them in a bottle. Despite its bitterness and unpleasant odor, Samarth swallowed it quickly and without complaint.

Like the rest of them, the boy had to sleep in the open, their tent having been claimed by the Tibetan generals along with the captain's possessions. Balram wrapped a blanket tightly around Samarth, already bundled in his coat, drawn up to keep the wind from raking his cheeks and his hair that had grown quickly after the tonsure at Mansarovar. He slept with the blanket over his face and would wake up with frost on his hair.

A great sound startled Balram and caused Samarth to sit up in panic. Balram saw torches flickering on the distant walls of the Gyantse fort whose architecture followed the triangular shapes of the hills on which it was perched. The earth seemed to be flickering too, a slow vibration that reached his bones. Samarth gripped his elbow on one side and Gyan shuddered on the other side. Dust clouds bounced up the path. A group of Tibetan soldiers approached their camp on horseback, carrying matchlocks. Affixed to the barrels of their guns were red flags, stars peeping through the holes in the worn fabric. "Must be a new group appointed to relieve our current guards," Balram said to Gyan. "They won't hurt us," Samarth too reassured Gyan as if Gyan was younger than him.

One of the soldiers swung himself off the horse to the ground, and Chetak stepped out of the dark toward him, a torch in his hand. Behind him was a woman, dressed in a Tibetan robe but carrying herself like a memsahib, the wife of a Survey officer who wore native clothes for private amusement. Next to her was a youth affecting the solemnity of a monk, a big bundle slung over his back, a slight limp in his gait. Balram remembered then that he had seen the two of them at Mansarovar after the storm. He hadn't noticed the woman's face at the time, and now he realized that she could pass for a memsahib or a native or a half-caste. Had her father been a man like the captain?

"Why is a bandit accompanying a memsahib?" he said to Gyan as if Gyan would answer. "And I thought I had seen it all." Gyan bit the hard skin below the tips of his long nails. Balram remembered now that in Mansarovar too the woman and the young man had been with Chetak.

Though his ankles were bound the captain stood up. Was it the sight of a woman that had lifted his spirits? He moved his hands, his wrists tied together, waving at the woman who wasn't even looking in his direction.

The soldiers conferred, gaping open-mouthed at the woman who stared back at them, forcing them to look away. In the torchlight Balram saw her lips were plump and her nose sharp. She seemed like someone who wouldn't brook any nonsense.

Chetak ushered her and the young man away from the soldiers. Balram pulled himself up to his feet and bowed. Gyan and Samarth remained sitting, and Harish and Rana were still asleep, but the woman didn't seem to mind their lack of politeness.

"This is Tara, and her guide, Mani," Chetak said. The woman looked embarrassed. "It's Katherine, actually," she said, and Chetak said, "I can't pronounce that." He could have been teasing her. She shook her head affectionately. Whether her relationship with him was maternal or amorous, Balram couldn't tell; her gray hair gave her a dignified look, yet her manner with the bandit was coy. "Tara suits you better," Chetak said, in a familiar tone no native would dare adopt with an Englishwoman. Then he told Balram, "She wanted to visit the Potala Palace, but the Tibetans wouldn't let her."

"They don't want you here?" Balram asked the woman. "Surprising."

Samarth touched the hem of the woman's robe as if to ascertain she was real. "What is a child doing here?" she said. Her Hindustani was perfect, and her diction much better than the captain's. "I'm not a child," Samarth said. He looked very small with the blanket over his knees.

The captain staggered toward them, his gait awkward and the rope around his ankles nearly causing him to fall face down onto the ground. He greeted the woman with such pleasure she turned toward her guide with raised brows.

"An explorer like myself, but a woman," the captain said in English. "What an unlikely encounter."

"A story for your journals, isn't it," the woman said; rather wryly, Balram thought.

The captain invited the woman to sit on his blanket, as if it was a throne. Chetak and the young guide seemed to be listening carefully to the flighty English words the captain and the half-caste woman spoke. The soldiers, now double in number, set up watches of two hours each until morning. Samarth went to sleep.

Balram looked up at the sky. At this very moment, hundreds of miles away, Durga must be sleeping under the same stars. His eyes fixed on the constellation of Seven Sages that he had shown her once. Tracing a line from it, he located the Dhruv, which the captain called the North Star, the star they relied on to calculate latitudes and orient themselves. But how unmoored he felt now. He didn't know the shape of the life that awaited him across the border or if there was a life.

Gyan intently observed the embers of the fire that were now more ashen than orange. If Balram shifted an inch, his body would press against Gyan's. These yearnings in him that could never be sated, but what did it matter now? All he wanted was for his friend to be returned to him, Gyan as he had been once, not in this frail form where sunlight could pass through him and leave no shadow.

"You must sleep," Balram told Gyan. Usually he seemed calmer at night without the harsh sunlight troubling his eyes, but the arrival of the soldiers had upset him.

The hills darkened as candles and lanterns were extinguished in the houses built on their slopes. Only stars marked the separation between the earth and the sky. To Balram it seemed that their quivering light was a silent incantation to revive the dead. There was so much he didn't understand—his son's grunts like the wind whose intensity he felt but couldn't parse for meaning; the abyss he glimpsed in a snow leopard's eyes, and the snow leopard itself like a creature from a dream that had strayed into his waking hours; and now his friend, his breath creasing the air in filaments of white, their history that had once spanned the length of their adult lives obsolete.

From the pocket of his coat Balram took out a length of fabric that he had sewn into a blindfold with needles and threads borrowed from the Tibetan soldiers. He touched Gyan on the shoulder, afraid of the reaction he would provoke, and predictably his friend recoiled, then slowly turned his head. Balram tied the blindfold over his own eyes. Hoping Gyan was watching him, and could see him in the starlight, he pointed to the slits he had cut into the middle of the blindfold so that one's vision wouldn't be fully obstructed. In shading the eyes from the sun, and thwarting snow blindness, it wouldn't be as efficient as the captain's wire-gauze spectacles, which now belonged to a general in Shigatse, but it served a similar function. Just as blinders made a busy street appear less frightening to a horse, Tibet's vastness seemed tractable when viewed through the gaps in the fabric.

Balram undid the cloth and placed it across his friend's wrist. Gyan picked up the blindfold and pressed it against his eyes as if it wasn't made of cotton but silk, a smile lifting the corners of his lips. The Milky Way like a dragon's breath arced across the night sky in a track of luminous and opaque clouds. What had these stars not seen before? Life and death, bonds broken and repaired, and men who drew maps who couldn't find their way home.

AUTHOR'S NOTE

WHILE THE CHARACTERS IN THIS NOVEL ARE FICTITIOUS, they have been inspired by people who once walked this earth. This novel begins with an epigraph from T. G. Montgomerie, who trained Indians in rudimentary surveying techniques in the nineteenth century. At the height of the Great Game, when the British feared Russian incursions into India through Tibet, the region became particularly important for both empires. As Tibetans barred all foreigners except Indian pilgrims and traders from entering their country, Britain's Trigonometrical Survey tasked "native spies" with mapping what was then a white space on British maps.

I first came across this story as a child, in Rudyard Kipling's *Kim*. Years later, in 2009, browsing in a secondhand bookshop in London's Leicester Square, I found a copy of A. Henry Savage Landor's *In the Forbidden Land*, whose first pages feature a photo of Landor with his "two faithful servants," whose names he spells as "Mansing" and "Chanden Sing." These men accompanied Landor on an expedition to Tibet in 1897. My novel took shape when I began to wonder why these two Indians had been "faithful" to a white man who wrote that "firm if not too severe a punishment administered in time is absolutely necessary with native servants, and generally saves much trouble and unpleasantness in the end."

Looking up explorations of Tibet in the nineteenth century, I found accounts of Indian surveyors such as Nain Singh Rawat, Kishen Singh, and Kinthup, whom British officials sent on surveying trips either to prove that the Tsangpo was the Brahmaputra, or to chart the routes to Lhasa and other parts of Tibet. They were seen as instruments rather than as humans with agency or autonomy. It seemed that the title of explorer was easily appended to the name of a white man, and sometimes a white woman, but never to Indians. At the time I was also reading about Sherpas clashing with Western climbers on Everest, and these contemporary events too informed the writing of this novel. My research led me to the stories of women who had traveled to Tibet in the nineteenth and early twentieth centuries, which in turn inspired Katherine's narrative.

While the novel's principal settings exist, I have taken some liberties with creating fictitious elements of the landscape to serve the narrative, though these are always rooted in the reality of Tibet's terrain.

The Tsangpo, which is the Tibetan word for river, is today known as the Yarlung Tsangpo in Tibet and the Brahmaputra in India. While Tibetans have different names for the river, for the sake of clarity I have referred to it as the Tsangpo, which also seems to be the preference of most Tibetans. Otherwise, landmarks in Tibet are mentioned by their Indian names, guided by how the characters in the novel would have referred to them. (Tibet itself was once called Bod by Tibetans; to Tibetans, Mount Kailas is Kang Rinpoche.)

The research for this novel alone would have proved insurmountable if not for the help of many others. My thanks to Professor Karl E. Ryavec for answering this stranger's email, and his book *A Historical Atlas of Tibet,* which has been an invaluable resource to me in the writing of this book. My thanks to the staff at the Survey of India, Dehra Dun; British Library, London; and the Royal Geographical Society, London, for their assistance in accessing the archives pertaining to Tibetan surveys and expeditions. Special thanks to those at the Survey of India for the explanations on the workings of nineteenth-century surveying instruments.

For primary research, I relied on the accounts of nineteenth-century surveys of Tibet published in the *Journal of the Royal Geographical Society of London,* particularly those penned by Montgomerie and H. Trotter. Nain Singh Rawat noted down a few journal entries himself while conducting a route survey in Tibet, which can be found in the book *Asia ki Peeth Par: Pandit Nain Singh Rawat, Jeewan, Anwesan tatha Lekhan (On the Back of Asia: Pandit Nain Singh*

Rawat's Life, Explorations and Writings), compiled by Uma Bhatt and Shekhar Pathak.

Books whose ideas influenced the novel include: *Mapping an Empire: The Geographical Construction of British India, 1765–1843* by Matthew H. Edney; *The Imperial Map: Cartography and the Mastery of Empire*, edited by James R. Akerman; and *Another Reason: Science and the Imagination of Modern India* by Gyan Prakash. Books on traveling to Tibet that aided my research include: *Western Tibet and the British Borderland: The Sacred Country of Hindus and Buddhists* by Charles A. Sherring; *Trans-Himalaya: Discoveries and Adventures in Tibet* (Volumes I, II, and III) by Sven Hedin; *Lhasa: An Account of the Country and People of Central Tibet and of the Progress of the Mission Sent There by the English Government in the Year 1903-4* (Volumes I and II) by Perceval Landon; *Three Years in Tibet* by Ekai Kawaguchi; *Narratives of the Mission of George Bogle to Tibet, and of the Journey of Thomas Manning to Lhasa*, edited by Clements R. Markham; *Trespassers on the Roof of the World: The Race for Lhasa* by Peter Hopkirk; *Adventures in Tibet: Including the Diary of Miss Annie R. Taylor's Remarkable Journey from Tau-Chau to Ta Chien-Lu Through the Heart of the "Forbidden Land,"* edited by William Carey; *My Journey to Lhasa* by Alexandra David-Neel; *On Top of the World: Five Women Explorers in Tibet* by Luree Miller; *A Home in Tibet* by Tsering Wangmo Dhompa; and *From Heaven Lake: Travels Through Sinkiang and Tibet* by Vikram Seth. For a more extensive bibliography, please visit www.deepa-anappara.com.

I wrote this novel over several years, and my thanks to everyone who read and offered advice at various points. My thanks to Professor Steve Waters at the University of East Anglia, whose dramaturgy lessons gave me a new lens through which to envision space in a narrative. Immense thanks to Professor Vesna Goldsworthy, Professor Anshuman Mondal, and Dr. Tom Boll for their invaluable suggestions, encouragement, and support over several years.

My love and gratitude to Avani Shah and George Newell, whose insightful comments helped me find a way back to my novel when all seemed lost. I am grateful to Kristien Potgieter and Taymour Soomro for their comments and support. Thanks to Samantha Allen for all the essential chats on historical fiction, and the encouragement. I am grateful to Roli Srivastava for her friendship, and for sharing her knowledge of her hometown, Dehra Dun.

My gratitude to Matt Turner, who is an extraordinary editor and agent, and Peter Straus, at RCW. I am especially grateful for their forbearance, generosity, and kindness.

I am immensely grateful too to have Caitlin McKenna as my editor. I always look forward to, and dread, her notes, which are incisive and demand from me the kind of rigor and skill that I worry I do not possess. While I bear sole responsibility for any errors and missteps, I believe Caitlin's comments have made this a better book.

At Random House, my thanks also to Naomi Goodheart, Erin Richards, Madison Dettlinger, and Andy Ward for their support. For a cover and text design that reflect the themes of the book, my thanks to everyone in the Random House production team. Thanks to Magali Cozo for the cover painting, jacket designer Elena Giavaldi, and text designer Barbara Bachman.

It is my privilege to be able to work with Juliet Mabey in the UK, and I am grateful for her suggestions, enthusiasm, and support. Thanks also to Polly Hatfield, Paul Nash, Margot Weale, Rowan Jackson and Lucy Cooper. Thanks to Sarah Terry for the copyedits.

My thanks to Manasi Subramaniam at Penguin Random House India, for the attention with which she read my book, and for her comments.

Last but not the least, my gratitude to Tibetans in Tibet and in exile who continue to remind me that we must always resist those who attempt to colonize our lands and our minds.

ABOUT THE AUTHOR

DEEPA ANAPPARA'S debut novel, *Djinn Patrol on the Purple Line*, was named one of the best books of the year by *The New York Times*, *The Washington Post*, *Time*, *The Guardian*, and NPR. It won the Edgar Award for Best Novel, was longlisted for the Women's Prize for Fiction, shortlisted for the JCB Prize for Indian Literature, and included in *Time*'s 100 Best Mystery and Thriller Books of All Time. It has been translated into over twenty languages. Anappara is the co-editor of *Letters to a Writer of Color*, a collection of personal essays on fiction, race, and culture.

deepa-anappara.com

Instagram: @deepa.anappara

ABOUT THE TYPE

This book was set in Fournier, a typeface named for Pierre-Simon Fournier (1712–68), the youngest son of a French printing family. He started out engraving woodblocks and large capitals, then moved on to fonts of type. In 1736 he began his own foundry and made several important contributions in the field of type design; he is said to have cut 147 alphabets of his own creation. Fournier is probably best remembered as the designer of St. Augustine Ordinaire, a face that served as the model for the Monotype Corporation's Fournier, which was released in 1925.